Death Writes

An Inishowen Mystery

Andrea Carter

CONSTABLE

CONSTABLE

First published in Great Britain in 2023 by Constable

13 5 7 9 10 8 6 4 2

Copyright © Andrea Carter, 2023

The moral right of the author has been asserted.

A CIP catalogue record for this book is available from the British Library.

ISBN 978-1-40871-847-6

Typeset in Bembo MT by Initial Typesetting Services, Edinburgh
Printed and bound in Great Britain by Clays Ltd, Elcograf S.p.A.

Papers used by Constable are from well-managed forests and other responsible sources.

Constable
An imprint of
Little, Brown Book Group
Carmelite House
50 Victoria Embankment
London EC4Y 0DZ

An Hachette UK Company
www.hachette.co.uk

www.littlebrown.co.uk

Andrea Carter grew up in Ballyfin, Co. Laois. She graduated in Law from Trinity College, Dublin, qualified as a solicitor and moved to the Inishowen peninsula. Having practised law for twenty years, more recently as a barrister, she now writes full time. She was shortlisted for the Irish Book Awards in 2019 and her first three books have been optioned for television. She lives in Dublin with her husband and dog.

By Andrea Carter

In memory of two kind, funny, brilliant men whom
I greatly miss. I think they would have
liked each other if they'd met.
Barney Power (1935–2016)
Dr Herby Sixsmith (1914–2007)

Chapter One

We stopped for petrol outside Monaghan. Just over halfway into a journey, which had seemed interminable already, taking us across the border into Northern Ireland, speeding through Derry, bypassing Strabane and Omagh and returning into the south at Aughnacloy.

'Can I get you anything?' Molloy asked, before climbing out of the car.

I shook my head, sitting hunched over in the passenger seat as if I were cold, hands clasped tightly in my lap. My eyes darted from the yellow fuel bunkers filled with logs and peat briquettes to the red LED sign proffering *Off licence*, *Car Wash* and *Coffee* – taking very little in.

In the rear-view mirror I watched Molloy fill the tank, his features illuminated by the ghoulish light of the garage forecourt. He was worried too. I could see it in the set of his jaw, his grey eyes troubled. It validated my panic, convincing me that I wasn't overreacting. Although I'd have preferred it if he'd thought I was.

We'd taken Molloy's car rather than the Mini. I was too stressed to get behind the wheel, plus I'd had a full glass of wine, supposedly the prelude to a relaxed Saturday night dinner; our attempt at a normal relationship without all the drama and mis-understanding that had marred our connection to date.

1

Until the call came, an unfamiliar Dublin number appearing on my phone's screen. The caller was Pat Barnes, a man who'd recently moved into the same housing estate as my parents, a new neighbour taking an interest in the older couple across the street, chatting with my dad while he mowed the lawn, passing the time of day with my mum.

With the low thrum of the petrol pump in the background, I replayed the conversation in my head, hearing again the hesitancy in the man's voice, treading that fine line between spooking someone unnecessarily and ignoring a red flag. *I don't want to come across as the nosy neighbour but . . . well, some people have moved in with your parents. I called over and they say they're fine but I don't know where they're all fitting. There are at least four or five of them . . .*

I'd thanked him, assured him he'd done the right thing and straight away rung my parents. I'd got voicemail. On all three numbers, the landline and both of their mobiles. I'd tried numerous times since with no success.

Molloy replaced the nozzle and crossed over to the shop to pay, his taut stride reflecting the urgency I felt. Was this four-hour mercy dash a ridiculously impulsive move on my part? I wasn't sure. But I needed to find out what was going on.

Molloy circled the back of the car and sat back into the driver's seat, tossing me a bottle of water for which I was grateful. I took a long draught, downing a quarter, feeling the cold liquid cut through my throat, which was dry and tight from alcohol and fear.

I offered him the bottle and he shook his head, starting the engine without a word as if sensing that I didn't wish to talk, overtaking a lumbering, belching oil lorry on the way out of the service station. I stared out of the window as we drove, rubbing condensation with my sleeve, vaguely aware of fields of cattle rushing by, houses with lush gardens, churches, a roadside sign for a school open day. It was May so a late dusk but the encroaching night felt ominous. As if we were driving from light into dark, from the warm possibilities of an early summer's evening to something far more sinister.

'Do you want to talk?' Molloy asked after a while, as we sped along a wide road, its hard shoulders lined with trees which looked almost black.

I shook my head. My mind was too cluttered to speak. Why the hell had neither my mum nor my dad answered their phones? Had something happened to them? We still had an hour and a half to go before Dublin, and I needed to stop my thoughts from spiralling or I would go crazy from inaction.

'Radio?' Molloy suggested, as if reading my mind.

I nodded. Radio.

He chose an arts show on RTÉ Radio 1, or maybe it was the first station he hit. A woman was being interviewed about a TV documentary which she was producing and presenting. I recognised her as one of the arts journalists who worked for the station, the easy intimacy making it obvious that she was talking to one of her own colleagues. I made an effort to focus, wondering if I needed music instead, something which didn't require me to think. I was about to suggest changing the station when something caught my attention.

'*Well, he's English but he lives in Donegal so we claim him,*' the woman laughed. '*About time we took one back! He turns seventy next year so it's a perfect time to do a retrospective. He was one of the youngest winners of the Booker Prize and he's also an IMPAC winner. There's no doubt that Gavin Featherstone is one of our best-known writers.*'

The interviewer paused as if checking something. '*His last book was what? Five years ago?* Violet, Green and Red. *Is that right? Is he still writing?*'

'*Word is he's writing a memoir.*'

'*Ah. So, you want to get in before him then?*'

Another laugh. '*Something like that.*'

'*And are you interviewing the man himself for this documentary?*'

'*I wish. He hasn't spoken publicly for years. The man's basically a recluse . . . It's what makes the documentary such a challenge and so fascinating. Obviously, we can access lots of archive footage but . . .*'

The host cut across her, hurrying the segment along as if he was running out of time. '*Sounds as if you've got your work cut out for you! We'll look forward to seeing the final product. Thank you to arts and culture presenter Gina Bailey for coming in to chat to us. After the break: film reviews.*'

Molloy chose that moment to overtake an articulated lorry at speed and I reached for the dashboard, gripping it with my fingers while the words 'All Ireland Championship. Congratulations to Monaghan Minor Ladies!' whooshed past. Despite the white-knuckle ride, I was glad he'd abandoned his usual cautious driving in favour of a more Starsky and Hutch approach, weaving in and out of traffic, breaking speed limits and lights and ignoring continuous white lines to overtake whenever he saw an opportunity. Displaying driving skills I didn't know he had.

When we'd returned to our lane, I glanced over at him. Tom Molloy, Garda sergeant in Glendara and my boyfriend, I supposed, yet that word felt strange even inside my head. I'd certainly never said it aloud. Years of running a solicitor's practice in the same small town had brought us together first as colleagues, then friends and eventually lovers. Although it had been anything but straightforward, not least because Molloy had been transferred to Cork for a time and I'd recently returned from six months working in Florida while a locum took over my own small practice in Glendara. But no matter where we stood in our personal relationship, Molloy had always been there for me, just as he was now. Literally taking the wheel.

A blue tractor sat crossways on the hard shoulder between Carrickmacross and Ardee. I felt Molloy suppress his instinct to pull over and give the guy a telling off, and my gratitude for this made me willing to talk.

Molloy turned off the radio and I filled him in on what I knew.

'And you don't know these people who've moved in?' he asked.

I shook my head. 'I don't think so.'

'Do they? Your parents?'

I shrugged. 'I don't know that either. They never mentioned anyone coming to stay when I spoke to them last, especially four or five people. They already have this guy Chambers living with them.'

Molloy shot me a quizzical side glance. I'd never had a chance to speak to him about this. Shortly after I'd returned from the States, which was only a couple of weeks ago now, though it felt like longer, there had been serious floods in Glendara, cutting off the town completely and taking up everyone's energy and attention. There'd even been a death. The town was still getting over it, slowly repairing the damage wreaked by the flood waters.

'When I visited them on the night that I came back from Florida there was a guy living with them who I'd never met,' I said, the memory causing my throat to constrict. *Did he have something to do with this?* 'His name was Stuart Chambers. They met him at a grief counselling group which they joined.'

Molloy knew my sister had been killed by her boyfriend years before I'd moved to Glendara, and that my parents had struggled for a long time with their grief. He had been the one who encouraged me to see them more often when my guilt had kept me away.

'They've been spending a lot of time with this group,' I added. 'They even went to Iceland for Christmas with them one year.'

'I remember.' Molloy indicated to join the huge roundabout which led onto the M1 motorway between Dublin and Belfast.

'I don't know much about the group but they seem to have got a lot of support from them,' I said. 'Anyway, this guy Chambers lost his wife and baby in a car accident. He's pretty young, barely thirty I'd say. My parents befriended him and he's been staying with them while looking for somewhere to buy. It's a little odd, but . . .'

Molloy raised his eyebrows. 'And the four or five other people this neighbour mentioned? Do you think they might be friends of his? That *he* might have invited them to stay?'

Unease crept across my scalp. It was this very possibility that had disturbed me since I'd got the call; strangers invading my parents' house, taking advantage of a vulnerable older couple.

'I have no idea,' I said. 'But six adults if you include Chambers, in addition to my parents, living in a small three-bedroomed house? That's going to be fairly crowded.'

I took another sip of my water. My mouth had gone dry again.

An hour later we turned in to the Chapelizod housing estate in West Dublin where my sister Faye and I had grown up. Darkness had fallen, although only just; it stayed bright until after ten in May. The amber streetlights illuminated an old beech tree on the corner which my daredevil sister used to climb, taunting her more cautious older sibling about the wonders to be found in its branches if only I had the nerve to follow her.

I suppressed the memory before it took hold and gave Molloy directions to the house. 'It's down at the end of this cul-de-sac on the left.' Suppressing, too, the general weirdness of arriving with him at my childhood home; the two halves of my life that had never met colliding without warning, without giving me a chance to prepare.

A plastic bag skittered across the road and a light rain stippled the windscreen as we drove past identical three-bedroomed semi-detached residences, each with a small front garden. Unsurprisingly most were lit, occupied by families who would be home on a Saturday night.

'This one?' Molloy asked, indicating to pull in.

I nodded, gazing up at my childhood home, a house so familiar to me, from which I'd come and gone maybe thousands of times.

'Well, they're in, at least,' he said. The front room was in darkness but there were lights on in the hall and upstairs.

'Or someone is.' I grimaced; my stomach tightly knotted. I glanced at the neighbour's house across the road and pointed to it. 'That's Pat Barnes's house.' Did I imagine a twitching curtain?

As we parked at the kerb, it occurred to me that if there were six extra people staying here, then we'd have to check into a hotel. Molloy couldn't drive back to Donegal tonight.

I felt a twinge at the thought of this house being closed to me, occupied by strangers. But I pushed away the thought; I needed to work out how I was going to handle this, assuming my parents were actually here. Because while I may have grown up here, in this neat 1940s semi-detached, this was my parents' house not mine. I couldn't just barge in and demand explanations as if they were teenagers having a party.

But yet, I knew they had been vulnerable since my sister Faye died. Vulnerable and a little lonely. I also knew that I hadn't been there for them as much as I should have been. I'd left Ireland straight after her killer's trial and when I'd finally returned, I'd moved to Inishowen, an almost four-hour drive away, leaving again more recently for my six-month stint.

The truth was I'd been absent more than I'd been present, dealing with my own guilt as well as my grief, guilt that arose from the fact that the man who'd killed my sister had been my boyfriend too, or my ex-boyfriend, a man she'd never have met if it hadn't been for me. A man who'd ruined our relationship and caused the falling out that had prevented me from answering her call on the night she died.

Molloy turned off the engine. For once, I was glad of the man's taciturn nature, his wordless squeezing of my hand before we got out of the car. The wind was chill and it was spitting rain as I walked to the door with him in my wake, somewhat relieved to see that my parents' old Nissan was the only car parked in the narrow drive.

I still had a key but it seemed wrong to use it when they were here. So, I knocked and waited for a minute, exchanging a glance with Molloy who stood calmly beside me on the doorstep. I was about to ring the bell, which I knew rarely worked, when footsteps sounded in the hall, and a figure appeared silhouetted in the door's glass panels.

It was opened by the man I'd hoped would have slung his hook long before now.

Chapter Two

Stuart Chambers was smooth featured, clean shaven and dressed just as he had been the last time I'd seen him, in chinos, a chequered shirt and a tie – *a tie* at ten o'clock on a Saturday night.

He smiled as if he'd been expecting me. 'Benedicta,' he said, insisting on using the full version of my name, which I'd shortened to Ben. 'Come in.' He opened the door wide, glancing over my shoulder at Molloy. 'Both of you. Welcome.'

As with the last time, I resented his ease in my parents' house. His use of 'welcome' grated with me. The man simply did not behave like a guest. Maybe it was rude but I couldn't bring myself to reply to his greeting or to introduce Molloy. I simply followed him down the hall and into the kitchen, passing the open door to the sitting room on the way. As we'd seen from the outside, the lights were off. The whole house seemed quiet with no evidence of the four or five extra residents the neighbour had described. But where were my parents?

My question was answered with merciful speed. The door to the kitchen, also ajar, revealed them both sitting at the kitchen table with a pot of tea and a huge slab of coffee cake between them. They turned as one when we walked in, and I wondered why one of them hadn't answered the door. It wasn't as if either of them was incapacitated.

'Ben!' My dad stood up, beaming, crossing the floor to enfold me into a big bear hug. 'Why didn't you tell us you were coming?'

He was followed by my mother whose smile quickly morphed into concern, the knitted brow of someone for whom the unexpected rarely brought good news.

'Is everything okay?' She switched her gaze to Molloy, questioning the presence of this stranger whose frame seemed suddenly too large for the small kitchen.

'Everything's fine.' I forced a smile, feeling a lump in my throat as I looked from one to the other – taking in my dad's salt and pepper hair, darker on his knuckles, and my mother's green eyes as familiar to me as my own. They looked well, well cared for, well fed, if a little older each time I saw them. I was filled with relief and I breathed properly for what felt like the first time in hours. But *was* everything fine? It didn't feel that way. 'I tried to ring but you weren't answering your phones.'

'Oh, we were at a meeting,' my dad said, easily. 'All three of us. We've just come back. We turn off our phones while we're there.'

I looked at Chambers, who seemed unruffled, beaming at this family reunion in an almost fatherly way, as if he'd had some hand in orchestrating it.

I introduced Molloy, beginning the sentence before figuring out how to finish it. 'This is Tom Molloy, a . . . eh . . . friend of mine from Glendara. He drove me down. Tom – my parents Margaret and Des.'

Molloy didn't flinch at the 'friend' description. He simply shook my dad's hand and then my mother's, smiling warmly at them both. I felt my eyes well and I pressed my palms against them before anyone noticed.

'It's good to meet you both,' he said. 'Apologies for landing in on you like this. Ben here suddenly had an urge to see you, so it was all a bit spur of the moment.'

My dad looked at me unconvinced. I'd only seen them a couple of weeks before, but I was glad Molloy had chosen to downplay our visit. Now that we were here, I wondered if I'd overreacted. Was that what he thought?

Chambers broke into my thoughts. 'You'll stay, won't you? It's a long drive from Donegal. You can't be planning on going back up again tonight.'

My annoyance flared again. Why was *he* the one issuing the invitation? But my parents looked eagerly at us both so I glanced at Molloy and he nodded. Maybe later we'd get an opportunity to find out what had been happening, not that it would be easy with Chambers's constant presence. I glanced over at him, his straight back, his combed hair, already reaching into the cupboard for two extra cups.

He caught me looking when he turned, meeting my gaze evenly. 'Have you eaten? I can whip up an omelette or something?'

We'd set off before Molloy had served up the food he'd been cooking and I was suddenly, unexpectedly hungry. Not that I wanted to tell Chambers that.

My mother, seeing my hesitation, said, 'Stuart's a great cook. He does all of it now. We're spoiled, aren't we?'

I stared at her, amazed. She never allowed anyone help her in the kitchen, claiming she worked better without people getting under her feet. 'It's fine,' I said. 'I'll make us a couple of sandwiches, if that's okay.'

While I rooted in the fridge for some cheese and ham and Molloy joined my dad and Chambers at the table, my mother crossed the kitchen to help me. She leaned in conspiratorially and, for a second, I wondered if she was about to confide in me, to ask for help like a kidnap victim passing a note. Instead, she glanced at Molloy and whispered, 'One bedroom or two?'

I flushed. 'You only have the one spare now, don't you?' I said, defensively. It was another thing I'd found difficult to handle, Chambers sleeping in my late sister's room. I knew that my parents couldn't keep it as a shrine forever and she'd moved out long before she died, but it was just another example of this stranger getting his feet under their table. I looked over at him now, seated at the head of it, in his shirt and tie like some dad in a 1950s sitcom.

My mother smiled, shrugging off the question. 'So, one then.'

I attacked some cheddar with the cheese slicer, her lack of reaction irking me more than was reasonable. 'Has he had any luck finding somewhere to live?'

'Not yet,' she said brightly as she lifted the lid off the bread bin. If she noticed the edge to my tone, she ignored it.

And then Chambers himself was beside her. I hadn't even heard him approach. He placed his hand on her shoulder with the words, 'I'll do that. You sit down.'

She moved meekly back towards the table while he lifted a loaf of sourdough from the bin and passed it to me. I was willing to bet that he'd baked the damn thing.

Molloy plucked the Nancy Drew mystery *The Hidden Staircase* from the bookshelf above his head the following morning, along with a very battered copy of *Every Girl's Handbook*. My old bedroom had been recarpeted and repainted many times since I'd left it for good as a first-year law student but the bookshelves still held most of my old books. There were even some from the 1930s, which my grandmother had given me, the flyleaves of *Deb of Sea House* and *Hans Christian Andersen's Stories* shamefully defaced by my childish hand in blue crayon.

'So, this is how I get an insight into the complicated psyche of Ben O'Keeffe?' He narrowed his eyes in amusement as he flicked through the dusty hardback with its cover image of Nancy the teen detective ascending a set of spooky steps with a torch. 'By finding out what kind of teenager you were . . .'

'I was reading those as a child not a teenager,' I retorted. 'And I'm hardly the closed-off one of the pair of us.' But the dig was half-hearted. I'd awoken feeling uneasy and out of sorts. Nothing had yet been resolved. Tomorrow was Monday and I needed to be back in the office, leaving my parents in the clutches of Chambers. Because that's what it felt like: 'clutches'.

Molloy was out of bed now, mooching around the room in white T-shirt and boxers, his morning stubble giving him a rakish look he didn't usually sport. I liked it but I was too distracted to let him know, or do anything about it.

He caught my troubled expression, placed the book on the bedside locker and sat on the end of the bed; a double to replace my old single with the broken spring around which I had to curve my teenaged body. He reached for one of my hands and held it. 'You're still worried.'

I chewed at my bottom lip. I was. I just couldn't put my finger on why.

'Chambers does seem to be pulling his weight,' he said. 'He cooks, he cleans, he was the one who left fresh sheets up for us last night.'

'I know,' I conceded. 'It does seem as if he is taking care of the house and my parents but I just can't shake the feeling that he's in charge, somehow. In charge of the house and *them*.'

Molloy examined my face. 'Do they seem any different to you?'

I thought about that for a few seconds then shook my head.

'On the surface, no. They're pretty much themselves, but . . .' I struggled to articulate what I was feeling. 'It's just not like them having someone to stay for this long.'

Molloy frowned. 'How long has it been?'

'Over a month, according to them. But I suspect it's longer. He moved in while I was in the States and, from what I can gather, rent free. He's a guest.' I made inverted commas with my fingers, a gesture I disliked when other people did it. I was beginning to irritate myself.

Molloy raised his eyebrows.

'That of itself doesn't bother me,' I added quickly, though it wasn't entirely true. It felt like he was taking advantage of them. 'It's their house, their decision. But my mother, particularly, has never really liked having visitors. She's very house proud. And that,' I waggled my hand at Molloy, 'what you just said about Chambers pulling his weight, doing all the cooking and clean-ing, that *is* odd. It isn't like her. Faye and myself had to pull our weight when we were growing up, taking turns doing the wash-ing up and making our beds, but my mum always preferred doing the important things herself so they were done *properly*.' I smiled at the memory. 'Her standards were high. Are high.'

'And the other people that neighbour mentioned staying here? Did you ask about them?' Molloy had gone to bed shortly before me in the hope of giving me time on my own with my parents.

I rolled my eyes. 'I didn't get the chance, did I? *He* was there the whole time.'

It hadn't been a long evening – it was after ten when we arrived – but Chambers's ingratiating presence, brewing fresh pots of tea and washing up the cups and plates, made it feel never-ending, his presence forcing our conversation into something stilted and banal. I was sure my parents were curious about my unannounced visit so late on a Saturday night and so soon after my last one, but they didn't press it. And I couldn't ask them the questions I wanted to, either.

The only memorable moment had come when my dad asked Molloy, 'So what do you do?'

'I'm a guard,' Molloy replied simply.

'He's the sergeant in Glendara where my practice is,' I'd added, unable to stop myself from glancing at Chambers. Did I imagine seeing his eyes narrow, betraying the first hint of something other than smug self-assurance? Or was that just wishful thinking on my part?

I withdrew my hand from Molloy's and lay back on the pillow. Even if I got the chance to speak to my parents alone, I still wasn't sure how to broach the reason for my visit. I didn't want to tell tales on the kindly neighbour. He'd clearly deliberated over making the call, not wanting to interfere, but unable to shake the feeling that something wasn't right. I knew how that felt. He'd gone as far as telling my mother that he was considering a holiday in Inishowen to get my phone number.

'If there were four or five extra people in the house, where did they all sleep?' I murmured. 'My parents are in their room. Chambers is in Faye's. Did they all sleep in here?'

Looking around me, I imagined that the room wasn't as pristine as it usually was, the carpet not freshly hoovered, the little bowl of potpourri missing from the dressing table. But that was hardly evidence of anything. They hadn't been expecting us.

I realised that Molloy had fallen silent.

'There's something familiar about Chambers,' he said eventually. 'I'm not sure what or why. Whether it's him in particular or just his manner.'

'Really?'

Molloy wrinkled his nose. 'Ah, I'm not sure. But I might see if I can have him checked out on the QT.' He gave me a wry smile. 'Bit tricky since he hasn't actually done anything illegal.'

'That we know of.'

'That we know of,' he agreed. He ran his fingers through his hair, a messy thatch of bedhead, also at odds with his usual neat appearance. If I hadn't been so addled, I'd have teased him about it. 'I don't think we should leave today without finding out more. That neighbour wouldn't have called you out of the blue unless he was seriously concerned, especially when he's never met you.' He studied my face. 'You'll need to speak to your parents properly before we leave. And that neighbour.' He paused. 'Or would you like me to do that?'

I felt my eyes glisten. Molloy understood how things were in my family better than most, and for the first time in my life, I had someone I could lean on. I gave a tight nod. 'Maybe. Or at least come with me when I do?'

'Sure.' He kissed me lightly on the lips. 'Anyway, let's get up. I can hear movement downstairs.'

I lifted the covers and climbed out of bed, grabbing a towel and Molloy's extra toothbrush; I'd nothing with me but he'd grabbed his and a spare. I was about to head across the landing in T-shirt and knickers when it hit me that I might meet Chambers so I tugged on my jeans.

The door to the bathroom was yanked open before I reached it. A toilet flushed, and my dad emerged wearing the same shabby blue and red checked dressing gown he'd always worn, a newspaper tucked under his arm.

'Morning!' he said cheerfully, squinting at me. In the harsh morning light, he looked a little washed out; deep lines on his forehead, shadows around his eyes, and his throat raw from shaving.

'Why are you using the main bathroom?' I frowned. 'What about your ensuite?'

He looked oddly sheepish. 'Ah, I like the bigger one. Anyway, your turn.' He did his ZZ Top impression to direct me inside, and I saw that he had toothpaste on his cheek.

I noticed that the bathroom was a little grubby. Last night I'd been too tired to pay much attention to it, but now I could see that the bath was grimy and the windows were greasier than I'd ever seen them. Another odd thing. My mother always said she couldn't stand a dirty bathroom, and Faye and I had been trained to scrub the bath each time we used it. If Chambers had taken over the cleaning, his standards weren't as high as hers.

I was surprised and pleased to find her alone in the kitchen when I went downstairs, standing with one hand on the kettle looking at her watch. She glanced up quickly when I appeared, her expectant smile fading when she saw that it was me. Not great for the ego.

'Oh, morning. You didn't see Stuart, did you?'

'No.' I shook my head.

She rubbed her neck; her face looked pinched and tired. 'He's usually up by now. Has his shower at eight, same time every morning, breakfast at half past.' She checked the clock on the wall as if hopeful it might show a different time, an earlier one maybe.

Apart from general bewilderment at my mother's concern that a guest wasn't up at nine o'clock on a Sunday morning, something else jarred, which took me a couple of seconds to figure out. And then it hit me – the only working shower was in my parents' ensuite. The shower in the main bathroom was an ancient one over the bath, which didn't work and my parents hadn't bothered getting replaced since they never used it.

'Where is he sleeping, Mum?' I asked, slowly.

17

'Oh, he moved into the main bedroom,' she said airily. 'He needed a shower first thing before work and, sure, what are we doing all day? Your father and I can have baths.'

'You've given him *your* bedroom?' I fought to keep my voice calm. She hadn't even called it *their* bedroom. It was now the *main* bedroom apparently.

'Not permanently.' She waved me away distractedly like some minor irritant. 'Just for a while.'

I felt a knot in my chest. Had this happened while those other people had been here? The house had only three bedrooms. Then a horrible thought occurred; was it possible that my mum and dad had been sleeping downstairs? In the sitting room?

My father burst through the kitchen door, cutting through my thoughts. 'He's gone,' he exclaimed.

My mother's frightened gaze flicked past him. He was followed closely by Molloy, now fully dressed and shaved.

Dad spread his palms in a gesture of confusion and hurt. 'His door is open. The room is empty and there's no sign of him. He's taken everything and just left.'

All colour drained from my mother's face. 'Everything?'

Molloy and I exchanged a look. I tried to remember if I'd noticed anything, but I hadn't even glanced in the direction of what I still thought of as my parents' room on my way down. 'It's the one at the front of the house, with the ensuite,' I told him.

Molloy headed back upstairs, and we listened silently to his heavy tread. A few minutes later he was down again, shaking his head. 'Your dad's right. It's been cleared out.'

'He didn't leave a note?' I said, appalled. 'Not even to say thank you for all the weeks he's been staying here?' *What the hell was going on?*

Neither of my parents spoke.

'Mum,' I said, 'did you have other people staying here recently? Other than Stuart?'

Her intake of breath was audible. 'Why do you ask?'

'Stuart mentioned something,' I lied, suspecting it was the last thing he'd have told me.

'Well, yes,' she conceded. 'But it was only for a few nights.'

'Were they friends of his?'

Her face darkened. She rounded on me. 'Why all the questions? Did you say something to him? Ask him to leave?'

'No, of course I didn't.'

Molloy shot me a warning look, but it was too late.

'I might have wanted to but I didn't,' I snapped.

'So why is he gone then?' she countered. 'He never mentioned anything to us about leaving. I knew you weren't happy with him staying here the last time you visited. But this is our house and it's our decision who stays here. We're not children.'

'I know that,' I said, flushing. 'I swear I didn't say anything. I'd never go over your head like that. I promise.'

My dad leaned back against the worktop and crossed his arms. Unlike my mother, his expression was hard to read, his head bowed as if he was trying to process what had happened. I felt a strange coldness seep through me as it hit me that, beneath my mother's annoyance, I could hear fear in her voice. Were they afraid of Chambers?

'Where does he live?' I asked.

My mother threw me a hard stare. 'Here. Until this morning.'

I held the stare, biting back the response I wanted to give, knowing this time it would be a mistake. 'I know that,' I said. 'I meant where is he from? Does he have family, other than . . .' I trailed off, deciding that now might not be the right time to mention the dead wife and child.

She turned away so she didn't have to look at me. 'Clare originally, I think,' she said dully. 'But he's lived in Dublin for a long time and his job is here – he said that his family are all far away.'

'Well, maybe he's gone back for a visit,' I said breezily. 'Clare is lovely this time of year.'

There was no response. All that could be heard was the slow and deliberate ticking of the kitchen clock.

Chapter Three

Molloy chose that moment to interject with a suggestion that he take us all out for breakfast, and I was grateful. His presence would help alleviate the uncomfortable atmosphere for which I entirely blamed Stuart Chambers.

The rain from the night before had cleared to a bright day, so we walked the short distance to Chapelizod Main Street and took a table outside one of the cafés. The old Dublin village looked pretty in the sunshine; a bike with a wicker basket was propped up against the old phone box and the horse chestnut under which we sat was lush, a watery sun dappling through its quivering leaves. It should have been a treat, having breakfast under a blue sky with my parents and Molloy, but everything felt askew and wrong. Why were my usually sensible mother and father so distraught that a stranger who'd been effectively living off them had upped and left? Why weren't they annoyed instead, that he hadn't thanked them or left a note?

A tiny, hairy-faced dog who was flat out, nose down, snoring on one of the tables would usually have given us all a laugh but the most I got when I pointed him out was a weak, unconvincing smile from my dad.

Once we'd decided what to eat, I went inside with Molloy to

order, the sweet scent of roast coffee giving me a much-needed boost. But as we waited in the queue for the counter, I revealed my fear. 'I don't want to leave them,' I blurted. 'I'm afraid Chambers will come back as soon as we're gone.'

'Can you stay?' he asked, brow furrowed with concern.

I shook my head. 'I've a ton of appointments tomorrow and we've court on Tuesday, remember?'

'Of course.' He nodded. Molloy would be there too; he prosecuted at the monthly district court in Glendara. He frowned in thought for a few seconds, then gestured towards the counter as we were called forward. 'We're up.'

On the way back out, both of us carrying cardboard cups of freshly squeezed orange juice, he nudged my arm and took me aside.

'Why don't you invite them up?' he said quietly. 'Ask them to stay for a bit?'

I looked at him, startled. 'To Inishowen?'

'Why not? They've never visited before, have they? You have the space.'

He was right on both counts. They hadn't ever visited before, and I did have a spare room in my cottage in Malin. It seemed a little odd now that I thought about it. Though we'd been partially estranged for a few years, things were a lot better now. At least until Chambers had showed up.

Molloy took a step back to allow a woman in a flowery skirt pass by, then lowered his voice another notch. 'In the meantime, I can arrange for the local guards to keep an eye on the house and I'll see if we can find out anything about this Stuart Chambers.'

'Oh God, yes, please do,' I said, spilling a little juice on the white tiled floor in my eagerness. The woman behind the counter waved to say she'd sort it out and I mouthed an apology.

'As I said earlier, I *will* need to play it carefully,' Molloy cautioned, sympathy softening his features. 'But I'm sure I can do a little light digging.'

We re-emerged from the café to find my parents deep in some intense exchange of their own. It came to an abrupt halt as we approached and I was sure I saw my mother quickly shove her phone back into her bag. Had she been trying to ring Chambers?

I said nothing as we retook our seats, leaving Molloy to chat to my parents, picking up the *Dublin Post*, a local newspaper which someone had left behind on a neighbouring table. I flicked through it while we waited for our food, suppressing the uncomfortable thought that the conversation was flowing more easily now that I wasn't part of it.

A wasp lurched drunkenly towards me and I waved it away as a headline caught my eye – *Liquid Cocaine concealed in Wine Bottles among €1 million drugs seizure in Dublin*.

I started to read.

Over €1 million worth of drugs have been seized from a residential premises in South County Dublin together with a substantial quantity of cash, believed to be the proceeds of drug trafficking. Garda National Drugs & Organised Crime Bureau (GNDOCB) personnel, assisted by Dublin officers, say that a number of champagne bottles were seized, which, following technical examination were discovered to contain cocaine in liquid form. The estimated street value is believed to be in excess of €1,000,000. Three men have been arrested and are currently being detained pursuant to drug trafficking legislation at Donnybrook Garda Station. It appears that a new method of concealing controlled substances has been identified and exposed.

I showed it to Molloy, and he raised his eyebrows. 'Seems a long way from Donegal, doesn't it?'

We turned as our cappuccinos, toast and eggs arrived on square wooden blocks, which I imagined would amuse Tony from the Oak, Glendara's pub.

After we'd finished, Molloy suggested that my parents and I go for a walk, saying that he had some calls to make before the drive back. I knew that he was giving me a chance to issue the invitation to stay and suspected he would double back and speak to Pat the neighbour in the meantime.

We strolled down to the Liffey walk, where the verdant, early-summer green of the riverbank felt like a cool oasis in the middle of a fraught morning. I'd always found the river to be calming, just as I now derived comfort from the rolling waves of the Inishowen coast; moving water reminding me that so much is out of our control, that sometimes we just need to let things take their course.

My mother had brought the tail end of her toast to feed to the swans, and she tore it into clumps before throwing it into the river. On the far side, a mallard attempted to corral a chaotic clutch of ducklings, and I remembered a grim photograph on the front of the *Irish Times* depicting a heron flying off with a baby duckling in her beak, pursued by an anguished-looking mother duck. I thought about a parent's instinct to protect their young and how mine must have felt when their daughter was killed by a predatory man. Though they'd taken care not to show it, I'd always wondered if they blamed me for bringing him into their lives. But how badly must it have shaken them? Shattering everything they believed in and questioning their ability to take care of their own child? How powerless must they have felt, and how vulnerable might that have made them to predators themselves? Was that what Chambers was? A predator?

I looked at them now, standing side by side to watch a set of double sculls slice through the water, while a man cycled along the path calling out instructions. There had been little conversation since we'd left Molloy. I wasn't sure what to say. The adult child's need to protect older parents was so much harder to manage, the need to balance it with a respect for independence, autonomy and agency. While I'd been in Florida, I'd worked in elder law and saw how difficult a line that was to tread, even for those whose motivations were pure. I recalled a woman whose son kept her a virtual prisoner after a fall; his love and concern for her almost killing her.

A commotion behind made all three of us turn. The tiny, hairy-faced dog who'd been asleep outside the café was yapping wildly and straining at the leash in a challenge to a black and white greyhound who was at least eight times his size.

'Sorry.' The owner grimaced and picked him up in her arms. 'He's a little barky.'

The greyhound owner smiled indulgently and headed on, and we watched them make slow progress along the river as the dog stopped every few yards to sniff the bank.

It was time to say it. 'How would you both like to come back up to Donegal with us?' I asked.

My mother turned to me in surprise. 'Now, you mean? Today?'

I nodded. 'For a visit. I'd love to have you.'

My dad's face lit up. 'Why not?' he said, and I felt a rush of shame that it had been Molloy's idea and not mine.

'But what if Stuart comes back?' my mother protested.

I bit back the response I wanted to give and said, 'He has your mobile numbers, doesn't he? He can call you and you can come back if you want to. It's only a drive.'

My mother looked doubtfully at my dad. 'I don't think we . . .'

It was all I could do not to throw up my hands in frustration. And then I remembered something. I took out my phone, did a quick search, and found that, yes, next weekend was Glendara's biennial literary festival: Glenfest. A reason for them to visit. Assuming, that was, that our local bookseller and the organiser of the festival, Phyllis Kettle, had managed to finalise the plans for it. Her bookshop had been seriously damaged in the floods and the repairs had been taking up most of her energy of late.

I told them about it, hoping that it might hook my mother, who was a retired librarian, in particular.

'You'd want us to stay a whole week?' she asked, looking amazed.

'Why not?' I said. 'You've never visited before. And that's my fault for not inviting you. It'll be a chance to see where I've been living all these years.'

I chose not to point out that *they* had just had a visitor stay for a whole month, probably more.

Molloy offered to drive: there was plenty of room in his car and we, at any rate, had no luggage. The same could not be said for my parents who, once they'd agreed to come, decided to pack for every eventuality in both weather and occasion.

But my dad insisted on driving their ancient Nissan. It had just passed its NCT, he said, and would be well able for it. 'Be good to give it a decent run out.' My impression was that he was happy enough to go, my mother being more reluctant, but he'd persuaded her.

Waiting downstairs while they packed, I felt as if I could breathe in the house for the first time since we'd arrived and I began to hope that Chambers's absence would be a permanent one. Still, it was a relief to set off.

'Did you speak to the neighbour?' I asked Molloy, once we were alone in the car. 'I should have gone over and thanked him, but Mum and Dad would have wondered what I was doing.'

'I did that,' Molloy said, checking the mirror for my dad's car as we pulled out of the estate. 'He couldn't really tell me anything further. He noticed four or five extra people coming and going from the house for about a week. They used keys, were clearly staying there, and seemed to know Chambers well. When he decided to call over, he found the house full of people and your parents looking overwhelmed and a bit lost, which was why he went back the next day to ask for your number.'

The thought of my mum and dad in any kind of distress, especially being bullied in their own home, made me livid. They'd been through enough in their lives.

'Maybe his visit triggered their leaving,' I said. 'Maybe Chambers anticipated Pat might call and tell me what was going on and got them to go. Did you get the sense that he was half-expecting us when we arrived last night?'

'A little. It was brave of Pat to call in. People don't usually stick their noses in like that.'

'They don't in the city,' I said wryly. 'They do in Glendara.'

'See?' Molloy reached out to pat my knee in a gesture he knew I'd find patronising. 'Not always such a bad thing having the neighbours knowing your business.' But then he paused, and I knew something big was coming.

'Go on,' I said, eyes narrowed.

'More importantly, I haven't been able to find any record of a car accident involving the wife and child of a Stuart Chambers.'

I spun around to face him. 'What?'

'That doesn't mean it didn't happen,' he added quickly, hearing my sharp intake of breath. 'Just that I haven't been able to find it.'

'I knew it,' I cried. 'I *knew* he was a fraud. What the hell is he up to?'

Molloy shook his head. 'I have no idea. But you might need to find out some details about that grief support group where they met him. Do you know the name of it?'

I shook my head. I'd never asked. Now, that seemed very care-less of me.

'What does he do for a living?' Molloy asked,

'He's a civil servant,' I said through gritted teeth.

'Okay, well that's pretty vague.' Molloy indicated to overtake a slow-moving car, checking in the mirror again before he pulled back in to see if my father was following.

'I know. I should have asked more but it felt intrusive as if it was none of my business. Although my mother still picked up on the fact that I didn't like him,' I said ruefully.

'Now, there's a surprise,' Molloy said with a smile.

We stopped in Monaghan for something to eat; a sort of late lunch, early dinner. We'd lost my parents somewhere along the M1, but they arrived only minutes after us in the square, making it feel like some weird family road trip. I was impressed. GPS wasn't my parents' thing and four hours' worth of directions wasn't exactly practical, but my dad seemed to be enjoying the drive and my mother had a map open on her knee, navigating, her finger glued to the route.

She was quiet over the meal, which worried me a little. It was less than twenty-four hours since Molloy and I had last been on this road, and while my stomach was no longer somersault-ing as it had been on the way down, nothing had actually been resolved. Having my parents visit would only be a temporary solution, especially if they weren't prepared to discuss things.

We ate quickly and set off again, reaching Derry at around half five. The city looked fine in the evening sunshine as we drove along a glimmering River Foyle, past the expansive white of the Peace Bridge and the handsome Guildhall. Once through the village of Muff we emerged onto the east side of the Inishowen peninsula to make our way along the estuary, accompanying the river on the last leg of its journey to the North Atlantic.

I was sorry I wasn't travelling in the same car as my parents at this point. I'd have liked to see their reaction to the drama of the Muff strait, the broad wide road that ran alongside the shore, at times so close you felt as if you could skim stones from the car. The sea was almost turquoise this evening, a pleasant change from its usual gunmetal grey; the horizon a thin line beyond the expanse of the lough, above which a few ragged scraps of cloud floated, casting shadows across the green water. Early summer in Inishowen was sweet.

At Quigley's Point, we turned inland and upland, crossing over a temporary replacement for the Riverside Bridge erected by the Defence Forces after it collapsed during the devastating floods. It would take some time for the area to recover completely. Many bridges had been damaged and some roads were still closed. I'd heard on Highland Radio that the infrastructure repair was likely to cost Donegal County Council over fifteen million euro.

We continued along the road hewn from the mountain, at times winding and narrow, then wider and straight, overlooking the valley on our left through which the Glentogher River meandered. After a fifteen-minute drive the purple-coloured mound of Sliabh Sneacht would come into view, followed by farmhouses and a thatched cottage. And then, finally, downhill into the little town of Glendara. We were on the home straight.

Suddenly I couldn't wait, impatient to show my parents my beloved Inishowen. I breathed out audibly, catching Molloy's sympathetic smile in response. We'd only been gone one night but it felt like a hell of a lot longer, and I suspected he felt the same.

He checked the rear-view mirror. 'Where are they?' My parents had fallen back again.

I wasn't concerned. 'They don't know the road so they're probably just taking it slowly. They can't go wrong, it's a straight run.'

We passed a wide section of road with a sweeping turn before the road narrowed again to trace a route thorough rocky fields filled with sheep and heather and furze.

Suddenly, out of nowhere, a car was approaching, hurtling towards us at high speed. A blue BMW with two people in it, on the wrong side of the road. Molloy pumped the horn. My heart leapt in my chest, terrified. We were done for. It was coming straight for us. There was nowhere for Molloy to go. On one side of the road, the land rose above a deep ditch while on the other it fell away steeply to the river glen below.

With no choice, he swerved and braked at the same time. At the last minute, the BMW swung back into its own lane, clipping our side mirror. But it was too late for us. Molloy braked again, desperately. He succeeded in slowing the car down but not enough. We were heading straight for the ditch.

Chapter Four

The car nosedived into the ditch, jolting us to a shocking and jarring halt. My seatbelt snapped taut and caught me in its grip but didn't stop me from falling to one side and whacking my head against the passenger window.

Momentarily dazed, I heard Molloy's voice, urgent and frightened beside me. 'Ben, are you all right?' His hand on my shoulder. 'Ben. Jesus.'

I blinked and opened my eyes. I hadn't realised I'd closed them. I nodded slowly as he looked at me, his face next to mine, his gaze intense. 'Speak to me. Say something.'

'I'm fine,' I said, but my voice was trembling. I tried to sit up but the car was tilted forward, and I couldn't get my balance.

Molloy took off his seatbelt and opened the driver's door, slipping as he climbed out, coming around the back of the car to open mine. I sensed someone with him, then heard a voice I recognised as Maeve, my friend and the local vet. What was she doing here?

They helped me out of the car and onto the grass verge. I swayed a little when I got to my feet, but I was unhurt. I sat down unsteadily onto a hillock.

'Are you okay?' Maeve asked, her voice full of concern.

When I nodded again, I saw that she was dressed in her work gear, a boiler suit and heavy boots, and her jeep was parked behind ours with its hazard lights flashing.

'Bastards,' she said, shaking her head. 'They overtook me a few minutes ago, and they must have been going nearly ninety. It's not the first time it's happened to me in the past few weeks either. One of my clients found a car burned out on his farm last week. Someone's going to get badly hurt.'

Molloy wasn't listening to her. His attention was completely focused on me, regarding me with an intensity that made me flush, conscious that we weren't alone.

But Maeve appeared oblivious. She glanced at his car, still tipped into the ditch at a strange angle. 'I can pull you out. Doesn't look like there's a lot of damage, but if you need, I can tow you all the way back to Glendara?'

Molloy still didn't respond. Wordlessly he pulled me to my feet, and with an odd expression on his face he wrapped me in his arms. He whispered something in my ear, something I would later wonder whether I had imagined, and released me just as my dad's ancient Nissan appeared around the corner.

It's not something you particularly want your parents to witness, the aftermath of a car accident you've been involved in. But at least they could see that I was all right. They'd been lucky; the BMW had missed them completely, my dad having stopped for a serendipitous pee, unaware of how close we were to our destination.

Maeve towed Molloy's car out of the ditch without too much difficulty. Apart from a few scratches it appeared undamaged and she went on her way, muttering about being late for her next call. I could have sworn she'd said something about a bear with a

32

sore head, but assumed I'd misheard, putting it down to delayed shock.

We continued on to Glendara, considerably shaken but unhurt, Molloy falling back into Garda mode as soon as we set off. Amazingly he'd managed to get part of the BMW's number plate and he called it in while I sat beside him, feeling as winded as if I'd been punched. The last part of the journey was a blur.

In Glendara we parked in front of the Garda Station, and my dad pulled in behind us, stretching luxuriously as he climbed out of the car.

'So, you weren't joking when you said you lived at the top of the country.' He grinned and then frowned suddenly as if remembering what had happened. 'How are you both?

'Are you sure you shouldn't see a doctor?' my mum added, tugging on a cardigan as she emerged from the warmth of the car.

I shook my head and smiled. 'The vet examined me.' Which was true. Maeve had checked my head to make sure I wasn't cut, and confirmed that I hadn't lost consciousness.

'Lucky you weren't driving that,' Dad remarked, nodding towards my very recognisable Mini, which had been parked outside the Garda Station all weekend. It occurred to me that it was just as well we'd decided to go public with our relationship. 'I suppose it's the safest place in town to park,' he chuckled.

I watched him survey the tiny Garda Station, before switching his attention back to Molloy, looking him up and down. 'Don't tell me *you* live here?'

Molloy laughed. 'No, there's a sergeant's house behind the station.'

The little terraced house from which I ran my practice was just about visible from where we stood, and I pointed it out now. I'd recently caved to town pressure, painting it a deep plum and adding a little swinging sign with the words *O'Keeffe & Co., Solicitors and Commissioners for Oaths*.

My parents exchanged a look of pride and I beamed. I couldn't help it, despite seeing Molloy's bemused expression. I was like a five-year-old showing her mum and dad around her infant class-room. Then I felt my throat constrict at the thought of how it would feel to have Faye here too. For the four of us to be together again.

'I can show you around tomorrow,' I said, feeling a sudden wave of tiredness, and convinced they must be feeling the same or worse. There was also the beginning of a headache now that the shock was wearing off. I needed some paracetamol. 'Let's get back to my house. It's in Malin, a ten-minute drive from here. But I need to pick up some food first, if you give me a few minutes?'

'We'll come with you.' My mum looked at my dad and he nodded. 'Could do with stretching our legs.'

'And I need to find those idiots before they kill someone,' Molloy said, before taking his leave and disappearing into the Garda Station. No kiss. Not a man for public displays of affection. Normally.

The rest of us set off up the hill towards the little supermarket, stopping for a few seconds when we reached the square. I wasn't the only one who'd painted my building a cheerful shade, and in the evening light there was a touch of Portofino about the blues, pinks and yellows of the town's businesses and residences.

'Pretty town,' my mum said. Her eyes narrowed. 'Ooh. Is that a bookshop?'

I looked and was surprised and pleased to see it was open. Phyllis's hours were always a bit erratic, dependant on her mood and penchant for travelling to far-flung, less visited places. And the shop had been closed completely for repairs since the floods. I'd checked myself just the morning before.

'Can we have a look?' my dad asked.

'If you're not too wrecked,' I said. In truth, I was curious to see it myself. 'I know the owner. She's organising that festival I mentioned.'

Before going in, my dad stopped to examine the sign above the shop. 'Is Kettle an Inishowen name? It's unusual.'

I smiled. 'It's a nickname. Phyllis's surname is Doherty, but it's so common here that nicknames are used to distinguish families. Her grandfather sold pots and pans in the square.'

Dad grinned. 'Ah, brilliant. I remember a mate of mine in the bank who was posted to Donegal telling me about that. He couldn't get a handle on it at all.'

As we spoke, I spotted Phyllis herself on the other side of the shop window, perched on her stool at the counter. She was wearing a salmon-pink dress to her ankles with a green leaf print, which trailed up the skirt and sleeves, and she was clearly busy at something, her frantic movements creating the impression of a wild shrub quivering in the wind.

I pushed the door open and an old-fashioned bell tinkled, announcing our arrival. Whatever Phyllis had done with the shop, I was glad to see that she'd kept that. The place was empty of customers but we were welcomed with gusto by her scruffy border collie Fred.

The bookseller herself was tapping on her phone with a biro clenched between her teeth and a stack of messily arranged papers in front of her. She gave me startled look, and greeted me without bothering to take the pen from her mouth. 'Yes, Ben, how are you doing?'

I started to introduce my parents but she stopped me with a

couple of raised fingers and muttered, 'Give me two wee seconds. I have to write this down before I forget it.'

While she scribbled, my mum and dad drifted off towards the shelves and I took the opportunity to take in the work that had been done to her shop. Kettle's bookshop had been a treasure trove, completely disordered and overstocked with an eclectic mix of new and second-hand books piled on floors and spilling off the stacks; Jackie Collins paperbacks nestling alongside first edition P. G. Wodehouse in a space that had the scent of an antique library. The last time I was in here, it was two feet deep in water, the bookshelves heartbreakingly warped and everything ruined. Despite that, we had managed to rescue all the books by moving them upstairs to Phyllis's flat.

Now I glanced around me in wonder. Phyllis had somehow managed to completely recreate what had been here before, including the mess. I could hardly believe it.

'Well, what do you think?' Phyllis followed my gaze with interest, chewing the tip of the biro.

'Wow,' I said. What I really meant was – *it looks exactly the same.* Absolutely no effort had been made to put any order on the chaos.

She put her phone down, extracted the pen from her mouth and beamed. 'It's perfect, isn't it?' Blue stained her lips, blooming in one corner of her mouth and making her look like an ink-guzzling vampire.

'It is,' I agreed, moving back towards her and surreptitiously glancing down at her untidy pile of papers. 'You're looking a bit frazzled, if you don't mind me saying.'

'Aye, you could say that.' She raked her hand through her hair, causing it to stick up like she'd had an electric shock.

'Festival plans?' I asked, hopefully. I'd always been good at reading upside down – it's amazing how useful a life skill it can be – and I'd caught sight of the word Glenfest. I really needed the festival to go ahead if I had any hope of keeping my parents here for the week.

Phyllis sucked in her breath and said in a voice that was almost doom-like. 'Gavin Featherstone is coming.'

It took me a second, but I got there. Gavin Featherstone was the writer about whom that documentary was being made, the one we'd heard about on the radio. I had a feeling now that we'd studied him in school. Surely this was good news, I thought. So why then was Phyllis wearing that troubled expression? Why did she look as if this was something that had been foisted on her which she didn't want?

'But that's great!' I said. 'Well done.' I was just relieved that the festival was going ahead.

'I can't really claim much credit,' she said. 'I left more to Tony than I should have while I was trying to get this place up and running. I asked him to help with the invites, but of course, Stan can't keep his nose out of anything.' She rolled her eyes. 'He invited Featherstone without even checking with me. Cuts his assistant's hair apparently.'

I grinned. So that explained it. Phyllis had briefly let go of the reins and the horse had bolted. Glenfest had always been her baby, but as a local publican Tony Craig would have an interest in attracting visitors to the town too. Stan, his half-brother, ran the hairdresser's salon above the pub.

'Still, in fairness, we needed someone like Featherstone. I was in danger of losing my funding if I didn't get a big name. I was tempted to cancel after the flood but . . .' Phyllis took a deep breath. 'Anyway, the bold Stan managed to pull the rabbit out of the hat, snatch victory from the jaws of defeat.'

'Well, that's good, isn't it? You've *got* a big name.'

'The biggest,' she said firmly, as if still trying to convince herself.

I tried to recall what I'd heard about Gavin Featherstone in the radio interview. 'Doesn't he live in Donegal?'

Phyllis's eyes widened. 'He lives here, in Inishowen! Didn't you know?' I shook my head and she leaned forward, arms crossed, resting her not inconsiderable frontage on her notes. 'Have you ever done the Moville to Greencastle shore walk? Well, you know that wee pebbly beach about halfway, where you have to watch your footing? With the pointy rock. The one they call the Monk, or some people think it looks like Winnie the Pooh . . .'

From what I could remember, there were a few such beaches along that walk. And quite a few pointy rocks. I stopped. Suddenly I remembered my parents. I cast my eyes about the shop and saw them happily perusing the piles of books stacked willy-nilly on the floor with Fred flopped between them, chin resting on his paws.

Phyllis was still speaking. I wondered if I should tell her about the ink stain, but knew I'd have to wait for her to take a breath, which didn't look as if it was about to happen anytime soon.

'If you're walking from Moville, there's a big house. You wouldn't know it was there because you can't see it with all the trees. A small wooden gate with a *Beware of the Dog!* sign. Slightly weird wee pillars. You must have noticed them?' Her eyes narrowed and she waited for mine to widen in recognition. 'That's Gavin Featherstone's house,' she finished with a flourish, straightening herself with a groan.

'At least he doesn't have far to come,' I said brightly. And then I recalled something else from the radio interview; the memory of that awful car journey slowly returning. 'But isn't he . . . ?'

Phyllis nodded vigorously and cut across me before I could finish my question. 'He's a complete recluse. Never leaves the house. Hasn't done an event in ten years. That's probably why you didn't know he lived here. His last public appearance was when he won the IMPAC.'

I raised my eyebrows. She was referring to the International IMPAC Dublin Literary Award, worth 100,000 euro. 'Right. Well done Stan on convincing him.'

'Aye, well, I'm not sure what persuaded him,' Phyllis said begrudgingly, sticking the pen back in her mouth, spreading the stain even further. 'I'm assuming it was this assistant fella that Stan knows. Featherstone usually doesn't respond to anyone. I don't think he even has an agent any more. Then out of the blue, a week before the festival is due to take place, Stan tells me he'll do it. To put him on the programme.'

'And can you?'

She snorted. 'Well, I can't turn him down, that's for sure. It's huge that he's agreed to do it at all.' Her eyes drifted to somewhere over my head. 'I don't know what happened to him. He used to love the attention. He was on everything; a real media whore.'

'Phyllis!' I pretended to be shocked.

She grinned. 'Anyway,' she clapped her hands together, 'now that the shop is up and running again, I've taken back the reins. This'll give the festival nationwide, if not worldwide, publicity.' She glanced down at her notes with a sudden look of concern. 'Although now I have the problem of fitting him into the schedule. It's full up. I'm going to have to shift someone.' She sucked in her breath. 'I won't be popular but there it is, I've no choice. We'll have to put him in on Friday evening. Thank God the programmes haven't been printed yet.'

She ran her fingers again through her dishevelled hair. 'I also have to find someone to interview him. Someone who's read his books or is willing to read them in a week.' She looked at me, with a baleful expression. 'I don't suppose . . .'

I laughed. 'Lord, Phyllis, I've never done anything like that in my life!'

Her shoulders slumped. She riffled through her notes, drew out a particularly crumpled and much scribbled-upon sheet and wrote something on it.

A laugh from my mum as my dad gave Fred a tummy rub caused her to look up again, and she seemed to notice for the first time that I wasn't alone. The dog usually never strayed too far away from Phyllis and I wondered if he'd picked up on her anxious mood.

'Who are they?' she whispered. 'Did they come in with you?'

'They're my parents,' I stage-whispered back.

'Ach.' Her face softened and then lit up. 'Isn't that lovely? Mr and Mrs Ben up for a visit.'

'Please don't call them that,' I begged, before inviting them over for a second attempt at introductions.

After they were done my mum said, 'Can I pay for this?' and I saw that she had *Violet, Green and Red*, Gavin Featherstone's most recent novel, in her hand.

'Ooh, good choice,' Phyllis said, rubbing her hands together. If there was one way to get into the bookseller's good books it was to buy something. 'I must get a proper display together before the weekend.' She added that to her list, sticking the biro back into her mouth immediately after.

'I think that pen's leaking,' my mum said with a half-smile.

'I've never read this one.' My mother turned the book over in her hand as we walked back to the car. She'd eschewed Phyllis's offer of a bag when she failed to find one after much rummaging beneath the counter. 'It's about an artist, apparently.'

'It got lousy reviews, that's why you didn't read it,' my dad retorted.

She nudged him. 'I'm glad you didn't say that in the shop. I must read *The Peering of Things* again; the Booker winner. I loved that one.'

'Did you hear what Phyllis said about the festival?' I asked, surprised when they shook their heads, assuming that was the reason for the purchase. 'Gavin Featherstone is coming.'

My mother gave a squeal of delight, and my dad grinned.

'Featherstone is your mother's pin-up boy. Looks as if we'll be staying the week after all.'

Chapter Five

Sunday was an early night for all of us. By the time we arrived back to my cottage in Malin, we were all bleary-eyed and my head was thumping. We had something to eat and watched some television; no one seemed in the mood to chat. I suspected that the last hour of *Fatal Attraction* wasn't exactly the right choice of viewing material, but no one seemed to have the energy to change the channel either. My parents seemed particularly subdued. I hoped they weren't questioning their decision to come because I was glad that they had. For the moment I felt better having them close, happy that they were committed to staying the week thanks to Gavin Featherstone.

Still, on Monday morning I was relieved to have the kitchen to myself when I arrived downstairs suited and booted and ready for a day at the office. When I say 'to myself', I mean myself and my rather grouchy cat Guinness, who wasn't about to forgive me too easily for disappearing for the weekend and then reappearing with two strangers in tow. He'd given my parents a wide berth the night before, but the three of them would have to learn to get along this week while I was at work. Ignoring me did not include refusing to eat, so I let him in through the window, fed him, then made myself some breakfast.

I rubbed my neck while I filled the kettle for coffee; it was a little stiff but no longer painful. We'd been lucky, Molloy and I. A near escape. Was that what prompted his declaration by the side of the road? He'd taken me by surprise but I knew I felt the same, unsure how I'd have got through this weekend without him.

Sitting down to eat, I contemplated the day ahead. Most of my appointments were connected with the district court sitting tomorrow; some licensing stuff, road traffic offences, a couple of drugs charges. The usual mixed bag. Bread and butter for a country solicitor. Or toast, I thought as I crunched on my second piece. Doherty's white sliced pan. No Chambers-baked sourdough for my parents this morning.

The book my mother had bought in Phyllis's shop was sitting on the table where she'd left it, and I reached for it now. The cover of *Violet, Green and Red* was like an abstract painting; a wash of colour with a silhouetted paintbrush dripping blood. I turned it over in my hand while I sipped my coffee, reading the short bio on the back.

Gavin Featherstone won the Man Booker Prize at twenty-seven and has twice been shortlisted since. His novel *Spirit of an Intruder* was the winner of the IMPAC in 2009. He lives in Co. Donegal, Ireland.

The author picture on the inside flap showed a ruggedly handsome man in his fifties – tanned with grey hair brushed off his face, heavy salt-and-pepper stubble, and wearing a corduroy jacket over a denim shirt in a shade of blue that perfectly matched his eyes. I understood now why he was my mother's pin-up boy, though the picture must have been taken a good decade ago.

I jumped suddenly, heart pounding, as Guinness took a flying leap from the floor onto the dresser behind me. The cat knew he wasn't allowed up there, but he did it sometimes just to annoy me, to show me that he could. This time he knocked something over and sent it skittering across the floor. I stood up to check what it was and he fled, expecting a telling off.

I cursed inwardly when I saw that it was a mobile phone, one of my parents', I presumed. I hoped it wasn't broken as I scooped it up from the floor, and was about to place it back on the dresser when the screen lit up with a text. I glanced at it, relieved when I saw that it wasn't personal, just a marketing text from a hair-dresser my mum must have been to, giving notice of a 10 per cent discount off colourings and tints.

I was about to put it back, I swear. But something made me tap the home button at the bottom of the screen. It took me straight in – no code needed – and a list of outgoing calls appeared. Eight calls all to the same number, yesterday morning, afternoon and evening. Calls made by my mother to a number assigned to *Stuart* in her contacts. With a sinking feeling I remembered returning to the table at the café and thinking she'd just made a call. I found a pen, quickly noted down the number and put the phone back on the dresser, feeling duplicitous and duped at the same time. What the hell was going on between this man and my parents?

Unable to finish the rest of my coffee, my stomach now sour, I rinsed out my plate and mug and went back upstairs to brush my teeth. The door to the spare room was closed. Before leaving the house, I left a note on the kitchen table with a spare key, suggest-ing they meet me for lunch at the Oak in Glendara, and giving directions to Lagg, my favourite beach, in case they fancied a walk, instructing them to look out for the sign for Five Fingers Strand.

The morning was clear as I drove in along the coast, the sky rinsed blue with smudges of clouds, and seagulls wheeling and squabbling overhead. It felt like an immeasurable privilege to have this as my daily commute. The sea changed almost hourly, switching in colour and consistency with the seasons and the weather. Today it was teal, with an orangey wash where the water blurred into sky on the horizon, and the day held the promise of early summer, a promise more broken than kept. But I adored living so close to the sea and hoped that my parents would get to see the Inishowen that I loved.

Leah greeted me cheerily when I walked into reception at O'Keeffe & Company Solicitors; my firm, since taking it over from my retiring predecessor years before.

'Morning,' I replied. 'You're looking rested.'

My legal assistant was five months' pregnant and had a neat bump. She'd had a rough time with morning sickness but it was beginning to pass.

'Did absolutely nothing all weekend. I must have slept about thirty hours.'

It hit me suddenly that if Leah's morning sickness had gone, then I should soon be lining someone up to take over during her maternity leave. She'd mentioned it to me more than once but I'd left it on the long finger, the prospect of running the office without her too terrifying to contemplate. I made a mental note to do something about it this week.

'Can't say the same for you,' she added, eyes narrowed as she examined my tired face.

'I'll fill you in later,' I said, lowering my tone when I noticed there were two people in the waiting room. 'Who are they?' My first appointment wasn't till ten and it was still only a bit past nine.

'First two district court appointments for tomorrow,' she whispered. 'The drugs cases. Bit anxious, both of them.' She handed me a bunch of files. 'These are all your morning appointments.'

I breathed in. 'Better get started so.'

The two drugs cases were followed by an adopted young woman who wanted advice on how to trace her biological parents. I was glad to be able to tell her about the new Birth and Tracing Act, which enshrined in law the importance of a person knowing his or her origins. Until now, people who were adopted were given a Certificate of Adoption, which had the legal status of a birth certificate but didn't contain details of the birth parents. The new Act hugely broadened the information given to adopted people, providing for 'the full release of birth certificates, as well as the full release of birth, early life, care and medical information as defined in the legislation, to all relevant persons who have attained the age of 16 years.'

Having provided her with the necessary contacts to go about applying for this information I saw the young woman out, feeling more than usually affected by her story. Maybe it was because my own parents were, for once, close by, but her plea that 'I just want to know the name I was given when I was born' had brought a lump to my throat.

She was followed by a farmer wanting to consult about a long-running boundary dispute with his neighbour, and a domestic assault case, which would require a barring order. The breadth of expertise required by a country solicitor could sometimes be overwhelming.

I finally got a break about eleven o'clock and came downstairs to leave the drugs charge sheets and my attendances on the counter for adding to the district court file. I needed to speak to Molloy before tomorrow to see if I could negotiate a plea in either case.

Leah was on the phone so I went off to make coffee, returning with a decaffeinated one for her and an extra caffeinated one for me. Finding her still on the phone I left her mug on the desk and wandered into the now mercifully empty waiting room in search of a newspaper. The national *Irish Times* and local *Inish Times* (one letter difference in name, a world of difference in content) were on the coffee table. Leah collected them in Stoop's newsagents on her way in each morning.

I grabbed the local one and took it back to reception, flicking through it on the counter while waiting for Leah to finish her call. *Good news on the jobs front!* trumpeted the front-page, head-lining an article about the expansion of a digital communications company providing employment in Glendara and Moville. The fourth and fifth pages were taken up entirely by a feature on Glenfest, which was supported by all the local businesses. We'd paid for an advertising square – *O'Keeffe & Co. Solicitors, for all your conveyancing, criminal, and probate needs, wish Glenfest every success!'* – along with Liam McLaughlin's Estate Agency, the Oak pub and of course Phyllis's own bookshop.

In the middle was an article whetting the appetite for the festival – *Full programme free with Thursday's edition!* There was no mention of Gavin Featherstone. Phyllis would be frustrated by that but the paper must have gone to print too early. At least he'd make it into the programme.

Even without Featherstone there was a full schedule of events: workshops for adults and children, panel discussions, music and an open mic event in the Oak on Friday night. I wondered who was going to be shafted in favour of Featherstone for the prime spot on Friday evening. The biggest name and the one presently listed on Friday was Róisín Henderson, a feminist short story writer and essayist from Belfast who'd gained notoriety (I knew this from the

47

weekend supplements) from proclaiming that the novel was dead, and the true form of fiction was the short story. I wondered how she'd take being moved aside for an older male novelist.

'Are you going to any of it?' Leah had finished her call and was looking over my shoulder while sipping her decaf.

'Yep.' I closed the paper, refolded it and put it back in the waiting room. 'It's a bit of a godsend to be honest. My parents are up for a few days and it will give them something to do.'

Leah gasped. 'Seriously? Your parents are here?'

'You'll probably meet them later. I'm hoping they'll come in and join us for lunch.'

'Ach, that's lovely. I have a doctor's appointment at half one so I'll have to just grab a sandwich but I'll hang around to say hello.'

After years of living in Inishowen without a hint of a relative, I could understand why people were curious. But seeing Leah's eyes narrow and knowing she was about to ask me the reason for their visit after all this time, I quickly re-routed the conversation back to Glenfest.

'I saw Phyllis yesterday. That writer Gavin Featherstone has agreed to come to the festival. I think he's going to headline it now.'

Leah made a face. 'Really? He's supposed to be a bit of an oddball. '

'Is he?' I shrugged. 'My mother's a big fan. I know he's a recluse, that he never does interviews.'

She nodded. 'Aye. He lives alone in that huge house with his assistant, Robbie something or other. He's from Belfast, I think. Featherstone's marriage broke up years ago. The wife left him, taking the kids, and he went a bit funny after that. His wife was from around here,' she frowned as if trying to remember. 'Or her family was, but he's English, I think. Never leaves the house, apparently. That assistant guy does all his shopping, all his . . .' she waved her hands about vaguely, 'business or whatever. I think he walks along the shore but that's it.'

'How old is he?' I asked, spotting an uncomfortable parallel with my parents' situation, which made me flinch. Featherstone's assistant doing everything for him? Was that caring or control?

Leah shrugged. 'Sixties, seventies?'

I nodded, remembering that the documentary was to celebrate his seventieth birthday.

She rested her chin on her hands. 'How strange is that, though? Never leaving your house. You can't say that's healthy . . .'

She trailed off at the sound of the front door being flung open, its handle whacking against the inside wall. I knew who it was before I saw him. Liam McLaughlin, our local estate agent and auctioneer, always made an entrance.

'You know I'm going to have to charge you for the paint job on that wall,' I called out.

Liam appeared in reception. 'You need to get one of them spring doorstops.' He dropped the leather folder he was carrying onto the counter and yanked some sheets from it. 'I have those sales advice notices for that farm at Bocan. I've taken deposits, and all the details are in here. How soon can you get contracts drawn up? Buyers are raring to go.'

'Lovely to see you too, Liam.'

'What? Oh aye. Sorry.' He grinned. 'Bit hassled.'

I took the sheets from him and scanned quickly through. 'No buildings on it, am I right?'

He nodded. 'Just land. Two parcels. Sixty acres in total.'

'Okay. They're coming in towards the end of the week, aren't they?' I looked at Leah for confirmation and she checked the appointments register.

'Thursday at ten,' she said. 'I've spoken to them, and they're bringing in deeds and maps. There's no mortgage on it so they have everything they need.'

'Great.' Turning to Liam, I said. 'I'll do them on Friday but it might be Monday by the time they go out? That do you?'

He looked satisfied. One thing off his list apparently.

I crossed my arms. 'So why are you so hassled?'

He blew out through his teeth. 'Phyllis. This bucking festival of hers. She's roped in half the town to give her a hand, and now she has me organising a marquee for her. Hope the bloody weather holds.'

'A marquee? Where?'

'The grounds of the Beacon Hall. Out the back. Now that this guy Featherstone is appearing she's decided the hall isn't big enough to accommodate the hordes of people that she thinks are coming, so she's insisting on a marquee.'

'Is there room for one?' I asked.

'Aye, just about. We can attach it to the big back door.' He raised his eyes to heaven. 'I think she might be overestimating the town's interest in some old hack who never sticks his nose out to speak to anyone.'

I laughed. 'He's fairly well known, I think. Internationally as well as in Ireland. And there's the fact that he hasn't done an event in so long. She might get people travelling to see him. That'd be good for the town, wouldn't it?'

Liam gave me a look that said he wasn't convinced.

'I know she's up to ninety,' I conceded. 'I saw her in the shop last night.'

The estate agent allowed himself a grin. 'Aye, well, if you thought she was in a flap last night, you should see her today. There's a crowd from RTÉ doing a documentary on him. It's being done without his cooperation, but they've got wind of him appearing at the festival so they're coming up.' His phone rang and he took it out of his pocket and checked the number. 'Right. I'm away. That's the marquee boy.'

Chapter Six

Open Mic on Friday night!! 9 p.m. after Gavin Featherstone event. Flash fiction! Slam poetry! Memoir! Anything goes. Just keep it to five minutes!!!

The poster, which had been handwritten in marker by someone with an appreciation for exclamation marks, was sellotaped to the window of the Oak pub alongside a more professional-looking printed one advertising the festival itself. Judging by the walk up from the office, Phyllis had papered the town with them or, more likely, got one of her minions to do it.

'Nice pub,' my dad remarked appreciatively, casting his eyes around the bar with its dark wood, exposed brick and the open fire, which Tony insisted on keeping lit for most of the year. In the cosy gloom of the interior, it could be any season, although he did put tables outside on the rare occasions it was warm enough.

The publican himself was behind the bar, chatting with his brother Stan who was perched on a high stool having lunch. The pair had found one another only a few years back, but were now inseparable. Stan sometimes even helped his brother out behind the bar, mainly, I suspected, because he liked being the centre of attention. Cocktails often made an appearance when Stan was on duty.

Both gave my parents the same curious but warm reception they'd had elsewhere.

'Drinks on the house for your first visit,' Tony announced. 'What'll you have?'

My dad's eyes widened with pleasure and I was sure he'd have ordered a pint had my mother not reminded him that he was driving. Instead, we ordered sandwiches, soup and coffee, my dad going for the Donegal crab toast with avocado and apple.

While Tony went to get our drinks, Stan twisted around on his stool to chat. The complete antithesis of his sober-looking older brother, today he was decked out in a chequered yellow waistcoat and pinstriped trousers. 'Will ye be here for the festival?' he asked, indicating yet another poster behind the bar.

'Looks like it,' my mother said. 'Are you involved?'

'Stan's responsible for Gavin Featherstone coming,' I offered.

My mother's face lit up. 'Really?' she said. 'Do you know him?'

'Never met the man. I cut Robbie's hair. Robbie's his assistant.' Stan grinned and tapped his nose. 'Robbie has a very specific kind of haircut, which needs a regular maintenance.'

'How'd you manage to persuade Featherstone to come?' I asked.

'Ach, that was down to Robbie,' Stan replied. 'I think he convinced him that if anyone was going to buy that book that he has coming out next year, then he'd have to come out of his cave sometime. And maybe for Featherstone, a small local festival like our wee one is an easy place to start. God love him,' he shook his head sadly, 'I don't think the man's that well.'

I wondered if he meant physically or mentally, remembering what Leah had said about staying in your house not being particularly healthy.

'Anyway,' Stan sat up straight on his stool, stretching his back,

'I've done my bit. From now on unless anyone needs an emergency cut-and-blow-dry, I'm staying well out of it! But I might be tempted to get up and do a turn for the open mic.'

'Indeed, you will not,' Tony returned with our coffees. 'We'd need a crowbar to get you off the stage.' He nodded to me. 'I'll bring your food down if you want to grab a table.'

When the three of us had settled ourselves at a table far enough away from the fire to enjoy the look of it without the heat, I asked, 'How was your morning? Did you get to Lagg?'

'We did,' my mother replied, wide eyed. 'It's spectacular. We had a lovely walk. We thought we might do that shore walk tomorrow; Moville is it? The one your friend in the bookshop mentioned? If you can give us directions.'

'Your mother wants to have a nosy at Featherstone's house,' my dad said with a grin.

I'd told them what Phyllis had said about where he lived.

'Sure. It's very easy to get to.' I said, looking up as our food arrived.

While Tony distributed the plates, I looked at them both properly, noting with relief that they looked considerably better than they had done last night: I hoped it was because they'd slept well and not because they'd heard from Chambers. I'd pass his phone number on to Molloy later when I talked to him about tomorrow's court. Another of the cases I'd thought was going on had turned into a guilty plea after the morning's appointments, which meant tomorrow would be a shorter day than I'd thought, giving me an idea.

'If you can wait till the afternoon for your walk, I might come with you,' I said, once Tony had departed back up to the bar. 'I'm in court in the morning but I should be out by lunchtime.'

'Excellent,' my dad said, biting straight away into his crab toast and pointing to it after he'd placed it back on his plate with full cheeks. 'This is really good.'

'The forecast isn't too bad.' My mother reached for the black pepper, brushing her knife off the table with her elbow in the process and causing it to fall to the floor with a clatter. I offered to fetch a replacement, but she insisted on doing it herself.

While she headed up to the bar I glanced at my dad, contentedly chewing his food. Should I grab this moment to bring up the subject of Chambers, I wondered? There was no way for me to ask about the calls my mother had made without admitting to snooping.

In the end, I hesitated too long and Dad spoke first, swallowing his food, then smiling and reaching out to pat my hand. 'It's good to see you happy, part of a little community.'

'Thanks, Dad.' I felt my eyes glisten, and then, as if hearing the summons, the door opened and Maeve walked in. As usual she was on the move, running in to grab a coffee and sandwich to eat on her way to a call. But she spotted us and came over.

'How are you all doing after yesterday?' She grinned. 'Not every day you have to pull the sergeant out of a sheugh. Hope he remembers it the next time I park on the footpath.'

'Fully recovered,' I said, smiling at the sight of my dad frowning and mouthing the word *sheugh* to himself. 'Did you say something about a bear with a sore head yesterday or was I imagining it?'

She nodded. 'Yep, turned out to be a toothache. We might have to get a specialist dentist over from the UK.'

Before I could respond, my mother reappeared. 'Nine on Friday,' she announced. 'Oh, hello Maeve.'

Suddenly I felt as if I was in some kind of surrealist play with absolutely no idea of what was going on. 'Sorry? What's nine on Friday?'

Mum retook her seat and placed her clean knife carefully on the table. 'I've an appointment with Stan to get my hair cut at nine o'clock on Friday morning.'

While Dad teased her about getting dolled up for Featherstone, Maeve grinned. 'You pair seem to be settling in, anyway.'

After lunch my parents left to buy groceries while I walked back to the office alone. Unbelievably the sky was still blue, flecked with wispy white clouds, and the square was a riot of colour, not just from the brightly painted buildings but the flower pots, which were bursting with the blooms of early summer: primroses, marigolds and bluebells. It was the perfect time for a festival with the town looking so well.

I needed to be back in the office for an appointment at two with the parents' committee for the local primary school, but I thought I'd try to catch Molloy at the Garda Station first.

Andy McFadden, the only other guard in Glendara, was at the front desk when I walked in, scratching his head and cursing at the computer.

He looked up at me with a pained expression on his face. 'Why can no one invent a simple wee printer? An ordinary good-humoured machine that does exactly what you want it to do, without having a feckin' screaming match with you every time you want to print something. Why are they always so thran?'

I grinned, imagining my dad's confused face at the word *thran*. I had a particular soft spot for thran, meaning awkward or contrary and there was never a shortage of opportunities to use it. 'I have no idea,' I said. 'Leah seems to have the magic touch in our place.'

'Maybe you can send her down here.' McFadden shook his head in frustration. 'You looking for Molloy?'

I nodded. 'Is he here?'

'Nah, he's gone over to Buncrana . . . Not sure why.' He rolled his eyes. 'You know the sergeant. Won't tell you anything unless he absolutely has to.'

I grinned. McFadden knew Molloy pretty well.

'Will I ask him to give you a shout when he gets back?' he said.

'Do. Thanks, Andy.'

As I was leaving, he called after me. 'I hear you two had an accident? You all right?'

I nodded and smiled. At least Molloy had told him that, I thought. And that I was with him.

The committee were a punctual lot and once I'd finished with them, I went downstairs to chat to Leah at reception. A sneering laugh from the waiting room alerted me to the fact that we weren't alone, and a glance in there revealed two seated young men, knees spread so wide they were almost touching despite being two seats apart.

'More district court,' Leah said. 'Both up tomorrow. They're together, same charges. They've fallen out with their solicitor and want to know if you'll represent them.'

I frowned. That was never a good start. 'Who's their solicitor?'

'Thompson's.'

I sighed. Thompson was the other solicitor in town. The last thing I wanted to do was get into a wrangle over clients. 'Give me a minute then send them up.'

A few minutes later, after handing over a clutch of crumpled and stained charge sheets, the pair sat back with their arms crossed, adopting the same splayed-knees position they'd taken downstairs. They could have been street dancers; it was so choreographed.

One was older, but only just, early twenties perhaps. He was tall and pale, with a bony face, protuberant eyes and a helmet of greasy black hair. The younger one was stocky with a hard square face and coarse red hair. Both wore expressions of defiance and irritation, creating the impression that they had much more important places to be.

'So, you're usually represented by Thompson's?' I asked.

'Aye, but them's new charges,' the older one said, uncrossing his arms briefly to wave a nicotine-stained finger at my desk. 'He doesn't know anything about those.'

I sighed. So that was the reason for switching. If they thought they could escape previous convictions by moving solicitor they were wrong. If convicted, it would be the first thing the judge would ask. Still, it did mean I could represent them if the charges were fresh.

I smoothed the sheets out on the desk. They had about fifteen charges between them: criminal damage, section 112 unauthorised taking, car theft, and a variety of road traffic offences such as no insurance or tax. I counted four different dates and felt a creeping unease. What if the two men in front of me had been in the BMW that had driven us off the road the day before? What would I do then?

Of course, I wouldn't be able to represent them. There'd be a conflict. I'd be a witness, a victim. But those two hadn't been caught, and the dates on these charges were weeks ago. So, I suppressed the niggle, told them I might not be able to represent them both if there was any conflict in their evidence, took down my *Offences Handbook* and got to work.

After about twenty minutes of the pair of them talking into their armpits and giving me the bare minimum of instructions – they weren't there, it wasn't them, they had no idea why they had been charged, that guard was a crabbit aul bastard – I ushered them downstairs and saw them to the door. There was nothing much I could do yet. I'd look for copies of all witness statements in court in the morning and the case would be adjourned until we had time to consider them and decide on a plea.

The afternoon continued in the same busy vein. I missed Molloy's returned call and when I rang back he was gone again.

Emerging from the office at half past five, I spotted his familiar figure speaking to a woman in a pink jacket across the road. So I hung back and waited till they'd finished, feigning doing something on my phone, then crossed the road to meet him.

He looked up, his features softening when he saw me. 'Hey, how are you feeling?'

I flushed. I knew he meant physically, but I couldn't help but think about his declaration to me the day before on the side of the road. Should I mention it? Here on the footpath, with the woman in the pink jacket still looking at us. What if he regretted saying it?

'I'm grand,' I said, inwardly rolling my eyes. And I thought he was repressed.

He nodded. 'Good. We still haven't found that car by the way. It was stolen from a publican in Buncrana. I'm sure we'll find it burned out somewhere.'

'Right.'

'There's a whole gang of them, doing doughnuts at night, playing chicken. Knocking over road signs. We've charged some of them, some cases coming up. But if I get my hands on those two arseholes from yesterday . . .'

I couldn't meet his eye. What if they were the same two arseholes that had been in my office this afternoon? Smalltown problems, I thought. Wouldn't happen in a city.

Thankfully, Molloy didn't seem to notice my discomfort. 'And how are the folks getting on?'

Relieved at the change of subject, I smiled. 'They've already met half the town, and Stan's cutting my mother's hair on Friday.'

'That's great. Hang onto them as long as you can, I'd say. Their house is fine – the local guards in Ballyfermot are driving by it every few hours.'

'Thanks,' I said gratefully.

'Did you find out the name of that counselling group?'

I shook my head, and it hit me that this was what I should have asked my dad when I'd had the chance. 'Not yet. I'm sorry. Any luck finding out anything more about Chambers?'

'No. Nothing. The problem is not knowing for sure if it's his real name. If he did actually lose his wife and baby in a car accident, then it isn't. If I had the name of the group, then I might be able to find out more. It might have accounts, a premises, might be registered as a charity. Might even have got a licence for fundraising at some stage.'

'Okay. Noted. I'll ask. I promise.' I paused, unsure what his response would be to my next snippet of information, or rather how I'd come by it. 'I have Chambers's number if that's any help?' I offered him my phone with the screen open at my contacts where I'd input the number I'd taken from my mother's.

Molloy gave me a shrewd look. 'And how exactly did you get that?'

I shrugged and said nothing, grateful when he took the phone from me and made a note of the number. 'I'll see what I can find out,' he said with a sigh.

'Oh, and about the district court tomorrow,' I said, moving on quickly before he decided to interrogate me any further. 'Pleas in those two road traffic cases, the careless driving and the insurance. And any chance you'll drop the supply if we plead to possession on the drugs charges?'

His eyes narrowed. 'Which ones are those?'

I gave him the names of the accused. 'You'll find the intent to supply difficult to prove; there's no evidence of it in either case and the quantity is borderline.' Switching from defence to mitigation I did my best to change my expression and tone to match. Conciliatory. 'And they're both first offences.'

'All right. I'll talk to the prosecuting guard and see what she thinks. I'll let you know in the morning.' Molloy paused. His own expression changed, and he looked at me in that way that made my spine tingle. His tone lowered. 'So, are we going to see each other this week? And I don't mean on the street or in court. Or with your parents in the room next door. Much as I like them.'

I smiled. 'What are you suggesting?'

'Why don't you come over some evening? I still have those steaks I never got to cook on Saturday night—'

He never got to finish his invitation. Our conversation was drowned out by the snarl of a loud engine, and we looked up to see a huge, sleek, Harley-Davidson roar past, all chrome and engine and noise. There was a friendly wave from the motorcyclist, a huge guy with a beard in full leathers.

'And look who's back,' Molloy said, returning the wave. 'Phyllis will be happy.'

Chapter Seven

The same Harley was impossible to miss parked in the square the next morning, as I made my way to the courthouse. I was running a little later than usual having been accosted at the office by yet another late addition to my list; this time, a severely hungover older man on a serious assault charge, a case I hoped wouldn't scupper my walking plans with my parents in the afternoon.

It was cooler than it had been the day before; a veil of clouds drifted across the sun and it was blustery as if it might rain, the usual unpredictable weather of early summer.

Phyllis was standing in the doorway of her bookshop as I passed, breathing in the fresh air, dressed in a sky-blue smock with massive pockets and a yellow paisley scarf tied around her hair.

'Morning,' I said, indicating the huge motorbike. 'I see Jude is back.'

I was surprised to see her flush; Phyllis is not normally easy to embarrass.

'He's staying in my spare bedroom,' she said, quickly.

'Is there room?' I smiled. Phyllis lived in a cosy but not very large flat above the bookshop, a space usually filled with the overflow of stock from the floor below, and Jude was not a small man. Plus, there was Fred the dog.

'He's here to help with the festival,' she said defensively. 'You remember he's a trained paramedic?'

I did. Jude Burns had originally come to Inishowen in precisely that role as part of a Malin to Mizen charity cycle, which had been scuppered by the floods. Rain turned out to be the least of the charity's problems but Jude and Phyllis had struck up a friendship, which appeared to have lasted, and I suspected was on its way to becoming something more.

'I thought it would be good to have him at the events. Health and safety, you know.' She waved her hand about vaguely. 'And, he's a reader, so he'd have probably come anyway.'

'You don't need to explain yourself to me.' I laughed. 'I like Jude.'

'So do I,' she said, suddenly beaming.

'How are the plans going, anyway?' I asked, sneaking a peek at my watch to ensure I had time to listen to the reply and deciding that I had. Just about.

Phyllis sniffed with exaggerated self-importance. 'Apparently, I am the woman who has just pulled off the most impressive coup in the Irish literary calendar. Possibly the literary world full stop.'

I knew she was joking but I was amused at how easily Phyllis had progressed from resenting Stan for inviting Gavin Featherstone, to claiming full credit for it today.

'We got a mention in both the *Independent* and the *Times* this morning. Did you see it? Our wee festival!'

I shook my head. My early client had meant I hadn't yet had a chance to read the papers either. Not a problem for Phyllis. She reached inside the shop to grab a copy of the *Irish Times* and handed it to me already open at page seven, where there was a small column with the headline, *Reclusive writer Gavin Featherstone to come out of retirement after twelve years.*

'That's fantastic,' I said, handing it back to her, deciding I'd read it later. 'I hear that he's got a new book coming out next year.'

'He has. A memoir.' A slight shadow crossed Phyllis's face. 'Pity it's not a novel. Still, if he reads from it, we'll get an exclusive.'

I caught sight of my watch. Twenty-five past. Definitely time to go.

But Phyllis was still talking. 'We're nearly there, I think.' She looked skywards, listing out categories on her fingers. 'Tony is doing food stalls and a bar for the launch on Thursday night. That's in the marquee; it'll allow us to test it before Gavin Featherstone's event on Friday. Programmes have been printed, posters are up, tickets are selling like mad. He's on the English course for next year's Leaving Cert so the school have booked twenty—'

I cut across her, mid-flow. 'That's great Phyllis, but I'd better go. I'm going to be late for court.'

'Ooh, take one of these with you.' She drew a shiny programme from the pocket of her smock. 'Just printed. Hot off the press.'

I saw that she had a sheaf of them in there. Probably the real reason why she was standing in the doorway of her bookshop, and why she was wearing a smock. I ran my eyes quickly down the list of the main events on the front page, curiosity briefly overriding the urgency of getting to court. 'I see you've moved Róisín Henderson.' *As I'd expected.* 'How did she take it?'

Phyllis smiled mischievously. 'Well, she wasn't happy, I thought I might have a lawsuit on my hands, until . . .' She lowered her voice to a mock whisper. 'Look at Friday's schedule.'

I flicked inside to where there was a more detailed breakdown of each event. Featherstone's author picture was there, alongside a black and white one of a woman in her forties, with glasses, a round pale face and a splash of freckles across her nose. The caption beneath read: *6 p.m. Friday. Gavin Featherstone in conversation with Róisín Henderson. The novel versus the short story. Clash of the Titans or David and Goliath?*

'Ooh, nicely done,' I said.

'I know.' She grinned. 'I made it look like a two-hander to keep her happy, but let's be honest, everyone will be there for him. Plus, I've asked her to do a short-story workshop on Saturday afternoon, which means she'll get paid twice; so she's not going to turn that down.'

'Phyllis, I really have to go . . .' I shoved the programme into the side pocket of my briefcase.

'Shall I put you down for tickets?'

'Do,' I said, walking away.

'With Mr and Mrs Ben?' she called after me.

I winced. I had a feeling that nickname was going to stick.

The usual crowd of solicitors, guards and punters congregated outside the little courtroom, which had also served as the town library until a shiny new one was incorporated into the county council offices. I spotted my two car-theft clients smoking and messing about on the steps, but there was no sign of the assault guy. I hoped he'd appear to meet his bail and hadn't retreated to his hungover pit.

Inside, Molloy was in his usual spot on the front right facing the judge, chatting to the district court clerk. No sign of the judge himself yet, thankfully. I took my place on the left with the other defence solicitors, dumped my files on the table and slid over to him.

'Section Three assault. First time in the list. I've just got instructions.' I gave him the name of my new client. 'What's happening with it?'

He checked his own papers. 'Six weeks for a book of evidence. Circuit court.'

'Okay.' I paused. 'Also, two other new cases . . .' I gave him details of the car thefts I'd avoided mentioning the day before and he frowned, just as a familiar snigger was heard from the back of the court.

Molloy turned. 'Those two bucks?'

I nodded. 'I'll be applying for statements.'

He shook his head, clearly unhappy. 'That pair are part of that gang of thugs I was telling you about yesterday. Terrorising the place. The older one is a particularly nasty piece of work. Has previous for breaking his girlfriend's arm because she was talking to a fella from Derry. Be careful.'

I raised my eyebrows at him. I hadn't asked about previous convictions, so this was crossing a line. It was possible I would find myself conflicted if they were charged with the accident in which we'd been involved, but there'd been no mention of that yet. If it happened, I'd pull out. In the meantime, I didn't need Molloy protecting me from my own clients.

'Anyway,' I said, again firmly, 'statements. Okay?'

He nodded dismissively and I slid across the bench to my seat. Taking a note on my file, I glanced back to see him already negotiating with one of the Buncrana solicitors. I felt a flicker or irritation. We might be getting closer personally but profession-ally he could still rightly piss me off.

Court was busy, fast and frantic. Summary justice, dispensed summarily. My assault client made an appearance at twelve o'clock just in time to hear his case being called, which meant that, as expected, I was completely finished by lunchtime. So I headed back to the office intending to drop my files and head straight out to Malin; I never took appointments on court days because I never could be sure when I'd finish.

I was about to leave again when the door opened and a young man in jeans and green Converse runners walked into reception. Early twenties, I guessed, with scruffy dark hair and troubled eyes, a cleft chin and the tiny trace of a moustache, which my dad would have called bumfluff. He was wearing a T-shirt with graphics from *The Thing*, the science-fiction horror movie from the eighties, which a cousin of mine made me watch as a child, giving me nightmares for weeks.

There was a wariness about him as he gripped a large brown envelope in narrow fingers. Solicitor's offices have that effect sometimes; as frightening as a horror movie in some people's books. His eyes darted from Leah to me and back again as if he was unsure whom he should be addressing. 'Em, I was told to drop something in here?'

It occurred to me that if one of us was a man he wouldn't have been so conflicted, but maybe that was my own prejudice speaking. Feeling sorry for him, I stepped forward, volunteering to take the envelope. 'What is it?'

A phone rang in his jeans pocket and his eyes widened; an old-fashioned ringtone which kept ringing, though he made no move to answer it.

'Don't you want to take that?'

He shook his head, the phone stopped and he handed me the envelope.

'It's a release form,' he said, his words tumbling out in a rush. 'For the Gavin Featherstone documentary. We usually get them signed straight away but Gina forgot this one, so she said to drop it in here and your woman will pick it up later today . . .' he trailed off, hopeful that this was sufficient information to allow him to drop and run.

It wasn't. But I did recall that the arts presenter I'd heard interviewed was Gina Bailey, and that Liam had said they were coming up to film the event. This young man must be part of the crew.

The office phone rang and Leah answered it. It sounded as if it had the potential to be a long one so I ushered our new arrival into the waiting room. Once there, I slid a one-page document out of the envelope and scanned through it. It was a standard release form for a contributor to a television programme, consenting to allow whatever material was gathered or footage was filmed to be used for broadcast.

'Okay,' I said slowly. 'To be clear, this is just to be collected? I don't need to witness the signature?'

He shook his head and then nodded. Crystal clear, then.

I tried again. 'Because I won't be here this afternoon. I was about to leave when you came in.'

His face cleared. 'Oh. No. You don't need to do anything. It's just to be collected.'

'And *who* is it for?' I asked, presuming that it must be a client of the office if they'd asked for it be dropped in here. The form was blank; no name had yet been filled in.

'Mrs Featherstone,' he replied.

I raised my eyebrows. A bit off for someone I'd never met to use the place as a post office but, in the circumstances, I supposed I was prepared to let it go. I put the form back into the envelope and took a pen from my pocket. 'And what's your name?'

'Ollie.' He paused. 'Oliver Connolly.'

I wrote the date and the words, *For collection by Mrs Featherstone. Dropped in by Oliver Connolly* on the envelope.

'Is that okay then?' he asked anxiously.

He reminded me suddenly of an overwound clock; taut and nervous, afraid of making a mistake. The T-shirt revealed how painfully thin he was, his skinny arms, the chest almost concave. Before I could respond his eyes closed, he inhaled then sneezed, loudly and repeatedly. Five, six, seven times. I watched the spray plume through the air and, when he'd finished, I said, 'Yep, it's fine,' and he fled.

Hearing the front door slam, I returned to give the envelope to Leah who'd finished her call. 'Can you give this to Mrs Featherstone when she calls in?'

'*The* Mrs Featherstone?' she said, her eyes widening.

Chapter Eight

Driving across the bridge into Malin and parking outside my cottage, it was impossible not to smile at the sight of two familiar figures sitting on a bench in the green enjoying the weather. My mum looked up from her book as I approached, putting her sunglasses on her head, while my dad continued snoozing, his head tilted back, hands clasped on his stomach.

'You two look like you're properly on holidays,' I said, surprised to see Guinness sunning himself at their feet. He'd thawed considerably towards them since they'd been bribing him with salmon. I'd caught my dad feeding him some the evening before.

Dad blinked awake. 'Oh, hi.'

'Still up for that walk?' I said. 'We could get something to eat in Greencastle before walking back? It'll take us two, two and a half hours. That okay?'

My dad looked doubtful but my mother said, 'You'll be grand. It's all on the flat, isn't it?'

It was a while since I'd done it but I risked a 'Pretty much,' with my fingers crossed behind my back.

'It'll be good for you.' My mum nudged my dad. 'You've been eating too much of Stuart's cooking.' She looked startled as if

70

she'd said something taboo, but I wasn't displeased. It gave me permission to mention him later.

The Moville shore walk is a two-and-a-half kilometre coastal path that follows the shores of Lough Foyle between the towns of Moville and Greencastle. I opted to drive. With three of us the Mini was a little crowded but we pulled into the old market town of Moville, once a port of call for transatlantic liners, about half two and stowed the car in the sloping car park across the road from St Eugene's Society Temperance Hall.

A brisk sea breeze snatched at our hair when we clambered out of the car, and we zipped up waterproof jackets before turning left to set off down the hill. The path soon split and we chose the route closer to the shore; the waves thudding in our ears, prominent lifebuoys and signs warning of strong currents, a reminder of the power of the sea, even on a day when it was relatively calm.

Passing a Little Free Library at the start of the walk prompted me to ask my mother how she was enjoying Featherstone's book.

'Ooh well . . .' she said. 'It's keeping my attention anyway. But it's quite a strange book.'

'How do you mean, strange?'

'Featherstone's other novels have a good mix of characters, but I can't warm to a single one in this one. They're all hideous; especially the protagonist, the artist.' She gave a half laugh. 'It's turning me off him a little.'

We passed a black and white house with large windows taking advantage of the views, and a lookout building with the waves lapping peacefully below.

'Turning you off Featherstone?' I asked. 'Why?'

She shrugged. 'Don't they say that writers put a little piece of themselves into all of the characters they write?'

'But don't they also say that crime writers are charming because they get all their aggression out on the page?' Dad interjected with a grin. 'That would imply the opposite. The worse the characters, the nicer the writer.' My dad liked his thrillers. Retired bank manager that he was, he said he liked things to actually happen in his fiction.

'Ah, maybe it was just the frame of mind he was in when he was writing it. He hasn't lost me yet.' Mum smiled. 'And I doubt Gavin Featherstone rates crime fiction. He's a bit of a literary snob, I imagine.'

A seabird sounded, piercingly shrill, as we picked our way along the route dictated by the vagaries of the rocks, tracing an undulating path around their shoulders. Wildflowers bloomed to the left; bracken, dandelions and dog daisies, and fuchsia not yet in bloom. To the right, there was the lap and whoosh of the sea as it caressed the seaweed-covered rocks, and in the middle distance, the land of Derry on the other side of the estuary.

We saluted some dog walkers, and once they'd passed, I picked up the thread of the conversation again. 'Featherstone might meet his match on Friday. The woman who is interviewing him is a short-story snob.'

My dad harrumphed. 'They've little to fight about.'

'It'll be interesting to see what he's like in person,' my mum said.

'That's assuming you don't see him today, stalker!' Dad took out a handkerchief to mop his brow. Despite the breeze, the sun had a little heat in it. Though possibly not for long.

'I'm not stalking him,' she retorted. 'I've been reading the man for years and I'm interested in seeing where he lives. That's all.'

She turned her gaze to the sea where the dark silhouette of a bird with a long neck and pointed beak dived into the water. A cormorant, I guessed.

'You have great bird life here,' she said, shielding her eyes. 'I noticed it on Lagg yesterday.'

'There's a reserve on Inch,' I said. 'Depending on how long you stay you might get to visit it. They have whooper swans and greylag geese who visit during the winter.'

I hadn't really been suggesting they stay for six months but I was still taken aback by the silent response. Maybe now was the time to bring up Chambers? I thought, get it over with. But we found ourselves having to walk in single file and, again, I delayed too long, not wanting to spoil the walk. Because it really was something special. The air was so fresh it was almost mint. And while we passed some houses, large and expensive with lush gardens sloping down to the shore, at times it was only ourselves, the sea and the birds, swooping and chiding one another overhead.

Rounding a path between two large rocks, spatters of rain began to fall, though the sun still glinted on the water – what Irish weather forecasters are so fond of calling 'sunny spells and scattered showers'.

'So, where's Featherstone's house then?'

I could see my dad was beginning to tire, so I looked ahead to get my bearings.

A wash of light brought the protruding land into silhouette like the spine of some ancient sea creature, waves crashing in the distance. I had a feeling there was a little cove coming up; possibly the one that Phyllis had mentioned.

'I think we might be nearing it now,' I said.

And sure enough, after a jutting rock we arrived at the sliver of a stony beach, strewn with dulse and bladderwrack. Half a tyre and other detritus had washed up too, along with sticks and branches. But no pointy rock.

I shook my head. 'It's not this one. We've a bit to go.'

My dad sighed and we rounded the shore again. The wind was sharp, whipping our hair and bringing a real chill. Even the sea was rougher here, all black rocks and thrashing water. Scraps of ragged clouds crossed the sun and cast shadows over the sea, dark patches moving across the water. It reminded me of a video I'd seen of a blue whale beneath a boat, ominous yet stunning, a seemingly endless mass shimmering beneath the waves.

Through a passageway overhung with furze we walked, emerging onto a patch of perfect sand like a beach in miniature, bookended by rocks. One of them was pointed. A gull perched on it while a woman tossed seaweed for her excited dog.

A high fence to our left corralled shrubs and plants, which seemed to be reaching their limbs out to the sea, with a little gate and steps leading down to the shore.

My mother sighed wistfully. 'Imagine being able to walk down to your own beach every morning.'

'Actually, this is it, I think,' I said. 'Featherstone's house.'

My parents turned as one, and we walked in the direction of the gate, stepping around rockpools with cockles and mussels, causing my dad to burst into a rendition of 'Molly Malone' and my mum to shush him as if he were about to disturb Featherstone's creative muse.

'Did I mention there's a TV team doing a documentary on him?' I said. 'They've got wind of the event on Friday and they're coming up to film it.'

'He won't appreciate that if he likes his privacy.' My dad whispered his response in a comically hushed tone. 'Does he know?'

'He might do now. But the documentary is being made without his cooperation, apparently.'

We strained our eyes to get a glimpse of the house. Though built on a rise it was almost completely hidden, surrounded by a grove of mature trees. The only part visible was a tantalising slice of window below one of the eaves.

'I wonder why he stopped going out?' My mother gazed upwards. 'He used to be happy enough to do interviews. He was a bit wild in his youth; a player and a heavy drinker.'

'I believe it happened after his marriage broke up,' I said. 'And I guess if he kept that going into his marriage maybe that's *why* it broke up.'

My attention moved from the house to the gate, which was locked, a large padlock hanging from it with a sign that said *Keep out! Beware of the Dog!*

'That's welcoming,' my dad remarked.

The sky darkened suddenly and it began to rain, properly this time.

I shivered. 'Let's keep going,' I said, and we headed back across the little beach. We were about twenty metres further on when the squeaking of a gate made us stop and turn.

'Ooh, is that him?' my mother said, eagerly.

I narrowed my eyes, squinting. A man was emerging from the little gate followed by a second, both in silhouette. It looked as if one was showing the other out. This seemed odd, because while all the houses along here had pedestrian access to the shore, the main entrance would be along the main road that ran parallel. I couldn't tell if either of the figures was Featherstone, but then I'd only seen his picture on a book jacket.

My mother was better informed. She shook her head. 'They're both too slight. Featherstone's a large man.'

I looked at her, surprised. You couldn't tell that from his author picture. She was a proper fan.

I was suddenly conscious that all three of us were watching the two men, but at least we were too far away for them to notice us. The shorter of the two roughly shoved the other, who pulled on huge headphones and stalked off, while the first one went back in through the gate, giving us a brief glimpse of his face when he turned briefly to lock it. The figure with the headphones stopped for a few seconds to look towards the sea, threw something at one of the rocks in temper and then strode off back in the direction of Moville, breaking into a lolloping run along the shore before disappearing from view.

'That didn't look too friendly,' my dad remarked.

'I wonder if that was the assistant going back in?' my mother mused. 'I might ask Stan about him.'

Amused at her curiosity, I suggested we keep going. A narrow sandy path, soft under foot but forcing us to walk in single file again, halted all conversation for a while. We passed a boat house with a slipway, a tiny bridge with a stream tumbling beneath, and a huge anchor on a lawn. And then the path became narrower and stonier, causing my dad to grumble that he'd been promised it was all on the flat. But when the lights of the fishing village of Greencastle came into view with the Irish Coastguard building and Maritime Museum, all was forgiven.

It stopped raining just in time for us to buy some fish and chips in the place opposite the post office and eat them sitting on a bench facing the shore. I found myself smiling at my parents' contented and weather-warmed faces. With a salty tang on my tongue and grease on my fingers, the last thing I wanted to do was to bring up Chambers.

'What's that over there?' my dad asked. 'Is that more of County Derry?'

Red and yellow buoys bobbed about. The land on the far side

was a dusky blue, the line between land and sea blurred. The sun was trying to break through, white rays shooting down onto the water like the hand of God.

'That's Magilligan prison. You can get a ferry across.'

'Oh right,' my dad said with a shudder.

As the sky clouded over again I gathered my nerve. 'Any word from Stuart?' I forced myself to use his first name.

Their expressions became visibly more tense but they shook their heads.

'Would the counselling group know where he's gone, do you think? What was it called again?'

'It's called See the Light,' my dad said, scrunching up his chip bag which wasn't yet empty, seeming to have lost his appetite. He threw the chip he'd been about to eat into the air and it was immediately caught by a swooping gull, with two others in pursuit trying to steal it. His expression lightened for a second as he watched them squabble, then darkened before he spoke. 'We're thinking of leaving it actually. It might be time. We might have got what we need out of it.'

He got to his feet to put the chip bag in the bin, while my mother wordlessly tilted her face to the sun, breathing in the salty air and finishing her food as I surreptitiously texted the words 'See the Light' to Molloy.

Chapter Nine

On Thursday morning I sat alone in my silent kitchen working my way through a second mug of coffee. My parents were still in bed. I suspected they were waiting for me to leave, giving me a chance to gather myself together before work. It had been their pattern all week and I was grateful for it – they were usually early risers.

I'd enjoyed having them here far more than I'd expected. We'd eaten together each evening and they were definitely more relaxed, getting out and meeting people, and exploring the area in a way I hadn't since I'd moved here, reminding me of places I'd forgotten. But it meant that I hadn't seen as much of Molloy as I usually did. We hadn't spent a night together since the weekend. And after irritating each other in court – an occurrence which wasn't exactly unprecedented – neither of us had got back to the other about dinner.

Though he'd acknowledged my text he hadn't come back on the counselling group. So, the day before, in the office, I'd done my own online search for See the Light. I'd found the website easily enough. It was professional looking and informative, describing the organisation as a grief recovery support group for people who needed help and healing for the hurt of losing a loved one. *A friendly and caring group of people who will walk alongside you throughout the grieving process, ensuring that you are never alone after losing someone you love.* The group had branches in Dublin, Cork and Galway, and seemed trustworthy enough; there was certainly no shortage of testimonials. But who could tell from a website? I'd explored the site, searching for anything that jarred, clicking on the section for funding where it stated that 'We rely heavily on donations – we wouldn't be able to do what we do without them'. Had my parents donated, I'd wondered?

I drained my coffee and stood at the sink to wash my mug, gazing out at the watery sky and hoping that it would hold for Phyllis's big festival launch later that evening. As Tuesday's walk had shown, the weather was fickle in early summer – if you optimistically wore sandals, your feet were blocks of ice; pessimistically throw on a jacket and you overheated. But a marquee would be miserable with the rain hammering down outside.

Guinness appeared at the window. So I let him in and fed him, or attempted to – he turned his nose up at the dried food I shook into his bowl in the hope of scoring some more fish from my dad. Then I headed into Glendara.

It was impossible not to notice the TV cameras in the square. A tall, slim woman in her forties wearing high heels, crimson lipstick and a scarf to match, stood outside the Oak pub speaking to a camera which was hoisted onto the shoulder of a bearded man with a cap, while Ollie, the young man who'd been in the office, held a furry boom mic on a pole. I was pretty sure the woman was Gina Bailey, the arts presenter I'd heard interviewed on the radio. She appeared to be intercepting people at random. Most hurried on, lowering their eyes and shaking their heads as if she were collecting for a charity and they were out of change.

Liam stood outside his estate agency on the other side of the street with his arms crossed and his feet planted firmly on the foot-path, watching what was going on. I parked and went over to him.

'So they're here,' I said, standing beside him, feeling like one half of Statler and Waldorf from *The Muppet Show*.

'Interviewing the locals apparently,' he snorted. 'Or trying to.' A woman scurried around the cameras, giving the crew such a wide berth that a car had to swerve to avoid her. 'I asked what they were doing and they said they they're capturing the town atmosphere. Gavin Featherstone's *home*.' Liam made inverted commas with his fingers. 'I told them Gavin Featherstone's home is Moville not Glendara.'

I smiled. The rivalry between the two Inishowen towns always amused me.

'Cameraman's decent enough, though. Joe something or other. Played a round of golf with him yesterday. Wife's expecting so he keeps jumping every time the phone rings.'

I grinned. All you needed to get Liam's approval was to play golf.

'She's a right wee harridan. Watch this.' He nudged me as Gina shouted at Ollie, causing him to drop the mic and take off. 'And she's his aunt, apparently.' He raised his eyebrows.

No wonder he'd appeared like an overwound clock, I thought. Gina was the one who'd overwound him. I wondered now if she was the one who'd been calling him, the phone call he'd refused to answer. He ran to a black van parked by the bank, and it struck me that there was something familiar about that hunched, lolloping run. When he pulled on headphones I had it. It was Ollie that we'd seen being shown out of Featherstone's back gate on Tuesday. Had Gina sent him there to persuade Featherstone to participate in the documentary? If she had, it looked as if he'd got short shrift.

'Anyway,' Liam inhaled deeply as if to calm himself, 'are you still seeing the vendors of that farm this morning?'

'Ten o'clock. If there are no issues, I should have contracts out at the beginning the week. But I'll let you know.'

'Great.' He rubbed his hands together. 'I'll tell the purchasers to get on to their solicitors. I told you it's Thompson's, didn't I?' I nodded and he turned to go, reaching for the door of his office. 'See you at the big launch tonight?'

'I'll be there. I hope your marquee holds up!'

He made a rude gesture in response.

Leah was on her hunkers behind the reception desk, dust flying everywhere. I wondered if such a position was a good idea in her condition, but knew better than to say so. Instead, I coughed and waved my hands about. 'What are you up to?'

She looked up, rubbing her eyes with her sleeve. 'Oh, hi. I've a bit of time on my hands this morning; I'm all up to date with the typing until you give me those contracts for Liam, so I thought I'd do a clear out.'

She groaned as she got to her feet, using the desk to haul herself up, and I saw that the door to the wills safe, a huge fire-proof thing under the stairs that had been there since I'd bought the practice, was ajar, its contents spewed out all over the floor as if from an open mouth. All too often, problems arose with locating the original will after death. Wills needed to be kept in a safe place where they couldn't be damaged by flood or fire or tampered with. So, after they'd been drafted and executed, we always gave clients the option of storing their wills in our safe.

Leah coughed and placed her hand on the reception desk to steady herself. 'I'm going to rearrange things a bit, to make some more room. It was getting a bit cluttered. And I keep meaning to consolidate the wills registers.'

As well as our own wills, we also had those that had been drafted by the previous owner of the practice, which was why we had two registers.

'Are you sure you should be doing that?' I said, frowning.

She took a sip from the bottle of water she always kept on her desk, and waved away my concern. 'I'm grand. I'm just trying to get everything sorted for whoever takes over when I go on maternity leave.'

Another subtle hint. Time to take it.

'Right,' I said, reversing out of the room. 'I'll leave you to it.'

Upstairs, I turned on my desktop computer, opened up the website for the *Inish Times* and quickly drafted an ad for the jobs section. Leah had already given me her dates so it was totally straightforward; I really should have done it weeks ago.

A few minutes later I headed back downstairs, taking the ad with me. The floor was now clear, the safe closed and Leah was back at her desk with the two wills registers in front of her. How on earth was I going to find someone to replace her for six months?

I handed her the ad. 'Can you send that into the paper?'

She took it, read through it quickly and smiled. The relief on her face made me feel pretty guilty. 'I'll do it this morning. We might be in time to get it in for Monday's edition.'

I pursed my lips, sulkily. 'You are coming back, aren't you?'

'Oh aye,' she said. 'Sure, who'd lift your sleeve out of your soup if I didn't?'

I grinned. I had a habit of reaching for something over lunch and dipping the sleeve of my suit jacket into my soup. Leah knew me so well that she'd learned to anticipate it. I pictured my mother knocking her knife to the floor in the Oak, and it hit me that I'd probably inherited my clumsiness from her.

Before we had a chance to get too sentimental, the farm vendors arrived for their appointment; I took instructions and spent the rest of the morning drafting the contract.

At one o'clock Leah and I left the office to head to the Oak for lunch. Festival fever had taken hold, and there was a buzz of excitement about the town which was infectious. Even the weather had decided to cooperate and it looked like being a sunny weekend.

We stopped to have a look at Phyllis's window, where there was a colourful display of the books whose authors were taking part, dominated by Featherstone's. A poster indicated that signed copies would be available after the weekend for those who couldn't make it to the live events.

Leah clicked her fingers. 'Sorry. I forgot to mention it but Mrs Featherstone never came in to collect that form on Tuesday.'

'Didn't she?' I raised my eyebrows.

'Nope. And you forgot to get that guy Oliver Connolly's phone number. I googled him in case it was on the RTÉ website to let him know, but it's not there. He must be freelance or something.'

I shrugged. 'Oh well. She might come in eventually. We'll hold onto it for the moment.'

Leah nodded. 'That's what I thought. There was an Oliver Connolly who won an award for a horror short a few years back at the Galway Film Fleadh, but I thought that couldn't be the same guy . . .'

She trailed off as the bookshop door opened and we turned together to see an extremely large man reverse out carrying a free-standing banner. He plonked it down on the footpath, before straightening himself with a groan, rising to his considerable height.

He smiled broadly when he saw me. 'I was wondering when I'd run into you.'

Leah had never met Jude. So, it was fun to see her eyes widen when I introduced this bearded giant wearing motorcycle leathers and a silver stud earring in the shape of a book. He gave her what I could see from her expression was a hand-crushing shake, then bent down again to pull up a cheery-looking banner in silver and blue. Cartoon books on legs chased one another between the words *Glenfest! Books! Workshops! Fun!*

'What do you think?' he asked, crossing his arms to survey the results.

'Eye catching.'

'Well, that's what we're after. Are you coming to the launch tonight?'

'I am.' I smiled. 'It's good to see you. I'd a feeling you might be back.'

'Me too.' He winked. 'On duty again, with my first aid kit.'

'How are your daughters?' The last time I'd seen Jude one of them had just been hospitalised after a drug overdose.

He beamed again. 'They're both brilliant. And the grandson is flying.'

'Glad to hear it.'

As we were turning to go, I saw that Phyllis had stuck a sticker across the top of the banner with the words *First appearance in ten years by Gavin Featherstone!*

'You a fan?' I asked, waving a hand towards it.

He rolled his eyes. 'The Steve McQueen of the literary world. Isn't everyone?'

Arriving at the Beacon Hall with my parents that evening, we were directed around the side of the building to the back, where a huge white marquee had been erected, large enough to host a wedding, although maybe not a Donegal one. Jude was sitting at a table just inside the entrance booking people in for the workshops taking place over the weekend, his height and bulk making him look more like a bouncer trapped behind a desk than a paramedic. After brief introductions to my parents, he waved us through.

Once inside, I could see that the marquee had been erected in such a way as to allow the audience to file in from one end, while writers and performers could come directly onto the stage through the back door of the hall, without having to walk through the tent. I had to admit the space looked pretty smart, with a raffia floor, some spider plants in pots and silver and blue bunting – what I now knew were the signature colours of the festival. A band played discreetly at one end on a small stage, which I presumed would be the one used for the main events, including Featherstone's big one the next day.

The tent was about half full. People mooched about with plastic glasses of wine, beer and soft drinks, and little plates of food from a stall at the side manned by Tony from the Oak. I spotted townspeople and clients, and assumed most of the writers taking part would be here too. The same thought seemed to occur to my mother and she began to spot them, producing her programme and using it like a catalogue in an art exhibition. I half expected her to go around plonking red dots on people.

'There's that poet Ann Marie what's-her-name. Ooh, I like her coat. And that critic. Oh, and there's Róisín Henderson. The one who's interviewing Gavin Featherstone tomorrow.'

I followed her gaze in the direction of a woman who was talking to Phyllis while gesticulating wildly, it was hard to tell whether in enthusiasm or displeasure. Slim and slight with short poppy-red hair and black-framed glasses, she'd paired a pale green dress with a denim jacket, a pair of Birkenstock sandals and long dangly earrings. Phyllis listened and nodded silently, which wasn't very Phyllis like, but then maybe she needed to keep the woman onside.

My mother was still author spotting. 'And there's that children's writer who's doing the reading with the kids in the library on Saturday.' She pointed out a laughing woman with blue hair and a huge tote bag with what looked like a unicorn's head poking out.

'Ooh.' She nudged me so excitedly that I almost yelped. 'Isn't that one of the men we saw coming out of Gavin Featherstone's house?' She lowered her voice. 'The one who went back in, not the one who was turfed out.'

Had Ollie been 'turfed out'? I supposed he had. It was hardly surprising. If Featherstone had already said no to the documentary, then Gina had sent him into the eye of the storm.

I looked at the man my mother had pointed out and thought that she was probably right; that he was the man who'd gone back in through the gate. He was holding a glass of orange juice, and he wore dark jeans, a white button-down shirt and a green parka with a furry hood. A brown leather bag was slung across his body. His slightly protruding ears accentuated the mod haircut he sported. Now I knew what Stan had meant when he said, 'Robbie has a very specific haircut, assuming this was Featherstone's assistant.'

'Someone should tell him the sixties called and they want their clothes back,' my dad muttered. An ex-bank manager, he'd always been a conservative dresser.

'I wonder if Featherstone himself is here?' Mum said, looking around her excitedly.

'I suspect he sent his assistant along instead. I imagine doing tomorrow's event would be enough of a challenge for a recluse,' I said.

'Hmm. Maybe,' she said disappointedly, continuing to stare at the man so intently that I was sure he would pick up on it and turn in our direction. She tapped her programme against her chin, thoughtfully. 'I wonder what that was all about on Tuesday?'

'Do either of you want a drink?' I asked, mainly to distract her but also seeing that my dad was yawning, and suspecting that he'd happily have gone home if he'd been let. I took orders for a glass of white wine and a beer, and made my way over to Tony's bar.

'Yes, Ben,' he said, throwing a tea towel over his shoulder.

I gave him my order and turned to survey the crowd while he fetched our drinks. People were still arriving, I saw. Liam and Stan walked in together, and I watched as Stan made his way over to my mother who seemed delighted to see him. Her hair appointment was for the following morning but they already seemed to be friends. Stan was fun, equally flirtatious with men and women, seeming to like the ambiguity, and I smiled, wondering if he'd try flirting with my dad.

It crossed my mind that there was no sign of Molloy. Then I spotted the TV crew, Gina Bailey, Joe the cameraman and Ollie, huddled together near the entrance – no cameras or mics this evening. Ollie saw me and gave a small wave before saying something to Gina and ducking outside.

I turned to collect my drinks from Tony. As I lifted them there was a tap on my shoulder, which made me jump, and I spun around, hands full, coming face to face with Gina Bailey herself. Her perfume wafted towards me, strong and expensive.

'Hi, sorry for disturbing you. I just wanted to say thanks for letting my nephew leave that release form in with you. It was all a bit last minute. Barbara Featherstone did some filming with us in Dublin but somehow that fell through the cracks. It happens sometimes. She asked us to drop it into your office . . .'

'She didn't come in,' I said, as soon as I could get a word in.

Gina's chin jerked back, her sleek hair moving as one. 'What do you mean?'

'Mrs Featherstone. She didn't come in to collect the release form. It's still there in the office. Feel free to collect it whenever you want."

Her eyes flashed. 'You can stick it in the shredder for all I care,' she snapped. 'It's useless to me unsigned.' She shook her head as she strode off muttering 'Shit, shit. Shit.'

I steadied myself once she'd brushed past me, trying not to spill anything. I was irritated by her rudeness but more amused at how at odds her language and tone were with her polished appearance, and I felt another rush of sympathy for her browbeaten nephew.

I started back in the direction of my parents, now chatting to both Stan and Liam.

'Nice manoeuvring,' Liam said as I delivered the drinks.

I laughed. 'Carrying three glasses at the same time is probably the most useful thing I learned in college.'

'Shall we go?' Stan said eagerly, giving my mother an elbow. 'Go on. I'll do it if you do.'

'You're on.' She handed my dad her glass of wine and set off to navigate her way through the crowd with Stan in her wake.

'Where are they off to?' I asked my dad as we watched them go.

'They're signing up to do Róisín Henderson's short-story workshop on Saturday,' he said, looking pleased.

My eyes widened. 'I didn't know Mum wrote.'

'She used to,' he said, taking an appreciative sip of his beer. 'A long time ago. Had a few short stories published before you were born.' He lowered his voice. 'By the way, that Paul Weller clone *is* Featherstone's assistant Robbie. Your mother asked Stan.'

Our conversation was interrupted by the appearance of Phyllis, who was looking quite spectacular in a colourful book-print dress and matching headscarf. I told her this, but she had other things on her mind, ushering me to one side, looking worried.

'I saw you talking to Gina Bailey just now. Featherstone has agreed to allow them to film the event tomorrow just as long as he doesn't have to speak to them.'

'That's good, isn't it?' I said, surprised. Had Ollie been a more successful emissary than it appeared?

She scrunched up her nose. 'That woman makes me nervous. She's supposed to be an arts journalist but there's something really intrusive and persistent about her. Almost tabloid-like, as if she's digging in places where she has no business being.'

I looked over to where Gina was locked in intense conversation with Joe her cameraman. I hadn't liked her much either.

'I'd much prefer to have a local journalist covering the event,' Phyllis said. 'The national media will happily screw you over because they know they never have to see you again, whereas the local guys at least have an interest in getting things right because they have to live in the same community as you.'

'You mean they're more generous,' I said with a smile.

'Aye, maybe.' She sighed, snuck a last glance at Gina and then rubbed her palms together. 'Anyway, I'd better get up and say a few words. Get this baby launched.'

I watched as she climbed the steps to the stage, motioned to the band to stop playing and then tapped the microphone. Once there was a lull in conversation, she looked down. For a second, I wondered if she'd lost her train of thought. Her expression froze, and I saw a slight shake in her hand. Nerves, I wondered? I willed her to pull herself together.

She cleared her throat. 'Evening everyone. Thank you all for coming to the launch of this year's Glenfest. I'm particularly excited about this year's festival and I hope we have something for everyone this weekend. There are events for kids of all ages in the library on Saturday morning, a short-story workshop, an open mic event and of course, the *pièce de résistance* and the highlight of the weekend: Gavin Featherstone in conversation with Róisín Henderson tomorrow evening, here in the marquee at six o'clock.'

She paused for applause, which came obligingly.

'There'll be a signing afterwards in the bookshop. And if anyone doesn't know where that is, I can give you directions . . .' She winked, and there was a polite laugh. 'Now there are a *few* tickets left for the event so let's make it a sold-out gig. It's being filmed for a documentary to be shown on RTÉ in the autumn, so you might even appear on the telly. If anyone would prefer not to be featured, please declare yourself to the producer.'

A shadow crossed her face again as she shielded her eyes with her hand to search out the TV crew. I turned with the rest of the crowd to see Ollie and Gina sharing a surreptitious cigarette at the entrance to the marquee. Realising the crowd's gaze was on her, Gina held hers behind her back and waved and smiled in acknowledgement.

Chapter Ten

The following morning, I offered to drop my mum into town for her haircut with Stan, though it was earlier than I would usually go into the office. My dad said he would collect her afterwards.

'Wow. Look at the colours out there,' she breathed, rubbing condensation from the passenger window to peer out at the encroaching tide of Trawbreaga Bay.

'It's not a bad old commute,' I agreed, as I flipped the indicator to overtake a slow-moving tractor on the coast road. 'I'm delighted that you've signed up for the short-story workshop, by the way. When did you start writing?'

'Oh, I've done bits and pieces over the years. But I'd like to start sending some work off again, so I reckon I should do the odd course. I've read some of Róisín Henderson's stories and she's really good.'

We passed the turn off for Culdaff where the road dipped towards the sea. I remembered it completely submerged during the floods, though it had escaped any serious damage.

'No sign of your sergeant last night?' my mother said, tearing herself away from the view and turning to face me.

I shook my head and smiled. That was how Maeve used to

refer to Molloy before anything had even happened between us. My sergeant.

'Are we cramping your style? Staying with you?'

'No,' I said quickly. Though it wasn't entirely true, I didn't want to give them an excuse to leave. 'Of course not.'

'Would you not usually see him during the week?'

My mother could be persistent when she wanted to be. But how could I explain the erratic nature of my relationship with Molloy? Our mutual workaholic tendencies; the fact that we'd only just sorted ourselves out after years of crossed wires. And that despite an intensity I'd never felt for anyone else and suspecting that Molloy was the same, we didn't actually share our lives. We'd sound like a pair of teenagers.

'Sometimes,' I shrugged, non-committedly, choosing not to mention the recent squabble in court. There was a beat and I primed myself for another searching question.

None came. Instead, my mother said, 'It's your dad's birthday on Sunday. Maybe we could do something to include him?'

This was something I had remembered. I was planning on taking them both to the little bistro in Malin, assuming they were still here. But I hadn't thought of including Molloy.

'I'll ask him,' I said, surprised at how pleased I felt.

I dropped her at Stan's salon and walked down to the office. We didn't open till half nine so for once Leah wasn't there before me. I turned the key and pushed the door open to blessed silence. I always liked the office at weekends. With no phones ringing and no clients, I could usually get lots of work done. This felt similar.

I made myself a coffee and headed upstairs. A text came from Leah saying she would be fifteen minutes late. No rush, I told her, I was here early for a change. I opened a litigation file with which I'd been struggling but I couldn't concentrate. The other side's affidavits were badly drafted and unclear, and I found myself getting irritable.

Finally, I took my coffee and went to the window to drink it. And there was Molloy, striding past in full uniform. I dropped my mug onto my desk and ran down the stairs, opening the door and calling out to him. He turned, and with a very odd expression on his face he came over; it was the expression of someone who'd been caught out.

I laughed. 'Why are you looking so guilty?' He'd been walking alone along the street of a town where he was sergeant. What on earth could he have to feel guilty about?

He gave me a tight smile. I had been joking but now I could see that he *was* concealing something. Molloy was a crap liar, which was something I liked about him. I realised that for days now there'd been something distracting him. I'd had the sense that I didn't quite have his full attention, that part of his mind was elsewhere. But this was different. I didn't like him hiding things. And anyway, I'd thought we were past that. I was about to include him in my dad's birthday.

'I'm sorry. I need to go.' He glanced at his watch. 'There's something I need to talk to you about but not now. I don't have time.'

'Go,' I snapped, already turning to go back into the office.

The man couldn't get away from me quickly enough.

The marquee was stuffed to capacity that evening for Gavin Featherstone's event. Rows of chairs had been set out on either side of a narrow aisle, as many as could fit, and every one of them was occupied by the time we arrived, despite thinking we had fifteen minutes to spare. If Phyllis hadn't stuck reserved stickers on the entire front row and told me that three of them were ours, we'd have been in standing room only at the back.

The TV crew had set up a camera to the left of the stage. Gina Bailey gave me a curt nod, and my mother muttered that she hoped they wouldn't be blocking our view. She was looking particularly sharp this evening with her new pixie haircut. When she'd called into the office after, to wait for my dad, she'd been on a high, as much from the laughs with Stan as the actual cut.

She whispered to me now, leaning across my dad. 'Stan said he's very nervous.'

'Why's Stan nervous?' my dad quipped.

My mother clicked her teeth in irritation. 'Featherstone. Robbie told him he was beginning to regret persuading him to do it. Poor man. I hope he's all right. It's a lot of pressure coming on to a crowd this size.'

My father rolled his eyes, while I surveyed the stage. Two bistro-style bamboo chairs had been placed in the centre with a low table in between and huge amps on either side. A carafe of water with two glasses sat on the table together with copies of Gavin Featherstone's most recent book, *Violet, Green and Red*, and Róisín Henderson's collection of short stories.

Conversation hummed in the tent and there was a real sense of anticipation and excitement, but it was very warm. Around us programmes were being used as fans, and my dad quickly ditched his jacket and my mother her cardigan. Beads of perspiration prickled my neck and trickled down my back.

'Do you want some water?' I whispered over to them, checking my watch. We still had at least ten minutes. 'I have time.'

My dad shook his head but my mother nodded gratefully and I stood up again to walk back out the way we'd come in, around the side of the hall to the front entrance. It was only once I got there that I realised there was nowhere to buy water unless I left and went up town, which I didn't have time to do before the event. Tony's food and drinks stall had been for the launch night only.

I spotted Jude, directing cars. He waved at me and I called out to him. 'I'm after some water for my parents. It's really hot in there. Any ideas?'

'Go into the kitchen,' he said, gesturing towards the main door. 'I assume the stuff in the tap is drinkable.'

I thanked him and went inside, hurrying down the long corridor, afraid the event would start before I got back. I knew my way around the Beacon Hall since I'd been involved in the local drama club which met there. The building had also been used to accommodate people during the flood, the tiny kitchen proving invaluable.

I almost collided with Phyllis coming in the other direction. She looked stressed, beads of sweat stippled her brow and her hair was standing on end again – never a good sign.

'Everything okay?' I asked.

'Ach, Ben,' she said, wringing her hands. 'His whole family is here. I wasn't expecting that. They've all come. His ex-wife, his kids . . .'

'Anything I can do?' I said, confused as to why Phyllis would find this particularly trying, given that there were so many other people here. 'I'm just getting my parents some water from the kitchen. It's hot in that marquee.'

'Oh,' her eyes widened. 'You wouldn't get him a wee Coke would you? He has to take some tablets and there's only water on stage, which he doesn't drink.' She rolled her eyes. 'There should be a few cans in the fridge.'

I nodded. 'Of course.'

'Thanks. I need to get back to him and have a few words before I introduce him.' She started to walk away, so addled that it appeared the lower half of her body was already departing while the upper was still talking to me. 'Can you leave it on the windowsill by the back door at the stage entrance? I'll give it to him before he goes on.'

'Sure.' I hurried into the little kitchen, found a couple of reasonably clean glasses in a cupboard above the sink, filled two with water from the tap, then opened the little fridge. At first glance it seemed empty, then I spotted one solitary can of Diet Coke in the door. I took it out and carried it along with the glasses of water to the back door of the hall.

I heard raised voices as I approached, quickly lowered to angry whispers. Two people were having a heated exchange, which they clearly didn't want anyone else to hear. One of them was Phyllis. She sounded upset and emotional. The other, I could see now – though they both had their backs to me – was a tall male figure with grey hair brushed back from a high forehead. In contrast to my friend, he sounded offhand, almost disdainful. Neither saw me, so I quietly put the can on the windowsill and tiptoed back out of the hall, returning to the marquee the way I'd come.

When I got back to my seat, Róisín Henderson was already on stage. She'd chosen the seat on the left behind her book, and she appeared nervous, biting her lower lip as she flicked through her notes and rearranged them on her lap. She took repeated sips from her glass of water as if afraid her mouth would go dry when she began to speak. I knew how that felt, remembering my own early appearances in court.

As we waited for the main attraction, I glanced around me, surveying a crowd who I could see weren't just from Inishowen. There were readers and journalists here from all over; some with notebooks, some with copies of Featherstone's novels for signing.

And then Phyllis herself bounded on stage with a huge smile plastered across her face. 'Good evening, everyone, and welcome to the highlight of our festival this year. Firstly, a huge thank you to Róisín Henderson, our wonderful short-story writer, for doing the honours this evening.' She looked towards Róisín, who smiled graciously. 'And in case I forget, for those of you who want to flex your own literary muscles, Róisín will be running a short-story workshop tomorrow here in the Beacon Hall, upstairs. There are still some slots available. Róisín is a wonderful teacher and it's an excellent opportunity for anyone beginning to write or who has been working on something and needs a little help. Róisín not only writes in English but in Irish too, so feel free to show her your *cúpla focal* if you prefer.'

She followed this with the emergency escape drill and the turn-off-your-mobile-phone speech, which sent everyone rummaging in pockets and bags.

'And now, without further ado . . .' She paused dramatically before launching into a prepared bio. 'Gavin Featherstone is one of the world's foremost literary novelists. His first book, *The Peering of Things*, published when he was only twenty-seven years old, won the Booker Prize, making him the youngest ever winner. Since then, he has written fourteen books, two of which were shortlisted for the Booker and the twelfth of which, *Spirit of an Intruder*, won the IMPAC prize. He was professor of creative writing at Queen's University Belfast, and has been writer-in-residence there. His most recent book was *Violet, Green and Red* and a new book, a memoir, is due next year, which I'm sure we're all very excited about.

'And finally, as some of you may know, this is Mr Featherstone's first public interview in many years so we are all very privileged to have him here. Can you all put your hands together for Gavin Featherstone?'

Phyllis strode off, and the man I'd seen her arguing with backstage walked on to applause and whistles more appropriate to a rock concert than a literary festival. He bowed and waved, and blew kisses at the audience. Not a hint of the nerves Stan had described.

'The man thinks he's bloody Hemingway,' my dad muttered under his breath.

Chapter Eleven

My mum shushed my dad, eyes shining with delight and anticipation. Tall and rangy, still handsome despite the corrugated
forehead which gave a hint as to his age, and the designer stubble
I'd seen on his author pic now grown into a full beard, Gavin
Featherstone was dressed in faded jeans, a green corduroy shirt
and walking boots. A silver sleeper glinted in one ear. It hit me
as I watched him greet his public that while the event had been
pitched as a conversation between two writers, this was very
much Featherstone's gig, and I wondered how Róisín Henderson
felt as she stood to clap along with everyone else.

He shook hands with her before taking his seat. She began by
welcoming him, adding that, really, he was the one who should
be welcoming her since he lived in Inishowen. I was relieved to
hear that her voice was steady although I wondered if that was a
dig at him for taking her slot.

If it was, he responded affably enough. 'True. Yet I think I
still count as a blow-in even after thirty-odd years. Maybe if I
die here?' He looked to the audience for confirmation and there
were nods and grins. 'I *am* sixty-nine.' His accent was English,
with a tiny trace of Donegal, which you'd miss if you weren't
looking for it.

'I'm sure that's not true,' Róisín laughed. 'But it does lead me on to my first question which is – since we are where we are, geographically, how location has fed into your work? I know that your first book *The Peering of Things* was set in the north of England, Northumberland, wasn't it? And you were still living there at the time.'

Featherstone nodded. 'Hexham. A small market town. I was born and brought up there and I moved back for a few years after I finished my degree.' He rolled his eyes. 'Thought I'd write the great English novel.'

'But you did, didn't you?' Róisín said. 'It won the Booker when you were only twenty-seven.'

Featherstone glanced down at his hands, picking at one of the frayed cuffs of his corduroy shirt. I saw that he wore a silver band on his right hand, though not on the wedding finger.

'They say the past is another country,' he said. 'Well, that book is in the past *and* in another country. It feels to me now as if it was written by a different person. However,' he smiled, 'it is unusual, I suppose: a young man's novel about something other than himself. Maybe that was why it was a success.'

'But your other books have been set here,' Róisín continued, 'in Donegal, or at least Ireland.'

Featherstone nodded. 'Yes, location very much does feed into my writing. For a long time, Ireland has been flowing through my veins so when I bleed onto the page it's Ireland that comes out. I walk as much as I can, I fish. I swim in the sea close to where I live. I'm sure people have seen me traipsing out in my dressing gown and hauling my ungainly body onto the rocks like a walrus . . .'

The audience laughed and Featherstone took the opportunity to lean forward and take a small sip from his glass. So much for him not drinking water, I thought. Maybe he *was* nervous.

He put the glass back down with a half laugh. 'What was the

question again?' His forehead was beginning to glisten, tiny beads of perspiration peppering his brow.

Róisín smiled. 'I think you've answered it.'

'Good.' He produced a handkerchief and rubbed it across his hairline. The marquee really was very warm.

Róisín consulted her notes. 'Before I ask you about themes in your writing, I'd like to talk about style. You've been described as writing in clear, sparse prose—'

Featherstone cut across her. 'You write in Irish, don't you? Did I hear that mentioned in the introduction?'

His interjection appeared to take her by surprise, as if she didn't expect the 'in conversation' bit to actually happen, but she seemed pleased. 'Erm, yes. I write in both Irish and English.'

'What's that like?' he grinned, reaching for his glass again and taking another drink, a longer one this time. 'I mean, I assume you don't have many readers in Irish.'

Róisín's expression darkened. 'You'd be surprised,' she said, tersely.

Featherstone bowed his head in mock humility. 'I'm sorry. That didn't come out the way I intended. I'm sure Irish is a lovely language but let's face it, it is rather in a coma, even if it's not quite dead yet.' He looked to the audience for support but they remained silent, some stony faced.

'Read the room, man, for God's sake,' my dad hissed under his breath.

As if hearing him, Featherstone held up his hands in protest. 'Okay, okay. It's not something an Englishman should say. I know that. But, I suppose, I wonder why you'd bother if no one is going to read it. I mean, don't we all want to be read? Isn't that the whole point?'

'Despite the best attempts of your country to destroy our

language – which by the way is one of the oldest in the world, and considerably older than English,' Róisín said, coldly, 'sometimes English is simply inadequate for what you want to say. It lacks the poeticism and musicality of Irish.'

Featherstone laughed and bowed his head. 'Touché. Look, let's not have a row about Irish and English – we're supposed to be arguing about the novel and the short story, aren't we? Isn't that how this dogfight was pitched?' He sat back and crossed his arms. 'Tell me about your story writing. Why do you write short stories? Why not novels?'

A shadow crossed Róisín's face. She paused before responding, choosing her words carefully, and I had the strangest feeling that she was on the verge of tears.

'I think there's a purity to the short story, an emotional reach that the novel rarely has. Every word must count. It's the most demanding form of fiction. A novel would be easier for me to write, but I write stories because it's how my characters emerge on the page, in short form.'

Featherstone snorted derisively. 'Ah come on. I've no time for that bullshit. The tortured writer. The muse.' He leaned forward to take another deep swallow of his water. Róisín flinched as if she'd been slapped, but Featherstone ploughed on. '*You* choose what and how you write, not your characters. You have to sit at your desk every day and work. Treat writing like a job if you want to make a bloody living out of it.'

'Is that what you told your students?' There was ice in Róisín's voice.

Featherstone's face clouded for a second. He looked at her, frowned, then recovered quickly. 'I've always wanted to make a living out of it. I don't see the point otherwise. You'll never make a living out of short stories.'

Róisín silently twisted and twirled her pen in her fingers.

Featherstone raised his eyebrows. 'Well, what do you say a writer should do? Marry someone with a proper job?' He gave a sudden wry grin as if trying to break the tension. 'I mean, I guess you could say that's what I did.' There was a ripple of relieved laughter from the audience. He had them back.

Róisín did not laugh. Instead, she shuffled her notes again, pushing her glasses up the bridge of her nose as if struggling to keep her emotions in check. 'Let's move on to the themes you choose for your novels. It seems to me to be the beauty and terror of the human condition, marriage, cruelty, narcissism . . .' Despite the drama of her words, her voice was flat as if all she wanted now was for the interview to be over. It was as if, in controlling her negative emotions, she'd also excised the positive; the excitement she'd shown at the start.

'Guilt,' Featherstone added. 'Regret. Even if that probably only emerged in my later writing. I'm interested in exploring the notion of personal guilt; how long a shadow it can cast if one doesn't face up to things, take responsibility for what one has done.'

Róisín raised her eyebrows. 'Can you elaborate?'

'Well, sometimes we get away with things, don't we? We don't always get what we deserve. But even if we aren't punished, do we ever truly get away with anything? Sometimes a life can be ruined by a failure to take responsibility for something we did when we were young. Something we then have to live with.'

Róisín sat forward with renewed interest. 'Are you talking about conscience, or karma?'

I noticed Featherstone was tapping his left foot. The fidgeting had moved from his arms to his legs.

'Probably both,' he said. 'I read about a case once where a

thirteen-year-old girl falsely accused someone of assaulting her. She was believed and he was convicted. But she was lying. Many years later she confessed, and the reason she gave was that every good day after she told the lie was tainted by what she'd done. Every accomplishment, every relationship had been stolen by what she called her cancerous guilt. That stayed with me. I can understand that.'

Róisín's eyes narrowed. 'Are you saying you feel guilty about something?'

He looked startled for a second, and then smiled. 'Don't we all have something we feel guilty about? Ah, maybe it's to do with getting older, vanishing horizons. The possibilities becoming more and more limited with each year.'

'Of course, your horizons are going to be limited if you never leave your bloody house,' my dad muttered, and my mother shushed him again. The rest of the crowd was hanging on the Featherstone's every word.

'I'm interested in the notion of crossroads.' Featherstone reached for his glass which was now nearly empty, put it to his mouth and gulped back the remaining contents. 'How you may never know that you've negotiated one of the major junctions of your life until afterwards, when it's too late to go back.'

'Do you draw on your own experiences in your writing?' Róisín asked, her voice softer now. Had she forgiven him for their earlier spat?

Featherstone sat back and crossed his arms. 'All writers draw on their own experiences. Don't believe anyone who tells you otherwise because they're lying.' He made a comical face at the audience and they laughed.

'Questions will always be asked about appropriation,' he continued, more seriously. 'Is this your story to tell if it's also someone else's? Do you need their permission to tell it? Well, I believe you don't. It's my choice to tell *my* story. It may impact on you, but I have the right to tell mine just as you have the right to tell yours.' He stopped suddenly and touched his chest as if he were in some discomfort, but it seemed to pass quickly. 'Anyway, didn't Kingsley Amis say if you can't annoy someone there is little point in writing?'

Another laugh. Featherstone seemed to be enjoying himself now although he did look very warm, his skin flushed and slick with perspiration. I noticed a slight tremor in his hand as he refilled his glass from the carafe, rubbing his face as he took a drink.

Róisín looked pleased, as if her best prepared question had just come up in an exam. 'Ah, but didn't Christopher Hitchens say that the booze got to Amis in the end, robbing him of his wit and charm as well as his health.'

Featherstone chuckled. 'Very possibly. I think he did give it up though. Just like I did.'

'Which I presume we'll be able to read about in your memoir coming out next year,' Róisín said with a flourish. 'Isn't that right?'

'Neat segue.' Featherstone bowed his head. 'And yes, you will.'

'So, will you read a little section from it for us then? I'm sure we'll all promise to keep whatever you tell us to ourselves,' she mock-whispered, glancing at the TV camera. 'Them too I'm sure . . .'

I watched the cameraman work the lens, going for a crucial close-up as Featherstone played along, smiling enigmatically before rooting in the pocket of his shirt and producing a pair of glasses, which he donned to peer at the crowd. 'Don't tell my publishers.'

His words were greeted with thunderous applause and he reached into the pocket again. Suddenly his expression changed. His face fell and he appeared distressed. 'I have it here somewhere,' he muttered.

'Maybe we'll take a few questions from the audience?' Róisín said, hurriedly.

Featherstone didn't respond; there was a shake in his hand as he fumbled to find what he was looking for. For the first time, I felt sorry for him.

Meanwhile Róisín was all business, clapping her hands together and taking control. 'So, we'll quickly throw it open to the floor, folks. I think we have a roving microphone somewhere?'

Jude materialised with a mic and a number of hands shot up. The first question came from a quivery female voice in the row just behind where we were sitting. 'If you could give one piece of advice to a first-time writer, what would it be?'

'Don't,' Featherstone replied. 'It's the road to misery.' He'd recovered his composure, and was looking relieved, having found a couple of sheets of paper in the back pocket of his jeans. 'No, I'm joking, of course. I'd say read a lot, write a lot and finish everything that you write.'

'Are any of your books going to be made into TV programmes, to reach a wider audience?'

'Oh God, I hope not.' There was a laugh.

I spotted Phyllis at the side of the stage, gesturing to Róisín and making a T sign with her hands.

'Last question, folks,' Róisín said firmly. 'And then we'll have a reading.' She squinted. 'I think there's a hand up down at the very back.' The person had already started speaking. 'Can you wait for the microphone to get to you?'

Jude strode down the middle aisle, Featherstone following him with his gaze. When he got there, the question was repeated but it still couldn't be heard. Had the mic failed? Jude conveyed it in his own booming voice. 'The question is – it's been said that writing is incompatible with having a family; what do you think of that?'

Featherstone's eyes narrowed as if he was trying to see who had asked the question, his hand moving to his chest again as if he was in pain. He managed a smile but seemed detached, his reply flippant. 'Everyone has challenges.' Then he turned back to Róisín. 'Shall I read?'

'Please do.'

Featherstone opened the pages out on his knee and the audience fell silent. He swallowed, Adam's apple bobbing. He cleared his throat. A few seconds passed. The tension was unbearable. Unexpectedly, and shakily, he got to his feet.

He reached out to touch the table in front of him but he was too tall, and his hand met nothing but fresh air. Something was wrong. He swayed, looking suddenly stricken, as if he was gasping for air. His face contorted in pain. He gripped his left shoulder and let out a shuddering breath. As the sheets of paper fluttered to the floor, his legs buckled and he keeled over completely, collapsing onto the stage.

Róisín leapt to her feet, hands clasped to her cheeks in panic, her face drained of colour. Out of nowhere Jude appeared, climbing onto the stage in one swift movement, surprisingly nimble for a man of his size. He kneeled down beside the felled writer. He checked Featherstone's pulse and heart, then started applying CPR while shouting for someone to call an ambulance and the cameras to stop filming. Phyllis joined him within seconds, looking distressed.

Someone else rushed forward. It was Featherstone's assistant, the man we'd seen at the launch the night before.

'Is he breathing?' he asked urgently, his face a picture of cold, sick dread.

But Jude didn't reply.

Chapter Twelve

There was a wee boy from Moville.
who was always eating his fill,
Slow down, said his ma, or you'll end up like your da,
and find yourself under the grill.

The young man grinned triumphantly from the makeshift stage in the Oak pub. His bloodshot eyes darted about the crowd gathered for the open mic competition and he was sufficiently encouraged by his mates' jeering down the back to produce another scrap of paper with a second limerick. This one about a 'wee woman from Buncrana'.

'Give me patience,' Liam groaned in my ear.

I spoke out of the side of my mouth. 'I think he's working his way around the peninsula. You'd better hope he's sticking to the towns; we're in trouble if he starts on the townlands.'

Liam made a face. 'How many more of them are there?'

'Entries or limericks?'

'Entries, you tube.' The auctioneer rolled his eyes at me.

I glanced at the list. 'Three.'

'Thank the Lord.' He folded his arms to wait, sneaking a glance at his watch. 'No news?'

I took my phone from my pocket even though I'd checked it ten minutes beforehand, and shook my head. I was sure we'd have heard something by now.

After his collapse, Featherstone had been taken to Altnagelvin hospital in Derry, which was closer than Letterkenny, his distraught assistant Robbie travelling with him in the ambulance. If his family were in the marquee, they didn't make themselves known, but then everyone was ushered out fairly quickly once the urgency of the situation became clear. Phyllis had followed on to the hospital with Jude, asking Liam to take her place and compère the open mic competition. I'd promised to help, assuming she would text me when there was any news, or simply appear and take over if Featherstone was okay. As yet, neither had happened.

My parents had gone back to Malin, ostensibly for something to eat, having said they might come back in later. I was drinking fizzy water in case I needed to collect them but I suspected they'd remain put; they'd been pretty shaken up by what happened. It had been a sudden and appalling end to the event for everyone, but they'd had front-row seats.

The rhyming genius finished his set and Liam went back up to the mic. 'Thank you, Jimmy. Always room for a limerick. Or three. Next we have . . .' He paused to check his list, then looked up again to make the introduction, faltering as his gaze moved to the back of the pub.

I twisted my head to see what had distracted him.

Molloy was standing in the doorway of the pub, glancing around, clearly looking for someone. My first thought was, what the hell was he doing here? It was unlikely he'd come to watch the open mic in full uniform; he stood out like a sore thumb. My second was more personal; a wave of embarrassment washed over me at the memory at our last encounter. My strop had probably been a bit of an overreaction.

I waved to get his attention. He spotted me and began navigating his way through the crowd; no parting of the Red Sea for him. A look of concern flitted across Tony's face as he pulled two pints of Guinness behind the bar, followed by relief when Molloy walked past.

Onstage Liam gripped the mic, clearly making an effort to focus. 'Next we have Seamus Hegarty with a song that he's written himself.'

A youth with a mullet bounded on stage with a guitar to whoops and cheers of encouragement to 'give it welly'.

Molloy appeared on one side of me just as Liam returned to the other. Molloy's face was grim. 'Featherstone's dead,' he said in a low voice.

'You're joking.'

He shook his head. 'I wish I was.'

'What was it?' I asked. 'A heart attack?' It *had* looked like one. All that gripping of his chest during the interview. And he'd been sweating, though he wasn't alone in that with the heat in the marquee.

He nodded. 'Certainly looks like it.'

'Hang on,' I said, suddenly. 'Why are *you* involved if it was a heart attack?'

'The hospital wants further investigation. A pathologist is travelling up to do a post-mortem first thing in the morning.'

'Why?' I persisted.

'They want to discount the possibility that it was triggered by something he ingested. Something he was allergic to or perhaps some sort of poison.'

Liam was leaning in, straining to hear. If he hadn't picked up the rest of what Molloy said, he certainly caught the last word. 'Poison?' he exclaimed. 'Someone *poisoned* him?'

'I didn't say that.' Molloy said warningly, shushing him. 'I said the hospital think *it's possible* he may have ingested something that brought on a heart attack. They're not committing themselves until after the post-mortem.'

Liam's eyes were wide. The song on stage came to an end and he reluctantly left the conversation and returned to the mic.

'Featherstone died shortly after he arrived at the hospital. Never regained consciousness after he collapsed,' Molloy added quietly to me.

I breathed out, reeling. There had been something desperately sad about seeing a man, who was so full of bluster and bonhomie at the start, become weak and dejected. I was upset for Phyllis too. Her 'wee festival' would now be remembered as the one at which the writer Gavin Featherstone had died. I knew I should feel more for the man's family and friends, but I didn't know them, although his assistant Robbie had seemed beside himself.

There was a tap on my shoulder and I turned. Maeve. I hadn't expected to see her here.

'I just heard what happened to that writer,' she said, aghast. 'Is he all right?'

I shook my head.

Before I could elaborate, Liam was back again and Molloy grabbed the opportunity to take me to one side, while the other two watched us with interest. They weren't alone. The local sergeant in full uniform in a crowded pub on a Friday night attracted attention, and I felt my neck burn as if the spotlight was above our heads instead of on stage.

'We need to secure the hall and the marquee,' Molloy said in a hushed voice. 'Ensure nothing is cleared away, anything he drank or ate from. The Garda Tech Bureau are on their way, but McFadden's there now and I need to get down to him.' He lowered his voice even further. 'I just wondered if you'd seen anything. You were in the front row, weren't you, with your parents?'

How did he know that? I wondered. Had Phyllis told him? Was that why he'd come looking for me?

'Nothing in particular,' I said. 'I wouldn't say he looked unwell, particularly, until the end. He did grip his chest once or twice as if he had heartburn, and he was fidgeting quite a lot and overheating, but then everyone was. The marquee was very warm. And he had those lights on him too.'

'And you didn't notice anything strange before he collapsed?'

I forced my mind back, trying to remember. 'Not really. He was a little confused, maybe, and then he collapsed when he was about to read. There were some questions from the audience before that. There was one about family, which seemed to irritate him a little.' I wondered suddenly if that had been asked by his estranged ex-wife or one of his children. 'Jude had the mic.'

'Okay thanks.' Molloy turned to go, and I called after him in a loud whisper. 'Are you going to have to close down the festival?'

'Probably.' He nodded towards the stage where another poem was being recited, this time by a young woman with dyed black hair and a nose piercing. She looked a little familiar. 'I'd say this will be the grand finale.'

He disappeared into the crowd and I returned to Liam and Maeve, now standing side by side with drinks in hand watching the performance. The pub seemed to be rapt. I realised that the woman onstage was one of Maeve's veterinary nurses, which was presumably the reason why she'd come in.

'She's good,' I whispered.

'I know.' She smiled. 'Just as well you can't make any money from poetry or I'd be afraid she'd give up the day job.' Her smile fell away. 'Liam's just told me what happened. Poor man. And poor Phyllis. What a shit end to her festival.'

'I know,' I agreed.

She poured herself a refill from the bottle of Coke she was holding in her other hand. I assumed she was driving. *Coke.* The four white letters on the distinctive red background blurred in front of my eyes as Molloy's words 'anything he drank or ate from' echoed in my ears. In my mind's eye I saw a can of Diet Coke fetched from the fridge in the Beacon Hall kitchen. *Had I given Featherstone the drink that had killed him?*

I ran out of the pub after Molloy, catching him just as he was getting into the squad car in the square. He motioned for me to sit into the passenger seat. I told him what had happened and he listened without comment until I was finished.

'And where did you leave the can?' he asked.

'On a windowsill. Phyllis asked me to leave it there and she'd give it to him. The high one just to the left of the hall exit leading straight into the marquee.'

'Okay. It's possible it's still there. Or maybe it's in one of the bins. I'll call McFadden and get him to look.' He paused. 'And you're sure there were no other cans of coke in the fridge?'

I shook my head. But, of course, now I was beginning to doubt myself. What if there had been another one in there? I didn't look very hard. I'd been anxious to get back with the water for my parents before the event started. What if I could have chosen a different can?

'My impression is that the fridge was empty and the can was in the door,' I said. 'Phyllis said he needed to take some tablets and that he didn't drink water.'

Molloy nodded. 'He was on heart medication. Statins.'

I looked up. 'Should that not have prevented a heart attack? Is that why you're investigating his death?'

He made a sound that was non-committal. 'You say Phyllis said he didn't drink water?'

I nodded. 'But he did. He drank the water on stage. He was drinking it all through the event. He even finished his glass and poured himself another one. But the marquee *was* very warm.'

Molloy's eyes narrowed. 'Who poured the first glass?'

I shrugged. 'I'm not sure. I assume it was Róisín Henderson, the writer who was interviewing him.' I tried to think. 'There was a carafe with two glasses on stage when I left to get water for my parents. I can't remember if they were full then. But when I came back two glasses of water had definitely been poured because Róisín was drinking from one of them. Featherstone drank from the other during the event.'

'Right.' Molloy reached out for my knee. 'Don't panic about the Coke. You did an errand as a favour, that's all. But thanks for letting me know.'

I got out of the car, and watched him drive around the square back in the direction of the hall. It was then that I remembered something else; the heated conversation I'd half-witnessed between Featherstone and Phyllis backstage. Should I ring Molloy and tell him about it, I wondered? No, I decided. Phyllis was bound to tell him when she got the chance, and it would be better coming from her.

I stood for a minute before going back inside, inhaling the night air. The clouds moved away from the face of the moon; pearl-like in a velvet navy sky. It was dusk, still not quite dark at ten o'clock on a Friday night, the street lights just coming on. Early summer was a time of year I usually loved in Inishowen. But I had a feeling this one was going to be different.

Chapter Thirteen

My parents were in bed when I got home and Guinness was out on his night-time rambles. I didn't see the point in sitting up alone ruminating over everything that had happened so I went to bed too, although I didn't sleep particularly well.

The following morning, woken by jackdaws making a racket outside my bedroom window, I came down early, pleased to find them both in the kitchen. I guess they assumed I didn't need my pre-work headspace on a Saturday, or maybe they'd found it difficult to sleep too. A pot of tea and a plate of toast sat on the table between them, with a jar of coarse-cut marmalade. I don't particularly like marmalade but it had been touching to find these remnants of my childhood popping up in my cupboards and fridge over the past week.

Guinness was curled up on my mother's knee. My parents had somehow managed to find a softer side to the cat, which had always eluded me. But then he was highly susceptible to bribery.

They looked up expectantly when I appeared, knowing I'd have news of Featherstone since I'd been out so much later than they were.

'How'd you both sleep?' I asked, postponing the inevitable for a few seconds.

'Your dad was grinding his teeth,' my mum said. 'He sounds as if he's eating crisps in the middle of the night.'

'Maybe I am,' my dad said, glancing at me. 'So? How is he?'

I watched their faces fall as I told them about Featherstone's death, wishing I didn't have to. Their visit had been going well so far; the years falling away from their faces as they enjoyed the good weather and the sea.

'Could it have been some kind of allergy?' my mother asked, absorbing what Molloy had told me the night before. She looked at my dad. 'Remember that kid with the nut allergy on the flight to Reykjavik? How he looked before his mother produced the EpiPen. Confusion, difficulty breathing . . .'

My dad nodded. 'It was very frightening to watch. Poor kid.' Then he frowned. 'But Featherstone wasn't really like that. It looked more like a heart attack to me. Did you see the tremor in his hand when he poured out that glass of water?'

I'd noticed it too but I'd put it down to nerves, or getting older, but then he hadn't been displaying any other signs of nerves or old age. He'd seemed totally at ease. In fact, he'd seemed to become more confident and excited as the event went on, until near the end that was. It struck me now that maybe that *was* a little strange for a recluse like Featherstone. Surely, he'd have found his first appearance in ten years more difficult. Hadn't my mother heard that he was nervous?

'And if Featherstone had an allergy,' my dad continued, 'then he'd be prepared. Surely it would be part of his assistant's job have an EpiPen. He hardly just types for him.'

'True.' My mother nodded.

'I imagine Featherstone typed his own stuff,' I said. 'Most people do these days.'

I looked at the clock. It was half-past nine. The post-mortem would have started by now, along with tests on the various vessels and containers they'd found. I shook my head to dispel the image of a Diet Coke can in the door of a fridge that had haunted me since last night.

I opened the cupboard over the sink in search of some coffee but we were out. Turning back towards the table, I asked, 'Fancy heading into Glendara for a paper and a coffee?'

Both looked nonplussed. My parents came from a generation that didn't go out for breakfast, and they'd been out with Molloy and me just the Sunday before. That would usually have done them for a few months, but I needed a distraction, and some decent coffee.

'The sun's shining so Tony might have tables and chairs outside the Oak?' I said encouragingly, adding, 'And we might get some news.'

Which turned out to be the clincher, causing them both to stand up and grab their jackets. The apple doesn't fall too far from the tree.

This time my dad drove, the memory of hunkering down in the passenger seat of the Mini on the way to the shore walk still too fresh in his mind.

Crossing over to the Oak from where we parked in the square, I was glad to see my promise hadn't been hollow. Four or five tables sat on the footpath under the awning, Tony having deemed the pale pink sun of the morning sufficient for outdoor dining. Three tables were taken: one by a group of people I didn't know, Phyllis and Jude sat at another with Róisín Henderson, and the TV threesome occupied a third a small distance away, Gina in a cherry-coloured dress and a pair of cat's eye sunglasses which were far too big for her face.

Jude pulled up a few extra seats so we could join them at

theirs, while my dad insisted on fetching the drinks from inside. I decided to leave it a few minutes and then follow him in to help carry them out.

It was only when we sat down that I saw that Phyllis's eyes were red-rimmed. Phyllis doesn't often cry, so I found this slightly shocking. I was glad to see Jude place his arm around her when he retook his seat, even if it was also odd to see her lean in to him. While Phyllis was an integral part of the community in Glendara she tended to be the rock for other people, choosing to live her own life in a rather solitary fashion.

Apart from Fred of course. My foot touched something soft under the table and I saw that the dog was stretched out at Phyllis's feet. He looked up at me, yawned, and flopped his head back down again on his paws.

'I'm so sorry, Phyllis,' I said. 'What a terrible thing to happen.'

She nodded and sat up straight, clearing her throat. 'Thanks for helping Liam with the open mic last night.'

'How did it go?' Róisín asked, slicing into a huge fruit scone.

'Bit of a mixed bag,' I said.

'I'll bet,' she grinned, scraping butter out of a foil wrap and slathering it all over the scone. 'They've cancelled the rest of the festival,' she sighed. 'No short-story workshop. And it was booked out.' She shot a semi-accusatory glance at Phyllis.

I said nothing, but apart from being inappropriate, her annoyance was misdirected. It hadn't been Phyllis's call. It was Molloy's.

My mother nodded. 'I'd signed up for it. I was looking forward to it but I guess you've no choice. It wouldn't send out a great message to go ahead regardless.'

Róisín shrugged as if she would have, if the choice were hers. She bit into her scone with relish. I couldn't help wonder at how unaffected she appeared to be. It was difficult not to recall the tetchiness of her exchanges with Featherstone the evening before, which few people could have failed to notice.

'Did you know him?' I asked, curiously. 'I imagine the Irish writing community must be pretty small.'

She shook her head, finished chewing and then swallowed. 'First time was when he walked on stage last night. He didn't want to meet beforehand. Claimed it would make the interview fresher if we met for the first time onstage.'

So that was why she'd been on before him, I thought. I tried to work out if this demonstration of ego had annoyed her, but her expression remained neutral. Róisín Henderson was a far more difficult person to read this morning than she had been last night. I wondered if she was masking the same concerns that I was. I'd fetched Featherstone's Coke, but it was probable that she had poured him the water which he'd drunk onstage.

Jude leaned in suddenly. 'Maybe keep your voices down,' he whispered, casting a surreptitious look in the direction of the TV crew.

I risked a glance and saw they had completely stopped their conversation. Gina met my gaze brazenly and gave me a wave, while Ollie looked away and pulled on headphones. Making a point of disengaging. I wondered if he was embarrassed by the insensitivity of his aunt and boss, no longer wishing to be here but having no choice but to stay till the bitter end.

'Why are they still here?' I whispered.

'They obviously think they've got a scoop,' Jude said harshly, not bothering to lower his voice this time and glaring in their direction. 'I imagine it's rare enough to be doing a documentary on someone and have them die during the making of it, let alone actually film their death. Although it seems pretty crass to me.' He paused. 'Those are journalists at the other table too.'

I cast a quick look, remembering what Phyllis had said about the contrast between local and national journalists, and wondered if were we about to get a taste of it. I saw that she herself kept looking at Gina Bailey, her eyes darting in the direction of their table every few minutes. Did they know each other, I wondered? Have a history? Phyllis certainly had strong opinions about Gina on Friday night, when you'd think she'd have been glad of the interest being shown in her festival. She didn't seem as bothered by the actual news journalists at the other tables.

At that moment my dad reappeared carrying three takeaway cups and I stood up to help, having forgotten to follow him into the pub. Tony had given him a cardboard carrying tray, so he waved away my help, plonking it onto the table.

I reached for my cup and gratefully took a sip of the strong hot black liquid. As I did so, my phone rang. Molloy. I walked away to answer it, my coffee in my other hand.

'Morning,' he said. 'Sorry I didn't get back to you last night.'

'That's okay. How's everything going?' I perched on the edge of one of the flowerbeds and put my cup on the ground.

'All right.' He sounded tired. 'The post-mortem is in progress. Toxicology will take a while, I think. The Tech Bureau have examined the scene. Various glasses and jugs are being tested for contents. The glass he drank from on stage, of course. Which by the way wasn't water; it was fruit juice of some description, lime cordial or something diluted with water.'

So that was why it had looked clear, I thought. And why he'd been happy enough to drink it.

'And, we found the Coke can. Or at least we found *a* Diet Coke can in the bin by the exit where Featherstone would have gone on stage, so we assume it's the same one. That's being tested too.'

I swallowed, but said nothing. There was a loud guffaw from the TV crew table where the cameraman was taking a call. 'Did you get the TV footage by the way?' I asked. 'They must have filmed the whole thing.'

'We did. They were surprisingly cooperative actually.' Molloy took a deep breath in. 'I think they're hoping for an interview for their documentary, official Garda line, etc.' He snorted. 'They haven't a hope. Anyway, I've watched it but I might get you to have a look too – see if you notice anything you didn't see on the night. If anything jogs your memory.'

'Sure.' I paused before asking the question, 'Was Featherstone murdered?'

Molloy sighed. 'It does look as if it wasn't a natural death. Of course, the post-mortem and toxicology reports may confirm otherwise.'

'Do you think it could have been the can of Coke?' I couldn't stop myself.

'Too early to say,' he said. 'At this stage it could have been anything. You mentioned Phyllis saying he wanted to take some tablets before he went on stage. It seems he was on medication for various things, not just his heart.'

Was it possible he'd just had a bad reaction to medication? I wondered. But that was just wishful thinking. From what Molloy said next, he was thinking otherwise.

'If someone slipped him something, it's likely to have been in what he was drinking on stage. The footage shows him drinking a lot before he keeled over. He drained the first glass and poured himself a second one.' He paused. 'We're going to need to talk to that other writer, the one who interviewed him, Róisín Henderson. Any idea where she might be? She's not at her hotel and she's not answering her phone.'

'She's here,' I said, 'with Phyllis and Jude. I'm at the Oak.'

'Okay, good. Can you ask her to come down to the station? Soon as she can. I'm here now.'

I hung up and walked back to the table to deliver the message.

My mother was chatting to Róisín about her cancelled workshop while my dad and Jude were talking amicably. But Phyllis was staring off into the distance, eyes filled with unshed tears. I couldn't help thinking that her reaction seemed more like grief than disappointment at the collapse of a festival into which she'd put a lot of work. Had she known Featherstone better than I thought? I wanted to ask her, but I couldn't. Not here, with Róisín and Jude present. And not yet, when it looked as if things were still too raw.

Chapter Fourteen

My opportunity came earlier than expected. On Sunday morning I awoke early. I'd forgotten to close my curtains and the sun streamed in the window of my bedroom, giving the room a lemony glow. Today was my dad's birthday, but the house was quiet when I got up so I decided to take a quick run out to Lagg before breakfast and have a dip at Five Fingers Strand.

Turning off the road to Malin Head, I drove down the sandy lane leading towards the shore, through velvety, green tussocks dotted with rabbit holes and grazed by sheep, and past the pretty, white St Mary's church. I parked about a hundred metres from the beach, grabbed my towel and togs, and made my way across the shingle onto the smooth and undisturbed sand, standing still for a few seconds to breathe in the sea air that I loved. The beach was deserted, not surprising this early on a Sunday morning, golden sand stretching as far as the eye could see; Glashedy Island and the Isle of Doagh just about visible on the horizon.

Despite the pale blue sky, it wasn't exactly warm and there was a sharp wind coming from the sea but the day had the potential to be a good one. The sun glinted off the water, the waves making their way inexorably towards the shore, and the five rocks which gave the beach its name were stark in the distance, jutting up from the sea like a submerged giant's hand. Seagulls shrieked and wheeled overhead, riding the air currents above the spine of Knockamany Bens.

I dropped my stuff and quickly stripped off, folding my clothes and leaving them on top of my runners, then ran along the cold wet sand to the water's edge. Wading in up to my midriff, I hesitated for no more than a second before I launched myself in, breath catching in my throat as I submerged my shoulders, the stinging cold almost paralysing me.

Experienced sea swimmers say you must stay in till it stops hurting, that your body becomes accustomed to the cold, and if you go in a second time it's even easier. I knew this to be true but I wasn't looking for pleasure when I swam – it was the short sharp shock that I was after; the jolt to my system, which was invariably followed by an improvement in mood and clarity of thought. This morning I'd awoken with myriad thoughts swirling around my head; concern about my parents and how long they would stay now that the festival had come to an untimely end, and Phyllis – what was really going on with her.

I managed three or four strokes before dragging myself out, shivering and stomping like a sea monster to shake off the icy droplets and get some feeling back into my toes, then hobbling back out to my clothes. Though it was early summer, the sea warmed up rather later in Inishowen than more southerly areas. Not that you could ever call it warm.

I was towelling myself dry, rubbing myself vigorously to get the blood flowing again, when I saw that I wasn't alone on the beach after all. A lone figure dressed in grey was walking in my direction, tracing the shoreline while gazing out to sea and the steadily breaking waves. A black and white dog circled excitedly as a stick was thrown, fetched and returned. Fred and Phyllis.

I pulled on my tracksuit bottoms and sweatshirt and gathered up my things, shaking the sand from my towel as I made my way over to her, my hair hanging in damp tendrils feeling cold against my neck. She didn't see me until I was almost alongside her so I called out her name, not wanting to startle her. I knew she'd been going for walks lately in an attempt to lose weight and reduce the pain in her hip but this didn't seem like one of those walks. Something about her made me think that her mind was somewhere else entirely; trying to get her attention felt like waking a sleepwalker.

She didn't hear me at first but when I called a second time, she turned, hair buffeted by the sea breeze. It seemed to take her a second or two to register my presence, before she mustered a half-smile and pushed a strand out of her eyes. 'An early morning swim?'

'Seemed a good day for it.' I shaded my eyes with my hands. 'Haven't done it in a while.'

She nodded distractedly. 'It's a fine day all right.'

I fell into step with her along the water's edge. She was wearing a pair of grey trousers and a loose top, and she was barefoot, carrying her sandals in her hand. She looked strange out of her usual palette of clashing bright colours. Not herself.

'You're here early,' I said.

She grimaced. 'Couldn't sleep. Too much on my mind.'

'I can imagine.'

The foaming water crept in further with each wave. One washed over Phyllis's feet but she didn't seem to notice or care.

'I really am so sorry. You always put so much work into the festival; to have something like this happen is absolutely unthinkable.'

Phyllis nodded but she didn't respond, just tilted her face to the sun while breathing in the salty air. Fred returned with the stick and dropped it at her feet but she didn't react. Looking down at his expectant, loving face – Phyllis had rescued him after his old owner died and he adored her – I picked up the stick and threw it for him myself. He bounded off, kicking the sand up behind him.

I touched Phyllis lightly on the arm. 'Do you mind me asking you something?'

She blinked and looked at me.

'Did you *know* Gavin Featherstone?'

She stopped walking.

'I mean, I know he was invited to the festival but you seem more . . .' I trailed off, unsure how to put what I was thinking into words.

'More upset than I should be?' She gave me a watery smile. 'I did know him, a long time ago.' She looked around suddenly as if she'd lost something, then spotted Fred barrelling towards us and started walking again. When he dropped his stick this time, she threw it for him, giving him a scratch around the ears before she did so. 'Good boy.'

He hurtled off and she straightened with a groan. 'About a hundred years ago, I did an English degree at Queen's.'

I looked at her with interest. 'I didn't know that.'

She waved my curiosity away. 'Ach, I never did anything with it, unless you count opening a wee bookshop.'

'I certainly do count opening a wee bookshop.'

She smiled. 'So do I. Anyway, Gavin Featherstone was writer-in-residence. It was a few years after the Booker Prize so it was a coup for the university to get him. I got to know him a little, attended some of his workshops. He was a bit of a rockstar back then. Very handsome.'

'Handsome, eh?' I raised my eyebrows, teasingly. 'How well did you know him, did you say?'

'Nothing like that.' She bowed her head. 'I was only eighteen then. Anyway, shortly after that he bought Shore Lodge here in Inishowen. I think he used prize money from something, or maybe an inheritance from his parents. And when I came back here after college – I did a master's after my degree – and I wasn't sure what to do with myself, he offered me a job.'

'A job?'

'Well, not really a job, more like a few weeks' summer work. I'd done a short typing course; he was writing a new book but he'd hurt one of his hands so he couldn't type for a while. He'd dictate his chapters into a Dictaphone and I'd type them up.'

'And you did that at his house?'

She nodded. 'I did. It was all a bit chaotic with the kids running around, but he had a study at the back in a converted stables, which is where we used to work.' She stopped. 'Have you ever been out there?'

I shook my head. 'I walked past it with my parents when we did the shore walk but you can't see anything. Too many big trees. I wouldn't have even known it was there had you not told me.'

'It's an amazing house. Way too big for him on his own, God knows why he stayed there after they left, but brilliant for a family.' She looked wistful.

Now her knowledge of its location made sense, I thought. 'So, you were friends,' I said, with sympathy. Her grief made more sense now too.

She shrugged. 'Ach, it was a long time ago. I went travelling after that for a few years. Got a taste for it. It took me a long time to find my way back here to open the bookshop.' She looked away. 'I haven't had any contact with him for decades. Sure, he hardly ventured out of the house in the past few years.'

I narrowed my eyes. 'Why do you think that was?'

She shook her head. 'No idea. He could be difficult. Thran,' she said with a smile which faded quickly. 'Always did whatever he wanted and damn the consequences, for him or anyone else. Didn't give a fig what anyone thought of him.'

'Maybe he'd changed,' I said, remembering what he'd said about guilt during his interview with Róisín, how the weight of it could taint your life.

'Not that much, I suspect.'

Despite her flippant tone, there was an edge there, which prompted me to ask what I'd been wondering about since Friday. 'You know when you asked me to fetch that Coke for him?' I said hesitantly.

'I do.' Did I see a hint of concern in her face?

'While I was leaving it on the windowsill as you asked, I over-heard you and Featherstone having some kind of an argument.' I tried to read Phyllis's expression but couldn't. 'It's none of my business, but Molloy asked me if I'd noticed anything odd that evening and well . . . I haven't told him about it. I thought you might have. Or if I was going to, I wanted to speak to you first.'

Phyllis smiled. 'It's fine. I'll tell the sergeant.' She turned her head away to gaze towards the horizon again. 'We *were* having a row. It was about the book signing that he was supposed to do in the bookshop after the event.'

'Oh?' I said.

'He didn't want to do it. I insisted he'd agreed when he said he'd do the festival, that it was a big part of going to a literary event for people, getting a book signed by the author. But he said he didn't want to speak to people, that it was enough he was doing the interview, that he didn't like meeting people any more.' She made a face. 'He even accused me of wanting to make money. I said of course I wanted to sell books; I was a book-seller. Anyway, you get the picture. He could be an awkward old bugger. Although I guess he was a wee bit anxious about his first event in so long.'

He didn't show much anxiety onstage, I thought. Not at first anyway. But I was relieved, the weight of duplicity off my shoulders.

I checked my watch and, seeing it was after nine, asked, 'Do you want a lift back?' wondering suddenly how Phyllis had got here. Mine had been the only car at the entrance to the beach, but maybe she'd parked at the far end.

She shook her head and looked out to sea again; Fred was now splashing about in the shallows. 'I want to stay a wee while longer.'

Chapter Fifteen

Back at the house in Malin, my parents were now up. I produced a card and a good bottle of whiskey for my dad. My mother and I sang 'Happy Birthday' to him over tea and toast, much to his embarrassment, and the suggestion to have lunch in the bistro was greeted enthusiastically. I was glad my mother didn't suggest including Molloy again. Though our squabble had been smoothed over by Featherstone's death – how awful that sounded – it seemed easier with just the three of us. Plus, I knew he would say no, barely two days into a murder investigation.

And there was still a tiny niggle left over from Friday morning when he'd told me he needed to speak to me about something; I had the feeling that whatever it was, it wasn't good news. But I parked that concern for the moment. Today was about my parents, in particular my dad. Lunch would be an opportunity to ask them about their plans; I was hoping they'd stay a bit longer, particularly since there'd been no resolution of the Chambers problem.

In the end, I didn't have to say a word. Lunch was a success, made all the more so by the fact that they both liked seafood.

'It's so fresh here,' my mum said, forking a piece of turbot with romesco sauce and lifting it towards her mouth.

'Wouldn't it be great if we could eat it for a bit longer?' Dad said with a wink, before turning to me. 'Do you think you could tolerate your old pair for a few more days?'

And so, it was decided that they would stay until Wednesday, without my having to do anything. Although I suspected the extended visit had as much to do with following the investigation into Featherstone's death as spending time with their daughter, or eating fish for that matter. The relish with which they devoured the Sunday newspapers that afternoon, handing each other sections and pointing out inaccuracies, was evidence of that. The news of Featherstone's death had come too late to make the Saturday editions, but the Sundays relished it – the tabloids full of exclamation marks and puns: *Final Chapter! Booker Prize winner Featherstone collapses and dies at first event in twelve years.*

The following morning, Monday, I was in town at twenty past nine, ten minutes early for work. So I texted Leah to tell her not to bother collecting the papers, that I'd do it.

Stoop's newsagents was cool and dark, as soothing as a library. The newsagent himself was nowhere to be seen but the papers, as always, were fanned across the counter, allowing me to scan the headlines. Those with no Sunday editions all mentioned Gavin Featherstone's death, and the *Irish Times* indicated the presence of an obituary inside. Excellent.

Stoop emerged from the bowels of his shop with a pricing gun held aloft like a weapon. 'That TV lot are still here.' He had a habit of launching straight into whatever was on his mind without any preamble. 'Bucked if know why.'

I smiled. 'I don't know either.'

'Thought they were just covering the festival. Festival's over, isn't it? Don't know why they need to be still here snooping around the place.'

'No,' I agreed, picking up the *Irish Times* and *Inish Times* and indicating that I'd like to pay for them.

He lowered the gun and slipped in behind the counter. 'They're staying out in Ballyliffin. My niece works as a receptionist there and she says they've extended their stay. Everyone else who was here for the festival had the decency to leave on Saturday after what happened.' He clicked his teeth. 'Vultures.'

'I'm sure they'll push off once they have what they need,' I soothed.

He looked at me dubiously, but took my cash.

Jude was in the window of Phyllis's shop dismantling the festival display when I passed. He happened to look out as I was walking by and waved, so I stopped for a few minutes, leaning against the open doorway to chat. I saw that he was removing Featherstone's books, taking them from the window and placing them into a cardboard box.

He followed my gaze and looked down at the book in his hand. 'She doesn't want people to think she's profiting from his death. But, of course, you and I both know that his books are the only ones anyone is going to be asking for in the next few days. Just because they're not in the window doesn't mean she's not going to have to sell them.'

I held up the two newspapers I'd bought. 'He was all over the papers yesterday. Publicity he'd probably have killed for while he was alive. Or at least his publishers would have.' I paused. 'I wonder if the memoir will still come out?'

Jude gave me a cynical look. 'Oh, I imagine so. It'll sell bucket-loads now. I can see the publishers bringing it forward. It's not supposed to be out till the new year but I'm willing to bet it'll make an appearance before then.'

I nodded, thinking he was probably right. I glanced into the shop. There was no sign of Phyllis. Or her dog. I asked after her. 'I met her on Lagg yesterday. Is she okay?'

Jude shook his head, deep lines of concern appearing across his forehead. 'She's there again now.' He glanced at his watch. 'Been gone nearly two hours. Poor Fred will be starving.' He gave me a sad smile. 'It's like she's avoiding me.'

'I'm sure that's not true,' I said, wondering suddenly if she'd spoken to Molloy yet, if maybe the prospect of that conversation was bothering her, but it didn't seem likely. Phyllis wasn't intimidated by Molloy.

Jude dropped another couple of books into the box. 'I was supposed to go on a trip to West Donegal with some biker mates today after the festival was over, but I pulled out. Wanted to stay here for a bit, help if I could.'

'That was good of you.'

'We leave all phones behind; it's one of our rules.' He smiled. 'One of the lads has a CB radio. But I didn't feel comfortable leaving Phyllis and being out of contact.'

'I'm sure she's glad to have you here.'

He shrugged. 'I'm beginning to wonder if there's any point. She's not talking to me. I know she's not sleeping; I hear her in the kitchen in the small hours. But anytime I try to talk to her she shuts me down.'

I tried to think of something to say that might help but I was stumped.

We looked out onto the street, each immersed in our own thoughts. It was a typical Monday morning in Glendara; kids in uniforms messed about, oblivious to the fact that they were late for school and Stan chugged on a takeaway coffee from the Oak, looking particularly flamboyant in purple cords and a pink shirt. Gina Bailey walked by with Ollie trotting behind her.

'He was in yesterday,' Jude remarked, nodding in their direction. 'Caught him trying to pinch a book. Powell and Pressburger. At least the kid's got taste.'

We watched them cross the square, *Despicable She* and her minion.

'What did you do?' I asked.

'I let him off.'

'You old softie.'

'Ah, Phyllis has enough on her plate without having to deal with reporting shoplifters. Can't imagine Molloy would appreciate it either. Plus, I felt sorry for him; I don't think that woman pays him. He's on some kind of work experience.'

They disappeared around the corner.

'She's his aunt, I think.'

'Is she now?' Jude crossed his arms. 'He told me he studied film in Ballyfermot. One of my girls wanted to do that. He's rightly bullied by your woman. He must be twenty-five but she treats him like a kid.'

'I've noticed,' I said. 'Stoop was complaining about them still being here at all.'

Jude nodded. 'Phyllis doesn't like it much either. I guess they're a reminder of what happened. Not that she's likely to forget too quickly.' He stretched and rubbed his lower back. 'Which is why I'd better finish this. I'd like to have them out of sight before she gets back.'

Arriving into the office, I found Leah staring at a long brown envelope that was sitting in front of her on the reception desk. She looked up at me eagerly when I came in; not my usual reception, if I'm honest.

'What?' I said.

'What do you mean, what?' she replied tartly. 'Where's my good morning?'

135

'You're clearly dying to tell me something. What is it?'

She pushed the envelope towards me. 'Have a look at that.'

I recognised it as the type of stiff envelope we used for wills, but the handwriting on the label was neither mine nor Leah's. I assumed it was my predecessor's, the solicitor from whom I'd bought the practice.

I read the words *Last Will and Testament of Gavin Featherstone, Shore Lodge, Greencastle, Co Donegal*. I raised my eyebrows. 'Right. So, we have his will.'

Leah seemed disappointed by my response, her own eyes still brimming with excitement. 'I was sure I'd spotted it in the wills safe on Friday when I was doing that clear out, and when I heard what happened on Friday night, I couldn't get here quickly enough this morning to check. And there it was.' She flipped her hand at it like a magician producing a silk scarf from someone's ear. 'His last will and testament.'

I checked the date on the envelope; more than twenty years ago. 'Unless he's done a new one,' I said. 'It's pretty old'.

'That seems unlikely, doesn't it?' Leah said, making a face. 'I mean, he still lived around here. You'd think he'd have come back in if he wanted to do a new one. It would have been the safest thing to do, to make sure the old one was destroyed.' She gave a shudder. 'Unless he did one of those homemade ones.'

'Let's hope not. Or if he did, let's hope we're not the ones who have to administer it.'

For a will to be valid it needed to be properly drafted, dispose of all assets and be properly signed and witnessed, or it would be rejected by the Probate Office. Homemade wills, or the pre-drafted forms that were sold in some stationers, were notoriously problematic.

'What do you want me to do with it?' Leah asked, resting her chin on her hands.

I slid the envelope back to her. 'Let's leave it a few days and then write to the executor, if no one contacts us. Have you checked to see who it is?'

She nodded. 'His wife, Barbara.' Then grimaced. 'Ex-wife, isn't it? Shit, that'll cause problems anyway, won't it?'

I shrugged. 'Maybe not. Let's wait and see. It's early days. The post-mortem only happened yesterday so there may not even be a death certificate yet . . .' I trailed off as it hit me that, surely, they'd have finished the post-mortem by now, have a cause of death even if they didn't have toxicology results. Why hadn't Molloy called me?

My alarm must have shown in my face.

'Are you all right?' Leah asked.

I nodded. He'd have called me if I had anything to worry about. Wouldn't he?

Leah handed me a couple of envelopes, which had been hand delivered over the weekend, and I took them upstairs along with the newspapers.

At my desk, I flicked through the *Irish Times* to find the obituary. I'd just opened the centre pages, dominated by a huge photograph of Featherstone looking ruggedly handsome and outdoorsy with a cigarette in his hand, when there was a knock on my door and Leah appeared.

I looked up, surprised. She had been avoiding using our steep winding staircase this last while, choosing more often to communicate with me on the internal phone. Now she came into the room and closed the door behind her with a quiet click, clearly concerned about being overheard. She carefully placed the brown envelope she'd shown me downstairs on my desk.

'Guess who's in reception,' she said, her eyes wide.

137

Chapter Sixteen

A moment of panic ensued when I remembered the newspaper still on my desk, open at the huge photograph of Featherstone. I shunted it quickly into the wastepaper bin at my feet, just moments before his widow and son came into the room.

As I stood to greet them, shake their hands and offer my condolences, my immediate impression was one of stature; I am not a tall person and both Barbara and Patrick Featherstone were nudging six feet. Barbara was younger than her ex-husband, I guessed; she looked to be in her early sixties. She was an attractive woman with almond-shaped eyes and shoulder-length grey hair framing an intelligent face, and she wore a long summer coat of emerald green, embroidered at the cuffs and collar. Her son, I found it difficult to take my eyes off because, and there was no other way of putting this – he was the absolute spit of his father. He had the same blue eyes, a similar beard, and dark hair instead of grey brushed back in a similar style. I guessed his age as early thirties but he was a considerably more conservative dresser than Featherstone, wearing a blazer and dark trousers.

They took the seats I offered, and I watched them settle themselves, Barbara putting her bag on the floor while her son unbuttoned his jacket. I'd been curious about Featherstone's estranged family ever since his event. The narrative of the woman who'd left the handsome and charismatic author without a backward glance, turning him into a broken recluse, hadn't fitted when I heard him speak. But now my sense was that neither of the people sitting across from me was as affected by the man's death as Phyllis had been yesterday morning. Although maybe they'd had a chance to pull themselves together for a meeting with a solicitor, while I'd caught Phyllis unawares, trying to clear her head.

Still, Patrick reached for his mother's hand when they sat down in what I assumed was a gesture of support. He wore a wedding ring, I noticed, a gold band, which matched a rather expensive-looking, gold watch. His mother did not. She didn't allow her hand to stay in her son's, retrieving it quickly and clasping it to the other one in her lap.

'I'm sorry to just turn up without an appointment,' she said, 'but we believe Gavin's will is here. I remember him coming in, to have it done, to your predecessor of course. And I'm assuming, or hoping, that it's still here.'

I remembered what Leah had said about her being local, or at least her roots being from here, but her accent held very little trace of Inishowen.

I nodded, holding up the envelope. 'You're correct. I have it here. I haven't had a chance to read it yet, so I can't guarantee there are no issues, but my assistant tells me you're the executor. So I'm happy to read it to you, if that's what you'd like.'

She seemed relieved, casting a glance at her son, who gave her a brief smile. 'Yes please.'

With both pairs of eyes upon me, I slid the will from its envelope. It was common practice these days to have an attendance sheet recording instructions for a will in case there was a dispute as to the meaning of its contents. Not so much twenty years ago. This envelope contained just one typed double-page of thick will paper with a blue line down the left-hand side.

I looked up, fixing my gaze on Barbara. 'You know when this will was drafted?'

She nodded. 'Yes, it was when the children were small. Patrick has a sister who lives in the States,' she added, glancing at her son.

I unfolded the will and smoothed it out on my desk. 'Are we sure this is his last will? That he hadn't had one done more recently?'

'I don't think so,' Barbara said. 'He certainly never told me that he had. We didn't speak much but I think he'd have mentioned that.'

So they weren't completely estranged, I thought. 'Okay. I'll go ahead and read it. You're free to take it elsewhere, of course, but if you do want me to administer it, you'll need to come in and see me again, so we can have a proper introductory meeting.'

'Understood.' She gave me an apologetic look. 'I know it seems very early to do this when Gavin only died on Friday. But we both live in Dublin so it seemed to make sense to check. I didn't even know if we'd be able to see you today.'

'Understood,' I echoed her, and smiled.

'And actually, I would like you to administer the estate. I'm assuming Shore Lodge, the house, will make up the bulk of it so it makes sense to have a solicitor here.'

'I'd be happy to. Will you be here for a while?'

Barbara looked at her son. 'Another week maybe? We're going to visit some old friends. Some old haunts. Patrick hasn't been here since he was a teenager.'

I nodded. 'Leah will give you an appointment after this, and we'll let you know what you'll need to bring in. The first stage is a Schedule of Assets and Liabilities for the Revenue Commissioners, so we'll need to establish what Mr Featherstone owned, property, bank accounts, shares, that kind of thing. And work out any tax due.'

I was about to start reading the will when Patrick reached over and gently tapped his mother's hand as if to remind her of something. I couldn't help but appreciate the supportive role he'd chosen to take – all too often I was forced to listen to adult children talking over their older relatives in the guise of being helpful.

Barbara gave a tight nod, then squared her shoulders as if steeling herself for something unpleasant. 'We had a call this morning about the post-mortem . . .'

I swallowed. The elephant in the room was Featherstone's cause of death, which could very much affect the administration of his estate. 'What did they say?'

'They're still waiting on toxicology results.' She paused and shot a glance at Patrick, who looked down as if he too found the subject distasteful. 'But it looks as if there's going to be a criminal investigation into his death.'

Bloody Molloy, I thought, pushing away the image of a Diet Coke can. He knew I was anxious about the part I'd played. Why hadn't he contacted me?

'Okay,' I said slowly, forcing myself to focus. 'We can't prepare any papers without a death certificate, which won't be issued until cause of death is established. And,' I hesitated, not wishing to be the one to say this directly, 'if someone was involved in his death . . .'

'No one can profit from a death they have caused.' Patrick spoke for the first time since the introductions.

'Well, yes,' I said, glancing from him to his mother. I expected to see a dipped head, but she looked at me levelly. 'Were you there when it happened?' I asked quietly. 'At the event?'

Barbara nodded. 'Yes. We both were.'

I wanted to ask why they didn't go to him, make themselves known when he was fighting for his life. But it didn't seem to be my place.

My job was to read the will, and so I began.

'This is the last will and testament of Gavin Featherstone of Shore Lodge, Greencastle, Co. Donegal, made by me on the twelfth of August 2000 hereby revoking all wills and other testamentary dispositions previously made by me . . .'

In my peripheral vision I saw Patrick reach for and this time hold on to his mother's hand. I knew how strange it was to hear the voice of a loved one after they were gone, albeit in legalese. *Had* Gavin Featherstone been loved by the two people in front of me? It was hard to tell.

In the event, the will turned out to be very straightforward, leaving everything to Barbara, Patrick and Susie.

'The house wasn't in your joint names?' I asked Barbara, folding up the will again.

She shook her head. 'Gavin bought it before I met him and we just never got around to it. He used to come here on his own to write while he was working in Belfast and when he left Queen's we all moved here permanently. I kept my house in Dublin, which I'd bought before I met him. I rented it out while I lived here, and the three of us just moved back in when Gavin and I separated. I didn't want anything from him so the deeds to Shore Lodge just stayed in his name.'

'Are you divorced?' I asked, taking out an attendance pad, thinking ahead to any possible complications with the probate.

Barbara shook her head with a sad smile. 'Never got around to that either. We don't even have a legal separation. It didn't seem important somehow. I didn't want or need anything for myself and Gavin was generous with maintenance for the kids, far more generous than a court would have been. I'd been teaching in the secondary school here but I went back to university work. I'm a history lecturer,' she added.

I must have betrayed something in my expression.

'You're wondering why I'm not more distressed at the possible murder of my husband. The father of my children.'

I shrugged my shoulders and gave a half-smile.

She closed her eyes briefly. 'It's the latter which upsets me, that the children have lost their father, that there's no hope for reconciliation now.'

Patrick was staring at the floor again, his expression unreadable.

Barbara took a deep breath. 'But he was estranged from them for a long time. Had been since we split up. His decision. Gavin always did precisely what he wanted and damn the consequences for anyone else. Even his family.' She was clear-eyed but her voice was solid with contempt. 'The way he treated people, it was always going to end this way; it was just a matter of time. I know how awful it sounds but it feels as if the other shoe has finally dropped.'

I tried to align this damning indictment with the affable indi-vidual who'd charmed his audience on Friday night and failed, yet it echoed some of what Phyllis had said on the beach.

'Let's have another meeting in a few days,' I said. 'Leah will give you an appointment. While we wait for a death certificate, we can be getting on with gathering information about the estate. Was Shore Lodge his only property? Land or buildings, I mean.'

Mother and son looked at one another, shrugged and nodded.

'Maybe you can double check that? In the meantime, we'll need to get a valuation done on the house.'

'Can you arrange for that to be done?' Barbara asked. 'I don't know any estate agents around here.'

'Of course. There's an auctioneer called Liam McLaughlin who should be able to do it. I can ask him if you like?'

'That would be great. Thank you.' They stood up to go, Barbara gathering her bag from the floor and Patrick refastening his jacket.

At the door I let my curiosity get the better of me. 'Do you mind my asking? If there was such a long estrangement, why did you come to the event on Friday? Neither of you live close by . . .'

Barbara smiled. 'That's an easy one. Because he asked us to.'

Not the answer I expected. I'd assumed she'd been asked by the documentary crew. I was about to ask her why he'd asked them to come but she turned and left before I got the chance. Probably just as well; it was none of my business.

I gave the will another once-over to make sure it was properly executed and had all the necessary clauses, not an easy thing to do while you're reading aloud to an audience, even an audience of two. Then I made my way downstairs.

Leah glanced up. 'I gave them an appointment for Friday morning – is that okay?'

'Perfect.' I handed her the envelope with the will. 'Set up a probate file, would you? They want us to go ahead with the administration. I'll draft a letter with an outline of the procedure and a list of everything they'll need, and we'll get it out in this evening's post.'

'Will do.' She made a face. 'I know the son, by the way. Patrick. How weird is that?'

This time it was my eyes that widened. 'How on earth . . . ?'

'He was friends with my cousins in Moville when we were kids. He was always in their house, when we used to be sent there for a fortnight every summer. I haven't seen him in about twenty years but it's definitely him.'

'What was he like?'

She smiled. 'He was a bit of a nerd actually. We were running about the shore like headers playing football and fishing while he spent his time writing. Plays and poems and things. I didn't know who his father was at the time, and it wouldn't have meant anything to me if I had. But now I wonder if he was trying to impress his dad.'

'Maybe.'

'Seems a bit sad now the way things turned out. Having no contact with him for so long and then he dies so suddenly.' She stood to grab a cardboard drop file from the shelf behind her. 'Does the divorce complicate things? For the administration, I mean.'

'They weren't divorced,' I said. 'They weren't even legally separated. They've just lived apart for all these years.'

Leah looked startled. 'Jesus.'

I smiled. I knew she'd find that bit difficult to understand; Leah liked her i's dotted and her t's crossed. 'I know. Nowt so strange as folk.' I paused. 'I'm not sure what to make of her. For all Featherstone's macho image, she strikes me as the one with the steely core.'

I wondered now what could have happened to make her leave. It must have been something pretty extreme for there to be virtually no contact ever again. Another woman? But would that really have resulted in a permanent estrangement from his children too?

Leah was looking at me curiously.

'Ah, I'm just thinking aloud. She said a couple of strange things, that's all.' I sucked in my breath. 'But then what is the appropriate reaction to your estranged husband dying suddenly and mysteriously in front of you and half the peninsula?'

'True.'

'Anyway, I need to ring Liam – we have to get a valuation done on the house.'

Leah grinned. 'He'll like that. A chance to have a nosy around Shore Lodge. No one usually gets past those big gates.'

I didn't know the big gates, having only caught a glimpse of the house from the shore side, but that had been enough to whet my appetite. 'Maybe I'll go with him,' I grinned. 'He might need someone to hold his measuring tape.'

Chapter Seventeen

Leah was spot on. Despite being 'wile busy' the last time I'd spoken to him, Liam was suddenly available the following morning. Stupidly, it hadn't occurred to me until he asked that he'd need keys, so I rang Barbara and left a message.

And then, I needed to get some work done. Having drafted the introductory letter to the Featherstones, I began to plough my way through witness statements which had arrived on the car theft cases. Reading them left me uneasy. The lads, if they were guilty, and let's face it, there was a distinct possibility that they were, had a fondness for nicking BMWs and it had been a beamer that drove us into the ditch. But I parked my disquiet for the moment and dictated a letter asking them to make an appointment.

Mid-morning, I took some work down to Leah. Despite my best efforts I hadn't been able to get Barbara Featherstone's mention of the post-mortem out of my head. On checking the appointments book I discovered I was free until twelve, so I decided to walk down to the Garda Station, using the excuse that I needed to find out when we'd be able to request a death certificate.

Gina Bailey was coming out of the station as I approached, reminding me that we still had that release form Barbara was supposed to collect. I should have mentioned it to her when she was in. I found it hard, now, to believe that she would take part in a documentary about her estranged husband. She might not have liked him very much but she struck me as a rather private sort of person.

Thankfully Gina didn't see me and I watched her stride off in the other direction. A figure waved to her from the other side of the road and she crossed to speak to them. Hearing a laugh, I squinted to see who it was and I caught a glimpse of red hair. Róisín Henderson. Were they *friends*?

I pushed open the door of the Garda Station to a stressed-looking Molloy. He looked up sharply, and when he saw it was me, flung his pen down on the desk. 'That woman is a complete pain in the arse.'

I grinned. 'I thought you said she was surprisingly cooperative. Giving you footage of the event?'

'She's just been in here pretending to look for permission to use that footage for the documentary. Firstly, I don't think there's anything we can do to stop that, as long as they don't show his actual collapse and, secondly, they won't be broadcasting the bloody thing till the autumn if at all, so there's hardly any urgency on it.'

'Maybe she needs to know well in advance,' I ventured, wondering why I was defending a woman I hadn't particularly liked.

He waved his hand dismissively. 'Ah, that wasn't why she was in here at all. She was digging for information. I basically had to push her out the door. I feel like they're breathing down my neck the whole time, lurking around corners and waiting for me to make a mistake.' He took a deep, calming breath. 'Anyway – why are *you* here?'

'Oh thanks!'

'Sorry. I'm having a day of it. Stuck in limbo until we get toxicology results. But yes. What's up?'

'I've just had instructions to administer Featherstone's will and I wondered when we could get a death certificate.'

He raised one eyebrow. 'So the vultures are circling already, eh? That didn't take long.'

'And,' I added, ignoring that remark, 'the executrix said she got a call about the post-mortem.'

Molloy nodded, closing his eyes briefly. 'Yes, yes, sorry. I meant to call you. The post-mortem results aren't actually confirmed yet. Toxicology on his blood and stomach contents aren't back. But we may have established what killed him.'

I held my breath.

'And before you ask, it wasn't the Coke – it was the water. Or rather the lime cordial.'

I breathed out audibly. 'You could have told me.' I tried not to look too relieved. Gavin Featherstone was still dead. 'What was in it?'

'Liquid cocaine.'

I frowned. 'The stuff we were reading about in the paper in Dublin? Remember I showed you the article – there was a load of it seized in champagne bottles.'

Molloy nodded. 'I remember. So much for it being a long way from Donegal. It's a new way of smuggling it. Less easy to detect. Dissolved into liquid, then extracted and turned into powder again. Sometimes it's sprayed on fabric.'

'God. Where would someone get hold of that?'

'Someone who was dealing in a fairly big way? Import, export. Or more likely, holding it for a dealer? Someone with a drug debt or money problems who was being forced to stash it?'

'So basically anyone?'

'Anyone with access. Proximity and a bit of recklessness. A dangerous move to help yourself, I'd have thought. Anyway, there was a concentrated quantity of the stuff in Featherstone's drink on stage.'

'Could he have been taking it voluntarily?' I asked, recalling the man's demeanour during the interview, his increasing confidence. My mother's reference to his wild times when he was younger.

Molloy shook his head. 'There are a lot of variables that influence how much would be a lethal dose: a person's age, cardiovascular health. But there was enough in there to kill at least two men. No one who knew what they were doing would willingly take that amount.'

I stopped him. 'Hang on. You said cardiovascular health. That's the heart, isn't it? Didn't you say Featherstone was on heart medication?'

Molloy checked his notes. 'He had atherosclerosis, which is a hardening of the arteries. Not unusual in a man of his age. Neither is a heart attack for that matter.' He looked up. 'But, while the cocaine would have created euphoria and boosted his confidence, it also stimulates the cardiovascular system, flogging the heart, causing arrythmia and making a heart attack very likely.'

'Okay.'

'He'd have had chest pain, high body temperature, rapid heartbeat, difficulty breathing . . .'

I nodded, remembering. 'All of the above.'

'Plus, we found it only in his glass, not Róisín Henderson's and not in the carafe they shared. The lime must have helped to conceal the taste.'

'Did you get to get to speak to Róisín?'

He nodded. 'She says she didn't pour out his glass, only her own, that his was already poured when she got on stage. That sounded odd to me, but the video confirms it. Featherstone's glass was full when the tape started rolling.'

'I don't think they use tape any more. I think it's all digital.'

Molloy ignored that.

'Who the hell would have put cocaine in Featherstone's drink?' I mused.

'Someone who wanted to kill him,' Molloy said flatly. 'Hence the criminal investigation into his death. Featherstone collapsed in a tent full of people – there must have been two hundred there. You'd think someone would have noticed who left his drink on the table.' He gave me a look as if to say, you'd think *you* would have noticed.

I wracked my brains trying to recall if Featherstone's glass had been full when we'd first arrived but I couldn't remember. Although I was sure there had been two full glasses when I came back from the kitchen, because Róisín Henderson was on stage and drinking from hers.

'Sorry.' I grimaced. 'Maybe it was done before anyone came into the marquee?'

Molloy scratched his head. 'If so, would there not be a risk that she would drink it and not him? Was it clear which side they'd each be sitting?'

I thought for a second. 'The camera was on the side where we were, presumably to capture Featherstone from the best angle. And,' I remembered now, 'there was a copy of each of their books on the table in front of their seats. So I guess the seating must have been decided in advance. Have you talked to Phyllis about it?'

'I have.' He checked the screen of his mobile, 'As a matter of fact, I've missed a call from her, so she may have remembered something else.'

I said nothing, but I was pleased that the bookseller had been as good as her word in contacting him about the row. 'I'll ask my parents if they saw anything.'

Molloy looked down at his notes, clearly anxious to get back to what he was doing. I'd like to have asked if he'd found out anything about the See the Light counselling group but now didn't seem to be the time. So I made my way towards the door.

He called after me. 'Ben?'

I turned. He came out from behind the desk and put his hands on my shoulders. 'I'm sorry I didn't tell you that the Coke can was clear.'

His touch was welcome. It had been over a week. And then, as if reading my mind, he kissed me, full on the lips. Right there in the Garda Station where anyone could have seen us. I felt myself flush, grinning stupidly when we parted.

And then the door opened and McFadden came in. I fled.

There was a man waiting for me when I returned to the office, legs crossed, mod haircut, white button-down shirt and a parka. A man I knew was not my twelve o'clock appointment.

'Is that who I think it is?' I asked Leah, quietly.

She leaned over the counter and whispered. 'It's Robbie Cahill, Gavin Featherstone's assistant. He says he's brought Mr Featherstone's will.' She bit her lower lip. 'Will number two.'

'Uh-oh.'

'I didn't know what to say to him.'

'It's fine. I'll talk to him.' I opened the door to the waiting room. 'Mr Cahill? Do you want to follow me?'

He looked up, a tight expression on his face. A leather satchel rested on his knees.

I brought him into the front room. Before we sat down, I said, 'My assistant has told me why you're here, Mr Cahill. I'm very

sorry about Mr Featherstone, but I'm afraid I can't represent you
– I'm already instructed by someone else in relation to a will we
had at the office.'

'An earlier one,' he said. It was a statement not a question. The
existence of the first will wasn't a surprise to him.

He drew a document from his bag and handed it to me. I
didn't need to unfold it to recognise a pre-drafted will of the type
they sold in stationery shops.

'This one was made this year,' he said. 'It's the most recent
will.'

'That may be so,' I said hesitantly. 'I can't, at this point, say
which one is valid; it's not up to me. But you *will* have to instruct
another solicitor.'

'Can you suggest anyone?'

'Maybe the other solicitors in town. Thompson's?' I saw no
need to give directions to their office. If he lived locally, he would
know.

Seconds passed. Neither of us spoke. He looked at me, stalling,
as if waiting for me to change my mind, his foot tapping on the
floor, knee going up and down like a piston.

There was something twitchy about him that I found discon-
certing, over and above the naturally uncomfortable nature of
two competing wills. So I was relieved when he finally dropped
his shoulders.

'Okay. I'll do that,' he said, and he was gone.

The expected phone call from Thompson came about an hour
later.

'Don't tell me,' I said, wearily, after the preliminaries were out
of the way, 'this will leaves everything to *your* client.'

'Well, yes,' he said patiently. 'As a matter of fact, it does. And yes, before you say anything, it is a homemade will, but I understand it's later than the one you have. Considerably later. And it's properly executed with a revocation clause. It looks perfectly valid to me.'

I sighed. 'Okay, I'll talk to my clients. I suspect they'll fight it. But even if yours is valid, you know the wife will have a case to claim her legal right share?'

'Okay . . .' he said slowly.

I heard the confused hesitation in his voice and I smiled. 'They're not divorced.' I said, with some satisfaction. 'Not even legally separated.'

He was the one sighing now. 'I see.'

'And the son and daughter will have a section 117 case, I suspect. Write to me formally and we'll get things going. Send me a copy of your will, and I'll let you know if I'm briefing counsel.'

'Will do.'

I was about to hang up when I remembered something. 'Oh, I have instructions to get Liam McLaughlin to value the house – is there any possibility we can agree it? Run with the one valuation?'

The other solicitor paused. 'I'll check with Mr Cahill but I imagine that should be okay. It's not the valuation we're going to be fighting over,' he said dryly.

Chapter Eighteen

I was gifted the perfect excuse to accompany Liam on his visit to Shore Lodge the following morning, when Thompson rang to say that Robbie Cahill had taken off to Derry leaving a set of keys with him in Glendara. At this point, the estate agent was already on the other side of the peninsula putting up *For Sale* signs at a cottage in Moville, so with no appointments till noon, I offered to drive out with them.

Not that I was fooling anyone. Liam grinned broadly as I pulled in to the entrance, which I might not have found had his Merc not been parked in front of it. Leah was right about the huge gates, but they were heavily camouflaged by lofty coniferous trees, reaching their long fronds over the wall.

He stood to one side to allow me to tuck the Mini in behind his enormous car, making it look very much as if one had given birth to the other. Liam was always telling me to get myself a 'proper' car.

'Why do I get the feeling that you're not going to just drop these off and run?' he said, holding his hands out for the keys.

Dropping them into his palm, I made a grand show of looking at my watch. 'I might have a few minutes before I have to get back for my next appointment, all right . . .'

'Aye. I'll bet. Come on,' he said with a laugh, tapping a code – conveniently scribbled on a tag on the keyring – into a panel on one of the pillars. He gave me a side glance. 'I presume it's okay for us to tramp around in here, by the way? The guards have finished searching the house or whatever?'

I nodded. I'd checked with Molloy before calling Liam. I didn't want to be stepping on anyone's toes.

'Does he have a dog?' Liam asked. The same *Beware of the Dog!* sign which had been on the shore gate was here too.

I grinned. 'Apparently not – Thompson said it's to deter visitors.'

Liam muttered something I couldn't hear.

The gate swung open with a low hum and we walked in. My first impression was one of trees, and not just the coniferous trees of the entrance; mature oaks, sycamores and birch in the fresh green of early summer filled the acre or so plot, along with pampas grass, laurels and rhododendrons, and a beautiful lilac with blossoms in a delicate shade of pink, the scent of which was heady and sweet.

A short, curved avenue threaded through the garden in the direction of the house, which was not yet properly visible. The sun dappled our feet as we followed it, littered with helicopter seeds twirling from a huge sycamore busy with birds. A wooden swing was a surprise addition underneath, hanging from one of its low branches, and Liam raised his eyebrows as he glanced at it. 'I thought Featherstone was estranged from his kids?'

'He was. They're adults now anyway. Maybe he just never took it down.'

'That hasn't been there since they were wains. That's new.'

He was right. Bright orange rope, fresh clean wood. An amateur job – it looked as if Featherstone might even have made it himself.

'Maybe he was hoping to get the grandkids up here?' he said.

I shrugged. I wasn't sure if Patrick or his sister had children but they were of an age where it was likely.

We rounded the tree and found ourselves in front of a fine old Victorian family home, large enough to accommodate four or five bedrooms; red brick, steeply pitched roof, canted bay windows and churchlike ornate eaves, which drew the eye upwards. A creeper with emerald leaves cloaked about two thirds of it.

'Hoo,' Liam whistled. 'That's a wile big house for one person.'

'Two,' I corrected him. 'His assistant Robbie lives here too.'

Liam turned the key in the lock and we stepped into in a cool entrance hall with fine staircase, paintings and prints along the walls and a floor covered in geometric black and white tiles. The air smelled stale and, despite the sunshine outside, the impression was one of gloom. I hunted for a light switch and found one behind an old-fashioned coat stand, wondering if the corduroy jacket hanging from it was the one Gavin Featherstone had been wearing on the cover of his book. The low-watt bulb made little difference other than to illuminate the dust motes dancing in the dry air.

We stood for a few seconds to get our bearings. A couple of doors led off the hall and a corridor to the left appeared to lead towards the back of the house where I assumed the kitchen must be.

A low door under the stairs turned out to be a cloakroom when Liam pulled it open. He withdrew quickly but I stuck my head in after him and saw that it was full of random objects; a watering can, slippers, an old typewriter. A second coat rack was weighed down with coats and scarves, far more than you'd expect for two people. It took me a few seconds to notice that these were kids' clothes, a little girl's red raincoat, a blue striped scarf and a pair of pink wellington boots. Unlike the coats on the stand in the hall, these hadn't been touched in a while – there was a sprinkling of dust on the shoulders of each one. Had they belonged to Patrick and Susie when they were children? And if so, why had Featherstone kept them? I'd thought they'd departed this house when they were teenagers.

With the strangest sense that I was shutting the door on a museum exhibit, I joined Liam in one of the reception rooms: a large, fusty sitting room with a high ceiling, which looked as if it was rarely used. The curtains were drawn but he'd switched on some lights; there was no overhead lighting, just low standard lamps in corners. A decorative cast-iron fireplace with a large brass mirror and an overstuffed couch and armchairs gave the impression of ornate clutter. But it was ill-maintained, the paint blistered in parts; carved wood panelling and a carpet patterned with curling flowers were both worn.

Once Liam had taken some measurements, I followed him back through the silent entrance hall to the room on the other side; this one a formal dining room with a mahogany table and eight chairs, a huge sideboard and more heavy drapes, also drawn. Rugs covering the hardwood floors exuded a slightly musty smell, which didn't help the gloomy unlived-in feel of the place.

'It's not really what I expected,' I said, eventually, looking around me.

Liam looked up from his notes. 'Why?'

'I don't know. It's sort of fussy. It doesn't really fit Featherstone's image.'

'It's in keeping with the house,' Liam said, tracing his hand along the grain of the wood. 'The house is Victorian. I'm no expert but it looks as if someone's been careful to source furniture from the period.'

I remembered what Barbara Featherstone had said about being a history lecturer and I wondered if it had been her? If it had been hard to leave a house she'd put so much work into?

'I'm sure it would be lovely if it was lived in,' I said, glancing at some dusty glasses and place mats decorated with old sketches from *Punch*. 'But it feels as if they didn't use this part of the house.'

Liam wiped his fingers on his handkerchief. 'You'll have to get someone to value the contents separately. I don't know enough about antique furniture, and there could be some fairly valuable items here.'

'Okay. Noted.'

When he'd finished with the two front rooms, I followed him down the hallway to a considerably more light-filled space at the back, where a kitchen extension with a skylight and French doors, a couch and a TV, felt much more lived-in. And cleaner. An Italian coffee maker, a bowl of garlic and tomatoes, and a knife block with olive green handles sat on the countertop.

And then, as if continuing the story of the children's clothes in the older part of the house, I spotted an egg cup with feet, pushed into a corner. Once I'd seen that, I noticed torn cartoon stickers on the fridge, a cracked, faded noticeboard with a purple fur-topped pen, and a mug bearing the legend *Best Ever Dad!* Remnants of family life like loot from a museum. Was Featherstone trying desperately to cling on to a family life that he'd lost, or had he just not bothered to clear anything away?

While Liam took notes and measurements, speaking into his phone as he walked, I opened the fridge, surveying shelves stocked with fresh food and a plastic tub containing some sort of green liquid.

'Nosy!' he called.

'I wonder where he worked?' I mused, closing the fridge and

wandering over to the French windows to peer out at a patio with plants, a garden table and chairs.

Liam shrugged, but when we went out through the back door and emerged into a little courtyard surrounded by restored out-buildings, he said, 'I think you might have your answer.'

An open door revealed a selection of rusty kid's bikes, with warped wheels and detached spokes, abandoned and forgotten on a carpet of wood shavings and turf mould. A second outbuild-ing with a half-door was locked, and I remembered what Phyllis had said about Featherstone having a study in a converted stable. A path led away through dense shrubbery, to the sea, I assumed, hearing the low, insistent roar of the waves from where we stood.

Liam hunted for a key and when he found it, he unlocked the half door and we walked in. Light streamed in through a skylight similar to the one in the kitchen, creating a neat yellow square on a rug, which divided the room into two halves. On one side sat a long blue couch, an old reading chair and lamp, and floor-to-ceiling bookshelves bowing under the weight of the books with a stepladder to reach the top shelves. The other half of the room was taken up by two huge desks: a computer sat on one while the other was buried in notebooks, foolscap pads and Post-its, all with the same neat handwriting in black ink. I had a sudden overwhelming sense that while there was very little of Gavin Featherstone in the rest of the house, he was here, in this room, just as if he was standing in front of us. This was his lair.

I ran my fingers over the books; a thesaurus, multiple diction-aries. *Bartlett's Unfamiliar Quotations*. There was one whole shelf for Featherstone's own books, including translations. But I was sur-prised to see a copy of Róisín Henderson's short-story collection.

An old bottle of Glenfiddich whisky sat on a shelf above one of the desks, open with about one measure taken out, the label curled at the edges and dust on the shoulders. It hit me then that there had been no alcohol in the rest of the house, not even a bottle of wine in the kitchen. I'd read somewhere that alcoholics sometimes kept a bottle as a kind of talisman. The last drink they'd had. Was Featherstone a recovering alcoholic?

On the floor below the computer sat a top-of-the-range printer. A page had become caught in its teeth and I kneeled down to pull it out, recalling McFadden's cursing in the Garda Station. It was the title page of a manuscript. *Redemption. A memoir by Gavin Featherstone.* I looked around the desk. Where was the rest of it, I wondered? Had the guards taken it?

Featherstone had been about to read from this at the event at which he collapsed. Was it possible there was something in it that someone hadn't wanted revealed? Something in Featherstone's past? But that didn't make sense. The memoir was due for publication in the new year. Killing Featherstone might have prevented him from reading from it that night but it wouldn't prevent the book from being released. Quite the opposite, as Jude had said.

'What are you poking about in?' Liam was at my shoulder and I jumped.

I pointed to the sheet. 'Featherstone's new book. The memoir.'

He whistled. 'I imagine there are plenty of people would kill to get hold of that.' Realising what he'd said he gave a sheepish grin and returned to what he had been doing.

I strolled around the room, picking things up and putting them down, knowing I should get back to the office, but not wanting to miss this opportunity to peer into Featherstone's life. I ran my fingers along a windowsill crammed with reference books, a kettle and chipped mug, a tub of teabags, an empty Bushmills cannister with rulers and pens; stones and shells from the shore; twigs and cones from the garden. A clothes brush.

A spider lowered itself on its thread, spinning a silvery web across a bowl of fruit, its contents just on the turn. The man clearly spent a lot of time in here.

It was then that I noticed the photographs, just about hidden behind a pile of books. They were pictures of Featherstone's kids when they were children, in fancy dress for Halloween, on the beach, formal school portraits. I recognised the local community school uniform. I saw the son I'd met, a young girl who was presumably his sister and Barbara herself, younger, happy and smiling. There was only one of each child as an adult; both were wedding portraits and I wondered if Barbara had sent them to Featherstone after each event. It seemed desperately sad, this huge gap of ten to fifteen years; the man's relationship with his children coming to a shuddering halt.

Returning to the house and heading upstairs, only two of the five bedrooms were in use. The master, at the front of the house, seemed to have been abandoned by Featherstone in favour of a room looking out over the sea, while his assistant occupied a smaller one to the side. As expected, the kids' rooms remained a shrine to their teenaged occupants, with posters, books and clothes; Patrick's still had a *Star Wars* duvet cover. I thought about what Leah had said about the son writing poetry to impress his dad.

Liam blew out a breath. 'Lord, it's like bloody Pompeii.'

He had a point. I felt a wave of sadness again for a man who seemed unwilling to let go of the family life he'd had, even now that his children were adults.

On the landing, my phone buzzed with a text from Leah reminding me about my twelve o'clock appointment and I left Liam to finish up in the house, walking back along the drive to the gate.

A postman was shoving envelopes into the letterbox, and he looked at me curiously as I emerged. I greeted him with a smile, although he wasn't someone I knew; we had a different man in Glendara.

He nodded towards the house. 'Sad what happened. Do they know what it was?'

I shook my head. 'I don't think so.' I took my car keys from my pocket, ready to depart.

'Maybe it was the stress of getting up to do something in public after all those years.'

Something about his tone made me pause. 'Did you know him?'

He crossed his arms. 'Aye, we'd have a wee chat sometimes. He'd come out if he was expecting something, hear the van. He ordered a fair bit of stuff online.' He smiled. 'Suppose that's what you do if you don't leave the house.'

'What was he like?' I decided I wasn't really in that much of a rush. If information was flowing in my direction, I wanted to be there to catch it.

'Ach, he was friendly enough. We'd talk about the weather and the garden.'

I nodded. 'It's a beautiful garden.'

'That assistant of his, Robbie, was out in it all the time. Real green fingers, that boy.' He clicked his teeth. 'Wile sad all the same. I'd say the old man was lonely.'

'At least he wasn't on his own. He had Robbie.'

'Aye. And they did get on well enough most of the time.' He paused for a few seconds as if making his mind up about something. 'They had a bit of a row a few months back. I heard them shouting. Robbie's wile quiet mostly, but . . .' He shook his head, frowning.

'But?' I made an attempt at nonchalance, but I was incapable of hiding my interest.

He lowered his voice. 'They must have been at it in the front garden because I could hear them through the gate. I was afraid it was about to turn nasty. Violent even. I wondered if I should call the guards.'

'But you didn't?'

He dropped his chin guiltily, and I got the sense that his conscience had been bothering him. Maybe since Featherstone died, in particular. 'Nah. They stopped. So, I just kept my head down, delivered my letters and took off.' He frowned. 'Do I know you?'

'I'm Ben O'Keeffe,' I said. 'I'm a solicitor in Glendara. What were they rowing about?'

His eyes widened as if I'd just told him I was an undercover guard. 'Ach, bucked if I know. That was months ago anyway. I saw them both after that, about a week later, and they seemed grand.' He closed over his post bag, as if already regretting what he'd revealed. 'Anyway, I need to be away.' He retreated to the post van post haste.

I walked slowly back towards the Mini. Had I been right about Featherstone's assistant when I'd seen common ground with Chambers and my parents? Was Robbie Cahill violent? Had he forced Gavin Featherstone into making that will in his favour?

I'd barely put the keys into the ignition when my phone rang. Molloy. I blurted out what the postman had told me without any preamble and he listened without comment.

'I'll look into it,' he said, when I'd finished.

Something about his tone was off. It hit me suddenly that he was the one who had called me, not the other way around.

'Is everything okay?' I asked.

'No, not really,' he said. 'It's your parents.'

Chapter Nineteen

The pause that followed lasted too long. Long enough to unnerve me completely. 'What do you mean, it's my parents?'

'Sorry,' Molloy said quickly. 'I mean their house.'

I swallowed down my fear, reminding myself that they weren't in their house. They were safely at mine in Malin, at least till tomorrow. I'd intended speaking to Molloy later to see what he thought about them returning there, and if there was anything we could do.

'It's Chambers, or whatever the hell his real name is. He's made a reappearance. The local guards caught him trying to sneak back into your parents' house last night.'

'Oh, for Christ's sake.' I tried to keep my voice steady. 'They're planning on going home tomorrow. I was hoping we'd seen the last of him.'

'He had a key, which I suppose isn't surprising,' Molloy said. 'He fled when they tried to speak to him. Made some excuse. But he's said he'll be back. I'm wondering if they should arrange to have the locks changed.' He paused again. 'Do you want to tell them about this or should I?'

'I'll talk to them. I know you're busy.' I tried to keep the edge from my voice. I couldn't help feeling that he'd let me down somehow, though I knew that wasn't fair. The man was managing a murder investigation. 'I don't suppose you've discovered anything more about Chambers or the counselling group?'

'No, I have,' he said, immediately making me feel lousy for doubting him. 'I just didn't get the chance to tell you. See the Light seems legit. They're a properly registered charity who pay their dues, follow the regulations and do what they're supposed to do, for the most part. Chambers, though, is another matter.' He clicked his teeth in irritation. 'I still can't still find any record of him, either his involvement with the counselling group or the car accident in which his wife and baby were supposed to have died. I think he must be using an alias.'

'Shit.'

'Maybe you could try to get them to stay a little longer till we get a handle on this?'

'I'll try.' I turned the key in the ignition and the Mini growled into life.

'Okay. But, Ben?' Molloy was still speaking. 'There's something else.'

I flipped the indicator, ready to pull out. 'Yes?'

'He's claiming the house belongs to him. That they transferred it to him as a gift.'

I drove away from Featherstone's house, hands gripping the wheel. Was this why my mother and father had appeared so reluctant to speak about Chambers? Did it explain the weird dynamic between them? Because he was what . . . their *landlord*? I had so many questions. I thought about the elder abuse cases I'd come across in the States, and kicked myself for not spotting it in my own life, feeling a chill at the hold Chambers had gained over my bereaved parents.

I drove downhill into Moville, past the fine old houses on either side, fizzing with anxiety. Taking a right in the square and heading in the direction of Glendara, I slowed down suddenly when a herd of sheep appeared, a woman with a stick and a sheepdog not dissimilar to Fred driving them on. While I waited for them to turn into a field, I spotted a sign for Kinnagoe Bay – a stunning beach with the wreck of a Spanish Armada ship in its shallows. It occurred to me that my parents would love it, that I must tell them about it. Then I remembered what was happening and my worry returned.

My phone buzzed on the dashboard and I checked it, afraid it was Molloy again with more bad news, but it was a text from Leah to say that my next appointment had cancelled. Suddenly I was desperate to see my mum and dad, so I cut off towards Culdaff and headed for Malin, relieved to see the old Nissan parked outside the house when I drove onto the green.

They were surprised to see me home in the middle of the day. My dad was drinking a glass of orange juice and reading the paper at the kitchen table, while, beside him, my mother folded some clothes she'd taken from the laundry, preparing to pack, I imagined. I hoped to God that what I had to say would deter them from leaving.

'What are you doing back?' my mum asked, lifting a shirt to give it a shake. Then, on seeing my expression, she lowered slowly it to the table. 'Is everything okay?'

I sank down into one of the kitchen chairs. 'I've just had a call from Molloy. Stuart Chambers tried to get into your house last night with a key.'

They exchanged a look which was impossible to read.

'Well, yes, we gave him a key,' my mother said. 'He was staying with us. He needed one.' She went back to folding the shirt, apparently unconcerned.

'Did he let you know he was coming back?'

They shook their heads, slightly uncomfortably, I thought. Even they must concede that was rude behaviour on his part, leaving without a word and then using his key to sneak back in without any notice. There was an uneasy pause, during which something seemed to occur to my dad.

'How would Molloy know that Stuart came back?' he asked, his eyes narrowed, glasses halfway down his nose. 'How would he know that from up here?'

Now it was my turn to look embarrassed. 'He asked some of the local guards to keep an eye on the place, just while you were here.'

My mother stopped her folding again. 'To stop Stuart from getting back in?'

'They didn't stop him.' I said defensively. 'He left as soon as they confronted him.'

'I'm not surprised,' she said, her cheeks burning with indignation. 'Guards greeting him on the doorstep. Why would they *confront* him? What's it to do with them?'

I looked down at my hands, picking at a cuticle with a nail and wondering how to broach this next bit. 'He said the house was his. That you'd transferred it to him. Is that true?'

My dad shook his head quickly, 'No, it's not.'

I felt a wave of relief. Then he paused and the relief ebbed. 'Not *yet*. He asked us to and we said we'd think about it.'

I was stunned. How could they be so casual about giving away their house, their home? The house in which they'd brought up their kids, including their late daughter?

'But why?' was all I could manage.

'For the group,' my mother said, finally pushing aside her pile of laundry and sitting down to join us at the table. 'To give those who are grieving like we were somewhere to stay, or just be, to talk to others who have been through the same hell that we went though. As a sort of refuge, to do some good for those who have helped us.'

'But why transfer the house to *him*, then?' I persisted. 'Why not to the group?'

She opened her mouth to speak but Dad got there first. 'That was what was making us hesitate,' he conceded. 'Stuart has some issues with the organisation, and he's been talking about setting up a breakaway group. See the Light provides support and coun-selling, it puts on events and talks, organises outings and trips like that holiday to Iceland we went on last year. But it doesn't actually advocate living together. Stuart wants to take that next step. He says that community living helps to heal grief, especially when it comes to the loss of family members. He says he's gained so much from staying with us.'

'I bet he has,' I muttered.

My mother gave me a warning look, but my dad spoke evenly. 'It seems a very laudable idea in principle, but the truth was that we didn't much like the idea of people moving in with us. That's the problem really, we still want to live there. And I know we said we were okay with those people staying, but it did get a bit much after a few days.'

My mother nodded. 'It did.'

'So,' my dad continued, 'we'd pretty much decided that we were happy to leave the house to See the Light in our wills, to use after we were gone but to hold on to it during our lifetimes.'

'We knew you wouldn't mind – your life is up here; you won't need the house,' my mother interjected, her voice calmer now.

It was true. I didn't.

She traced the grain of the table with her finger. 'But Stuart wasn't happy about that.'

All her anger with me had dissipated, and I saw with sickening clarity the fear I'd caught a glimpse of in Dublin. I preferred the anger.

'No, he wasn't,' my dad agreed, taking off his glasses and rubbing his eyes. 'He was becoming quite insistent. He was always polite, never rude, but insistent.'

'Was he bullying you?' I asked, wondering too late if my own hectoring tone might count as bullying.

Neither of them replied, which told me all I needed to know.

'Why didn't you tell me?' I asked, my voice softer now, heartbroken that they hadn't confided in me before now.

'There was nothing to tell,' my mother said. 'We understood why he was trying to persuade us. It was because he knew how much it would mean to have somewhere for people.'

'But you need *somewhere to live.*'

'Well, yes,' my father said, twisting his now empty glass around in his hand. 'Exactly. He said we could continue to stay there, but as I said, it wasn't really what we wanted, a house full of people we didn't know.'

I wanted to say that was very bloody decent of him, allowing them to live in their own house, but I resisted. 'Look, do you want to talk to Molloy?' I said, instead. 'There may be something that can be done. Some criminal proceedings against him. Coercive control or something.'

They looked astounded. 'Absolutely not,' they said in unison.

'He's a good man,' my dad insisted. 'He's just a bit driven when it comes to this cause, because it's so close to his heart. '

'Which is understandable,' my mother said in a slightly accusatory tone, as if I didn't understand grief. They may have lost their daughter, but I'd lost my sister too. 'And,' she added, pointedly, 'we don't particularly want to be treated like some doddery old pair who aren't capable of making their own decisions.'

I looked down. 'That's fair enough,' I said, 'but anyone can fall victim to a conman.'

My dad looked as stung as if I'd said it about him. 'He's not a conman.'

'I'm afraid he might be,' I said gently. 'Molloy had him checked out and he can find no record whatsoever of the wife and child of a Stuart Chambers having been killed in a car accident in the past few years. He thinks he might be using a false name.'

There was silence. They didn't even exchange glances this time. Instead, they both stared down at the table. I had a terrible feeling that this wasn't as big a shock to them as it should be, that they'd had their suspicions all along that Stuart Chambers wasn't who or what he claimed to be. But they just didn't want to believe it. It was as if there was a veil there, stopping them from seeing clearly.

'Look, I have to go back to the office,' I said, getting to my feet and realising how much time had passed since Leah had sent that last text. 'We can talk about this later if you like.' I paused. 'I know you were planning on going home tomorrow but, please, I'd really like it if you stayed a few extra days.'

Neither of them replied, and I wished I could tell what they were thinking.

Chapter Twenty

I was glad to find the office quiet, the waiting room empty and Leah on the phone. I waved to her and headed upstairs, sinking heavily down at my desk.

I hadn't handled the conversation with my parents well, I knew that. I was itching to protect them, but my fear had translated into something that was maybe a little too close to control. My mother's words, *we don't particularly want to be treated like some doddery old pair who aren't capable of making their own decisions*, echoed in my head.

It was up to them what they did with their property *and* who they chose to have live with them, and the last thing I wanted to do was to strip them of that agency, tear at the very fabric of their independence. But I knew they'd found the trial of my sister's killer completely overwhelming; my dad had taken early retirement from the bank soon after, finding it impossible to manage the stress of a busy job. And I wondered if that made them more susceptible to a bully like Chambers.

I was glad to be hauled away from my own thoughts when Leah buzzed me to come down and sign some post, the last of which was a letter to Barbara Featherstone, the follow-up to her attendance on Monday. When I'd rung to tell her about the second will, she hadn't seemed especially shocked, especially when I told her who'd been in possession of it. But she was convinced that it was either a forgery or had been done under duress, and would be proven so, while accepting that would probably have to be decided by a court.

'Oh,' Leah said, putting the letter into an envelope once I'd signed it, 'I nearly forgot. Pregnancy brain. Mrs Featherstone rang earlier to know if she should still come in on Friday, and if so, her daughter Susie will be home from the States, and can she come too? I told her Liam was doing the valuation this morning.'

'Tell her yes,' I replied. 'I still need to take instructions in relation to the estate, although there's probably only so much that she can do without Robbie Cahill's cooperation. God, this is going to be messy.'

Leah gave a smug smile. 'A tasty job for my replacement, whoever that is.'

'Ouch.'

At lunchtime Leah took off for a pregnancy massage, so I trudged up to the Oak on my own, feeling at a bit of a loose end. I'd wondered if there would be a text from my mother, maybe even a suggestion to meet for lunch, but there was nothing. I didn't even know if they were still leaving tomorrow. Tempted though I was to ring, I decided to give them space.

Passing the bookshop, Phyllis spotted me and beckoned me in. 'On your way to lunch?'

Fred was flat out on the floor with his chin on his paws, looking morose.

I nodded. 'On my tod today. Do you want to join me?'

She shook her head. 'No thanks. If you fancy it, there's a huge pot of broccoli and stilton soup upstairs in the flat that I'll never get through on my own. Jude made it before he left. I think he's worried I won't eat if he's not here.' She gave a half-smile. 'You'd think the man had never met me.'

'Jude is gone?' I said in surprise. 'I thought he was staying for a few more days?'

'Ach, I told him to go on his trip. I've been on my own too long. Sometimes I need a little headspace.'

I paused, not wanting to be intrusive, but something must have showed on my face.

Phyllis smiled. 'Don't worry. He's coming back. I haven't driven him away for good.'

It hadn't been her relationship with Jude that concerned me. It was whatever was troubling her, but clearly, she hadn't felt ready to confide in him either.

'So?' she said brightly. 'The soup? Do you fancy it? It's not quite as good as mine but it's not bad. I'd be glad of the company.'

'Please,' I said gratefully, knowing if I had lunch on my own in the Oak that I'd brood too.

She put the *Closed for Lunch* sign on the door and I followed her up the narrow staircase that led to her cosy flat. Fred came padding up after us. Phyllis put a bowl of water and some food down for him and gave him a good rub, which seemed to perk him up a bit. Then she laid out bowls of soup and a big loaf of homemade bread on the table in her kitchen, and set about making a pot of tea: Phyllis's house blend, a mix of Earl Grey and Barry's.

While she turned away, I lifted a book from the little dresser. Phyllis's flat was nearly as full of books as her shop, although she seemed to keep her kitchen for cookbooks. This one was on Georgian cooking, a chunky, colourfully illustrated hardback I assumed she'd picked up on one of her travels. Underneath it were some drug information pamphlets. I frowned, glancing over at Phyllis, but she still had her back to me. I picked one up, remembering the difficulties Jude's daughter had suffered in that area, and hoping she hadn't relapsed. Maybe that was the real reason he had left?

Phyllis turned with a steaming pot of tea and I replaced the book.

We sat and ate quietly for a little while. I considered broaching the subject of whatever was bothering her but, in the end, it was she who spoke first. 'You're a bit quiet yourself.'

I smiled. 'Family stuff. My parents are supposed to be heading back tomorrow but I'm hoping they'll stay longer.'

She looked at me with real sympathy. 'I imagine what happened at the weekend can't have been easy for them.'

'No.' It hadn't, but it occurred to me that they too were considerably less distressed about Featherstone's death than Phyllis was herself. I took a bite of my bread.

'I hear Gavin Featherstone left two wills.'

I coughed and swallowed my mouthful of bread with difficulty. It never ceased to amaze me how this kind of information got out in Glendara, and how quickly. 'You know I can't say anything about that.'

Phyllis had stopped eating too, her spoon resting against the side of her bowl, brow furrowed as if she was trying to make up her mind about something. I stayed quiet, hoping not to spook her. Was it possible that she was about to confide in me?

But, after a few seconds she picked up her spoon again. 'Róisín has asked if she can still run her short-story workshop. The one that was cancelled on Saturday.'

The moment had passed. I realised I'd been holding my breath. I took another mouthful of soup. 'Really? Is she still here? I assumed she'd gone back to wherever she lives.'

'Galway,' Phyllis said. 'Term's finished in UCG so she's in no rush. You know she teaches there? She has some friends she's staying with in Moville. She's coming in later to have a chat about the workshop. Says she's not in this part of the country very often, and she doesn't want to let down all the people who booked places.'

'My mother being one of them,' I said, wondering suddenly if the rescheduling of a creative writing workshop might be enough to tempt my parents to stay longer even if nothing else did.

'Oh, that's right. Anyway, we could have it in the hall now that the guards have cleared out. Or even the library. But I wondered if it might be insensitive? All the other writers have left, the marquee has been taken down, the festival is over.' She paused, reaching down to give Fred a pat. 'What do you think?'

'Maybe you could do it without mentioning Glenfest so it doesn't appear connected with what happened?' I said. 'You could also run it by Featherstone's family and see what they think, since they're the people you wouldn't want to upset?'

Phyllis nodded and looked away, agreeing with me in that distracted way people do when they haven't the slightest intention of taking your advice.

A dome of dark clouds covered the square as I hurried down the street half an hour later, hoping to make it back to the office before it started to pour. I did so, but standing on the steps rooting frantically in my bag, I realised that I'd left my keys inside on the reception desk, having pulled the door behind me when I'd left for lunch. Checking my watch I felt the first few specks of rain, and my heart sank. Quarter to. Leah wouldn't be back till five to at the earliest.

Within seconds it had started to bucket, fat drops of summer rain falling on the town. I put my bag on my head and ran, ducking into the library for shelter, standing for a few seconds underneath a sign looking for volunteers to shake myself off before going in. I nodded to the two librarians chatting at the desk before heading towards the bookshelves to kill some time while waiting for the rain to stop.

I was just flicking through the new Donal Ryan when a familiar voice caught my attention; Róisín Henderson was speaking to one of the women at the desk. The library was almost empty at this time on a Tuesday afternoon and I could pick up most of what she was saying even though I was lurking amongst the stacks.

'Can we arrange that for ten o'clock on Sunday then? Three hours or so.'

The librarian's voice was quieter but the response seemed to be in the affirmative.

'And the library will be closed so we can just use the main floor?'

When I heard Róisín taking her leave, I replaced the book and stepped out from behind the shelf, catching her as she was making for the door, hair flying, earrings swinging: a woman on a mission.

'Oh hi,' she said, clearly taken aback by my presence in what I assume she thought was an empty library.

I held the door open for her. 'On your way to see Phyllis?'

'Yes. Thanks.' A pause. 'Did she tell you about the workshop?'

I nodded. Did she guess that I'd overheard?

'She's afraid it'll be seen as insensitive. But I don't want to let people down. I know they were looking forward to it.'

'I guess that's a decision for Phyllis to make,' I said pointedly.

Róisín's voice hardened. 'Emerging writers need encouragement; they need nourishment. It's just typical that the death of a successful, wealthy, male writer would steal that opportunity away from them . . .' She faltered as if realising she'd gone too far, but there was no back tracking, just a slight change of direction. 'If I'm honest, the workshop would be an opportunity to sell a few copies of my short-story collection too. Since I didn't get to do the signing on Friday.'

Well, yes, I thought, because someone died. Thankful that the rain had stopped when we emerged onto the street, we crossed the road together, splashing through puddles.

'It would have been nice, the two of us signing together in the bookshop,' she said wistfully. 'Who knows, we might have increased each other's readership?'

'Was that the plan?' I asked, frowning. 'That you'd sign together?'

She nodded. 'He offered me a lift down after the event. Robbie was the one driving but he told me it came from Featherstone himself. We could have arrived together.'

I imagined her picturing a queue of excited readers stretching down the street, convincing herself they were there as much for her as for him.

'It turns out Robbie and I are from the same part of Belfast. He was a mechanic for a while in the garage where my dad got his car serviced. Small world.' She glanced at her watch. 'Anyway, I'd better get moving.'

With relief, I saw that there was a light on in the office. Leah was back. I knew something Róisín had said jarred with me, but a busy afternoon of appointments meant that I didn't have a chance to think about it again.

At four o'clock, Leah buzzed through a call. 'It's the sergeant.'

Molloy launched straight in. 'What are you doing this evening?'

'Nothing much.'

'Can you come over to the house? About seven?'

'I can.' I tried not to show how pleased I was at the prospect of an evening together, just the two of us. But Lord, we needed it. 'I have an hour or two of paperwork I can do after the office shuts, so I'll come over after that.'

'Good. I'll see you then.' He rang off.

I looked at the phone as I put it down. No warm words of affection. Not even a 'looking forward to seeing you'. Molloy was kind, loyal, with more integrity than anyone I knew, but when it came to expressing emotion, he was a challenge. But then there was his declaration on the side of the road, the one I hadn't yet returned. The kiss in the Garda Station. The man could still surprise me. If I wanted to be in a relationship with him, and I very much did, then I'd have to accept that I couldn't change who he was.

I texted my mother to let her know that they'd have the house to themselves for the evening, and she replied to say they'd been thinking of going back to the little bistro and would see me later or tomorrow. So, everyone was happy. I decided I'd pick up a bottle of wine after work.

The first indication that Molloy and I were at cross purposes came when he opened the door to me still in his uniform.

Chapter Twenty-one

'Okay . . .' I said, slowly, looking him up and down.

He clocked the bottle of wine in my hand together with my deflated expression, and looked confused. A metaphor for our relationship, if ever there was one.

'Are you still working?' I asked, wearily.

Realisation finally dawned, and, sheepishly, he took the bottle from my hand and led me into the kitchen where I saw that he'd set up a laptop, notebook and pens. He'd also made a pot of coffee and laid out two mugs with milk. Not even any biscuits. Clearly not the romantic evening I'd had in mind.

He put the wine on the countertop and turned to face me, wincing. 'Remember I mentioned to you on Sunday that I'd like you to have a look at the footage from the event? I didn't want to do it in the station in case anyone came in and saw me showing it to you. I'm sorry.'

'It's all right,' I said, gazing longingly at the bottle, then Molloy's grey eyes, thinking how different the evening would be if we opened it. I sighed. 'We can have it another night when things have calmed down, I suppose.' Work was something we were both driven by. That was never going to change, and there was no point in fighting it.

He threw me a grateful glance and I allowed him to pour us both some coffee. 'How were your parents when you told them about Chambers?' he asked, handing me a mug.

'As expected. Although they haven't transferred the house to him; that's a lie, apparently.' I took a deep breath. 'To be honest, I'd rather not think about it. I'll talk to you in the morning when I find out if they're still leaving.' I sat at the table, hands wrapped around the mug.

Molloy touched my shoulder as he moved to the chair beside me. 'We'll keep an eye on them. Don't worry.'

'Thanks.' I nodded towards the laptop. 'Anyway, let's watch this.'

He clicked on the video file to open it. 'I imagine they'd only have shown a short clip in the final documentary but they obviously decided to record the whole thing.'

He clicked play and the marquee's interior with its empty stage came into view. It gave me a shiver seeing it again, knowing this time how the evening would end. The video panned over the mix of strangers and townspeople in the audience; a man surreptitiously rolled a cigarette, ducking his head as he licked the Rizla paper, while the woman beside him stifled a yawn and a man in the row behind stretched his neck, making circles with his head. None seemed to be aware they were being filmed, or else they had forgotten.

'I remember reading somewhere that every hour filmed results in about a minute of edited material,' I said, taking a sip of my coffee.

'They're called rushes apparently.'

'Get you with all the telly jargon. Getting lessons from General Gina?'

Molloy rolled his eyes.

181

The camera moved back to the stage where Róisín Henderson had now taken her seat, and I leaned forward to watch her pour herself a glass of water from the carafe. You could see that Gavin Featherstone's glass was already full just as she'd told Molloy. But interestingly, it looked to me as if the carafe was brimming too before Róisín touched it, meaning that Featherstone's first drink hadn't come from there. I said as much to Molloy who agreed; he'd already noticed.

'I don't suppose the recording shows who left Featherstone's glass there?' I asked, knowing perfectly well what the answer must be, but feeling I had to ask.

He gave me wry look. 'That would be handy, wouldn't it? No, as you can see, the first time it appears in shot, it's full. And forensics show the only fingerprints on it are Featherstone's so someone wiped it first.'

Gina Bailey came into shot. She immediately ordered Ollie to go and do something, sending him scurrying off, before consulting with the cameraman who'd obviously left the camera running for this bit.

'That guy Joe is the director as well as the cameraman, apparently,' Molloy said. 'Though he seems content to take a back seat to her highness.'

Robbie Cahill walked into shot, dressed in the same parka he'd been wearing at the office – it occurred to me that he must have been every warm. I reminded Molloy of what the Shore Lodge postman had said about his row with Featherstone, and he nodded.

'We'll talk to that postman. I'm also looking into Cahill's previous convictions. He's a bit of an unknown, arrived here to work for Featherstone and just stayed. He has no record in this jurisdiction, but I'm waiting to hear back from the PSNI; he grew up in Belfast and spent a good chunk of his life there.'

We watched together as Cahill approached the stage and had a brief exchange with Róisín. She leaned down to chat to him, smiling as she took off her glasses and gave them a wipe. I wondered if this was when he'd offered her a lift to the bookshop. I hadn't seen it happen on the night. I wondered about this until the camera panned back over the audience and I saw my mother offering a mint to my dad, while the chair beside them was empty. It must have been when I'd gone to get their water.

Cahill returned to his seat, and behind him I saw Barbara and Patrick Featherstone come in. I'd wondered how Phyllis had known they were there, but it seemed probable now that Featherstone himself had told her, since he'd asked them to come. They took off their jackets as soon as they sat down. It was clear that everyone was getting warmer, fanning themselves with programmes and discarding layers of clothing.

'It was very hot in that marquee,' I remarked.

Molloy nodded. 'The Tech Bureau found that someone had interfered with the portable air-conditioning system so that it wasn't working properly. It may even have been heating the tent rather than cooling it.'

My eyes widened. 'Do you think that was to ensure that Gavin Featherstone drank on stage?'

'Possibly. And he continued drinking because it was lime, maybe he wouldn't have if it was just water.'

'He *was* that generation of men who don't drink much water. My dad doesn't drink it either despite my mother nagging him to do it.'

'If someone tried to kill him by putting something in a liquid he didn't usually drink, that might imply that the killer didn't know him very well,' Molloy said, frowning at the screen. 'Chances were that he wouldn't drink the water, even if it was warm in there. But lime cordial . . . ? Does that indicate it was someone who knew him, knew his habits? Or maybe the cordial was simply necessary to mask the taste of the cocaine?'

'Robbie knew him well,' I offered. 'He lived with him. Plus, Róisín said he worked as a mechanic. He could have tampered with the air conditioning.'

Molloy gave me a suspicious look. 'You're very keen on Robbie Cahill as a suspect. It wouldn't have anything to do with a second will, would it? One which happens to conflict with the one you're instructed to administer?'

'Of course not,' I said indignantly. Then more quietly, 'How do you know about that?'

'It's my job,' he said shortly.

I probably should have told him.

'In fairness,' he conceded, 'the most likely suspect *is* whoever benefits from the death so we are looking at Robbie Cahill. Along with your clients,' he added pointedly.

Applause drew our attention back to the screen; the camera was now fixed on the stage entrance through which Phyllis appeared to deliver her introduction. Molloy got up to refill our mugs and find some biscuits, while I kept on watching.

He glanced back just in time to see Featherstone's triumphant arrival on stage. 'He certainly seemed fine at that point.' Molloy emptied some chocolate digestives onto a plate, while shaking his head. 'I can't help thinking that whoever got their hands on liquid cocaine must have nicked it from a large stash. It's in that form for transporting, import and export. A pretty dangerous move, I'd have thought.'

'Hmm?' I barely heard what he said. My eyes had caught something fleeting on the screen that almost made me cry out.

Molloy had his back to me, making a fresh pot of coffee. So,

I quickly rewound, watched even more closely and there it was. Featherstone touched Phyllis's hand as they passed one another on stage. Just the briefest light touch with his fingers but somehow achingly intimate. Had Molloy seen it? It wasn't the first time he had watched this recording, so he must have, but maybe he didn't see anything odd about it.

'And, by the way, toxicology did confirm the presence of cocaine in Featherstone's system.' Molloy was still following his own train of thought when he came back to the table with two fresh mugs.

'Did you see this?' I stopped, rewound and played clip again.

'The hand-touch?' Molloy nodded, taking a sip of his coffee. 'I did wonder about that until Phyllis told me that she used to know him when she was younger.'

I said nothing. Molloy wouldn't win any awards for interpreting nuance in physical intimacy, but for me it was a far more familiar touch than would be normal for an old friend or employer. I decided it was something to ask Phyllis herself about.

We sat and watched the interview the whole way through. It was uncomfortable viewing; Featherstone reaching constantly for a glass which I now knew contained something that would kill him. I wanted to shout at the screen and tell him to stop, but he drank as if it was the very drink that was making him thirsty. Then the touching of his chest as if suffering from pain or irregular heartbeat, and his speech growing more rapid.

'Now I know what I'm looking for I can clearly see the effects of cocaine,' I said. 'All the things I put down on the night to charisma and adrenaline.'

Molloy nodded grimly. 'That's the problem. When you know what you're looking for, it's there right in front of you. If the hospital had known straight off what he had taken, they might have been able to do something. Still, it was complicated by his existing heart condition, so they may not have been able to save him.'

By now Róisín had thrown the event open to the floor and was taking questions. It was clear that Featherstone was getting worse, but he replied to the first couple of questions with a sense of humour, just as I remembered him doing. Then the last question came, inaudible, posed without the mic.

'Who asked that last one?' Molloy said. 'Could you see?'

I shook my head. 'It was way down the back. I don't think we could tell if it was male or female.'

Jude repeated the question. It seemed almost sabotage, now, to ask Gavin Featherstone about family, calculated to set him off balance. I wondered aloud if it could have been Barbara or even Patrick, remembering what Leah said about him trying to impress his father as a child.

'I'm hoping Jude can tell me,' Molloy said. 'I've been trying to get hold of him but his phone is off.'

'Oh, he's gone on a biker's trip,' I said. 'No phones apparently. I think he's coming back here after, though.'

Featherstone was preparing to read now. It was hard, seeing someone struggle like that, stand with such difficulty and then collapse. Fight to breathe, turn red then blue, and fall. We saw Jude running up to him, placing his two fingers on the man's neck, his look of concern conveying the urgency of the situation. Would it have changed things if he'd known it was a cocaine overdose?

Suddenly the screen went blank and I remembered Jude waving at the TV crew, making a slicing motion with his hand, ordering them to stop filming. I wondered if it was something he'd had to do in the past as a paramedic.

Molloy tapped the keyboard to close the file, then turned to me. 'Well? Anything?'

I shook my head. Something was nagging at me but I didn't want to say anything until I was sure what it was.

He sighed, and his eyes softened. 'Will you stay?'

I stayed.

I awoke with a jolt at 3 a.m. The thing that had been bothering me, nudging at the edge of my consciousness, had grown solid. I knew that it was connected somehow with Phyllis and Featherstone's touch as he walked onstage, and I tried to work out how. My mind reeled back to my conversation with Róisín while leaving the library, and suddenly I knew what had jarred with me at the time. She said that despite being issued by Robbie, the invitation to accompany them to the book signing had come from Gavin Featherstone himself. But Phyllis claimed that Featherstone had refused to do the signing, and that's why they rowed.

One of them was lying.

Chapter Twenty-two

When I came home to shower and change the next morning, my parents were still in bed but there was a note on the table propped up against the salt.

> We've decided to take you up on your invitation to stay a bit longer. But there's something we need to have a chat about. Mum and Dad xx.

Not exactly what you want to read first thing from your parents, without elaboration. I felt relief followed by concern, as if I was sixteen again and in trouble for something unspecified. Maybe staying out all night with my boyfriend.

Neither of them appeared by the time I left for work. Hoping they would continue to keep Chambers at arm's length, I was also happy to postpone 'the chat', so I didn't hang around in case I heard footsteps on the stairs. Guinness was at the kitchen window, also back after a night's prowling, so I let him in and fed him, grabbed a quick coffee and headed off, feeling discomfited and out of sorts. I was worried about my parents and after last night's bit of home cinema, I was worried about Phyllis too.

It was a typical Inishowen summer morning, blustery and

mild. The unsettled nature of it reflected my mood; a weak sun disappearing and reappearing from behind scudding clouds, causing shadows to come and go as if someone was playing with the light switches. The sea was a greenish blue, the wind making white horses of the waves offshore.

In Glendara, I made straight for Phyllis's bookshop. Thwarted by a closed sign on the door, I headed for the office.

Someone was rushing out the door as I was going in. It didn't take me long to recognise who it was; high heels and a cloud of expensive scent provided the biggest clues.

'Oh hi,' she said breathlessly, lighter in hand. Already lighting up on the doorstep.

'Morning,' I said, wondering what the hell Gina Bailey had been doing in my office.

She went to shove the lighter back into her bag, but missed it somehow and succeeded in upending it, tumbling the contents onto the footpath. She waved away my help, but I couldn't help noticing a syringe and alcohol swabs among the belongings that she gathered up.

'My nephew Ollie said that he saw Barbara Featherstone coming out of here on Monday.' She waved her hand in front of her face, fanning away the smoke. 'The little shit took until this morning to tell me, of course. That's what comes of taking on family instead of someone who knows what they're doing; directs a few horror shorts for college and thinks he's fucking Scorsese.'

I raised my eyebrows. Maybe the Oliver Connolly Leah had found online had been the same one. A bit of a comedown being his aunt's gopher, if he'd won an award for his film making.

I realised that Gina had stopped speaking and was looking at me expectantly. If she was waiting for me to respond to a question which she hadn't actually asked, she was out of luck.

'Well?' she said. 'Did she sign the release or not? Is that why she was here?'

I closed my eyes briefly in irritation. This woman was not my client. She'd simply used me as a post office. And now she was demanding information about an actual client's reasons for calling at the office. Confidentiality rules were strict; solicitors weren't even supposed to reveal that they'd been consulted by a particular client, let alone why.

'*You* told me to destroy it, if you remember,' I said, placing my hand on the door, ready to push it open.

Gina reached for it too, an aggressive move which took me by surprise and prevented me from going inside. I stiffened. She was taller than me so her hand was above mine, leaving me almost fully enclosed.

'Take your hand off my door,' I said, coldly.

She quickly removed it, as if realising she'd made a mistake. If Barbara Featherstone *had* come to see me then I must be acting for her and it made sense to keep me onside.

'Look,' she said, in wheedling tone, 'Barbara Featherstone gave us an interview in Dublin. She said that she would cooperate with the documentary and now she is being difficult. We need her. Especially after what happened.'

'That,' I said, 'is not my problem. *If* I see Barbara Featherstone, I'll give her the release form, assuming we still have it.'

She tried a different tack, one I assumed was an attempt at reasonableness. 'We know there was something unorthodox about the relationship between Gavin Featherstone and Robbie Cahill, and that it's connected with why Barbara left him. We want to give her the opportunity to tell her story.'

When I still didn't respond, she added, 'This documentary is going to be fully rounded, showing both sides. Not just some sycophantic piece about his work. Gavin Featherstone was a king, but that's over. No more sacrifices on the mountain.'

'You mean now that he's dead you're going to do a hatchet job on him?'

Her smile fell away; she was clearly unable to keep up the sympathy act for long. 'I know there's something in that man's past, something he was hiding. Someone wanted to kill him, for God's sake. Someone *did* kill him.'

I noted the change from 'we' to 'I'. Was this somehow personal to Gina Bailey? A vendetta of sorts? It felt like it was. 'You'll need to talk to Mrs Featherstone about this,' I said. 'I have to go.'

I made a break for the door, escaped inside and pulled the door firmly behind me, breathing heavily as I stood for a few seconds on the other side. Molloy and Phyllis were right. Gina Bailey was digging about in things that should not concern her as an arts journalist. She'd made me feel like some sort of prey. Was it people like her who had caused Gavin Featherstone to become a recluse?

If they wanted Barbara to play the wounded wife and share salacious details about the break-up of her marriage, I suspected they'd got her all wrong. Although I had to admit that Gina had a point about Featherstone's past. I remembered what he'd said during his event about a person being haunted by something they'd done. Was it possible his death was connected with something *he'd* done?

I suspected this wasn't what Gina Bailey thought — she'd implied that Featherstone was gay and in a relationship with Robbie Cahill. But Barbara had left him, and the sudden, brutal and permanent nature of their split seemed to imply that it was for a specific reason, rather than the accumulation of factors that usually led to the breakdown of a marriage. There was also the fact that despite having no relationship with his family, he had invited them to his event, and despite the estrangement, they had agreed to come. Assuming what Barbara had told me was true.

I thought back over the recording I'd watched with Molloy, and the strange way in which Featherstone had answered some of Róisín's questions. Then he'd been about to read from his new book, the memoir. I stopped. Hang on. *A memoir.* Was there something in that? I'd meant to ask Molloy about it after I'd been to Shore Lodge but forgotten all about it when he called me about Chambers. I pictured the sheets Featherstone was about to read from fluttering to the ground when he collapsed. You couldn't see them on the video – the camera was filming from the wrong angle and his body had blocked it – but I remembered it now.

Suddenly I felt that tiny give, like the loosening of a jar you're trying to open. That feeling you get when you're defending someone and you spot a tiny inconsistency in a prosecution statement that shows a witness is lying about something insignificant. And if they're lying about that, what else are they lying about?

I walked down the hall to the reception desk, reaching for it like a drowning man, half expecting to hear the door opening behind me and Gina Bailey following me in.

Leah gave me a wry look. 'She caught you, then?'

'She did. I presume she interviewed you too?' I had no fear for Leah's ability to keep client confidences. She was like a brick wall when it came to information.

'I hadn't even taken off my coat. Like a rat up a drainpipe, she was, in after me. Kept firing questions, thinking she'd trip me up if she asked enough of them.' She clicked her teeth. 'Even asked me when I was due to butter me up; cheeky wee wagon. I ran her.'

I grinned. 'Sounds like you handled her better than I did.'

'Ha. I'm from Donegal – whatever you say, say nothing! Do

you think she knows about the two wills? She'd have a field day with that.'

I shrugged. I wouldn't have been surprised if she didn't; if the story had spread widely throughout Glendara and Moville, but was blocked by the invisible membrane that existed between locals and outsiders. There were times when I'd been on the wrong side of that particular barrier myself although that seemed to have changed over time.

Leah handed me a huge pile of oblong brown envelopes, hand-written addresses, all of a similar size and shape.

'That's a lot of post,' I said flicking through them. 'What's going on?'

She smiled, smugly. 'People after my job.'

'Huh?' I frowned. My head was full of fluttering pieces of paper, memoirs, and long kept secrets.

Leah rolled her eyes. 'They're applications for my maternity leave.'

'Ah.' Realisation dawned. The ad had appeared in Monday's edition of the *Inish Times*. I'd wondered if it would get lost with all the coverage of Gavin Featherstone's death, but apparently not. I didn't know whether to be pleased or not. A little wave of dread washed over me every time I contemplated the prospect of running the office without Leah, of training someone else to do her job.

'I'll have a look now,' I said, without enthusiasm. 'Anything else?'

'Oh, you've to go and do a will in the nursing home.' She checked her notes. 'A Mrs O'Donnell rang to say that her brother wants to make a will – he's not well.'

'No wills for weeks and then three come along at once. They're like buses,' I said.

Now Leah looked confused.

193

'Sorry, Dublin joke,' I said. 'Who is the brother? Is he a client?'

She nodded. 'It's that nice old man, Peter McGonigle.'

'Oh.' I felt a prickle of sadness at the thought of a client I liked being unwell enough to need a house-call will. 'I'll go later today. Let me work out what time suits and I'll buzz you.'

At my desk, before doing anything else, I rang Molloy, launching straight in when he answered, taking a page out of his book. 'When the Tech Bureau searched the hall on the night Featherstone died, did they find any sheets of paper on stage?'

Molloy paused as if checking something. 'Nope,' he said eventually. 'Why?'

'Because Gavin Featherstone was about to read an extract from his new book. He'd taken a page out of his pocket and it fell to the ground when he collapsed. Are you sure it wasn't found?'

He checked again. 'No. And we secured the place before it was cleaned or swept, as soon as everyone cleared out.'

'Someone must have picked it up, swiped it while everyone else was in a panic.' Róisín was the closest, I thought. It would have been easy for her to do it without anyone noticing. 'When I was out with Liam doing the valuation of Shore Lodge for the estate—'

'You were what?' Molloy interrupted. 'When did you get a job as an estate agent's assistant?'

'I had to bring him out the keys,' I said impatiently. I wasn't about to undergo a telling off when I was trying to help him. 'Anyway, under Featherstone's desk in his study, stuck in the printer, I found the top sheet of his new book. The memoir.'

'Yes, we have it. There was a full print out there, which we seized.'

'Well, might there be something in there which would explain why someone would want to kill him?'

'Yes,' Molloy agreed. 'You're right. We've been waiting for someone to have the time to read it. But maybe we'll push that up the agenda.' A pause. 'Thanks.'

Slightly mollified, I replaced the phone in its cradle. What was in the section Featherstone had been about to read, I wondered? And was that why he'd invited his family up? To hear it?

My mobile buzzed. It was a text from my mother. *We've decided to go to Derry to take our mind off things, maybe see a film. Will you join us after work for something to eat? We fancy a Chinese.*

I texted her back, and then buzzed Leah. I could do Peter McGonigle's will on the way.

Chapter Twenty-three

The room smelled medicinal and stale at the same time; all the windows were firmly shut and the fluorescent lights fizzed as if they needed new tubes.

The old man in the orthopaedic bed, with his head propped up on a pillow, gave me a watery smile. Peter McGonigle was a long-standing client of mine, a bachelor farmer in his seventies of whom I'd grown increasingly fond. He was also a client of Maeve's; she'd remarked more than once about his decency to his animals. The woman who stood in the doorway beckoning peremptorily was someone I'd never met: Peter's sister apparently.

I ignored her until I'd had a chance to speak to him, pulling out a chair to sit by his bed.

'How are you?' I asked.

Unshaven and frighteningly thin, his sparse hair stuck up in messy spikes, but the eyes were bright and alert.

'Aye. I've been better, to be honest. This auld chest of mine could do with a good power wash.' His eyes narrowed. 'What are you doing here?'

'I thought you wanted me to come?' The first red flag; the man was surprised to see me.

He shook his head and his brow furrowed for a few seconds before he smiled again. 'Doesn't mean I'm not glad of the visit.'

A hiss came from the doorway. 'Miss O'Keeffe. I want to speak to you.'

Red flag number two.

Peter closed his eyes wearily. His voice was tired and cracked. 'You'd better go. That's our Maureen. She'll give you no peace till you do.'

I placed my hand lightly on his, got to my feet and made my way to the door. 'Yes?' My tone was clipped.

The woman steered me out into the corridor where a stench of old school dinners seemed to seep out of the very walls. A clang of cutlery and delph in the distance sounded vaguely ominous, getting louder as it advanced.

'I was the one that called you. He hasn't got long.'

A food trolley trundled by pushed by an acne-faced teenager in a green tabard.

The woman waited till it had passed, then lowered her tone. 'He wants to leave the farm to my son. He has money too, that's to go to my daughter.' She checked off her requirements on her fingers as if putting in an order at McDonald's.

Shuffling footsteps heralded the arrival of a young man, stopping me from responding straight away, which was probably just as well. He was close enough to hear what was being said but unlike the food-trolley pusher, his presence didn't seem to present a problem.

Maureen nodded in his direction as he slumped into one of the faux-leather chairs that lined the wall of the nursing home corridor, greasy fringe falling over his eyes. I sensed something familiar about him, though I couldn't see his face.

'That's my son. The one who's to get the farm.' She waved her forefinger at me, 'You'll need to take down their names,' clearly taken aback at my slow-wittedness.

I tried not to look at him. I really did. I didn't want to give these 'instructions' any credence, but there was something about the wide-legged seat, the dull, brooding presence, which drew me in. When I caught a glimpse of his face I almost laughed, even though it wasn't in the least bit funny. The son was one of my car-theft clients, the older one with previous for breaking his girlfriend's arm. He must have registered my presence too because he didn't lift his head to meet my eye. Had he omitted to tell the mammy about his own need to consult a solicitor?

'I cannot discuss Mr McGonigle's business with anyone but him,' I said shortly, turning on my heels to go back into the room.

Maureen's eyes flashed in anger. Little greedy, piggy eyes. 'Now houl' on there. I was the one that called you to come here and I'll be the one paying the bill.'

Out of the poor man's estate after he dies, I thought, bitterly. But I said nothing, just walked back to the bed where Peter looked as if he'd fallen asleep.

His sister trailed in after me like a burr from Robin-run-the-hedge, which sticks to your trouser legs after a walk in the fields. She crossed her arms defiantly. 'You'll need a witness. I know how wills work.'

'Please leave.'

She stood there for a few minutes as if unsure what to do, but I wordlessly stood my ground, and finally, she departed, marching furiously out of the room and leaving the door wide open.

I walked over to shut it. When I returned Peter had woken up, his eyes rheumy and red-rimmed. I didn't like the flicker of fear I saw in them, and I wondered if he'd feigned sleep to avoid a conflict he knew was coming. My heart broke for this strong and kind farmer who was now a frightened and vulnerable old man.

I left twenty minutes later having had a cup of tea with him when the trolley called around, somewhat comforted by the warm friendship that appeared to have developed between the old man and the teenager in the green tabard.

His sister reached out for me as I emerged from the room like the troll from under the bridge in the Billy Goats Gruff. 'Have you done it?'

I ignored her for a second time and carried on walking.

I drove into Derry feeling sick, the expression 'old age ain't for sissies' rattling around in my head. I'd suggested to Peter that if he wanted me to visit again, to ask a nurse or his teenaged tea-trolley buddy to call me and I'd come straight away. But I worried that the predatory sister might call another solicitor, someone who didn't know him, who didn't know the context. I imagined how difficult it would be for him to resist leaving his beautiful farm with its neat cottage, well-maintained fences and cared-for animals to that idiot nephew, if he were bullied into it. I'd also remembered what Maeve said about the burned-out car on one of her clients' farms and wondered now if it could have been Peter's.

Rain stippled the windscreen as I drove into the city, past the huge Sainsbury's, which we didn't have on the other side of the border, and through the roundabout onto the quays. Before I'd left the office there had been a further text from my mother to say they were seeing a film at four and would meet me in the Mandarin Palace Chinese restaurant at six. Checking my watch, I saw that I was early; despite the tea I hadn't spent as long with Peter as I'd expected.

Thinking I might catch them at the cinema I parked on the quayside to walk across to the Omniplex on the Strand Road. The rain had stopped when I got out of the car so I decided to take a wander up to the Guildhall to kill a little more time, and I gazed across at the elegant Peace Bridge twisting white across the river, linking the largely Unionist 'Waterside' and the largely Nationalist 'City Side'. Today a rainbow curved above it, creating a striking double arch.

I liked Derry a lot, a hilly city with settlements rising up on either side of the Foyle. I looked up now at the red sandstone Guildhall with its fine stained-glass windows reputed to represent everything from fishmongers to musicians, and its four-sided clock tower with the golden star. I remembered a Derry client of mine describing someone as having 'more faces than the Guildhall clock' and it occurred to me that the faces we show to the world are often no more than masks. Maureen O'Donnell was unlikely to reveal the ugly countenance I'd seen earlier outside of her family circle, and I wondered what those who were connected with Featherstone's death were hiding. Including, I realised with a chill, Phyllis.

Registering the time, and seeing that it was later than I thought, I turned to rush back, walking briskly along the Strand Road. A green parka with a furry hood burst out of a door just ahead of me, and it took me a second to recognise the man as Robbie Cahill. He looked distressed, rubbing his face and muttering under his breath as he turned left to cross the road.

Glancing at the door from which he'd emerged, I saw that it was a methadone clinic. With a prickle of uneasy memory, I pictured the green liquid in a plastic container, which I'd seen in the fridge at Shore Lodge, and recalled that you could get methadone weekly and keep it at home once you were trusted. Was it possible that Robbie Cahill was a recovering addict? What did that mean for his access to liquid cocaine? Was he the one who had spiked Featherstone's drink?

He slowed his pace on the other side of the road, and I ducked into a doorway in case he saw me. He was cursing under his breath now, his movements erratic and jerky as if he wanted to punch someone. Feeling uneasy, I scurried past the busy Trinity Hotel, hurrying on to the cinema.

I quickly got lost in the crowd at the Omniplex; Thursday evenings were busy and the multiscreen cinema attracted customers from Inishowen as well as Derry. I hadn't a hope of finding my parents, although the sweet, burned smell of popcorn made me relish the prospect of a Chinese meal. I was about to give up, buffeted by people emerging from the many screens, when my phone buzzed with a text from my mother. They were already at the restaurant.

I spotted them easily at a premium table, which looked out over the river, glasses of wine in front of them while they examined the huge menu. I sat down to join them. 'I called to the cinema thinking I might catch you.'

My mother looked up. 'Ah, we didn't go. We decided to go for a walk instead. We crossed the Peace Bridge and walked along the wall.'

'You're lucky to have such a lovely city close by,' my dad added. Small talk.

I played along, waiting till after we'd ordered to ask, 'So, what did you want to speak to me about?' said lightly, in an attempt to convey interest but not concern. Not at all the way I felt.

Both took a fortifying sip from their drinks, and my father spoke, almost as if it had been rehearsed that way. 'Remember we said that we were going to change our wills in favour of the See the Light group? Leave them the house rather than transfer it to Chambers like he wanted?'

Alarm bells should have rung at my dad using 'Chambers' rather than 'Stuart'.

'Well, the truth is we've already done it, changed our wills, I mean. Except it's Chambers himself we've named.'

I swallowed. 'Not the See the Light group?'

'No,' Dad said. 'He wasn't happy with that.'

My mother looked down into her wine glass. 'He sort of badgered us till we did it.'

I felt my anger ignite again, my mind reeling back to a woman bullying an old man in a bed. Death really did bring out the worst in human nature; grief and greed weren't just close to one another in the dictionary.

'We made it clear that we were leaving it to him for the purpose that we discussed,' my dad insisted. 'As a refuge for people who had been bereaved like we were.'

The waiter arrived at the table with prawn crackers and dips, halting our conversation for a few seconds. Once he'd left, I asked, 'Which firm did you go to in Dublin?' I hadn't known my parents to ever consult a solicitor. Even so, I knew they must have to buy the house.

'We didn't. He had a couple of those forms.'

I cursed inwardly. So, he was all kitted out. My parents would have received no independent legal advice – no protection. God knows what was in those wills.

'The problem is that he's told us that we can't now sell it. Not that we'd be intending to,' Dad added quickly. 'He said once you leave property to someone then it's tied up and you can't do anything with it.'

'That's not true,' I said flatly. 'He's lying to you. A will only deals with property after death. Same with bank accounts, shares, anything. You can do whatever the hell you want with your own assets while you are alive no matter who you've left them to in a will.'

They exchanged a look of relief, and my dad nodded. 'I *knew* that. I did. But he was very persuasive . . .'

I felt wretched. My dad had been a bank manager, dealing with probate on a regular basis. If he could be bullied and gaslit, what hope was there for anyone else? He knew what Chambers said wasn't true but part of him was afraid it was; he was *that* convincing. I tried to stay calm. Getting angry wasn't going to help anyone and the person I was angry with wasn't here.

'I'm not telling you what to do,' I said calmly. 'If you're happy with what you've done, that's fine. But, you should know that you can change your will at any time, simply by making a new one. You can make as many wills as you want. It's the most recent one that stands . . .' They both nodded slowly. 'Once it's validly executed and can't be challenged for some other reason,' I added quickly, remembering the Gavin Featherstone situation where we were about to challenge a more recent will. No wonder people became confused and frightened by this stuff. It was a maze.

'That's the thing,' my dad said, seeking confirmation from my mother and receiving a nod of consent. 'Since you told us what Molloy found out about Stuart, we're not sure we trust him any more. We've talked it through today and we've decided we'd like to change our wills. The problem is that he has them in his possession. The actual wills. He thought he should hold on to them in case anything happened to us.'

'Okay,' I said evenly, trying not to focus on the 'in case anything happened to us' part of that sentence. What the hell had Chambers been planning?

'So, what should we do? Don't we need to get them back?'

I shook my head. 'One way of revoking a will is to destroy it. But you don't need to. You just need to make a new one. The first line of a standard will revokes all previous wills.'

I had a sudden memory of my dad telling my mum that Chambers had taken everything with him when he'd left, and it hit me that it was the fact he'd taken their wills that frightened them. Was that why my mother had been trying to get hold of Chambers so obsessively?

'Can you make new wills for us?' my mother asked, looking hopeful.

I shook my head again, regretfully this time. 'As your daughter I shouldn't, even if I'm not named in them. But I can send you to the other solicitor in Glendara. Thompson. He's good. I can ring him now if you like. He's usually in the office late.'

'We don't need to tell *him*, do we?' my mum said, a shadow crossing her face.

No name was needed. I knew exactly who she meant.

Chapter Twenty-four

At half past nine the next morning, Molloy rang. First call of the day. Leah put him through and I answered it with my left hand, phone propped between my chin and shoulder while I opened the post. Not great for the neck.

'You might have been onto something with that memoir.' The sound of pages turning in the background was unmistakeable.

I put down the envelope I'd been working on. 'Have you read it?'

'It's a work-in-progress,' he said, with a sigh. 'The copy we got from the house has some pages missing. What's the betting they're the ones Featherstone was planning to read from at the event? The very pages that have now done a disappearing trick.'

'Was there a file copy on his computer?'

'It was deleted. And therein lies the problem.'

I switched the phone from one ear to the other so I could hear better. 'He didn't email it to himself? Or have a copy on a USB somewhere?

'Nope to the first question. And to the second; if he did, we can't find it.'

I was silent for a few seconds. 'I wonder who deleted it? Featherstone himself? Robbie Cahill?'

'Who knows? It's not there anyway.'

'But who else would have had the opportunity?' I persisted. 'The man was a recluse. No one went in or out of that house.' Although I suddenly remembered Ollie being roughly shown out through the back gate two days before the event. I told Molloy. 'I suspect he was sent there by Gina to hassle Featherstone into taking part in the documentary so I doubt he got a chance to sneak into the study to delete something from the computer.'

'True.'

'And if he did find it, I think he'd be more likely to steal a copy to feed his aunt's voracious appetite than delete it.'

'Also, true. We'll ask Cahill about it anyway.'

'Can you tell *when* it was deleted?' I asked.

'I'm not sure. We've seized the computer. There's a possibility our tech people can retrieve the draft. In the meantime, I'm waiting for his publishers to get back to me; I'm assuming *they* have a copy. Or hoping, I should say. The book was coming out in six months. I don't know what the lead-in time for these things is . . .'

'I don't know either,' I said, wondering if Phyllis might know and remembering that I really, really needed to speak to her.

'The publishers are in London. His editor is away and, apparently, she's the only one who can speak to me.' I didn't need to see Molloy's face to know that he was rolling his eyes. 'You'd think, considering one of their authors was murdered, that they'd be on the alert for a call from the police.'

'What about his agent?' I asked.

'Didn't have one apparently. Fell out with his last one a while back.'

'Right.' I paused. 'What part of his life did the missing bit cover? Can you tell?'

'It seems to be in the middle of his early time at Queen's. When he was writer-in-residence, rather than professor of creative writing. He was still in his twenties, after the early success of that first novel.'

My neck was beginning to hurt and I switched the phone back to the other side. 'Do you think something happened to him back then that someone else didn't want revealed?'

'It's a possibility. Though presumably it was going to come out eventually when the book was published. There's a later bit that's missing too, covering a more recent period.'

Molloy's voice became fainter as he turned away from the phone. I wondered if he had the actual manuscript in front of him, and I had a sudden urge to read it. 'Quite a chunk, in fact. About twenty pages,' he said, his voice returning to its usual volume.

'Well, he certainly didn't have twenty pages with him at the event,' I said. 'At most it was three. Maybe he took a couple of pages to Glendara, and someone else removed more from the manuscript at home.' I paused. 'It has to be Robbie Cahill, doesn't it? He could easily have pocketed the pages after he collapsed and he was probably the only one with the opportunity to swipe the other chunk from Shore Lodge, *and* delete the draft from the computer.'

Molloy was silent. Not committing himself.

'By the way, I saw him coming out of a methadone clinic in Derry yesterday.'

I was surprised by Molloy's lack of reaction. 'He's a long-term methadone user. He's on the Northern Irish register, which is why he gets it in Derry. He's been totally upfront about it: even told us that he had a relapse a couple of months back but he's clean again now.'

I wondered if the row the postman had overheard had been around that time. Had Featherstone been angry with him for relapsing?

'And his previous convictions have come through from the PSNI. Nothing for about ten years, and before that, just what you'd expect from an ex-addict: some possession, thefts, a small bit of dealing. A minor assault.'

I nearly dropped the phone. 'An assault?'

'A fight with another addict while he was living on the streets. A scrap over drugs.'

'So, he *is* violent?'

'Don't worry,' Molloy said. 'I'm not dismissing it.' He breathed in. 'In the meantime, I've got the job of reading Featherstone's memoir, what we have of it. Learn a bit more about the great man himself.'

'I guess it makes a change from books about dead presidents.' I pictured the tomes beside Molloy's bed.

He snorted. 'The man had an ego to compete with any dead president, I'll say that for him. Lots of humblebragging.'

I laughed, amused that Molloy even knew the word. 'That doesn't surprise me.'

A babble of voices followed by a door opening and closing indicated that Molloy had gone into his office at the back of the Garda Station. I imagined him leaning against the desk. 'So, I'm assuming your parents are still here?'

'They are.' I related our Mandarin Palace conversation, how they'd been manipulated into making wills in Chambers's favour. I'd made an appointment for them to see Thompson this afternoon.

Molloy clicked his teeth. 'That man is one nasty bit of work. But without his real name, I can't even check if he has a record.

If your parents decided to make a formal complaint against him, it would give me reason to pursue him . . .'

'I suspect they won't,' I said with a sigh. It hit me now, that maybe that was why Chambers had taken the original wills, because they included his real name. Had he somehow persuaded my parents to sign documents they didn't even get to read? The lawyer in me was appalled at the abuse of trust this would involve. 'I imagine they won't want to have anything more to do with him but I doubt they'd want him to go to jail.'

I put the phone down, moving my head in a circular motion to stretch my neck before returning to the post on my desk. The contract had come back in on Liam's farm, and there were a couple of more applications for Leah's maternity leave. Today was the deadline I'd given in the ad, and my intention was to call some candidates for interview on Monday, before the week-end. Not a task I was relishing, although I was grateful that Leah had volunteered to sit in. I added the new CVs to the pile but when I went to put the envelopes in the bin, discovered it needed emptying. So I picked it up to bring downstairs to the shredder.

Halfway to the door I spotted that the *Irish Times* from Monday was still in there, the one with Gavin Featherstone's obituary, which I'd hurriedly slid from my desk before his wife and son came in. I put the bin down, extracted the newspaper and opened it out on the desk, abandoning the task in hand.

Gavin Featherstone (born 25 August 1952) was a British novelist best known for his novels *The Peering of Things* and *Spirit of an Intruder*. At twenty-seven, he became the youngest ever winner of the Booker Prize and was later shortlisted twice. He won the IMPAC in 2007.

Born in Northumberland in the north of England to a working-class family, Featherstone excelled at school and went to Oxford, studying English Literature. After his degree he returned home for a couple of years during which he wrote *The Peering of Things*, which became one of the bestselling debuts of all time and winner of the Booker Prize.

Featherstone served as writer-in-residence at Queen's University, Belfast a few years later. In an interview with the *Guardian* newspaper, he said that early success did not do him any favours, that there were bouts of heavy drinking and philandering, and he admitted that there were times when he was drunk during tutoring sessions. In later life he shunned alcohol completely and claimed not to have had a drink for thirty years.

After the success of *The Peering of Things*, Featherstone received a massive advance (an alleged £500,000) for his next book, *Opium*, a tale of amorality and greed described as a black comedy. Despite talk of a film adaptation the book was not a success.

His later work pursued themes of personal guilt and retribution. He had a number of successes with subsequent novels, two of which were shortlisted for the Booker Prize, but he never won again after his early success. Featherstone said the rest of his life was spent chasing something he'd caught when he was young but didn't value. *Time* magazine included *The Peering of Things* in its list of the 100 best English-language novels of the twentieth century.

Some years after his time as writer-in-residence, Featherstone returned to Queen's to take up a position as Professor of Creative Writing, a role he filled for fifteen years, during which he purchased Shore Lodge, a large Victorian house in Inishowen, Co. Donegal, where he went regularly to write. He eventually moved there permanently with his wife and children.

In 2009 his marriage to university lecturer Barbara Doherty broke down. What followed were his missing years, the least productive of his career, during which he completed only two novels in ten years, both of which drew mixed reviews. He remained estranged from his wife and children, gradually withdrawing from the outside world at Shore Lodge, with locals saying that he was rarely seen.

He was due to publish a memoir early next year. Though details remain scant, it is understood that after many fallow years his publishers were hoping for a return to form. The first reading from this new book was to take place at the Glenfest literary festival in Inishowen where Featherstone lived; his first public event in more than ten years. Sadly, Featherstone collapsed on stage before he had a chance to read and later died in hospital. Cause of death is still being established. Featherstone is survived by his estranged wife Barbara, his son Patrick, daughter Susie and his grandchildren Saoirse, Luke and Orla.

So Featherstone was an alcoholic, I thought as I sat back in my chair, recalling the old bottle of Glenfiddich that I'd seen in his study. Was that why he had taken in Robbie, I wondered? Sympathy for another addict? Had they met at some support group, like my parents and Chambers? More and more, I found I was associating Stuart Chambers and Robbie Cahill in my head.

Though there was much in the obituary that I knew already, a picture of the dead man was beginning to emerge. I still couldn't decide whether I liked him or not. He was complex and full of contradictions, like all of us, I supposed. But unlike most of us he would live on in his books. Immortality in prose.

I snipped out the obituary with a pair of scissors before putting the newspaper back into the bin.

Chapter Twenty-five

That afternoon I walked my parents over to Thompson's office, quite a strange feeling it has to be said. During my years in Glendara, the town's other solicitor and I had built up a decent working relationship, but strictly speaking we still were still rivals for the same business. And yet here I was handing my parents over to him. In a manner of speaking.

Stan was leaning against the doorway leading to his hairdresser's salon upstairs, having a sneaky fag, and he called out to my mother as we crossed the road. It was a bright mild day and I could see he was wearing a huge pair of reflective shades.

Seconds later we ran into my neighbour Charlie from Malin coming out of the Oak with his little corgi Ash. Our relationship had never been helped by Guinness's taunting of his dog, but he seemed very friendly with my dad, who stooped to pet Ash while he and Charlie discussed the upcoming Irish Open golf championship. There was even a suggestion that they might play a few holes together in Ballyliffin.

Forced to remind Dad that their appointment was for three in order to get us moving again, I remarked, 'You pair will soon know more people than I do.'

My smile faded when I saw Robbie Cahill emerge from

Thompson's as we approached. I felt a twinge of unease, concerned that he might have seen me the day before, though he gave no indication of it, politely holding the door open for my parents as they went in. Today he was wearing a T-shirt and I noticed how the underside of his arms were criss-crossed with scars. Faded track marks, I wondered?

I waved my parents off but didn't accompany them inside. Then I turned away, purposely heading back through the centre of the square to avoid any interaction with Cahill. He reminded me too much of Chambers to be comfortable seeing him in such close proximity to my parents. Moving in with an older person, making himself indispensable and then the same type of homemade will in his favour, were too many similarities for my liking. And then there was Molloy's comment about whoever had access to liquid cocaine being someone who had a drug debt or money problems. Did Robbie Cahill owe money? Didn't drug users always owe money?

I was so preoccupied that I almost missed Phyllis sitting on a bench by the flowerbeds, despite her multi-coloured skirt and red Birkenstocks. I watched her for a few seconds before she spotted me – the light refracting off her hair as she raised her face to the sun, her beloved Fred at her feet – and it occurred to me how little I actually knew her. I knew that she travelled as widely and as often as she could, that she was an amazing cook, that she was warm and kind, and that she dressed in colourful clothes. But personally? Emotionally? Who she'd loved? Her past? I knew nothing about any of those things.

I sat down beside her, and she looked over at me and smiled.

'Have you someone minding the shop?' I asked.

'Nah. I can keep an eye on it from here. I needed a bit of vitamin D today.'

Her bookshop was on the shady side of the street; you could see it from where we were sitting.

'It's not busy at the moment anyway. The rush on Featherstone's book is over.' She gave me a wry look. 'We all end up as next week's chip paper eventually, no matter how famous we are.'

'Very true.' She seemed a little better, I thought, as if some weight had been lifted. The last thing I wanted was to upset her again, to make her feel as if I was accusing her of something, but I had to ask. 'I watched the recording of Gavin Featherstone's event,' I began, hesitantly.

She placed one hand in front of her eyes to block the sun while the other reached down to touch Fred, as much, it seemed, to comfort herself as him. As if he were her anchor.

'Molloy asked you to,' she said.

It was a statement, not a question. Phyllis knew about my relationship with Molloy, had seen it develop over the years and was aware in a peripheral way, I suspected, of a certain blurring of professional lines.

Still, I nodded. 'While I was watching it, I noticed something I hadn't seen on the day.'

'Go on.' Phyllis's eyes narrowed.

'After your introduction, when you were coming off stage and Featherstone was going on, you passed one another and . . .' I trailed off, seeing Phyllis nod defeatedly.

'He reached for my hand,' she said quietly.

'Well, yes.'

She gave a half-smile. 'Not something an author usually does to the organiser of a literary festival.'

I smiled back. 'Well, no.'

She withdrew her hand from Fred as he stretched out under the bench and she looked down, examining it as if she might see some trace of Featherstone's touch. Then she shook her head dismissively and clasped it with the other one in her lap. 'I wasn't entirely honest with you on the beach the other morning. Or at least I didn't tell you the full story.'

'Okay.' I waited.

'The thing is, I knew Gavin Featherstone a wee bit better than I admitted. A long time ago, just as I said,' she added quickly. 'There's been nothing between us for years, decades even.' She took a deep breath, as if steeling herself for what came next. 'I had a relationship with him. A romantic one. At least it was romantic for me. It was while I was working for him. It was brief, he was married and I'm ashamed of it.'

I wasn't massively surprised by this. It was pretty much what I had been expecting. It was the only thing that would explain Phyllis's sadness at Featherstone's death, the grief which appeared out of all proportion for an ex-employer from twenty-odd years before.

'But there must have been quite an age gap between you?'

'Oh aye. He was in his forties and I was only a few years out of college. I thought he was Hemingway,' she said wryly. 'He was probably the reason I opened the bookshop years later.'

I reached out to touch her lightly on the arm, remembering my dad's remark about Featherstone thinking he was Hemingway, but he hadn't meant it as a compliment. 'God, Phyllis, that must have been hard.'

She shrugged. 'Ach, I wasn't a child. I should have had more sense.' She looked at her feet, splaying her toes, the nails of which were painted in sparkly, purple polish. 'He was so good looking, so charming. But so brilliant too. I've always been attracted to people who could do things that I couldn't. I tried to write but I just didn't have the gift. But Gavin did. He was such a huge

216

talent, one of the writers of his generation. I could see it when I was typing for him, what a genius he was . . .' She gazed wistfully into the distance.

'But there was a sadness about him too. You know I'm a sucker for a sad tale.' She gave a half-smile. 'His father was a lorry driver, very macho, and his mother suffered from mental illness, was in and out of hospital all his life. He said he became cocky as a defence mechanism against all the "your mother's in the mental" digs. You know what kids are like.'

I nodded. I did.

'As he grew older, he said he wanted to win something to make her proud, give her a reason to live. But she died six months before he won the Booker. Suicide. He always said she beat him to it. I think he was very angry after that for a long time . . .'

'Did his wife know about your affair?' I asked quietly.

Phyllis shook her head. 'I don't think so. Most of the time she wasn't even there. He used to come down to write when he was working in Queen's and she stayed in Belfast with the kids. It didn't last long,' she said, again. 'And it had nothing to do with them splitting up,' she added quickly. 'That happened years later.'

I remembered the quite open reference to Featherstone's philandering in the obituary. If it hadn't been Phyllis, then maybe it was another affair that had ended the marriage.

'Did you tell Jude?' I asked gently. I wondered now if I'd been wrong about his daughter, if this was why he'd left; to allow Phyllis to mourn for an ex-lover in private without crowding her with a new relationship.

She shook her head. 'I couldn't. I wasn't happy with Stan for inviting Gavin. Of course, I couldn't say why. I just had to go ahead with it. But I wanted to be honest with Jude, until I

217

realised how he'd react. He can be pretty protective; he'd think Gavin had taken advantage of me. '

I thought Jude would be right, but I nodded. 'I remember what he was like with his daughters. A big bear who wore his heart on his sleeve.'

'Exactly.' She gave another half-smile. 'I didn't think he could have been civil to him when he met him if he knew. When Gavin died, it was too late. And I couldn't really grieve with Jude here – he'd have wormed it out of me eventually. So I sent him away.' Her chin dipped. 'I think I might have hurt him.'

'I'm sure he'll be back. All you need to do is say the word.' But I was suddenly distracted by a disturbing thought; a memory of Jude on his knees alongside Featherstone, calling for an ambulance while Phyllis flapped around them both. 'You didn't pick up a couple of sheets of paper from the floor after Featherstone collapsed, did you?'

Phyllis looked at me surprised. 'No. Why?'

'It was the extract from his new book that he was going to read. The memoir. They're missing. Molloy wonders if there was something in there which someone didn't want revealed. The draft on his computer is missing too – it's been deleted. Molloy is waiting for his editor to get back to him with a full copy.'

Phyllis breathed out heavily. 'Wow.' Then she turned to me, looking hurt as the reason for my question dawned on her. 'And you thought it was something about me, so I took the pages?'

'No, I . . .'

Her face softened at my distress. 'It's all right. I did lie to you about my relationship with him. But no, I didn't take them.'

'Would the publishers have a copy at this stage, do you think?'

'Probably. It would have to go through all sorts of edits before it's published.'

She trailed off and glanced over at her bookshop, as if suddenly remembering that she was supposed to be watching it. I followed her gaze. Ollie was looking in the window, his huge headphones and skinny frame making him look like some kind of life-sized insect. Phyllis's eyes narrowed and I wondered if Jude had told her about his shoplifting after all.

I cursed inwardly. There was something else I wanted to ask her but I needed to do it quickly before he went in and she had to leave.

'That row you had with Gavin Featherstone before he went on stage?' I said quietly. 'I know it wasn't about him refusing to sign books. Róisín said that Robbie Cahill offered her a lift down to your bookshop, and that the invitation had come from Featherstone himself.'

'No,' Phyllis agreed, distractedly, still looking at her shop. 'It wasn't about books . . .'

Ollie pushed open the door. He was going in. Phyllis stood up quickly, the sudden movement causing Fred to raise his head. And with a swish of her skirts both she and her dog were gone, without answering my question.

I sat there feeling frustrated as I watched her cross the square with her devoted dog at her heels. What was it that she still wasn't telling me? Phyllis was being evasive certainly, but there was pain there too; I could see it glinting sharply beneath the facade she was struggling to maintain. It was the only thing preventing me from sharing my concerns with Molloy, though I couldn't do that indefinitely.

I decided to stay put for a while. The day was pleasant and warm, the air heady with the scent from the flowerbeds and the square was a great place to people watch; I suspected that was why Phyllis was so fond of sitting here when the weather was good.

She might be private about her own life but she was intensely curious about everyone else's. And kind. Phyllis was one of the kindest people I knew. She'd been there for me in the past when I'd needed her, and always with discretion, leaving me reluctant to expose an aspect of *her* life without clearing it with her first.

I glanced around me, doing a 360-degree turn in my seat. I saw the hardware shop, Stoop's newsagents, the Oak pub with Stan's hairdressers above it. I saw Liam emerge from his estate agency to check something in the window, catch sight of Gina Bailey coming out of the Oak and duck back in. I saw the shades of red, yellow and blue of the buildings in the square, the bunting hung from the telegraph poles and the old phone box, now with a defibrillator inside. The little town to which I'd grown so attached.

And now my parents were here too. There had been no mention of a departure date since their revelation about the wills but the fact that they'd need to stay a little longer while their new ones were prepared gave me a strange feeling of security.

Raised voices behind me broke into my reverie, and I turned, recognising at least one of them; I'd been harangued by it on my own doorstep. Gina Bailey was talking to Robbie Cahill just on the other side of the flowerbeds. I watched them, peering through tulips and magnolias, unable to hear what they were saying but in no doubt that the exchange was a little fraught. Gina gesticulated wildly while Robbie stayed completely still. Was it her usual pushy journalist act or something more? Eventually Robbie seemed to lose patience and he walked away. For the first time I felt a glimmer of sympathy for the man.

Gina watched him go, her shoulders slumping. Then she swayed and fell to the ground in a faint.

Chapter Twenty-six

I leaped to my feet and rushed over, skirting the flowerbeds to find the woman still lying in a heap on the ground, unconscious. I kneeled down next to her, relieved to find she was still breathing, then looked frantically around for help.

Without warning, McFadden was beside me, pushing me aside to administer CPR. I hadn't even noticed him approach. Thankful for his presence, I left him to it and stood to call an ambulance, pacing uneasily until it arrived, my legs quivering in shock as I resolved yet again to do a first aid course as soon as I got the chance.

It arrived within minutes. Gina still hadn't regained consciousness as we watched it drive away.

'Did you see what happened?' McFadden asked.

I shook my head. 'Not really. I saw her come out of the Oak a few minutes before. One minute she was talking to Robbie Cahill, and the next she was on the ground.'

McFadden's brow furrowed. 'Where is he now? Cahill?'

I'd looked around for him while calling the ambulance but there'd been no sign. 'No idea.'

I assumed he'd have come back if he'd seen what happened. We'd been there almost a quarter of an hour, attracting the attention of other townspeople: Stoop standing in the door of his newsagents looking concerned, and Tony shouting over from the Oak to ask if there was anything he could do.

'He may not have seen her collapse,' I said. 'He was walking away at the time and she honestly didn't make a sound, just slumped into a heap. She was making plenty of noise before that, though. They looked as if they were having some kind of argument.'

'Right.' McFadden nodded. 'I'd better let the rest of her lot know what's happened. One of them might have contact details for her family.' He paused to check. 'There's what? A cameraman and a young fella, a runner or something?'

'Actually, the runner, Ollie, went into Phyllis's bookshop, although that was a while ago now.'

'Okay, thanks.' He stopped and shook his head worriedly. 'She didn't look good.'

'No,' I agreed. She hadn't. 'Actually, Ollie is her nephew,' I said quickly, remembering.

McFadden barrelled off towards Phyllis's shop and I saw him stick his head in through the door then leave again straight away. I followed more slowly in his wake, still feeling shaken as I walked back to the office along the footpath.

Phyllis appeared in the doorway of her bookshop as I passed.

'Did you hear what happened?' I asked. *How could she have missed it?*

'No,' she said, her eyes widening. 'I was upstairs when I heard the ambulance, then McFadden appeared looking for Ollie but he didn't tell me why. He ran off when I told him he wasn't here. Is someone hurt?'

'Gina Bailey collapsed in the square. She's on her way to hospital. She was still unconscious when they put her in the ambulance.'

Phyllis's face fell. 'Lord. I'm no great fan of the woman but I wouldn't wish that on her.'

'No. Me neither. She was having some sort of a row with Robbie Cahill before it happened.'

Phyllis massaged her temples, looking tense. 'It wasn't the same thing as happened to Gavin, was it?

'I don't know.' I wasn't sure how much Phyllis knew – I presumed it wasn't common knowledge that it was cocaine that had killed Featherstone. 'Maybe?'

I continued back to the office, the image of Gina Bailey tumbling to the ground replaying in my head. I hoped she was okay. Recalling what McFadden had said about family and wondering if she had children or a partner, I took my phone out to google her as I walked.

A Wikipedia page revealed that she had both husband and children. The search also threw up a number of YouTube clips. The first appeared to be an interview conducted by a considerably younger-looking Gina. The video had gone viral, with more than 400,000 views. Curious to know why, I clicked play, foolishly trying to watch it on the small screen of my phone as I walked. It took an age to upload. When it finally did and the camera panned to the interviewee, I stopped in my tracks, causing someone to run into the back of me and tread on my heels.

'Oh sorry.' I spun around in apology.

Maeve chuckled. 'What are you, fifteen? Staring at your phone and running into things.'

'Sorry,' I said again, closing the site and giving her my full attention. 'Bit distracted. That TV journalist Gina Bailey just collapsed in the square – she's been taken to hospital. '

Maeve whistled. 'Jesus, they're dropping like flies at the moment. Is she okay?'

'No idea. I hope so.' I shoved my phone into my pocket.

'I was just about to call in to see if you were around for lunch tomorrow?' Maeve and I often had lunch together on a Friday but I hadn't seen her much since my parents had been around.

'Sure. I'll see you then.'

I'd arrived at the door of the office so I pushed it open and went inside. Leah called after me as I made for the stairs – something about a phone call I needed to return – and I shouted a hurried response, saying I'd be back down in a minute, desperate to watch the rest of the clip on a large screen, with the sound turned up.

At my desk I quickly found the video again, pressed play and sat back to watch. It was a short clip lasting a little over three minutes from an arts show that had run on BBC Northern Ireland years before. Gina Bailey and Gavin Featherstone were sitting on a bench, which looked as if it might be outside Queen's, presumably sometime during or after his tenure there. His hair was tousled and threaded with grey.

A body-language expert would have had a field day, I thought. Featherstone was leaning back, legs crossed, arms stretching across the back of the bench, taking up space, while Gina was sitting at the edge with her knees together, a mic in her hand, almost curled in on herself.

I turned up the sound. Featherstone was in expansive form, gesticulating and laughing just as he had been during the event in Glendara. Gina asked him about his writing habit, how he found time to write alongside his duties at the university.

He snorted. 'Well, I've given up drinking for a start. I can't take the hangovers any more. I used to have to take four Valium, phone the fucking Samaritans and contemplate life for about five days just to get through them.' He grinned. 'So, I have a lot more time on my hands.'

He tilted his head, and the sun glinted on something in his left ear. When the camera zoomed in for a close up, I saw that it was the silver sleeper he'd been wearing at the event. There was a charm hanging from it, which hadn't been there then. I tried to make it out. A feather? A bird's wing? And then it hit me. It was a little silver quill. It was hard not to smirk. There was something embarrassingly self-aware about a writer having a quill hanging from his ear.

Picking up on Featherstone's easy mood, Gina appeared to relax. 'Other voices are starting to be heard in fiction, and I wondered if maybe writers like yourself are feeling marginalised, being white, male and heterosexual. You've had some criticism for your depiction of female characters . . .'

Featherstone's expression changed; all humour dissipated. 'It's a writer's job to live other lives, to channel other voices. How would it be if I just portrayed a male writer in his fifties, working in Queen's? I mean that's a *ridiculous* proposition.' His tone was contemptuous. Then he paused, a dangerous curl to his mouth. 'Have you actually read any of my books? Because it doesn't sound as if you have.'

Gina flushed. 'Of course.'

'I mean, I assume you wouldn't be wheeled out to interview me if you hadn't.' He crossed his arms as a venomous look flickered across his face. 'Name three, in order of publication.'

Gina became flustered, the flash of panic in her eyes all too visible under his penetrating gaze. 'Eh, *The Peering of Things* . . . eh . . .'

It was painful to watch. She started to riffle through her papers, dropping a sheet on the ground. Featherstone coolly picked it up and handed it to her, clearly enjoying himself immensely at her expense, the triumph of having exposed a young female reporter written all over his face.

The clip came mercifully to an end, and I switched off the video, unable to bear watching it a second time. Now it was Gina Bailey I had sympathy for. Featherstone could easily have rescued her by supplying the titles himself or making a joke out of it, but he stayed silent, watching her squirm like a worm on a hook.

It must have been a live interview or they wouldn't have broadcast it, but it was amazing that Gina had come back from it to have the career she had. Was that why she had been digging into Featherstone's past? Some kind of revenge for his humiliation of her? She must have leaped at the chance to do the documentary. Maybe that was why she'd been asked; the TV station knowing her history with him, a story coming full circle. It also explained why she'd sent her nephew to Shore Lodge rather than going herself. She must have been afraid that Featherstone would remember her.

I scanned quickly through the comments below the clip; most were cruel, and all were on Featherstone's side. *How naive and ill-prepared was the young woman? Who did she think she was?* I wondered if that would happen now – everyone siding with a powerful man who was bullying a younger female journalist. I had a horrible feeling it might be worse. There was also a number of home-made, spoof versions of the interview – one had Gina Bailey's head replaced by a panicking Beaker from *The Muppet Show*.

I closed down YouTube, mind whirring. Was it possible that Gina Bailey hated Gavin Featherstone enough to kill him? It was clear the man had a cruel streak. Had he made other enemies?

I stood up, feeling slightly grubby and went downstairs to see what Leah wanted.

Chapter Twenty-seven

By means of the highly efficient town grapevine, in other words, Stoop the newsagent, the following morning I learned that Gina Bailey had regained consciousness but remained seriously ill in Letterkenny General Hospital. According to Stoop, who seemed to blame it on the fact that she hadn't known when to go home after a party – or a literary festival in this case – she was diabetic and had made a mistake with her insulin. What McFadden and I had seen was diabetic shock cause by hyperglycaemia, or high blood sugar. I still found it difficult to get the image of the woman slumped in the square out of my mind.

When I made it to the office, Barbara Featherstone and her adult son and daughter were sitting in the waiting room. My heart sank a little as it always did when people were early for their appointments and the Featherstones were a full half-hour before their allotted time. I stuck my head in to say good morning, told them I'd be a few minutes and withdrew. Leah handed me a sympathy coffee, plus the probate file she'd set up for them, drawing my attention to Liam's valuation of Shore Lodge, which she'd clipped to the inside cover, and I took them both upstairs.

Once I'd brought in an extra chair and inhaled half my coffee, I buzzed Leah to send them up. Barbara immediately introduced her daughter Susie: a short, barrel-shaped young woman who looked a couple of years younger than her brother, dressed in American jeans, white runners and a flouncy blue and yellow blouse. She shook my hand before taking a seat alongside Patrick, who was less conservatively dressed this morning in black jeans and a short-sleeved shirt. Barbara took the seat nearest the door, giving the impression of someone who wished to remain on the periphery of things.

Now that I'd had a little exposure to them all, it was impossible not to notice the contrast between the Featherstone children and their parents. Despite his less attractive character traits, their father had been inarguably handsome and charismatic while Barbara was elegant and stylish. The children, on the other hand, despite Patrick bearing a striking resemblance to his dad, were somehow more ordinary. And it wasn't just in appearance. Looking at the three of them sitting across the desk from me, Barbara appeared calm and detached while I sensed an anxiety and insecurity in the children. Understandable, I guessed, given the circumstances. But their mother gave the impression that the whole thing didn't really concern her, that she was only here for them. Maybe that was true? For the first time, I wondered if she had a new partner.

I started things off by passing Liam's valuation over to her; she scanned it quickly, and slid it back across the table. She didn't appear to see any need to share its contents with her children, which was fine; she was the executor while they were merely beneficiaries. Assuming this will would stand, of course, an issue which must have been at the forefront of all of their minds.

Patrick was the first to bring it up, diverging immediately from his silent support of his mother on their last visit. 'So where do we stand as far as this other will is concerned?'

It occurred to me that this change might have been prompted by discussions he'd had with his sister, who leaned forward now with interest.

'At this stage it's still very unclear,' I said, choosing my words carefully. 'I haven't seen the other will yet; I'm still waiting for a copy from Mr Cahill's solicitor. You know as much as I do about the contents – I'm sure your mother has told you. But I've been told it has a revocation clause, that it's properly executed and is considerably more recent than the one in our possession.'

'What does that mean for us?' Susie asked, frowning. Her voice had a clear American intonation and I wondered how long she'd been away.

'Well, the revocation clause revokes any previous wills. So at first glance, it's the most recent will that stands,' I said. 'The last valid will made before death.'

Both Patrick and Susie shook their heads vehemently.

'But,' I cautioned, 'even if the new will *is* found to be the valid one, it's not as simple as that. There are challenges that can be made on your behalf.' The two were listening so intently that I found myself stubbornly switching my attention to Barbara. 'Firstly, a spouse has a legal right share of the other spouse's estate. You cannot disinherit a spouse. In a case where there are children, it's one third.'

Barbara shrugged. Her expression was so impassive it was almost blank.

'Also,' I turned back to Patrick and Susie, 'section 117 of the Succession Act allows a child to challenge a parent's will where the parent has not provided for them,' I quoted from the Act, 'under their will, or otherwise, in accordance with their moral obligation and in light of their means.'

Patrick and Susie exchanged meaningful glances at this and I wondered if one or both might be in need of money. It certainly didn't appear as if their mother was.

'A court will take into consideration the full circumstances of both parent and child in making a decision,' I added, remembering what Barbara had said about her husband being generous with maintenance for the children though she hadn't needed money herself. Gavin Featherstone might not have engaged emotionally with his children for many years but if he'd provided for them financially, they might be in trouble with a section 117 case.

'But it's only if the other will is found to be valid, that we'd need to do that?' Patrick said. 'Take a challenge under section 117?'

I nodded. He'd been paying attention. 'That's correct.'

'But that will,' Patrick indicated the original twenty-year-old will still in its envelope on the file, 'leaves everything to Mum and us. How do we ensure this is the will that stands?'

'Well, we can't "ensure" that, as you put it. My understanding is that we'd have to challenge the latest will, and leave it to a court to decide,' I replied. 'But I'll need to get counsel's opinion on that.'

'I don't care what's in it – we're challenging it,' he said firmly, his voice becoming embittered. 'That guy controlled Dad for years. It was Dad's fault for letting him move in but then he didn't leave; it was as if he had some kind of hold over him. But we certainly don't have to tolerate him now that Dad is gone. We'll fight him all the way.'

'Agreed,' Susie said. 'I'm assuming we *can* do that?' She fixed me with a penetrating look.

I leaned back in my chair. 'The grounds on which you can challenge the validity of a will are, firstly, that the will hasn't been properly executed. Now I understand that it's a homemade will, which can be problematic, but from what Mr Cahill's solicitor says, and I've no reason to doubt him, it has been.'

'What else?' Patrick asked, scowling.

'Other grounds are that the testator was not of sound disposing mind, did not know and approve the contents of the will, that he or she was unduly influenced, or that execution of the will was obtained by fraud.'

Patrick rubbed his cheeks, looking stressed. 'I should think the last three grounds could all be applicable and possibly the first one as well,' he said flatly.

'Proving a lack of sound disposing mind can be difficult. It's also possible that an affidavit of mental capacity was drawn up.' I was pretty sure this hadn't been done since the will was a homemade job but I wanted to manage expectations, something I often thought was a solicitor's main role. From what I'd observed, Gavin Featherstone didn't appear to have any mental capacity issues.

'Either way, I imagine we'll have to leave it to a court to decide,' I concluded. 'I'll brief counsel and see what they think, as soon as I get a copy of the other will.'

Barbara seemed content with that and was already gathering up her bag to leave, but her children gave no indication of joining her. I supposed it was hardly surprising they weren't ready to let the subject of Robbie Cahill go, when they regarded him as attempting to steal their inheritance.

'The man is a drug addict,' Patrick said, his face becoming flushed. 'Did you know that? I don't know why Dad allowed him into the house in the first place, let alone have him stay and work for him.'

Barbara reached across her daughter's lap to her son, to calm him, in a reverse of what had happened on Monday, although this move appeared more measured than affectionate. I imagined this wasn't the first time he'd said this.

'Your father had a habit of picking up waifs and strays,' she said. 'You don't remember that about him, but he did.'

'But not to have them to stay permanently,' Patrick persisted. 'Robbie Cahill was supposed to be his assistant, but Dad did his own typing. He always did, you said.'

'He wasn't that kind of an assistant,' she said, patiently, as if she were talking to a child rather than an adult son. 'He did other things for him. Your father was pretty useless when it came to taking care of himself or cooking or housekeeping.'

As if responding in kind to his mother's condescension, Patrick became more high-pitched, his eyes glistening from unshed tears. Monday's stoicism was long gone. 'He's probably dangerous, for God's sake. It was probably him who killed Dad, once he'd got him to make that will leaving everything to him.'

There was silence for a few seconds, a slightly embarrassed one, I thought. Even Susie was looking at her feet.

To break the tension I said, 'There's something I should probably mention.' I paused as I tried to work out how to phrase it. 'The court will likely look for evidence of Mr Featherstone's intentions so you might be asked questions about the family estrangement. I probably should put something about it in the brief I send to counsel.'

'Okay.' Barbara nodded slowly, but she didn't offer anything. Patrick and Susie looked at her expectantly and I wondered if they even knew the reason for it.

'Was it alcohol?' I prompted. 'Again, that might be relevant. Maybe even for testamentary capacity.'

Barbara shook her head dismissively. 'Oh, he didn't touch it. I left him thirteen or fourteen years ago, and he didn't drink for years before that. He tried to be funny about it but actually he was a chronic alcoholic. He couldn't handle it. He had a car accident while driving drunk so he didn't drive. One of the reasons he needed Robbie Cahill, I imagine. Once I'd left,' she added with a wry smile.

There was a pause. She was dismissing alcohol as a reason but not giving me an alternative, giving me the uneasy feeling that I was picking at a scab that wasn't yet ready to come off. It didn't stop me wondering though. Did Barbara know about the affair with Phyllis? Were there others? If it was their father's serial infidelity that had caused the split, I could understand her not wanting to discuss it in front of her children.

So I backed off, deciding to tackle things from the other direction – the rapprochement rather than the row. 'Do you know why he wanted you to come to the event?'

'Not a clue,' Barbara said brusquely before glancing pointedly at her watch. The implication was clear: she'd given enough time to this discussion. 'So, is that it? You'll come back to us when you get a copy of the other will and send a brief? Do you need a retainer? I can transfer some money if you do.'

I shook my head and all three of them stood up to leave. Barbara allowed her children to troop out ahead of her, before pausing to speak to me in the doorway. I found myself holding my breath. Was she about to answer my question now that we were alone?

'I forgot to say, they've released Gavin's body, finally, so we're waking him this weekend at the house. At Shore Lodge.'

'That sounds like a good idea.'

'It's what he would have wanted, I think.' She raised her eyebrows. 'Will you come? We're asking everyone. He was locked away for so long that we'd like to have as many people there as possible.' A half-smile. 'Fill the house for the first time in years, bring it back to life. Celebrate his life before we have to dismantle it. For Patrick and Susie.'

I risked the question, 'What does Robbie Cahill think of that? Will he be part of it?'

She shrugged. 'Not his call. He can be there if he wants to be.' She left and closed the door behind her with a quiet click.

I returned to my desk and tidied the file, readying it to give it back to Leah while we waited for a copy of the other will. Underneath Liam's valuation, I spotted the release form for the TV documentary, guessing Leah must have put it there.

I ran downstairs with it to see if I could catch Barbara before she left. Patrick and Susie had already gone, but she was emerging from the bathroom with freshly applied lipstick.

I handed her the sheet. 'I forgot to mention this the last time you were in. It's a release form for the TV documentary. One of the crew left it in here for you to collect.'

'Thanks.' She folded it and put it in her bag. 'Did you hear what happened to Gina Bailey?'

'I was there when it happened, as a matter of fact.'

She nodded, showing no further curiosity, said goodbye and left.

Back upstairs, I watched her cross the road from my office window. Once on the other side, she took the release form from her bag and, with surprising venom, tore it into strips and threw it into the bin. I crossed my arms. So, Barbara Featherstone was capable of emotion after all, albeit when she thought no one was looking.

The phone rang. I went back over to my desk and picked it up.

'It's Molloy,' Leah said. 'Will I put him through?'

His greeting sounded strangely tense, and I wondered if Gina

Bailey's condition had worsened. Was it possible he might have two unexplained deaths on his hands?

'What's wrong?'

'Featherstone's editor has just got back to me.'

'Oh?' I waited.

'He sent her a draft of his memoir the week before he died. Let me read you some of it.' I heard him tapping keys on a computer. '"I liked getting into fights. I know how that sounds but I did. It was a way of working off the alcohol, the rage I felt against my dad. The sense of injustice I felt at the world. The fear of being exposed as a fake, the insecurities I pushed down when I was sober—"'

Molloy was no orator. I cut across him, impatiently. 'Can we fast forward to the good bit? Or maybe give me the gist?'

His tone was grim. 'Featherstone killed someone.'

Chapter Twenty-eight

I was silent for a second. 'He what?'

'He admits in his memoir to having killed someone.'

Molloy spoke slowly with almost a full second's pause between each word. He was right to spell things out for me. I was struggling to take it in.

'His editor emailed me the two sections that were missing from the draft in his house. She said that she couldn't believe it herself when she read it. She warned him of what it might mean to bring out this book, but Featherstone was certain that he wanted it published, that he understood the implications. He said he was prepared to take the consequences, whatever they were.'

'But how? Where? Who? When?' My mind was full of questions, each one tumbling after the other like a troupe of acrobats. Did Barbara know about this? Was it the reason for the estrangement? Was this why Gavin Featherstone wanted his family to come to the event? So that he could read his confession aloud? I tried to imagine the reaction in the marquee if he had. All those shocked faces. And then I remembered that the documentary crew would have caught it on camera. What a scoop.

Molloy attempted to answer the questions I'd actually uttered aloud. 'It happened when he was working at Queen's for the first time, when he was writer-in-residence, rather than later when he was professor of creative writing. From what I can gather, it was a street fight at a time when he was drinking heavily. But I'll know more when I get to the second bit, the longer section later in the book. That part I started to read for you was what I presume he was going to read at the event.'

'Right. Wow. Did anyone else know about what he was intending to reveal?'

'His editor isn't sure. It was very early days – she hadn't yet shown it to anyone. Wasn't sure what to do about it until we contacted her.'

I breathed out slowly. 'Presumably this has huge implications for the investigation into his death? I mean, maybe it was revenge. Can you find out who he killed? Or claims he killed?'

It hit me that Featherstone may not actually have killed anyone, that this could simply be attention-seeking machismo for his new book. But I dismissed the notion as soon as it occurred. Why would anyone actually admit to killing someone when they hadn't? Surely the consequences, the very real risk of life imprisonment, would be far too serious for whatever shock value it might have.

'I hope so,' Molloy said. 'I'm going to drive to Belfast now, this morning. As soon as I've read the rest of the second bit. Speak to the PSNI. Hopefully I'll have a few more details before I go, a location, a date, maybe even a name. If not, I'll see if they have any unsolved murders around that time that fit the description. I could ring, but it's always better to be there in person.'

'Okay. That makes sense.'

There was a knock on the door and Leah interrupted me to bring in an envelope, something hand delivered. I nodded my thanks and opened it with the hand that wasn't holding the phone. It was the promised letter from Thompson's with a copy of Featherstone's new will. I scanned it quickly to confirm its contents were what I'd been told and put it aside to look at properly later on. As I did so an idea sparked in the back of my mind. It would certainly explain a few things.

Molloy was still speaking. He'd moved on to something else but I hadn't caught it. 'What was that?' I asked.

'I said that BMW that ran us off the road has been found burned out on a farm near Culdaff. The farmer says it's not the first time a car has been dumped in one of his fields.'

Uh-oh. 'What farm?' I asked innocently.

'Peter McGonigle's. He's in a nursing home at the moment. Of course, no forensics.'

No reference to the fact that Peter was my client's uncle, but if Molloy didn't know yet, it wouldn't take him long to find out.

I was relieved when he rang off saying he'd give me a shout when he got back from Belfast. Damn it, I thought. Withdrawing from the case didn't particularly bother me, but explaining why to the nephew might be an issue.

The morning was stuffed with appointments, which was just as well or I'd have spent the whole time staring out the window reeling from Molloy's revelation about Featherstone, asking myself question after question, none of which I had an answer for.

At lunchtime, I made my way to the Oak to meet Maeve while Leah headed off with her mother to do some baby-clothes shopping. Passing the bookshop, I wondered if Phyllis knew about Featherstone. Was this what she'd been keeping to herself? Had he told her what he was planning to read and that's what they were arguing about?

Molloy had sworn me to secrecy for the moment, so I hurried on past, afraid if she called me in that I'd be tempted to mention it. Averting my eyes from the shop, I spotted a huge motorcycle parked in the square; I was glad to see that Jude was back.

I arrived at the pub before Maeve to an unusually bad-tempered Tony who was stomping about behind the bar, clattering cups and plates. It took me a few minutes to work out that he was indignant at the pub coming under suspicion for Gina Bailey's collapse. By the time McFadden had come calling, all the cutlery, glasses and plates that she'd used had already been put through their industrial dishwasher at 180 degrees. Which meant he hadn't been exonerated either.

'Do they think I go about poisoning people?' he groused, using a tea towel to polish a glass with what seemed to be a little too much vigour. 'Wouldn't exactly be good for business, would it?'

'I thought it was something to do with her insulin? I'm sure that's what Stoop told me this morning.'

Tony rolled his eyes. 'I don't think they even know. I presume after what happened to Gavin Featherstone they have to investigate.' He plonked the glass onto the counter with a thump. 'But it's not just the staff under suspicion. It's the customers as well. The Featherstones were all here at the same time as that woman, minding their own business, having lunch. Last thing they need after what happened. She's a real lady, Mrs Featherstone,' he said wistfully.

I smiled. Did Tony fancy Barbara Featherstone?

He clocked my amusement and said hurriedly, '*And* that other wee girl.' He nodded towards the door through which Róisín Henderson had just come in. 'She was here too. First, she's the one interviewing your man and now . . .' Tony clicked his teeth.

No one seemed to have much sympathy for Gina Bailey, I noticed.

'Anyway,' Tony said abruptly. 'Are you eating?'

I ordered some soup and a salad and went to sit down, passing by Róisín who was taking off her denim jacket and rooting in the pockets for her wallet. Despite what Tony had said, she seemed pleased about something, smiling to herself and almost fizzing with excitement. It didn't take her long to tell me what that was.

'The workshop is going ahead. It's going to be in the library on Sunday morning,' she said draping her jacket over a chair.

I hoped she'd actually got Phyllis's approval for it, this time.

'It'll be great. We'll have a bit of craic with it.' She crossed her arms and rocked forward and back on her tiptoes, as if she needed to be moving to contain her glee. 'Can you let your mother know? I know she signed up for the last one.'

'I will.'

She headed up to the counter to order, while I found a table a reasonable distance away, not wishing to feel under pressure to share. I wasn't in the mood.

My food arrived, but there was no sign of Maeve. I ate. Still no sign of Maeve. I knew she sometimes got held up with emergencies so I waited till half one to ring and text but got no reply. I finished my coffee and at a quarter to two I gave up and went back to the office.

The phone rang at five to two before Leah had returned from lunch and I answered it, wondering if it was Maeve apologising for standing me up. But it was Molloy again. This time he sounded as if he was on a city street.

'Are you in Belfast?' I asked.

'Yep. Just a quick one. I thought you'd want to know. I've read both missing excerpts from Featherstone's memoir.'

I found myself holding my breath again. 'And?'

'And, he names the man he killed. Full admission. You'll never guess who the son is . . .'

'The son of the man he killed?' I stopped to think. 'I presume it was a *man*?' Realising how differently I'd feel if Featherstone had killed a woman, and what that said about me.

'Yes, and yes,' he replied.

'Robbie Cahill,' I said, without hesitation.

'Congratulations.' Molloy didn't sound surprised.

'Lucky guess.' This wasn't entirely true because, suddenly, when Leah had brought in the letter and the will earlier it had all made sense. The reason for the new will leaving everything to Cahill, disinheriting his family in the process. Redemption. What Featherstone had spoken about in the marquee on Saturday night.

There was a shout on the street on Molloy's side and he lowered his voice. 'So, the son of the man Featherstone killed has been living with him and working for him for nearly ten years.'

I blew out a breath. 'It's quite something all right. How on earth did it come about?'

'Not sure yet. We'll need to speak to Cahill about it. He was a child when his dad died, and his mother died from cancer shortly after so he ended up in various foster homes. Sounds as if he hasn't had an easy life.'

'And then the drug addiction.'

'Yes,' Molloy agreed. 'He was an only child, so no siblings to help take care of him.'

'Poor kid.' It was the second time in a few days that I'd felt sympathy for Cahill.

Molloy gave a grunt of agreement. 'But the big question is *does he know*? Featherstone says in the book that he hadn't told him at the time of writing. Was he waiting for Cahill to read it in the published book, or hear him confess at the event in front of all those people?'

'He must have told him,' I argued. 'It would have been too big a risk not to. Cahill could have accessed the draft of the memoir anytime in the house. And I imagine it was the reason for the new will.'

I remembered what the postman had said about the row between Featherstone and Robbie Cahill, and Molloy's mention of Cahill's relapse into drugs a few months before. It sounded as if they had both happened around the same time. Was that when Featherstone had told him, I wondered? I reached for Thompson's letter from my in-basket, and checked the date on the copy of the new will, which was clipped to it. February. Three months ago. That fitted.

Robbie Cahill must have been hugely shocked when his employer of ten years, with whom he lived, confessed to killing his father. Was the new will some kind of redemption for that? The same reason Featherstone had initially given Cahill a job and a home? Or was it blackmail on Robbie Cahill's part? But then how could you blackmail someone who was about to tell the world what he'd done.

'I'm inclined to agree,' Molloy was saying. 'We're going to have to bring him in.' A voice sounded in the background: someone was calling him. 'Look, I need to go. I'll talk to you later.'

He rang off just as Leah came in the door, with Maeve in her wake. They were laughing and chatting, but broke off when they saw me.

'I'm sorry for standing you up,' Maeve said with a grimace while Leah went to hang her coat up in the cloakroom. 'I had to go out to Peter McGonigle's farm. Some idiot was driving around his fields and they left the gate open, letting the cattle out. A bullock was hit by a car. I had to put him down.'

'Ah no.' If my decision hadn't been made before this, it was now. My loyalty would always be to Peter. I'd get a letter out today telling the nephew I no longer acted for him.

Once Maeve left, my phone pinged with the notification of an email to my personal account – Molloy had sent me on the excerpts from Gavin Featherstone's memoir. Although I guessed I was just getting an early read; in six months anyone would be able to read it once it was published.

I thought about his bringing in Robbie Cahill. While I understood that, added to the man's drug history, the row with Featherstone and the fact that he would benefit hugely from his death, this latest development would force Molloy to act, I was surprised to discover that I was beginning to have doubts about Cahill's guilt.

I made myself a coffee, printed out the excerpt and took it back up to my desk, beginning with the section that Molloy had started to read aloud on the phone.

I liked getting into fights. I know how that sounds but I did. It was a way of working off the alcohol, my rage against my dad. The sense of injustice I felt at the world. The fear of being exposed as a fake, the insecurities I pushed down when I was sober. I would provoke an argument with a stranger, for no reason. In Belfast that wasn't hard. I was English; all I needed to do was be in the wrong place. Or the right place, depending how you looked at it.

We were alone at the back of a pub. I'd gone out for a cigarette. He gave me a light when I asked him for one. I handed it back with a barb, knowing exactly what I was doing. He threatened me and I punched him.

Immediately I sensed something was wrong. He didn't fight back. He fell straight away, slumping onto the ground, unconscious. It sobered me up. I ran. And I kept running for forty years.

Chapter Twenty-nine

On Saturday morning I awoke early, Gavin Featherstone's words still swirling around in my head. After reading the first excerpt from his memoir about the fight in the pub car park, which lasted no more than a page or two, I'd gone on to read the longer section from later in the book, which Molloy had also sent me.

While the first – the one we assumed he'd been intending to read at the event – was brutal, direct and coldly matter of fact, the second was longer and more contemplative, covering a more recent period in his life; the time after his wife had left him and he was alone in Shore Lodge. In it he named the man he'd killed, admitting that he'd followed media accounts in the aftermath of the attack, learning that the man had died at the scene and that the PSNI were looking for the culprit. He'd spent years, he said, terrified that the knock on his door would come. He spoke about his regret, the guilt with which he lived and his decision decades later years later to seek out the man's son.

I picked up my phone from my bedside locker, opened Molloy's email and began to read again.

> I'd lived with it for too long. Every happy event, every writing success, every award had been tainted with

my guilt. Nothing helped. I'd given up drinking but it wasn't enough. I'd given up the pleasures of the flesh but it wasn't enough. I'd told my wife what I'd done but it wasn't enough.

Finally, I couldn't live with it any longer. I needed to make amends. So, I went looking for the man's family. The family I'd destroyed. And when I found them there was only one member left. A son. A son who was in trouble. Who sold drugs to make a living, and who took them to ease his pain, to fill the void in his life which I'd created.

The words on the screen began to blur. I replaced the phone and lay back again on my pillow. It was raining outside my window; the soft drumming on the roof was soothing, punctuated by the odd whoosh of a car circling the green.

I thought about the strange way in which Featherstone had chosen to take responsibility for what he'd done: approaching the dead man's son without telling him why, getting to know him, then inviting him to come and live with him, giving him a job and promising to help with his addiction on the basis that he himself had kicked one too. Most people, I imagined, would simply present themselves at a police station and confess. But then Gavin Featherstone wasn't most people.

He was living alone in that big empty house when he sought out Robbie Cahill. But there was no admission of guilt and there wouldn't be for years, and no mention of any attempt to heal things with his own family. Were his actions not still an exercise in avoidance? Despite all his talk about making amends, was offering Cahill a job not a way of making him feel better about himself, without actually taking responsibility and accepting the consequences of his actions? So why then had he decided to confess now?

For a little while, I allowed time to wash over me, letting the minutes fall away. Eventually I knew I wouldn't sleep any more so I hauled myself out of bed and took myself off to the shower, standing for a long time under the hot water, skin tingling. While many questions remained unanswered, I now knew why Featherstone's marriage had broken up. He said that he had *told his wife*. I stopped mid-shampoo when it hit me that this admission would implicate her too. If she'd concealed what she knew about the commission of a serious crime, then she was culpable and could be charged.

Downstairs I made coffee. Needing some fresh air, I opened the back door and stood in my little yard to drink it. The rain had stopped and the watery blue sky that replaced it was patched with scraggy clouds. I heard a mew and found Guinness sitting in a plant pot taking the air too. He studiously ignored me so I allowed my thoughts to drift back to Featherstone.

The reason Robbie Cahill was a suspect in his death would be made public eventually, whether people read the memoir or not. But was it he who had killed Featherstone? He had plenty of motive. Featherstone had killed his father, and possibly hastened the death of his mother, destroying his family and landing him in a series of foster homes. He was about to inherit Featherstone's estate. He also had opportunity; people wouldn't have questioned or noticed his leaving a glass of water on stage for the man he worked for and, presumably, he'd have had access to the drug that had killed Featherstone. Drug addicts didn't lose their contacts unless they tried very hard to do it. I'd discovered that through some of the criminal work I'd done.

Cahill had a difficult road ahead if he was to prove his innocence; the cards were well stacked against him. But somehow, despite my earlier leanings, I was no longer convinced. The first place to look after a murder is at those who benefit from the death. Surely then, he would know that he'd be an obvious suspect? Plus, he may not have owned Shore Lodge, but he was living there anyway; if what the postman said was anything to go by, he and Featherstone had been relatively content together. Would he really kill to inherit, knowing that he'd have to take on the family and might very well fail, losing his home in the process? And knowing that once it was discovered that his own father had been murdered by Featherstone, he'd be certain to be a suspect.

I stopped suddenly, mug halfway to my mouth. That would be a reason for not wanting the details in the memoir to become public after Featherstone's' death. What if Robbie Cahill swiped the pages from which Featherstone was about to read after he collapsed and deleted the draft from his computer, because he *knew* suspicion would fall on him? The publisher had a copy but maybe he didn't know that. If he'd been happy enough for it all to come out at the event, *until* Featherstone collapsed and died, then it must not have been something he'd seen coming. Because he didn't kill him. Damn it. The more I thought about it the more I was certain that Molloy had the wrong man.

I heard a noise on the stairs; my parents were up. I turned to go inside. Guinness extracted himself from the plant pot, stretched and reluctantly padded in after me, flopping down on the kitchen floor to sun himself in the only patch of light coming in the window.

When the door swung open and my parents came in, my dad made a beeline for him and the cat seemed equally pleased to see him, hauling himself to his paws to rub his body luxuriously along my dad's shins.

'Is that actually a purr?' I said, amazed. 'How do you get him to do that?'

'He's a cat. He likes affection.' Dad grinned as he stroked the cat's head.

'He doesn't ever seem to want it from me. He's usually pissed off with me for some reason.'

'That's because you don't treat him like a god. Cats need to be worshipped.'

I rolled my eyes. My mother put the kettle on to make tea, while my dad left to go and buy the papers, leaving Guinness to stretch out as if he'd just had a massage. I watched my mum take some mugs from the cupboard and find some bread to toast. There'd been no further mention of them leaving and I wondered what they were thinking. On Monday, they would be signing their new wills so I knew they'd be here till then, but what about after that?

My phone rang, breaking into my thoughts. It was Phyllis so I took it into the sitting room.

'Morning,' she said brightly. 'I didn't wake you, did I?'

I looked at my watch, and grinned. 'It's a quarter to ten, Phyllis. I'm not a teenager.'

She laughed. 'Aye well. Fair enough. It's still a Saturday.' She paused. 'Are you going to the corp-house later?'

'I think so. Are you?' In light of what she'd now told me about her relationship with Featherstone, I wasn't sure she'd want to go to a wake hosted by his family.

She sighed. 'I should show my face, but I don't particularly want to go on my own. Jude is going to mind the bookshop for me,' she added, before I could ask.

'I'll come into Glendara and collect you,' I said decisively. I'd been wondering how to show my support to Phyllis. Maybe this was it. 'It's not much out of my way. About two?'

'Oh great. Thanks.' She sounded relieved. 'See you then.'

249

I hung up and headed back to the kitchen. I'd be glad to have a little company myself. I'd never really relaxed into the Inishowen tradition of calling to people's houses after a death. In Dublin, only close family or friends called to the house while the rest went to the funeral. But then there wasn't going to be a funeral for Gavin Featherstone; he was to be cremated.

I told my mother of my plans for the afternoon when I came back into the kitchen. 'I don't suppose you want to come?' I asked. 'It's a tradition here that everyone goes to the wake. And they've said they want the house full.'

She shook her head. 'Ah no, we'll leave you to it. There's something your father and I want to do later.'

I looked at her curiously, but she didn't elaborate. Instead, she held up the teapot. 'Tea?'

I drove up to the entrance of Shore Lodge at around half past two with Phyllis in my passenger seat. The day had turned dull again and a misty rain was falling. Cars lined the roads on both sides and I spotted McFadden in a fluorescent yellow jacket directing traffic. This time the gates were open; people trooped in and out wearing waterproof jackets and carrying umbrellas, clearly grasping the opportunity that the rarity of this open house presented. I doubted many of them actually cared about the man.

With difficulty I found a parking space into which nothing larger than a Mini would have fitted, and pulled in. Unclipping my seatbelt, I glanced across at Phyllis who was clearly ill at ease, twisting a large red ring round and round her middle finger and making no attempt to get out.

'Are you okay?' I asked.

She nodded, her eyes glistening. 'I haven't been here in twenty-three years. Not since . . .'

I reached out to touch her hand. 'Let's get it over with then. We don't need to stay long.'

We climbed out and walked towards the house, drizzle blurring my vision and dribbling down my cheeks.

Before the gates, Phyllis stopped dead, her gaze directed across the road. 'Don't tell me they're filming the wake?'

In a slipway on the other side of the road I saw Joe and Ollie alongside their black van. The cameraman was concentrating on fixing a tripod while Ollie did his usual dipping of the head when he saw us. Phyllis's eyes welled. *Was she going to cry?* Maybe it wasn't such a good idea, her being here.

'I suppose it's an opportunity to get a couple of shots of the house for the documentary,' I said gently. 'Those gates are usually closed. At least they're not bothering people, staying well out of the way.'

Phyllis shook her head in disbelief. 'I wouldn't be surprised if Gina Bailey was directing things from her hospital bed.'

Which made me think I probably should enquire after the woman at least, since I had been the one to find her. I hesitated for a second, and then, to Phyllis's appalled cry of 'What are you doing?' I ran across the road.

Both men looked up at me in surprise. It was as if they hadn't expected anyone to actually acknowledge their presence, as if the camera made them somehow invisible.

Joe's phone rang and he rooted it out of his jeans pocket, pointing his finger at Ollie, eyes narrowed, and warning, 'Do *not* touch the camera,' before striding off to take the call.

Ollie regarded me from beneath heavy brooding eyebrows. 'His wife is expecting a baby. She keeps thinking it's coming.'

I nodded with a smile. 'Right. How's your aunt doing?'

'She's all right. Getting out in a few days.'

251

The cameraman returned. 'False alarm.' He nodded at me. 'The kid's looking for a backer for his horror flick if you're interested.'

'Really?' I asked, glancing at Ollie, but all I got was another dipped head. He wasn't a kid, but I understood why Joe had called him that.

Phyllis looked worried when I returned, as she waited for me at the gates. 'What was that all about?'

'Just asking about Gina. Come on. Let's go in.'

We waved to McFadden and made our way in and up the driveway.

Approaching the house, I had a very different feeling to the last time I'd been here with Liam. Despite the gloomier weather, the house and grounds seemed revived by the presence of people. And it occurred to me that the Robbie Cahill problem had been neatly solved for the Featherstones with him still in custody.

The front door was ajar to allow people to walk in freely. Once inside I could see that all the curtains were open; the carpets had been cleaned and the place smelled of furniture polish and flowers, thanks to the carnations and lilac picked from the garden and placed in vases in the reception rooms and entrance hall.

My eyes were drawn to a room from which people were filing in and out – the dining room from what I could remember – and I caught a brief glimpse of a coffin lying on the grand table.

'Should we join them?' I asked.

Phyllis nodded, looking as if she might throw up.

Two women in front of us in the queue looked around them furtively. Sagging features, salt and pepper hair. 'Where is she?' one of them asked. 'The wife.'

The response was a low hiss. 'She's a cold fish that one. Always thought a wile lot of herself.'

'Aye. You'd think marrying a famous author would do her. But even he wasn't good enough for her in the end.'

I glanced at Phyllis, who gave an embarrassed half-smile.

Then a voice behind us made me jump. 'You're all so good to come.'

Chapter Thirty

Barbara Featherstone was wearing a black maxi dress with a slim tulle skirt decorated in brown and gold swirls. It had to have been designer. She watched as the two women ahead of us shuffled into the room where her husband lay. They hadn't even noticed her presence.

'It's fine,' she said, delicately touching her collarbone. 'I know what they think of me.'

I flushed, as if I'd been the one who'd made the remark.

'He's going to be cremated on Monday, and his ashes scattered along the shore where he used to swim. His wishes. He included it in *both* wills so he must have meant it.' Her mouth curled into a smile.

Leah had scanned and emailed Barbara a copy of the second will at her request, but I was surprised that she had a sense of humour about it. Her children certainly didn't.

Her eyes narrowed as she transferred her attention to Phyllis. 'You run the bookshop in town, don't you? You were the organiser of the festival.'

Phyllis nodded, her discomfort written all over her face. 'I'm so sorry about what happened.'

Barbara smiled easily. 'It was hardly your fault. I'm just sorry your festival was ruined.'

It was clear there hadn't been any contact between the two of them before this. I supposed there would have been no need. Phyllis had followed Featherstone to the hospital after his collapse and I presumed Barbara hadn't. It suddenly struck me how odd that was.

'Would either of you like a drink?' Barbara asked. 'Wine, whiskey, tea? There are sandwiches too if you're hungry?'

Phyllis shook her head, her eyes searching desperately over my shoulder for some escape. I was glad to see her eyes widen in recognition, having seen someone she knew. 'Do you mind if I . . .' I nodded, and she seized her opportunity to bolt.

'Kitchen?' Barbara suggested, once she'd gone.

I was happy to avoid the queue to view the body, so I readily agreed.

'Have you been here before?' she asked as I followed her down the hall; the skirt of her dress swishing as she walked briskly, emphasising her height and slim figure. 'To the house, I mean?'

'Just the once, when Liam was doing the valuation. I brought him out the keys.'

'So, you saw the shrines, then?' Barbara turned and looked at me over her shoulder. 'The kids' bedrooms just as they'd left them. Their things in the cupboard under the stairs. Coats and wellies they'd already grown out of by the time we left.'

'I did.'

'When I said we'd have to dismantle Gavin's life, I never expected to have to dismantle our family life too. I assumed Gavin would have got around to that at some stage over the years.' She sighed. 'But then maybe he saw that as my responsibility.'

Emerging into the bright empty kitchen, I felt the same sensation as before, that of leaving a museum and entering the lived-in part of the house. Barbara went to one of the overhead cupboards and began to take out some glasses and cups. Randomly it seemed to me, as if she wasn't really concentrating. We certainly wouldn't need three glasses and four mugs.

'We were never very good at throwing things out here. We had too much space.' She gave a wry smile. 'Wouldn't happen in Dublin. But Gavin seems to have taken things out of the base-ment and put them back where they were.' She picked up the egg cup with the legs. 'I'm sure I threw that out years ago. It's like he turned into a hoarder after we left, retreating into himself as if he didn't want to lose anything else. Sad really.'

'I saw the swing,' I said. 'It looked new. I wondered if he was hoping to have his grandkids up here someday. Patrick and Susie have kids, don't they?'

She nodded. 'One and two respectively. Patrick's son is a bit of a handful.' She leaned back against the sink and there was emo-tion in her usually inscrutable face. 'I never thought Gavin would keep the house like this, like some kind of mausoleum. I know it probably sounds ridiculous but it's only beginning to hit me that in taking Patrick and Susie away from their father, I made a life-changing decision not only for myself but for them too.'

'They were kids then,' I said, 'but they've been adults a long time. They could always have got back in touch with him. I'm assuming you wouldn't have stopped that.'

'I suppose.' She offered me the kettle or a bottle of Glenfiddich, both of which sat on the counter. I wondered if it was the same one I'd seen in Featherstone's study with the single measure missing.

I chose the kettle. 'Driving,' I said. 'Tea would be great.'

She filled the kettle from the tap and switched it on, sliding over two of the mugs that she'd taken from the cupboard. 'I believe Robbie Cahill's been arrested.'

I nodded. 'So, I hear.'

She took a deep breath. 'And Gavin's big secret is about to come out?'

I paused. Molloy had sworn me to secrecy about that and still hadn't said any different, but I presumed he must have spoken to Featherstone's family about it.

Despite the fact that I knew the answer from Featherstone's memoir, I said, 'You knew?'

Barbara crossed her slender arms, and bowed her head. 'I did. He told me before I left him. I didn't know Robbie Cahill was the man's son, though.' She looked up again. 'I guess that was his big announcement, that he'd been forgiven by the victim's family?'

'I suppose.'

She shook her head in disgust. 'It was typical of Gavin to want to do a big public confession. Couldn't just go to a Garda Station and turn himself in like a normal person. He had to write a book about it. Talk about the meaning of guilt and conscience and regret, as if he was the only one ever to have experienced it. Get invited to all the festivals when he got out of prison, amid a flurry of publicity.'

'He was sixty-nine, so he was unlikely to get out if he was convicted of murder,' I said. 'Or manslaughter for that matter.' Although what she'd said wasn't a million miles away from what I had been thinking. And Barbara Featherstone knew her husband better than most.

'Maybe he thought being forgiven would get him a more lenient sentence,' she said.

'I'm not sure that works for murder,' I said dryly. 'Murder carries a mandatory life sentence. And if he was lucky enough to be charged with manslaughter, he'd probably have got a hefty sentence for evading justice for so long.'

'Right.' Barbara considered this for a moment. 'I wonder if he knew that? I wouldn't put it past him to just make an assumption.' The kettle clicked off and she turned away from me to make the tea.

'Was that the reason you left him?' I ventured. 'Because he told you he'd killed someone?'

She sighed, her shoulders slumping, before turning to hand me a mug. 'On the surface, yes. But it was more complicated than that.'

She grabbed some milk and sugar, gestured towards the table and we sat, she at one end and me on her right. The table was an old one, with stains and pen scratches. I wondered if this was the same family table she'd sat at with Featherstone and their kids, and how weird that must be for her.

As if thinking the same, she traced one of the indentations with her finger, making circle after circle with one perfectly manicured nail. 'I think the truth is that I grabbed the opportunity. I was tired of massaging his fragile ego, protecting him from anything difficult so he could write. Editing his work. Easing his self-doubt.' She gave a thin smile. 'Despite the fact that I also had a full-time job. I was teaching in the school here. I'd cut short my own university career so I didn't have to travel. Everything had to come second to the great Gavin Featherstone's genius.'

'Self-doubt?' I said, surprised, blowing on my tea, which was scalding. Two words I would never have associated with Gavin Featherstone.

'Oh yes,' she took a sip from her mug. 'There were times when he spent days in bed. Gavin's happiness was dependent on the sales of his books, which had been declining steadily.' She looked up. 'The public perception may be that he retreated from public life, but the reality is that public life rejected him first.

258

He'd had a couple of not-very-successful books, and the invitations stopped coming. Meanwhile I cooked, cleaned, took care of his kids and put up with his infidelities. Life was passing me by. I got tired of being "Gavin Featherstone's wife".'

I flinched inwardly on Phyllis's behalf at the mention of infidelities. And then it hit me: had Barbara not recognised the young graduate who'd done her husband's typing years before? Phyllis said that she often wasn't here but, surely, they had met?

My thoughts were interrupted by the door being roughly pushed open by one of the women from earlier. She saw us, looked startled, covered her mouth with her hand and retreated.

'Bitches,' Barbara said, coolly. 'And they'll be as nice as pie to me on the surface.'

'I'm sure not everyone thinks as they do,' I said uncomfortably. I couldn't think how else to respond.

She gave me a shrewd look. 'Wouldn't that be nice? Anyway,' she continued, 'when Gavin told me what he'd done I knew it was my opportunity. He, of course, expected me to accept it because I'd accepted everything else. Keep his secret. Tell him it was so long ago there was nothing he could do. Soothe his conscience when it pricked him in the night.' She closed her eyes briefly.

'Well, I decided not to. That I'd had enough. That it was the final straw. I told him that I could only accept what he'd done if he took responsibility for it and confessed. I knew he wouldn't, that he'd take the coward's way out just as he did in Belfast.' She gave a tight shake of her head. 'He may have given up the booze but his character hadn't changed. Despite all the bravado he displayed on the surface, Gavin Featherstone was the master of avoidance.'

'Why didn't you go to the police yourself?' I asked.

She nodded. 'I should have, of course. But I was desperate to get away from him at that point, and I knew if I reported it, I'd have to support him through the trial for the kids' sake. I wouldn't have been able to walk away knowing he needed me and that I'd caused it.' She took a deep breath. 'Instead, holding it over him seemed to give me a way out. I knew he wouldn't hand himself in. I guess you could say I did what he did, taking the coward's way out. Leaving him because I didn't love him any more, but using what he did as an excuse.'

'Understandable maybe.'

'Yes.' She bowed her head in acknowledgement. 'It was. But it wasn't truthful. I think he always imagined it was in his power to win me back. I imagine that's why he kept the house this way. Whereas the truth was that I'd never have returned here, no matter what he did.' She looked down, examining her hands. 'Maybe that wasn't fair on him. And I didn't anticipate the long estrangement from the kids. I didn't want that for him or them. But he saw us as a package. He turned in on himself, lost his courage to go out and face the world.'

'But he must have got it back?' I said. 'With the memoir? That was brave.'

She lifted her chin. 'I don't know what triggered that. I really don't. Maybe he was desperate for another literary success so he decided to use his trump card? Or maybe it was a last act of desperation to win us back? His final dramatic chapter,' she said wryly. She looked down at the table again, scratching at a yellow crayon mark with her nail.

Something had been bothering me and now seemed like the ideal opportunity to ask. 'Why did you agree to take part in the documentary? I know you changed your mind. But why cooperate to begin with?'

She looked up. 'For the kids, I suppose. I thought it would be good for them to have something for posterity, having lost touch with their dad. And I wanted to save them from participating themselves. I guess that was the main reason. That was the deal with Gina Bailey. That she wouldn't ask them if I took part. But then I found out what she was up to, digging for something unpleasant, snuffling about like a pig looking for truffles, and I pulled out.'

'Did they know? Patrick and Susie.'

'About what Gavin did? No. Not then. They do now, of course.' She sighed again. 'Maybe you're right. I've been thinking that it was selfish of me making such a huge decision for them. But as you say, they're adults, and even without knowing what he did, they've never shown the slightest interest in getting in contact with him.'

It didn't take long to discover how wrong we both were.

Chapter Thirty-one

Having finished my tea, I decided I'd better go and find Phyllis, so I made my way back up to the main part of the house. Relieved to see her chatting to a woman I knew from Glendara, and no longer swivelling the big red ring on her finger, I decided I'd do what I was supposed to do at a wake and pay my respects.

Reluctantly – for it was a thing I always dreaded – I walked into the room housing the coffin. I'd managed to avoid the rush from when we'd first arrived, and Patrick and Susie were alone now, sitting on dining chairs pushed up against the wall, whispering together, their gazes fixed on the floor. Because of the post-mortem and the length of time since death, the coffin was closed. Small mercies.

They looked up when I approached, both smiling in recognition. I tried to imagine how strange this must be for them, waking a father they hadn't seen in so long. Other than the event at which he'd died, this must have been the first time they'd been in the same room as him since they were teenagers. And Susie hadn't even been at the event.

As I made my way over, Patrick got to his feet. 'Thanks for coming. Did you see Mum?'

'I've just had a cup of tea with her in the kitchen.'

Our conversation was drowned out by a commotion in the hall, the sounds of more people arriving. Seconds later, a woman of about Susie's age came in. She hesitated for a few seconds in the doorway as if searching for someone, before her face brightened in delighted recognition. Susie stood up, beaming, then her face crumpled and she started to cry. The woman rushed over and hugged her tightly.

'Susie's best friend from school,' Patrick whispered to me. 'They won't have seen each other in years.' He paused. 'Have you a few minutes or are you rushing off?'

'I have some time.'

'Let's leave them to it. There's something I want to ask you.'

The two women pulled apart and sat down side by side, gripping tightly onto each other's hands.

'Will you be okay if I leave you for a bit?' Patrick asked his sister and she nodded, wiping her eyes with a tissue.

He ushered me out of the room, past Phyllis who eyed us curiously, then out through the front door and into the garden. Immediately he tipped his head back and inhaled deeply, breathing in the fresh air and letting the rain fall onto his face. 'Oh, thank God. I can hardly breathe in there.'

'Too many memories?' I asked, knowing that it couldn't be a physical thing; the windows in the dining room were open as was traditional at a wake so there was plenty of air in there.

'Something like that.'

He led me over to the old sycamore tree with the swing, where we could shelter from the rain. It was still spitting though it wasn't heavy. He produced a box of Silk Cut cigarettes and offered me one. I shook my head.

He withdrew one for himself and lit it. 'Haven't smoked in years,' he said ruefully, blowing out smoke into the damp air. 'I started again on Monday.'

'I think you'd be forgiven for that.'

He smiled. 'I used to pinch Dad's Rothmans when I was a kid. They were rough. God knows how we smoked them.' He gazed up at the house, which looked imposing and mysterious in the afternoon mist; orange blocks for windows, the gunmetal sky above. 'I love this place and I hate it. The antique furniture, the clutter, it's so different from where I live at the moment. My wife likes clean lines and white walls. She couldn't face coming up here and I'm glad she didn't.'

'It must be strange being back after so long.'

He took a deep drag on his cigarette. 'I feel like I'm a teenager again here. I keep expecting to hear his voice. His tread on the stairs.'

I knew what that felt like. I still heard my sister's voice in my head. Her laugh.

'It wasn't easy growing up here. Everything revolved around him. Everything was sacrificed on the mountain of Gavin Featherstone's talent.'

Though his words sounded bitter his tone didn't somehow, as if he was just stating a fact. It was a lot like what his mother had said, and I wondered if he was simply parroting something he'd heard growing up.

'Susie had ADHD as a child. She was always running around, making noise, annoying him. My son has it now too but he has meds which help. I don't know what we'd do without my mother. She minds him a lot now that she's stopped working.' He put his hand to his forehead as if he was tired and it hit me that he *was* actually grieving for his dad. 'I know my mother wasn't happy. But we loved him, myself and Susie. He talked to us, you know?'

I looked at him with interest as he flicked the ash from his cigarette onto the grass.

'Oh, there were times when we had to be quiet, when he was working and we had to stay out of his study, but he was still more engaged than many of our friends' dads. I guess because he was usually at home.' He smiled suddenly at the memory. 'He used to make up words. *Who's run off with the hoochiflicker?* he'd ask, with a completely straight face. We'd count his sneezes; he had this thing where he'd sneeze up to twenty times. I wonder now if it was an allergy. I've never seen anyone do it since.'

He fidgeted with the cigarette between his fingers, flicking it repeatedly and agitatedly, and I sensed he was about to broach whatever he'd wanted to speak to me about.

He looked at me levelly. 'When do you think we'll have it sorted? Honestly? The estate, I mean.'

'Honestly? I have no idea. These things can go on for years if no agreement is reached. I should warn you; it will also be expensive.'

'I was afraid you'd say that.' His furrowed brow made him look older than his thirty-odd years. 'The truth is, and we don't want our mother to know this, but we both need money. My business is in trouble and Susie is about to leave her husband in the States.' He squared his shoulders and took a deep breath. 'Dad promised to help us both but he died before he could.'

My eyes widened in surprise. 'You were in touch with him?'

Patrick nodded, looking down. His feet were shod in expensive loafers, which I saw now were scuffed and needed replacing. Something I hadn't noticed while he'd been sitting on the other side of my desk. Gold watch, battered shoes; a story of declining fortunes.

'We hadn't seen him,' he said. 'It was just phone and email, so far. I was hoping to talk to him properly when we came up for his event. Mum doesn't know.' He added quickly, 'And we don't want her to.'

'Why not?' I asked.

'We're afraid she'd see it as a betrayal.'

From what Barbara had just told me in the kitchen, that seemed unlikely. And I said so.

Patrick shrugged. 'She's very proud of never having asked him for anything. For herself, I mean – he paid maintenance for us, I think. I don't think she'd like it that we've both gone to him for money.' He looked sheepish. 'I thought it was just me. I didn't realise Susie had too until she came over this week and we talked. She didn't know I was having difficulties either.'

'But he was willing to help you out?' I asked. 'Your dad, I mean.'

He nodded. 'From what Susie says, he was glad we asked. Happy to have some contact with us at last. We know now why he stayed away, of course, in case Mum went to the guards about what she knew; I think she held it over him. So he was pleased to hear from us without Mum knowing.'

'I see.'

He took another drag and dropped his head, examining the burning tip. 'I don't know if your parents are still around?'

'They are.' I smiled.

He looked up again. 'Did you ever think that there are parts of them that you can never quite reach. Even as their child?'

'Oh God, yes. But then I expect it's the same for them.'

'True. I've always felt that about Mum, but Dad seemed more transparent; easier to read. You could always tell when he was happy or sad, or angry or jealous.' He smiled. 'I wanted to impress him when I was a kid, so I wrote some really bad poetry. But I soon discovered there was only one artist allowed in our family. He didn't quite put my efforts down but he didn't encourage me either. I think he was happy that neither of us were creative and he didn't try to hide it.'

266

Patrick's eyes drifted as he stared at the house again. 'So then to discover that he had this huge secret that he'd been hiding. That's been pretty shocking. I always assumed it was his infidelities that made Mum leave him. I never imagined anything like that.'

'But he obviously reached a point in his life where he was willing to admit to everything,' I said, 'writing that memoir.'

'Yes.' Patrick reached out to touch the swing, pushing it distractedly. 'I don't know why that was, when he hadn't been willing before. He lost all those years with us, and with Mum.'

I didn't say that his mother wouldn't have been willing to be with his dad even if he had done what she'd wanted.

'You don't think it was because he was hoping for a relationship with his grandkids?' I asked, gesturing towards the swing. 'That seems new, and you and Susie are certainly too old for it.'

Patrick looked at the wooden seat and the orange rope as if seeing them for the first time. 'Maybe. I hadn't thought of that.'

He finished his cigarette, taking one final deep drag before grinding it out in the grass with the heel of his shoe, then carefully picking up the butt between his thumb and forefinger. 'Suppose we'd better go back,' he said in a resigned tone.

Once inside, I left him to return to his post while I went in search of Phyllis again. This time I was definitely ready to leave, anxious to get back to my parents.

Barbara called to me from the midst of some people she was chatting to in the hall. They were clustered around a large sideboard, as if she was showing them something. 'If you're looking for your friend, she asked if she could go out and have a look at the shore.'

'Great, thanks.'

'Do you know the way?'

'I'll find it, thank you.'

I made my way to the back of the house, through the kitchen and the courtyard and along the path leading to the little gate that accessed the shore. The padlock was now gone, and I unhooked the catch to step out onto the rocks.

Phyllis was standing there alone, facing the sea, silhouetted against the wash of silver light that stained the horizon, seemingly oblivious to the cascade of spray that rose up around her. She didn't hear me approach, probably because of the seabirds, which whirled overhead, squabbling and chiding one another and making a racket.

I took half a step closer and I saw that she was crying, tears welling in her eyes and tumbling down her cheeks. I said her name and she turned. I'd startled her and she was immediately embarrassed, brushing furiously at her checks with her sleeve. There was something in her hand, which I caught a brief glimpse of before she shoved it quickly into her pocket.

She forced a smile. 'Are you ready to go?'

I made no comment, just nodded.

On our way back through the entrance hall, our attention was drawn to the sideboard where Barbara had been earlier. There was a display of pictures on it, which I presumed she'd taken out especially for the wake. They depicted Featherstone's life and his achievements, forming a sort of pictorial obituary – from the beginning of his career to the present day. The last time I'd been in the house, the only pictures displayed were of Featherstone's absent family.

There were photographs of him receiving the Booker Prize and the IMPAC. Another showed him as a very young man standing at a lectern, performing a reading as writer-in-residence at Queen's, and then years later, a group photograph with his class when he was professor of creative writing; in this one he was wearing a black gown.

'He'd some career,' someone behind us remarked, with a whistle.

Phyllis stayed silent. I sensed her holding her breath and I wondered if she was afraid that she was in one of the photographs. I scanned the class picture from Queen's, but couldn't find her.

Then I stopped dead. In the front row, another familiar face appeared: pale and thin, wearing glasses with long red hair falling in curtains around her face. Unlike the other students in the photograph, she wasn't looking at the camera. Instead, she turned her adoring face towards her teacher. It was Róisín Henderson.

Chapter Thirty-two

The same Róisín Henderson who claimed never to have met Gavin Featherstone until their event. I remembered her clearly telling me this on the Saturday we'd had coffee outside the Oak. The day after he died.

Without warning, Barbara was beside us. 'I see you've found my rogues gallery.'

I'd inhaled so sharply and audibly that she'd come over to investigate.

She smiled, reaching out to straighten one of the pictures. 'I went looking for photographs yesterday and I found these in a rusty filing cabinet in the cellar. Just shoved in there among the paint and the jam jars and the torn lampshades. All these treasures covered in cobwebs and rat droppings! I cleaned them up, found some frames and thought I'd display them today.' She crossed her arms. 'Impressive, isn't it, when you see it all together?'

I nodded vaguely but was too distracted to admire her work. 'Did you know Gavin had taught Róisín Henderson?' I pointed to the group photograph.

Barbara frowned. 'Róisín Henderson?' She repeated the name as if she didn't know who I meant. Then she peered in. 'Oh. Isn't that the woman who interviewed him last Friday?' She stopped for a second as if it suddenly hit her that it was only a week ago it had all happened.

'Yes. I think it is.'

Phyllis hung back and I sensed her stiffen again. Did she already know that Róisín had been taught by Featherstone? If so, why hadn't she said anything?

Barbara lifted up the framed picture to have a closer look, then transferred her gaze to me. 'It *is* her. She's still around, isn't she? I think I've seen her in Glendara in the past few days.'

I nodded. Why *had* Róisín lied about knowing Featherstone? I wondered. Especially in the context of their joint event. Surely a previous connection like that was the kind of thing that would amuse an audience, if nothing else?

'I'm not surprised they clashed a bit on Friday, now,' Barbara said, placing the picture back down onto the sideboard, positioning it carefully between the two awards pictures. 'Gavin could be a tough enough taskmaster. Had no difficulty in humiliating his students if he felt they weren't fulfilling their potential.' Her gaze moved to the pictures on either side, Featherstone's glory days. 'It was easy for him, of course. He didn't let them get away with using youth and inexperience as an excuse for underperforming. He could always point to his own early success.'

'No. *His* failures came later.' The voice behind us was bitter.

Barbara turned to see who was speaking.

I assumed Phyllis would immediately regret what she'd said, expecting to find her flushed, embarrassed face, but she persisted, waving her arm at the display. 'This makes him look as if he was always successful. But he actually wrote some pretty lousy books.'

There was a sharp intake of breath from some people nearby. Phyllis was breaking the etiquette of the wake, speaking ill of the dead, criticising a dead writer's talent while his body was still cooling across the hall.

But his widow didn't seem to mind. 'Well, yes,' Barbara admitted, reasonably. 'That's certainly true. They weren't all good and they didn't all sell. But he hadn't had any failures by that stage. While he was teaching, he was still very successful. And cocky,' she conceded, with a smile. 'Always cocky. Although his students still seemed to adore him.'

I looked at the picture again. Róisín Henderson certainly did. Her expression was unmistakeable. The student had a massive crush on her professor. So why, then, wasn't she here to say goodbye to a man she had so clearly adored?

The camera crew were gone from opposite the gate when we left. Phyllis glanced over as we pulled away, before she took out her phone and began tapping.

'What are you up to?' I flipped on the indicator to execute a wide U-turn to drive back to Glendara.

She clicked her teeth in disgust. 'I cannot believe that I missed that.'

'That Róisín Henderson was Gavin Featherstone's student? So, you didn't know? You weren't there at the same time?' I hadn't really thought they had been – there must have been ten years between Phyllis and Róisín.

She shook her head distractedly as the tapping became more intense, more urgent. What was she doing? Googling?

'I just thought she was a secret fan, despite all that novel-versus-short-story guff. She'd read all his books. But she never once mentioned that she knew him.' She gave me a sidelong look. 'And yes, I know that I lied about knowing him too. But I had good reason.'

I hesitated before I replied. 'Maybe she did too.' The same reason, I wondered?

Phyllis didn't respond to that. 'I was so distracted with getting the shop finished that I didn't do my usual research before inviting her to the festival . . . So stupid. I'd never normally have let that slip through the cracks. Left too much to bloody Tony and Stan.' She went back to peering at her phone, taking her glasses from her bag and slipping them on while she read something on the screen.

While we waited to take the right turn towards Glendara from Moville, I remembered that it was Róisín Henderson who'd made me suspect that Phyllis was lying about the row with Featherstone before the event. Now I'd discovered that Róisín was a liar too.

'Gotcha!' Phyllis's eyes widened as she took a sharp inhale of breath. 'So that's why you kept the connection to yourself,' she muttered. 'Because you were afraid someone would find what I've just found. And I would have found it earlier if I hadn't been so bloody distracted.'

'What is it?' I asked, very interested now.

'There's no way I'd have put the two of them together if I'd known this.' Phyllis turned to me, her glasses halfway down her nose. 'What year was that photograph taken? The group one from Queen's with Róisín in it?'

I shrugged. There hadn't been a date on it but from the obituary I'd read in the paper, I could guess. 'Early 2000s?'

'Well, a few years after she left college, Róisín Henderson's old professor, Gavin Featherstone, wrote a review of her first novel in the *Literary Times*.'

'Her novel?' I raised one eyebrow curiously. 'But I thought she only wrote short stories?'

'It looks as if this was her only one. With good reason.'

273

'Oh?' I made a face. 'Not good?'

'Not good. The weird thing is that he doesn't even mention that he taught her – surely you should disclose that in a review?'

I nodded. 'You'd think.'

'Well, he doesn't.' Phyllis looked at me over her glasses. 'I'd say he forgot he even knew her.'

'Oh dear.' I remembered Róisín's look of adoration in that picture. 'How bad is the review?'

Phyllis gave me a narrow look, then pushed the glasses back up her nose and started to read. '"Clunky plot devices, implausible dialogue, an unnecessary twist and a preposterous ending all serve to make this novel problematic. But the book's principal difficulty is that it lacks momentum; there are too many story threads, making it impossible to follow and slowing the pace to an almost interminable lethargy. Ms Henderson is either trying to be too clever or she is not as clever as she thinks she is. One thing is certain – whatever it is she is trying to do; she fails to pull it off."'

'Ouch.' I hit the indicator to overtake a cyclist.

'Ouch is right.' Phyllis took her glasses off and peered crookedly at me. 'Would you kill someone if they gave you a terrible review? I know Robbie Cahill has already been arrested but, Lord . . .'

She continued to scroll through her phone as I drove the rest of the way to Glendara, while beside her I conducted an internal battle with myself. Even if I now suspected that Phyllis and Featherstone's row on the night of the event was about his intended reading, and what it contained, I didn't know that for certain. I'd been fighting the urge to ask her about it, but Molloy had told me not to say anything, which meant I found myself in the uncomfortable position of having to keep something from both him and Phyllis. I was stuck in the middle, being duplicitous with both.

When I dropped her outside the bookshop, Jude came out to greet us, giving me a friendly wave and sticking his head in through the driver's window to invite me for something to eat. I declined reluctantly – his soup had been pretty good.

As I drove away, watching him wrap his arm around Phyllis as they walked back to her place, I was struck by how happy I was that she'd found someone who clearly cared about her so much. In all the years I'd known her, I'd never seen her with anyone in that way, and I wondered if that had anything to do with her relationship with Featherstone.

She wasn't the only young woman for whom an early encounter with the great novelist had long-term consequences. Featherstone's acceptance of the invitation to Glenfest had shifted Róisín from the spotlight. And while Phyllis claimed she didn't mind because she'd be paid for two events – her workshop and the interview – it must have hurt, being sidelined at the last minute in favour of someone who had mercilessly denigrated your writing. Someone you had previously idolised.

I recalled Featherstone's needling of her during the event, his querying of her writing in Irish, his sneering at her reasons for writing short stories, the irony being that it now appeared that he was the one who had driven her away from writing novels in the first place. I remembered thinking that she had been on the verge of tears while they were talking about it. Now that made sense. Featherstone had destroyed her feelings for him. But was it possible she hated him enough to kill him?

He certainly hadn't been much of a mentor to her. He'd baited her, searched for her vulnerable spots, then poked at them mercilessly with a stick. Just as he'd done to Gina Bailey in that interview. Was it a coincidence that two women he'd damaged were in the vicinity when he died? My eyes widened when I remembered seeing them sharing a laugh on the street that day before I'd gone into the Garda Station, only a couple of days after Featherstone's death. Was it possible that they'd worked together to kill him?

I pictured again that clip of his TV interview with Gina Bailey, replaying it in my head. A car sounded its horn behind me and I realised I'd slowed almost to a halt. An image swam towards me, driving all other thoughts from my head. Needing to catch hold of it, I pulled the car over and parked in the gateway to a field.

Suddenly, I knew what Phyllis had been clutching in her hand on the shore earlier before she'd slipped it into the pocket of her dress. And where it had come from. Now that I'd seen it in my mind's eye, I couldn't unsee it. It was the silver quill earring that Gavin Featherstone had worn in his interview with Gina Bailey.

Chapter Thirty-three

The next morning, Sunday, the sky was clear, evidenced by the lemony light sneaking in through the gap in my curtains. I discovered I really felt like a swim. So, I fed Guinness, grabbed a towel and my togs and headed off for Lagg before my parents were up.

I'd slept well but awoken with a mind overflowing with the information I'd gleaned the day before. I tried to piece everything together and have it make some kind of sense; Patrick and Susie approaching their father for money without their mother's knowledge; Róisín Henderson hiding the fact that she was his student. And, foremost in my thoughts, that little silver quill.

Where had Phyllis got it? I was certain that Featherstone hadn't been wearing it at the event. Had she come across it lying on the rocks? Or was it in her possession before that? Featherstone mentioned 'hauling my body onto the rocks like a walrus'. Had he lost the quill while swimming one day? And why had Phyllis been crying? Did they swim together in the past off those same rocks, she and Featherstone?

All of this raced through my mind as I submerged my own body into the sea at Lagg, and I resolved to try to speak to her today if I could get her alone, something which would be more difficult with Jude's return.

The full force of the cold water gave me an almost electric shock, and my legs were numb as I stumbled back onto the sand and rubbed them to get some feeling back. But the sun on my face was reward enough, and my head was clear. I dried myself off and pulled back on my clothes, remembering my last swim just two days after Featherstone had died; how I'd run into Phyllis on the beach, distracted and grief-stricken, and also how she'd lied to me, or at least told me only half the truth. I was convinced that she was still hiding something that could get her into trouble.

I tugged on my jeans as a tall figure appeared in the gap between the dunes, silhouetted by the morning light behind. Definitely not Phyllis this time – it was completely the wrong shape. I was startled to see that it was Molloy. Jeans and a light blue T-shirt. Sunglasses. Off-duty handsome. My heart skipped a beat as it always did when I hadn't seen him for a while.

He was carrying two takeaway cups and a paper bag, which he raised in greeting. 'Thought you might want some breakfast after your exertions. Cappuccino and almond croissant do you?'

'Very nicely, thank you.' I shook the sand from my towel and rolled my wet togs into it. 'How did you know I was here?'

'I brought coffee and pastries to Malin. Thought I'd treat you all to breakfast. Your parents told me you were gone when they got up so I took a punt.'

I was weirdly touched. 'You know my habits.'

'I know your habits,' he agreed with a smile. I shoved my towel under my oxter and he handed me a cup. 'Not sure how hot it is. It's done a bit of a tour of the peninsula.'

We sat on a rock to have our breakfast. The coffee wasn't hot but it was nicely warm, and after the freezing water it hit my bloodstream and travelled around my body like the water in a radiator. We said nothing for a few minutes, eating our pastries and gazing out to sea, appreciating the view.

The beach was deserted this early on a Sunday morning, and we had clear sight of the brooding and mysterious rock which was Glashedy Island, a place I was determined to get out to someday. We watched the gulls circle and ride the air currents – exuberant and joyful or squabbling, it was hard to tell – and the little oystercatchers wading along the shore. The white sand and blue sky so exquisite it made you want to cry. I'd been feeling more emotional than usual this week, thinking a lot about mortality. Maybe it was all the wills? Maybe it was Leah's pregnancy? Or maybe it was the fact that my parents were still close by and I'd discovered I liked it.

Molloy watched me as if reading my thoughts and then looked down, pushing at the sand with his foot, clouds of little sand-hoppers leaping away in response to the massive earthquake he'd caused in their world. 'I'm sorry I haven't been around much since your parents got here. God knows what they think of me.'

I smiled. It never occurred to me that this would bother him. 'They like you,' I assured him. 'And, anyway, you do have a murder to solve. You were in Belfast on Friday.'

'This is true.'

'Do you still have Robbie Cahill in custody?'

He nodded, taking a deep breath and a sip of his coffee. 'For the moment. We're going to have to release him later today; he's coming to the end of his detention period and his solicitor is getting antsy. He's not admitting to anything, but he has drawn our attention to a couple of things.'

'Such as?' I paused and raised my eyebrows. 'If you don't mind telling me.'

He grinned. 'It's a bit late for that, don't you think?'

An acknowledgement from Molloy of his operating outside the rules. I liked it.

'He's told us that Featherstone wasn't well.'

I nodded. 'The heart condition. We knew that . . .'

'Well, no, there was something more serious. Or more imminent. He also had pretty advanced lung cancer. Terminal. It was likely he'd be dead in a few years.'

'Right.' I recalled the man's slight breathlessness, his hand on his chest during the event. Patrick's mention of stealing his father's strong cigarettes as a teenager.

'His family didn't know because he didn't tell them. But Cahill was the one who had to drive him to appointments for treatment, collect his medication.' Molloy took a sip of his coffee. 'It did get a mention on the post-mortem report, but we didn't pay a lot of attention to it since it wasn't what killed him.'

I absorbed this latest information. It made sense of a few things. 'So that's why he was finally prepared to admit what he'd done. He was facing down the barrel of his own mortality.'

'That seems likely.'

'He could do all the interviews and festivals he wanted to publicise the book, soak up all the attention that came with the huge admission he'd made, and then, with a bit of luck,' I added dryly, 'he might even be dead by the time his trial came around.' I paused. 'Did Robbie know that Featherstone had killed his father?'

Molloy nodded. 'He did. Only recently, he claims. Featherstone told him while he was writing the memoir.'

That fitted too, I thought. It explained the row that the postman had overheard.

'He claims that's what caused his relapse. He was going to leave Featherstone and go back to Belfast but Featherstone wouldn't let him. He helped him get back on the wagon, and insisted on making a new will in his favour, to make sure he had somewhere to live after he died.'

My eyes widened. 'Wow.'

'Cahill swears it was something Featherstone wanted. That he insisted Robbie go out and buy the readymade will. They even had the postman come in to witness it.'

I'd checked the copy of the will Thompson had sent me but hadn't recognised the postman's name. Although it did explain his sudden reluctance to keep talking to me when he realised who I was, probably guessing that I was acting for Featherstone's family.

'Cahill claims Featherstone told him he'd made an earlier will in favour of his family but that this would override it,' Molloy said.

'Revoke,' I said, automatically.

'Revoke,' Molloy said, accepting the correction with a side glance.

'But he left everything to Robbie, not just the house,' I protested.

Molloy nodded. 'Robbie says he didn't want that but Featherstone insisted. He was uneasy inheriting money but Featherstone claimed that his ex-wife didn't want anything, that she'd always refused anything he'd offered, and that he intended taking care of his kids before he died.'

Was that true, I wondered? It aligned with some of what Patrick had told me, that his father was planning on helping him and his sister before he died. But why had Featherstone been so anxious to keep Cahill living with him, to stop him from returning to Belfast? Was he afraid Cahill would report what he'd done? Or was it the fact that he was dying and needed someone with him? Or was it a more laudable reason than that – that he'd witnessed how vulnerable Robbie was during his relapse and didn't want to wreck the guy's life all over again by leaving him homeless after he died.

Then I remembered what Barbara had said about Featherstone 'getting invited to all the festivals' after admitting what he'd done. About the invitations drying up before that.

'God, maybe Featherstone planned to have Robbie with him on the publicity tour for the memoir?' I said. 'As a kind of restorative justice thing.' I recalled a documentary I'd seen about an IRA bomber and the daughter of one of his victims who'd become close, and gave interviews together.

'Who knows? It's possible. In a way that's another motive for Robbie Cahill. I can't imagine it's something he'd have been keen on.' Molloy sighed. 'We've no shortage of motives for the man but somehow I just don't know if we have enough to charge him.'

I was silent for a few seconds.

'What are you thinking?' Molloy asked.

'I'm not convinced that Robbie Cahill killed Gavin Featherstone.'

Molloy frowned and crossed his arms, hooking his empty coffee cup on his thumb. 'You've changed your tune. Why not?'

I told him my thinking; that to claim his inheritance Cahill would have to take on the family with no guarantee of success and the risk of a great deal of expense, that he had probably been better off with Featherstone alive. He'd had a secure job and a home, important for a recovering addict. And that while I was pretty sure he'd taken the pages from the marquee and deleted the draft from Featherstone's computer, he had done both those things after Featherstone collapsed. He'd known that Featherstone had killed his father and been okay with his intended public confession *until* Featherstone died and he knew he'd be an immediate suspect. Which meant that he hadn't known that the man was going to die.

Molloy thought for a minute. 'Okay – those are reasonable points.'

'And,' my brain quickly processed the additional information I'd just gleaned, 'the fact that he was dying of lung cancer would be another reason for Robbie Cahill not to kill him. If his motive was inheritance, what would be the point if he'd be dead soon anyway? And if Robbie was the only one who knew that, then surely it puts those who *didn't* know in the frame instead.'

'That's everyone apart from Robbie Cahill and Featherstone's doctors,' Molloy sighed. He checked his watch. 'Do you want to walk for a bit?'

We stuffed our cups into the paper bag and set off along the beach.

'By the way,' Molloy said, 'that day you saw Cahill coming out of the methadone clinic, he'd just found out that a friend of his had died. Another recovering addict. A young guy, only eighteen.'

My heart sank. That explained his demeanour on the day. Had I misjudged the man completely?

'I went to the wake yesterday,' I said. 'I brought Phyllis.'

Molloy nodded. 'They asked our permission to do it, but I thought I'd give it a wide berth. Let them have their goodbye. How was it?'

'Packed. Lots of curious people. But they wanted it that way.' I paused. 'Did you know Featherstone taught Róisín Henderson in college? The writer who interviewed him at the event. There was a picture of him with his students in the house and she was in it.'

'Okay,' he said slowly, raising his eyebrows. 'This is the woman who's running the workshop your mum is going to this morning?'

I smiled. He'd had quite the chat with my parents.

'She didn't mention that when we questioned her,' he conceded. 'But was it a secret?'

'She told me that she'd never met him,' I said. 'And he didn't mention knowing her either, though I think *he* simply forgot. Phyllis didn't know when she scheduled the event and seems a bit put out about it.'

'I believe Phyllis knew him pretty well herself,' Molloy said in a voice heavy with meaning.

So, she'd told him that much, I thought, with relief, conscious that while I was sharing my suspicions of everyone else, I was avoiding any mention of those I had of the bookseller.

'Plus, he gave Róisín a very rough review a few years later, for her first novel. I can't imagine she felt too kindly towards him. She never wrote another one.'

'Enough to kill him?' Molloy said sceptically. I could see he wasn't taking this seriously.

I shrugged. 'Maybe not but I imagine people can feel very strongly about these things. He was also very rough on Gina Bailey; she interviewed him when she was just starting out. It seemed he didn't much like young women snapping at his heels. He tended to kick them away, and fairly viciously from what I've observed.'

'All right,' Molloy said. 'Noted. I need to go and speak with Gina Bailey tomorrow anyway. But I'll have a word with Miss Henderson too and see what she has to say.'

'How is Gina Bailey doing?'

'Better. No permanent kidney damage, they think. She says

she made a mistake with her insulin but the hospital says otherwise, they say she consumed so much sugar that she couldn't have done it by mistake – she's been a diabetic since she was a child. We assume it happened in the Oak but it was too late to find whatever it was.'

We walked along in silence for a few minutes, enjoying the sound of the steadily breaking waves, watching the gulls and kicking at the rags of kelp and bladderwrack that were strewn across the beach.

Until Molloy cleared his throat. Never a good sign. He did it when he wanted to broach a personal subject. 'There was something else I wanted to talk to you about.'

'Oh?' I felt a pinch. Was this what he'd mentioned on the morning of Featherstone's event?

'I'm not sure how you're going to react. But I thought I should discuss it with you.'

Formal language. It must be something emotional. My stomach somersaulted. Things had been good between us recently, or at least on an even keel. Were we about to go through one of our tunnels again?

'I'm about to be promoted to inspector.'

My face broke into a smile as I felt my heart leap for him. 'That's fantastic! Congratulations.'

Molloy had entered the guards late after a career in science, which meant his progress up the ranks had been slower than average for his stage of life. This was important to him.

I reached out to give him a hug and found myself babbling into his chest, my eyes welling. 'I love you too, you know. I didn't get a chance to say it to you on the side of the road after our accident, but I do. So much. And I'm really proud of you and pleased for you.'

I trailed off. Something was wrong. His body was stiff. I pulled back. Why was his face so clouded? He looked sad. Why did he look sad?

'What's wrong?' I asked, feeling panicked again.

'It'll mean I'll be transferred. Probably to the other end of the country. I might end up back in Letterkenny eventually if I can request a transfer, but I'll be gone for a long time.'

I closed my eyes and watched a showreel of our relationship to date. Molloy disappearing when he'd been transferred the last time, not answering my calls or texts. Losing contact. There had been a reason for it at the time but now I was filled with a churning disquiet. What if that happened again? And then I thought about where we were now, how he'd been with my parents, how supportive. I should have expected this promotion. Molloy was a good guard. I'd miss him like hell but if geography was all that was concerning him, then I should be able to handle that.

'But that's okay,' I said. 'You'll still be in the country. We can do long distance, can't we?'

He smiled and his face cleared. 'Do you really think we could last if I left for a while? We didn't manage too well before.'

'That's because you disappeared on me,' I said.

'And you went out with someone else.'

'*Because* you disappeared on me,' I retorted.

We both laughed, and somehow it felt okay. That it was going to be okay. He reached for my hand and we walked together along the sand, the sun on our faces. And I knew that we were in a very different place now and that I liked it here.

Chapter Thirty-four

Back in Malin, my dad had lit an unnecessary but welcome fire in my sitting room, settling himself in contentedly with the newspapers and a pot of coffee while my mum was at her workshop in the library in Glendara.

'Your sergeant was here,' he said looking up, glasses halfway down his nose. 'Did he find you?'

'He did.' I sat down on the other armchair.

'I asked him what his intentions were,' he winked.

'You're hilarious,' I said, getting up and returning to the kitchen to grab myself a mug before coming back in and pouring myself some coffee. 'As a matter of fact, he's getting a promotion.' I told him Molloy's news and the fact that he'd be leaving Inishowen for a while.

Dad's face fell, far more than I'd have expected it to. What did it matter to him where Molloy went? Until he asked, 'Are you going with him, wherever he's posted?'

I smiled. 'No, Dad. I'll be staying here. My practice is here. He's hoping to be reposted to Letterkenny at some point, but I have to be here in the meantime.'

His face cleared. 'But you're staying together?'

'We're staying together. What about you two?' I asked. 'What are your plans after you sign your wills tomorrow? You're welcome to stay as long as you like, you know. Consider it an extended summer holiday?'

'I'll need to speak to your mother and see what she thinks.' He avoided my gaze, returning to his sports pages, and I decided not to push it.

We were contentedly and silently immersed in separate parts of the newspaper when my mother arrived back, eyes shining and looking more excited than I'd seen her in a long time.

'How did you get on?' I asked, glancing up at the sound of the sitting-room door opening, although her expression was answer enough.

She sank down beside my dad, tumbling foolscap, notebooks and pens onto the coffee table and shoving aside Gavin Featherstone's novel, which she'd left there after finishing it a few days before.

'You know, she's really very good,' she said. 'She thinks I should keep going with what I'm working on, that I might have something.'

My dad beamed as proudly as if my mum was his little girl.

'Very constructive in her criticism,' she continued, 'but very encouraging. She loves Stan's crime novel with the hairdresser sleuth!'

I laughed. 'I'd read that.'

'And she's really generous with her time. She's leaving tomorrow to go back to Galway, but we're all meeting up for a drink in the Oak this evening so we can ask her any last-minute questions about our work. Once we've had a chance to absorb what went on in the workshop.'

'That is generous,' I said, amused to see that she had a copy of Róisín Henderson's short-story collection along with her notes;

Róisín's plan to sell a few copies of her books had clearly succeeded. I wondered if she'd replaced Gavin Featherstone in my mother's affections, until I spotted an old hardback of *The Peering of Things*, the Booker winner she'd expressed an intention to reread, which she must have borrowed from the library.

'I'll drop you in if you like. It'll save you driving and then you can have a drink.'

'That would be great.'

'What are you writing? Novel or short story?' I smiled, recalling the clash between Róisín and Featherstone.

'It's a sort of memoir.' She glanced at Featherstone's book and sighed happily. 'What a lovely library you have.'

That evening I dropped my mother at the Oak for her meet up with Róisín Henderson and the rest of her workshop attendees. I was about to pull away again from the curb when, in the rearview mirror, I saw Phyllis coming up the street. I waited for her, thinking that this could be my opportunity to speak to her alone, but she stopped, turned and Jude appeared, emerging from the door of the bookshop and locking it behind him.

They spotted the Mini and stopped to chat.

'Coming in for a drink?' Jude asked, nodding at the door of the Oak.

'We're just having a quick one before dinner,' Phyllis added. 'Jude's made a Spanish stew. Come and eat with us if you like.'

I shook my head and explained how I'd been dropping my mother off to meet with Róisín's workshop group.

Phyllis's response was classic festival programmer. 'Did she enjoy it?'

'She certainly seemed to.'

'Ah, good. Are you coming back in for her?'

I nodded. We'd joked on the way in about how our roles had been reversed with my doing the dropping off and collecting. I'd wanted to save my dad the drive, leaving him to relax with a bottle of red and Guinness on his knee, pleased to see that touch of contentment returning now that they had resolved the issue with their wills. My sister's death had infused every element of their lives for so long that I was grateful for this partial recovery. And loath to put it at risk by exposing them again to Chambers. Wherever the hell he was.

'Sure, you'll probably only be home when you have to come back. Come on in and have a chat,' Jude urged.

I liked Jude and I hadn't seen him properly since he'd been back so I agreed, unhooked my seatbelt and joined them as they went into the pub.

Róisín Henderson and her group, including my mother, were sitting at a big round table with notebooks and drinks in front of them. Stan was there too, gesticulating wildly beside my mother who glanced up at me in surprise, initially worried, before smiling when she saw who I was with.

Jude offered me a drink before going to the bar while I joined Phyllis at a smaller table. 'Non-alcoholic beer, please.'

There was a laugh from Róisín's group as we sat down. It was obvious that the writer was very much the centre of attention and admiration at her table.

'Did you get to speak to her about Featherstone?' I asked Phyllis.

She nodded, settling herself on her stool. 'I helped her set up the workshop in the library this morning. She just denied that she'd ever hidden her connection to him, as if it was somehow my mistake. But I *know* she did. I know she told me she didn't know him.'

I knew she had too. I'd asked her directly. But then I'd also asked Phyllis some direct questions, which she hadn't answered truthfully either. I glanced at Jude, his huge frame blocking my view of the bar. How long did I have, I wondered? He shifted slightly to one side to reach for his wallet in the back pocket of his jeans and I saw that he was waiting for a pint of Guinness to settle, which meant that I had a few minutes.

I lowered my voice. 'Phyllis, that row I overheard between you and Featherstone . . .'

She looked so stricken that I almost regretted mentioning it. But I persisted. 'You told me it was about him refusing to sign books, but Róisín said that he'd offered her a lift down so they could do it together. Was she lying about that too?'

Phyllis started twirling her red ring again, round and round her finger. I pictured that silver quill. Did she still have it?

'Please, Phyllis. Molloy is struggling with this investigation, trying to work out what happened and who was involved. I know there's something you're not telling me, so I'm caught in the middle. Either you or Róisín are not being wholly truthful. And I can't see why Róisín would lie about something like that.'

She sighed, a deep tense sigh. 'Róisín was telling the truth. About this anyway. The row Gavin and I had wasn't about the signing. It was about something else, to do with our history.' She looked at me, her eyes pleading. 'But it's nothing to do with his death, I promise. It's private. It's nothing anyone else needs to know.'

'Are you sure about that?' I leaned in so I could lower my voice even further. 'Gavin Featherstone was murdered. What if this is relevant and you just don't know it?'

She looked away. The shutters had come down. 'Please, Ben. Don't press me on this. Just take my word for it. I've kept your secrets in the past. Allow me this one, please.'

I fell silent. Because what could I say to that? She was right. And there was no point in asking her about the quill if she wouldn't tell me about the row. It was clear that she hadn't wanted me to see it.

Jude returned from the bar with our drinks and whatever opportunity I'd had was lost. We tried to chat, the three of us, but I was sure he could sense the strained atmosphere. I was almost relieved when my phone rang and I could go outside to answer it.

It was Molloy. 'We've tracked down Chambers.'

'You're kidding. How? When? Where?'

'Well, we don't physically have him yet but we know who he is. One of the Ballyfermot guards who saw him trying to get into the house took a photograph on his phone, not something he should have done, strictly speaking. He did his own bit of investigation, sending the picture around to a few colleagues, including the fraud squad, and he discovered his real name. Chambers is actually David Varian, and he's done this before.'

I blew out a loud breath. 'That's great news. I'm so relieved.'

'Good. Leave it with me.'

There was a tap on my shoulder. It was Jude. He and Phyllis were leaving the Oak to head back to her place. Phyllis wouldn't meet my eye when I waved goodbye.

Molloy was still speaking. Now I could hear a smile in his voice. 'I know they keep trying to leave but see if you can persuade your parents to stay a couple more days. We might have some progress by then.'

'Will do.'

Back in the pub I saw, gratefully, that my mother's group was breaking up, too, and I stood awkwardly while she and Stan and the others said goodbye, each one thanking Róisín in turn.

I was considering giving her a wave to let her know I'd wait in the car when the pub door opened and Robbie Cahill came in, released, presumably at the end of his detention period. He looked tired, older somehow, as if the whole experience had taken it out of him, and it hit me that they'd have had to get his methadone to him while he was in custody.

I half expected a general intake of breath at the arrival of a man suspected of murder but of course few people in Glendara knew who he was. Which made me wonder at his being in Glendara at all on a Sunday night, rather than returning to Shore Lodge. Then I realised he was here to meet Róisín.

She didn't seem in the least self-conscious about it. She gave him a friendly wave and the five-minute sign and he stood there, as I did, waiting for the leave-taking to be finished; Stan now clapping somebody enthusiastically on the back, while my mother laughed along.

Though we were only a couple of metres apart, I was surprised when Robbie spoke to me. 'That your mother?' he asked.

I acknowledged that she was, feeling a little wrong-footed until I remembered that he'd run into us together going into Thompson's.

'She do Róisín's class?'

'Yes.' I wasn't sure I really wanted to get into a friendly chat with this man. Not because he'd been arrested for murder but because he was someone else's client in a case where I represented the other side. I also felt slightly ashamed about judging him so quickly.

He didn't seem to bear me any ill will. 'Drink?' he offered. 'That looks like it might go on for a while.'

He was right. It reminded me of the long goodbyes of my mother's family. My dad would be sitting in the car with myself and Faye revving the engine while the hugs were still going on.

293

I declined his offer but this time I gave him a smile. Because something had just occurred to me. Robbie Cahill would know about that quill earring. If Phyllis wouldn't speak to me, there was nothing to stop me asking him about it.

I cleared my throat like Molloy about to tackle something tricky. 'While I was at the wake yesterday, I found something on the rocks behind the house. I thought it might belong to Gavin?'

He frowned. 'What was it?'

'You know that silver earring he wore, the quill?'

He looked at me blankly and shook his head.

'Hang on,' I said, taking out my phone and searching for the video of Featherstone and Gina Bailey. Finding it, I froze a close up of Featherstone's face, which showed the earring, and I handed it to him.

His eyes narrowed as he looked at the screen. Within seconds he'd handed it back to me. 'I never knew him wear anything on that earring – it was always just a sleeper. And I knew him more than ten years.'

Chapter Thirty-five

On Monday morning I was up early, mainlining coffee after a not-great night's sleep. Today would be mostly spent interviewing candidates for Leah's maternity cover and I'd been dreading it. I was grateful that she herself had agreed to sit in, despite having to close the office for a few hours to do it.

While I was thankful too that progress had finally been made on Chambers – that Ballyfermot guard was in line for a cracking bottle of whiskey from me – my parents had both been very quiet when I'd told them about it, although they assured me that they wouldn't leave until there was more news. Their appointment with Thompson wasn't till late this afternoon and, in their world, it would certainly be too late for them to drive back to Dublin today.

Letting Guinness in through the window, I poured myself an extra mug and searched for something to take my mind off things. The side of the Donegal Creameries milk carton didn't keep me occupied for more than a minute, so I went into the sitting room to fetch *Violet, Green and Red*, Featherstone's book, still lying discarded on the coffee table. Beside it was the older novel, *The Peering of Things*, which my mother had borrowed from the library. I brought them both back into the kitchen with me.

The blurb on the back cover of *Violet, Green and Red* indicated that it was about an artist, middle-aged and male, who'd had multiple affairs. Sounded familiar. I flicked through it as I sipped my coffee with one eye on the clock. I didn't have long; the first candidate was due in half an hour. I found myself becoming unexpectedly absorbed, wondering if part of the reason my mother hadn't liked this book was because the protagonist was too close to Featherstone himself. There were definite similarities.

As I got a sense of where the story was going, I wondered suddenly if there were truths to be found in Featherstone's fiction as well as his memoir. Truths he was less willing to reveal? The memoir was something he controlled, the telling of his own story massaged for the benefit of his family and public. But had his fiction revealed elements of his character and his past that he may not have intended? One plot thread in particular bothered me. If I pulled at it, would it unravel everything else?

I glanced across at the older novel turned face-down on the kitchen table, a much-borrowed, old hardback edition with a cracked spine. I picked it up, opening the back cover where there was a black and white photograph of a much younger Featherstone. With no beard and no stubble, he had the look of a young Kirk Douglas.

I froze, mug halfway to my mouth. Now I knew why Phyllis had stiffened when we were looking at Barbara's rogue's gallery in Shore Lodge. A tiny thing. But suddenly it all seemed so obvious that I drove to work kicking myself that I hadn't guessed it before.

'So, what do you like to read?' I asked.

Lord, these interviews were interminable. Although I knew my concentration wasn't helped by the fact that my mind kept drifting back to the revelation I'd had before leaving the house, which I'd had no chance to pursue since being greeted by a waiting room full of candidates.

The young woman sitting across the desk from Leah and me had put reading at the top of her list of pastimes, but she was wearing such enormous fake eyelashes that I wondered how she could see out of those spiders' legs to read anything.

'Oh, *Take a Break*, *Chat*, *Hello*. I'm mad for all of them magazines.' She waved a set of pink talons at me, lashes fluttering like the pampas grass in Featherstone's garden.

'Okay,' I said slowly.

'Oh, aye. That one too.' She beamed at me as if we'd found some common ground.

'Right,' I said, wearily, appealing to Leah for assistance but finding that she too was distracted, her gaze fixed on the floor.

I made myself focus. This was important. I'd have to work with whoever I chose for at least six months. 'And how would you handle client confidentiality, do you think? You know that if you worked here, you wouldn't be able to breathe a word of what happens in here outside the office.'

The girl nodded seriously. 'Oh aye. I understand that . . .' She trailed off, her eyes drifting to my left. She lowered her voice. 'Is she all right?'

I turned quickly. Leah was sitting with her eyes closed, rubbing her stomach. As if sensing our scrutiny, she blinked them open and gave a weak smile. 'I'm fine, thanks.'

I leaped to my feet. 'Thank you very much for coming and we'll be in touch soon.' I ushered the startled girl out of the room and through the front door, returning to Leah on a wave of guilt. She hadn't been herself all morning but I hadn't even asked her what was wrong, being too preoccupied by my own concerns. As usual.

I closed the door quietly. 'Are you okay? Seriously?'

When she looked up, her eyes were swimming with tears. 'I haven't felt the baby move in a few hours. I've been too busy.'

I felt sick. It had been Leah who had put together the applications and the CVs ready for each interview, everything done for me by the time I sailed in as usual.

'Come on, grab your coat and I'll drive you to the hospital.'

'What about the interviews? We've another four to go.' The objection was half-hearted. Her hand was on her bump. She was frightened.

'We can reschedule,' I said quickly. 'I'll ask them to come back.'

A couple of minutes later, I'd emptied the waiting room, rung the other candidates, and we were in the car on our way to Letterkenny. Speeding along the wide main road past the hilltop fort of An Grianán of Aileach I was reminded uncomfortably of the mercy dash a couple of weeks before to see my parents.

Leah left a voice message for her husband and he was there to greet us when we arrived, pacing the foyer of the hospital, panicked and ashen-faced. I watched them walk away from me, arms wrapped around each other, Leah with her head on Kevin's shoulder.

An hour later, he sent me a text to say that the scan had shown that all was fine but that they wanted to do a few extra tests. I breathed out in relief, feeling a sudden whoosh of exhaustion as my shoulders finally dropped from their hunched position. Sitting miserably in the waiting area I'd been feeling desperately guilty about overworking Leah, procrastinating for too long about her maternity leave and giving her additional stress in the process. I guessed Kevin assumed I'd gone home, which was why he'd sent a text rather than coming out, but I was grateful. I'd have completely understood if he blamed me for the scare. I knew Leah had been carrying too much at the office and I imagined he knew that too.

I also knew I should leave and go home but the practice was closed, all interviews were cancelled for the day and I had no appointments because of those interviews. It was warm in the hospital foyer. I felt my eyes close and wondered if I might fall asleep where I sat, despite the harsh artificial lights.

A phone rang beside me and my eyes snapped open. It was visiting time and the foyer was busy; the segregation of those who were allowed to leave and those who weren't marked out by what they wore, dressing gowns and slippers in the company of jackets and jeans and anxious faces carrying presents in plastic supermarket bags. I saw a pair of green Converse runners pass by, heading for the revolving doors. And immediately my mind scrolled back to what I'd discovered this morning.

I felt an urge to follow, until I remembered, Gina Bailey was in this hospital too. Had he been visiting her? *If I spoke to her, would she tell me? Confirm my suspicions?*

At the information desk, I asked what room she was in and headed up in the lift, emerging onto her ward, finding her room easily enough and pushing open the door.

She looked pale and washed out, in her blue and white striped hospital gown, out of her usual brash red palette. But her hair was blow-dried and she was sitting up, flipping through a magazine, not *Take a Break* or *Chat*, but *Cosmopolitan*. There was no denying she was surprised to see me.

'No grapes,' I quipped as I approached the bed. 'Sorry.'

'I don't think I could have them anyway,' she said. Her eyes narrowed. 'I can't say you'd have been top of my list of expected visitors.'

'I was here for something else,' I admitted. 'But then I saw Ollie leaving and I remembered you were here.'

A shadow crossed her face at the mention of her nephew. *Was it possible I was right?*

With an effort she shook it off. 'Getting out tomorrow,' she said brightly.

'Back to Dublin?' I asked and she nodded. Though she'd issued no invitation, I sat on the chair left for visitors beside the bed. 'So, what's happening with the documentary?'

'It's parked,' she said shortly. 'We'll wait for the memoir. See what it says. No point in us treading over old ground. I think it'll still happen, just in a slightly different way.'

Did she have some inkling as to what was in the memoir? I wondered.

I took my phone out of my pocket. 'I came across this,' I said, showing her the still from the interview with Featherstone. 'Made me feel a bit kindlier towards you, if I'm honest.'

She looked away quickly as if the very image caused her pain. 'He was a bastard, Featherstone. Five minutes before that interview started, when no one was looking, he put his arm around my shoulders and his hand just sneaked down to my breast.' Her face contorted in disgust. 'I can still feel the clammy heat of it. I don't think he even fancied me – it was a just a power thing. He made some crass comment about having my long legs wrapped around him.'

'Ugh,' I shuddered, closing the image and putting my phone away.

'That's why I was so fucking nervous. Why I couldn't remember his bloody book titles.' Her neck flushed, as if she was still ashamed of her screw-up, even now, years later. 'He liked playing with people. Especially women. Tomcat and mouse, you know? Pure gamesmanship.'

'Why didn't you report it, tell someone?' I asked, although I knew the answer. Back then, a powerful man and a less powerful young woman; no one would have taken her seriously. Might even be the case now.

She didn't even bother to answer my question, just laughed derisively. Her expression hardened. 'Did me no harm.' She sniffed. 'It was good lesson in how things worked. Taught me to be tough in a man's world.' Caustic, spiky Gina was back.

'Shortly after that, I left the BBC and joined RTÉ and I haven't looked back. I get to produce my own work. I have a lot more leeway as to what I work on and what I don't than most people in there. Now I'm the one with the power.'

'And you can do things like having your nephew work for you?' I hoped she wouldn't notice my swerve.

But she did. 'Yeah. That kind of thing.'

'That must be good. Being able to help out family,' I pressed.

She took a deep breath. 'I'm doing my brother a favour. Ollie did film studies in college, even won an award for a short he made after he graduated. But then he thought that he was some great talent, that the world owed him a living. He got a shock when he discovered that it didn't, that you have to work your tits off to get anywhere in the creative industry. Couldn't handle it. Anyway,' she gave a brittle smile, 'we needed to get him away from Dublin for a bit. Keep him busy.'

'Why was that?'

She paused, glancing down at her hands now resting on the magazine. 'Ah, he's been in a bit of trouble.'

'What kind of trouble?'

There was a beat, as if she was making up her mind about something. 'Drugs. I think it started off as a way of raising money for his next project – he was introduced to someone by one of the actors. But then he got to like it, or got sucked in. I don't know which. Either way became pretty heavily involved in the drugs scene in Dublin.'

'How?' I asked. 'What was he doing?'

'Holding them.' She reached for a glass of water from the locker beside the bed and took a sip. 'Keeping them in the house. My brother's house. My brother and his wife spoil Ollie, they always have. Infantilise him. Maybe because they were older parents.' She replaced the glass, taking the opportunity to look away again, avoiding my gaze.

I leaned in, holding my breath, afraid that if I said anything she'd stop talking, clam up. But that didn't seem to be happening. Now that she'd decided to talk it was as if she couldn't stop.

'Ollie's impulsive, immature; doesn't think things through. Hadn't the cop on to know that you don't get involved with these people. It's a spider's web; once you're in, they won't let you out.' She examined her fingernails and I saw that they were bitten to the quick, cuticles ragged and torn.

'My brother was an accountant and his wife a dentist. Both retired. They're too conservative for Ollie. He thinks he's in the wrong family.' She met my eye as if seeking reassurance. 'I guess we've all thought that at one time or another when we're young, haven't we?'

'I certainly did.'

She nodded. 'He gets fixated on things. Has a bit of a temper when he doesn't get what he wants. The snowflake generation, you know? Want everything without working for it.' She swallowed; that shadow crossed her face again and I wondered if what had happened to her hadn't been an accident after all. 'Anyway, they begged me to give him a job. So, I did. And when this documentary came up, he seemed determined to come along. It was a small op with only me and Joe so I could bring him.'

I took a punt. 'You're very different, you and Ollie. You've worked hard for your success.'

'Oh, he's adopted,' she said quickly.

And there it was: confirmation of what I'd suspected. Gina seemed to check herself, but it was too late. She knows, I thought. She bloody well knows. And she did nothing.

Chapter Thirty-six

My heart hammered against my ribcage as I raced back down the corridor and out through the busy hospital foyer. I knew Gina Bailey hadn't told me all of that by accident. She was too smart for that. She'd made a decision, grabbed her chance, and I just happened to be the one who was listening at the time.

I pushed at the revolving door, my heart sinking when a familiar face appeared on the other side: Maureen O'Donnell, Peter McGonigle's delightful sister. I ducked my head, but it was too late. She'd seen me. I'd written to her son telling him that I could no longer represent him but he could only have received the letter this morning. Was she about to ask me about it? Or worse, have another go at me about her brother's will?

I wanted to turn away but she looked so stricken that I couldn't help but ask if she was okay.

Although it was obvious that she wasn't; her eyes were blood-shot and she clutched a ragged tissue, bits of which fell to the ground like snow. 'It's my son. He's been in an accident.'

'Oh. Is there anything I can . . .'

She shook her head. 'He's in surgery. I've been told I just have to wait.'

I had a terrible feeling that I was going to have to accompany her back inside and wait with her, when a much younger woman came running across the concourse. 'Mam!' And it hit me that Maureen had been waiting for her daughter while she parked the car. The younger woman paid me no attention whatsoever, corralling her mother back in through the revolving door, nearly toppling a man on crutches coming through on the other side.

I made a beeline for my own car, diving into the Mini and speeding out through the gates of Letterkenny General Hospital like I was a little boy racer myself. Because now I knew. Maybe not how or why, but certainly who.

I made it to Glendara in record time, bursting in through the door of the bookshop and startling Jude who was carefully reshelving some biographies.

My eyes darted frantically around the shop. 'Jude, where's Phyllis?'

He regarded me strangely, brow furrowed, Michelle Obama's *Becoming* gripped in one large paw. 'She's gone out to the scattering of the ashes. Why?'

'Featherstone's?' I said stupidly, checking my watch. Because who else's could it be?

He nodded. 'It seemed a little odd. She'd said before that it was just for family. But she got a phone call and ran out of here like she was on fire.'

'Who was the call from?'

He shrugged and shook his head. 'She wouldn't tell me. I think they hung up. She kept on trying to ring them back as she left.'

I was out the door again before he could ask me anything else, hurling myself back into my car. My chest felt tight as I sped past my own closed office, my poor Mini bouncing around as we flew around corners and hurtled over potholes towards Moville.

I called Molloy on the way to tell him where I was going and why, choosing to leave a voice message, knowing he'd stop me if I spoke to him.

I thought again about *Violet, Green and Red*, Featherstone's most recent novel, which I'd picked up that morning, trying to slot it together with the other pieces I'd gathered, assembling the jigsaw to see if a full picture would emerge. In the book, the artist protagonist impregnates a much younger woman called Violet. Despite her request that he acknowledge the child, he immediately distances himself from her, pushing her out of his mind, returning to his art unaffected and hoping never to have to deal with the subject again. In the end, he is unsure if she even has the child, but he hopes that she's had a termination. Was that what happened to Phyllis? Had she been dismissed so callously by Featherstone?

Other images floated into my mind: an author picture on the inside cover of a much older book, leaflets on a kitchen table. I now knew why Phyllis had frozen on seeing the old photographs at Shore Lodge. It wasn't because she was afraid that she would see herself. She was afraid that she would see her son. And that other people would see him too, in a much younger Gavin Featherstone. His father. She'd been shocked by the resemblance, particularly the cleft chin, a feature which Featherstone and Patrick had hidden with facial hair in later life, but was clearly there in the older pictures.

Ollie was Phyllis and Gavin Featherstone's son. I was convinced of it now. Especially after my conversation with Gina Bailey. It must have been Ollie who had called Phyllis, and the reason she'd rushed out to Shore Lodge. Could she be in danger? I had absolutely no idea what he was capable of. He was a complete unknown to me, the kind of kid you didn't especially notice.

Was that his problem, I wondered? Had he also been brushed off, disregarded? I couldn't stop thinking about that film *Fatal Attraction*, which I'd watched with my parents on the night they'd arrived, and in particular, Glenn Close's famous line in which she tells Michael Douglas's character that she isn't going to be *ignored*. Phyllis's son had been ignored. I assumed there'd been no mention of him in Featherstone's memoir. Molloy had read it; if there had been he would have said.

As I approached Shore Lodge, I remembered seeing Ollie leaving that day from the back gate. Had he been trying to see his father? Had he succeeded? Or had Robbie Cahill asked him to leave before he had the chance?

The gates were open so I drove in, the wheels of the Mini crunching on the gravel as I parked behind the line of cars, which I assumed belonged to the family. I swallowed when I saw Phyllis's car. And then I spotted the camera crew's black van parked askew on the lawn.

The front door was unlocked so I pushed it open and ran inside, sprinting through the empty house, into the kitchen and out through the French doors into the courtyard, from where I could hear voices coming from the shore. I rushed down the path, my breath ragged. Opening the little gate, I saw a cluster of people down on the rocks. I stopped dead, not wanting to interrupt the scattering of the ashes. I could see Barbara, Patrick and Susie from where I stood, and I was surprised to see Robbie there too. But where were Phyllis and Ollie?

My eyes darted around me in alarm. Suddenly Phyllis came running towards me, badly out of breath, approaching from further along the shore, the direction of Greencastle.

'Oh Ben,' she cried. 'I think he's going to do something stupid.'

'You mean Ollie?' I had to be sure.

She didn't even register surprise. She was too distraught. 'He sounded so strange. I think he might have taken something. He said he wanted to say goodbye to his father, so I thought he'd be here.' She flapped her hand towards the little crowd who had neither noticed nor heard us, the waves and seabirds drowning out all other noise just as they had that day when Phyllis stood crying with the silver quill in her hand. Was it then that she knew?

Something drew my gaze towards the house and I turned, my eyes settling on the one upstairs window we could see. Did I see movement there?

'Maybe he's inside?' I said.

Phyllis nodded and we ran back in, entering the house through the kitchen and hurrying up the stairs. I remembered the layout from my visit with Liam and thought I'd figured out which room had the visible window. I was right. It was Patrick's childhood bedroom.

The door was ajar. Ollie was sitting on the bed, still with its *Star Wars* duvet cover, head bowed, fringe curtaining his eyes. In his right hand he gripped an olive-green handled knife, which I recognised from the block in the kitchen. He prodded the tip of the blade into his wrist, giving it little staccato jabs.

Phyllis stifled a sob. Her hand flew to her mouth, then very quickly she pulled herself together and approached the bed, her hands outstretched, palms facing down as if Ollie were a frightened dog. 'Oh, Ollie, don't. Please.'

He looked up at her, misery etched on his thin face. His eyes were glassy. Phyllis was right; he had taken something.

'What's the point?' he said, his voice full of despair. 'I've lost everything. And I've destroyed everything else.'

'You have me. You have your parents who brought you up, who love you.'

'I thought *he'd* love me. I thought he'd be proud to have a son like me. But he didn't care.'

He dropped his chin again. He seemed somehow both younger than his years and older at the same time. Immature yet world weary.

'Oh, Ollie.' Phyllis placed her palms together. 'It wasn't just you. He wasn't capable. He was a limited man.'

Ollie waved the knife around the room, his pupils no more than pinpricks, jabbing at the posters on the walls, at the teenaged books and gadgets; evidence of a childhood of plenty. 'He loved the others. Why couldn't he love me? I thought he'd be happy to know that I was like him. Creative.'

Phyllis was in tears. 'Oh, darling. Your father never supported anyone else's art, the only art he ever supported was his own. He didn't like competition.'

Ollie curled in on himself, folding himself up on his half-brother's bed. 'I showed him the quill and he didn't even look. Just told that guy to show me out. Like I was nobody.'

'How did you get the quill?' I asked, knowing the answer when Phyllis averted her gaze.

She answered for him. 'I put it in with his adoption papers. I wanted him to have something from . . .' She trailed off, sucking air through her teeth when Ollie stabbed particularly viciously at his wrist.

I winced too. That knife looked sharp enough to draw blood.

'I saw him wearing it in that interview with Gina when we were researching the documentary,' he said. 'The one where she made a fool of herself. I knew straight away he was my dad.'

No sympathy for his adoptive aunt, I thought, and completely blind to Featherstone's cruelty. Maybe Ollie and his father weren't so different.

As if reading my mind, he lifted his chin in bravado. 'I knew I'd got my talent from somewhere.'

And your issues, I thought. Ollie had become involved with criminality and drugs despite being adopted into a safe middle-class home.

'Did you kill him?' I felt Phyllis flinch beside me, but how could I leave it unsaid?

'I wanted him to suffer like I did,' he said, a touch of spite in his voice. 'Make a fool of himself onstage.'

'But you put enough cocaine in his drink to kill him. More than enough.' Impulsive, petulant, and as easily hurt as a teen he might be, but Ollie Connolly was an adult. And he'd committed an adult crime.

'I thought that would be a bonus if it happened.' His eyes glistened again and he rubbed his sleeve across his face. 'I told him I was in trouble. That there were people after me that I was scared of, and he said whatever money he had was promised to his *real* children. He rejected me, turned me away as if I was nothing.'

Tears finally spilled down his cheeks. I looked at him, defiance and miserable regret competing for dominance in his thin face. I couldn't work out what he really felt and I wasn't sure he knew himself. It was almost as if he hadn't meant to kill his father. But how could he not have? He'd poured in enough liquid cocaine to kill two men. Something wasn't adding up.

'Did no one see you interfere with the drink?'

He shook his head. 'I turned off the camera when Joe went to take a call from his wife, and I did it then, before anyone came in. I was able to adjust the air conditioning too. Gina was pissed off because she wanted to capture everyone coming into the marquee. She spotted the glitch in the rushes. She guessed it was me, but she said she'd fix it before giving it to the guards.'

I remembered the recording had started while I was fetching water for my parents, and that it had seemed an odd point for it to begin.

'She said she wouldn't say anything. But I didn't believe her.' Ollie poked his wrist with the tip of the knife again, making Phyllis whimper each time he connected.

Then a voice from behind made us both turn. 'She wasn't the only one who knew.'

Chapter Thirty-seven

Barbara Featherstone cut a striking figure in the same green coat she'd been wearing when I first met her. 'I can't stay silent. It would make me as bad as Ollie's father.'

Phyllis took a step towards me, almost a stumble, as if she were trying to distance herself from the sound of her son's name in this woman's mouth. Her face was deathly white.

Barbara was unflinching. 'Yes, I know who Ollie is. He told me. And I know what he did. I met him coming out of the marquee that night. It was early before anyone arrived. I wanted to speak to Gavin before the event. He was upset, weren't you, Ollie?'

Ollie pulled his knees to his chest like a child, wrapping his arms around them, the knife tucked in between.

'He told me about his father. I think he thought I could persuade Gavin to have some kind of relationship with him.' She shrugged. 'I told him that I'd seen what he'd done, switching the drinks. He still had the original glass in his hand, stupid boy. We talked and he asked me to fix it. He said that he was sorry and gave me the glass to switch back. Which I promised to do.'

'But you didn't,' I said, confused.

'No. I didn't. I thought Ollie's first instinct was the right one.

That Gavin deserved to die. Of course, I didn't know he was dying anyway. He might have told me.' She sniffed.

Ollie looked appalled. 'But you told me that someone came in, and that's why you couldn't change them back.'

'I lied.' There was something frighteningly calm and controlled about Featherstone's widow.

Ollie looked at her with wild eyes, brimming with accusation and hurt. 'Then it's *your* fault that he died. You told me—'

'Now, Ollie,' Barbara cut across him like a teacher correcting a pupil, 'I'm not going to take all the blame; I wouldn't have the foggiest notion about where to pick up a pint of liquid cocaine. That was all down to you, don't forget. If you're going to start pointing fingers, I might just . . . ' She turned on her heels, and then stopped.

'You thought I didn't mind that Gavin was your father. Young people think they're the only ones who feel anything. That little fool Róisín Henderson used to write him letters when she was a student and he bloody well kept them all. I found them in a shoebox along with a stack of *National Geographic* magazines when I went looking for those old photographs.' She laughed bitterly. 'Pathetic.'

The last word was uttered while looking at Phyllis with such an expression of loathing that I wanted to go and stand between them, but Barbara's poise and self-possession quickly returned.

'The only decent thing Gavin ever did was be a father. Decent enough for me to regret taking Patrick and Susie away from him, though he never showed any inclination to fight for them. But then I discover that he's fathered another child he wants nothing to do with?' She shook her head in disgust.

'I already felt sorry for Ollie watching him being bullied by that bitch of an aunt while we filmed in Dublin. So, I promised to keep my mouth shut about what he'd done. I think we all thought that poor idiot Robbie Cahill would take the hit for it. It would have solved a lot of problems and put Patrick and Susie in the clear when it came to the inheritance. God knows they need it. But when I found out that Gavin had killed his father, it didn't seem so fair any more.' She sighed. 'Gavin was a bit of a wrecking ball.'

So she knew about her kids' money problems, I thought. But how screwed up of her to think it fair for Robbie Cahill to take the hit. Blood was clearly thicker than water for Barbara Featherstone.

'I knew of course that he must have fathered Ollie while we were together, and I hated him for that. And then this bloody memoir.' She rolled her eyes. 'We'd all be exposed again. The Gavin Featherstone show back on the road. I knew it would be easier if he wasn't around when it came out. Gavin dying seemed to benefit everyone.'

There was a sob. Ollie had started weeping, the slow remorseful tears of someone for whom there is no way back. 'I killed my own dad.'

'He wasn't a proper dad,' Phyllis said, wretchedly, letting out a shaky breath. Tears streaked her own face as she made to walk towards her son.

Suddenly I felt desperately sorry for him, and heartbroken for Phyllis. He looked unbearably vulnerable as he rubbed at his face, the deep groove between his eyebrows indicating that he spent more time frowning than smiling. I wondered suddenly about his adoptive parents. They'd barely got a mention, other than from Phyllis.

Footsteps pounded on the stairs. Ollie's eyes widened. He gritted his teeth, and savagely ripped the knife across his wrist.

Blood spurted, soaking his arms and legs and the *Star Wars* bedspread. Phyllis screamed and ran to him, cradling him in her
arms and trying frantically to staunch the flow just as Molloy and
McFadden appeared in the doorway.

There was a lot of blood. The bedspread was torn for a tourni-
quet, the rest of the family on the shore oblivious to the drama
unfolding inside until the ambulance arrived. The paramedics
assured us that Ollie would be okay, that the cut wasn't as deep
as it looked. He was taken to Letterkenny, while Molloy and
McFadden followed in the squad car with Barbara in the back
seat.

'I'll bring you to the hospital,' I said, looking at Phyllis's
pinched face, her sleeves stained with her son's blood. 'You're not
fit to drive.'

She nodded silently and sat into my passenger seat. 'How did
you know Ollie was mine?' she asked dully as we drove out
through the gates.

'A couple of things. Gina confirming that he was adopted.
The quill earring. An old author picture of Gavin. There's quite
a resemblance.'

'I know,' she said. 'I hadn't noticed it until Shore Lodge. I
got so used to seeing Gavin with the beard that I forgot what
he looked like without it.' She breathed out shakily. 'Ollie came
looking for me about six months ago. He applied for his birth
certificate under that new Act.' A wry look. 'Can't deny parent-
age when you're the mother.'

'True.'

'Gavin's name isn't on it, of course. He didn't even know I had
the baby, and he wouldn't have agreed if he had.' She gazed out
the window, unseeing. 'But Ollie became fixated on knowing

who his father was. I thought I gave him enough information to discourage him from looking, but he wouldn't leave it alone. He convinced himself that his father was a writer because of the quill.' She looked down again, twisting that red ring around her finger. 'It was too big of a clue, especially when he could tell from his birth certificate where he was born.'

I recalled the young woman in my office seeking her biological parents, desperate to know what her birth name had been, and I understood not wanting to 'leave it alone'.

'Then he appeared up here to make the documentary, not knowing it was about his own father. Or so I thought. I was hor-rified when I saw him in the tent that night of the launch.'

I pictured Phyllis stalling during her speech, and wondering at the time what had distracted her.

She shook her head. 'But I was wrong. He'd guessed by that stage, especially when he saw that clip with the earring. I'd taken it from Gavin when he was asleep and put it in an envelope when I signed the adoption papers. I wanted Ollie to have something from his father.' She looked up at the roof of the car, eyes bright with tears. 'What a mistake that turned out to be.'

I reached for her hand.

'He couldn't cope with Gavin's rejection. That's my fault. I was the first one who rejected him.' Tears spilled over her lashes.

'From what Gina says, he had a perfectly happy home life with his adoptive parents,' I said.

Phyllis didn't reply, prepared to take the full blame rather than allow any to fall on her son. A typical mother.

'That day I did the shore walk with my parents, we saw Robbie showing Ollie out,' I said quietly.

'Did you?' she said, sadly. 'I wish I'd known. He wanted to confront him so he snuck into the house. But his timing was lousy. All Gavin could think about then was getting his family back, controlling his legacy; he couldn't cope with anything else. He was so limited emotionally; he'd combust if he had too much thrown at him.' Her eyes closed briefly.

'Was that what the row before the event was about?'

She nodded. 'He told me that a kid turned up claiming to be his son, said something crass about how it could be anyone's. He even joked about the kid being mine as if he'd forgotten that I was pregnant all those years ago. He just assumed I'd had a termination and put it out of his head.' She sounded desperately tired. 'He wouldn't tell me when it happened or what the kid said. He didn't even want to listen to me when I tried to tell him about Ollie, just said he'd talk to me after the event.'

'It was Ollie who asked that question about family, wasn't it?' I said. 'Featherstone recognised him. And Jude was the one with the mic so he saw Ollie too. You were afraid he'd tell Molloy, which was why you sent him away before he had a chance.'

Phyllis nodded and looked down, fidgeting with her ring again. 'I knew Molloy would talk to Jude eventually. Jude didn't see anything strange about it. He assumed that Ollie was Gina's plant to provoke Featherstone for the documentary. He was just annoyed about the way she treated him. But then Robbie was arrested and I thought we didn't have anything to worry about. I genuinely thought he'd done it.'

'So you weren't protecting Ollie all along then?' While I understood Phyllis's wish to shield her son, I'd have found it difficult to accept that she would allow someone else to take the blame for a murder he'd committed.

She shook her head. 'No. It was only when I found the quill glinting in a rockpool at the back of Featherstone's house that I guessed what he'd done. I'd been fiddling with this and it fell

317

off.' She looked down at her huge red ring. 'I've lost weight and it doesn't fit me any more. And there it was. The silver quill I'd stolen from my son's father to give to my son. He threw it away after Gavin rejected him.'

'Where is it now?' I asked.

'I got rid of it.' Her expression showed that she was fully aware she was admitting to destroying evidence.

I dropped her outside the hospital. This time I wouldn't go in. I'd spent enough time here today already.

Phyllis unhooked her seatbelt. 'This is where I gave birth,' she said sadly. 'I went to my aunt's house in Dungloe when I started to show and spent the last few months of my pregnancy there. But I came back here to have him. I had ten whole minutes with my son before they took him away.' She gazed up at the hospital entrance.

'The pain of having him nearly tore me in two. I couldn't bring him up around here, near a father who didn't want him, but the pain of giving him up was even worse.'

Epilogue

We drove down the steep incline to Kinnagoe Bay. Sheep wandered carelessly across the road in front of us and then suddenly the view opened up: a dramatic vista of golden sandy beach, turquoise sea and bright blue sky. We parked at the bottom of the hill and made our way towards the shore.

'So how was he?' I asked, shading the sun from my eyes with my hand. It was early evening and it was low in the sky.

Molloy had just come from the hospital. He knew I wasn't referring to Ollie, who had been released into Garda custody the day after he was hurt.

'Not good,' he sighed. 'It's likely he'll lose the use of his legs. He's made admissions on all the car thefts, including running us off the road with his mate. But no penalty could possibly be worse than the one he's inflicted on himself.' He paused, looking ahead at the deserted beach. 'Why exactly are we here?'

'No idea,' I said. 'They just asked us to meet them here.'

He stepped down onto the sand and reached his hand out for me in a show of chivalry. 'I hear your probate dispute has been resolved.'

I didn't even attempt to figure out how he knew that. Robbie Cahill and Featherstone's kids, the two older ones at least – I kept having to remind myself that they had a half-sibling – had reached a settlement. Robbie would keep the house while Patrick and Susie would inherit the majority of the money, which would be considerable once the royalties started to flood in. All Robbie wanted was a job and a home; he'd decided to run Shore Lodge as a writers' retreat in Gavin Featherstone's memory, managing it and living there.

'Sometimes it's not about money, it's about competing for love,' I said, thinking about that half-sibling as we navigated our way around the huge, jagged rocks, which cast long shadows across the sand.

Robbie had confirmed that he kicked Ollie out of the house on Featherstone's orders, but swore he neither knew who he was nor had ever seen him again. And maybe he hadn't; Ollie's habit of dipping his head, and the huge headphones he wore, meant that he'd stayed under the radar. Although I wondered if Robbie might not have wanted to complicate an already tangled inheritance situation with another child, and chosen to keep his mouth shut.

'So, Inspector Molloy,' I said with a smile, 'will everything be tied up at your end before you go?'

Molloy grimaced. 'It's in the hands of the DPP now. I'm glad I'm not the one who has to decide who is charged with what. That Barbara Featherstone is a cool customer.'

I nodded. 'Still, she didn't actually do anything. She wasn't the one who spiked Featherstone's drink.'

Molloy raised his eyebrows.

'What? I thought it was all Ollie.'

'She was the one who added the lime cordial, knowing her husband wouldn't drink it if it was just water. Always kept some in her bag for the grandkid, apparently.'

'You're kidding,' I said incredulously. 'So, if she hadn't done that, Featherstone might not have died? He might not have touched the drink at all.'

'Maybe not.' He paused. 'Ollie's legal team might try diminished responsibility but I doubt it will work. What he did was pretty cold-blooded too.'

I agreed. Phyllis was determined to stick with the 'hurt and lashed out' narrative, but there had been two full days between Featherstone's rejection of Ollie and the murder.

'Where *did* he get the liquid cocaine?' I asked.

'That's another story. He'd been ordered to hold on to a case of bottles, and he watered the bloody stuff down like some kid stealing his father's whiskey.' Molloy shook his head in disbelief. 'Did he really think it wouldn't be noticed? He didn't inherit his father's brains.'

'Or his mother's.'

'Or his mother's,' Molloy agreed. 'They'll have to keep an eye on him in prison. He'll have crossed some unpleasant people.'

Suddenly I remembered that call he'd ignored at the office. The look of fear on his face.

'Still, he's young,' Molloy added. 'A life sentence isn't a life sentence here. Phyllis may still manage to have a relationship with him.'

'You think?' I'd been spending more time than usual with the bookseller and I knew that she was hopeful of that. I felt bad that I'd been in the States when Ollie had contacted her initially, wondering if she might have confided in me if I'd been here. I looked down. 'I'm sorry I kept my suspicions to myself. It was the wrong call.'

Molloy snorted. 'It was. I understand, but it probably shows why it'll be good for us not to be in the same town, professionally at least.'

It occurred to me that if Molloy wasn't leaving, then he might not have been so easy on me. 'So, have you found out where you're going?'

'Sligo,' he said. 'Just heard today. Not too far.'

'Totally doable,' I said, confidently.

'Sure, what could possibly go wrong?' he grinned.

We walked a little further in silence, both thinking about what lay ahead. Small white-edged waves licked the sand.

'So where exactly is *La Trinidad Valencera*?' Molloy said, name checking the Spanish Armada ship that had sunk off this beach. 'Oh! There are your parents.'

I followed his gaze. My mother and father were standing about halfway along the beach, looking at something inland, which seemed odd. Surely the view was the sea.

'You told them about . . . ?' he asked.

I nodded. The day before, Molloy had informed me that once in possession of his real name, the guards had been able to track David Varian down to a house he owned in Leitrim. His modus operandi was to target legitimate counselling groups – See the Light was genuine, it was nothing more than a vehicle for him – infiltrate them and become close to couples who'd lost children, lonely, bereaved people who had no one to leave their money to. He became indispensable to them, burrowing in like a tic.

Molloy suggested that his plan would have been to wear my parents down, playing the long game, eventually persuading them to gift him the house by convincing them they were doing something good. If not, he'd hope they'd die early, gradually eroding their freedom and space until they couldn't do anything for themselves. I'd shuddered when Molloy said that Varian would have relied on my not seeing them very often because I lived so far away. The guilt was pretty overwhelming.

Less so now when I looked at their smiling faces. They'd seen us approach.

'Evening,' Molloy said. 'What are you two admiring?'

My mum beamed. 'Our house.'

'Your what?' I looked to where she was pointing. A pretty cottage sat on the hillside in the slanting light, above the car park and the rocks. What a view it must have, I thought.

'We're renting for the moment, just to see how we get on,' my dad said. 'We've taken out a six-month lease. But, if we like it . . .'

'Liam found it for us,' my mother said excitedly.

I felt my eyes well and it wasn't the sea breeze. 'So this is what you've been up to.'

'We wanted somewhere that wasn't on your doorstep, but where we could walk on the beach every day,' my mum said. 'It'll keep us fit. And I'm going to volunteer in the library.'

'Who knows, we might even find the sunken treasure from that Spanish ship,' my dad grinned.

Molloy reached for my hand. Seabirds chided each other over-head, and together the four of us watched the sun glittering and glinting off the water as it lowered itself in the sky.

Acknowledgements

In each of the Inishowen books I tend to focus on one particular part of the peninsula. Of course, I'm spoiled for choice with such a spectacular location, but the idea for this book came from Donegal man Liam Skelly, who sent me a beautiful, framed photograph of the gorgeous Moville shore walk. It seemed like fate when I ran into him on the walk while working on this book and he gave me some tips! While there is much that people will recognise, as usual I've fudged some of the detail for fictional purposes. Featherstone's house, in particular, only exists in my imagination.

I've also played around with timings in this book for the purposes of the story. The new Birth Information and Tracing Act only came into law in 2022, while in chronological terms (some of you may have already figured this out!) this book follows directly on from *The Body Falls* which was published in 2020.

Thank you to my great friend, and fellow writer, Henrietta McKervey, who always reads an early draft of my books. She helped to pummel this one into shape and kept me right on so many fronts. I honestly don't know what I'd do without her.

I'm very grateful to another great friend and fellow writer, Neil Hegarty, for his advice about Derry and the surrounding area. Again, I've played with the topography a little: for instance, there is no methadone clinic at the location in Derry that I've described.

Thanks also to my old college mate, Simon Mills, who always helps me with medical questions. This time he introduced me to Professor Bill Tormey, who was kind enough to speak to me and was very helpful. All errors are my own and departures from reality are for the purposes of the plot.

My parents will recognise elements of Featherstone's house. In particular, my dad's study (which I've always coveted) bears a striking similarity to Featherstone's!

The title for Featherstone's novel *The Peering of Things* comes from a line in a poem called A Cradle Song by Padraic Colum.

The case Featherstone cites in the public interview about the false accusation really exists. The citation is DPP v Hannon (2009) IECCA 43 and the judgment is well worth a read.

Thank you to Peter McGonagle for allowing me to use his name when I asked, although I did change the spelling. And to David Varian for the same reason (although he actually wanted to be a villain!).

I've been out of the legal world for a long time now but I still have a crew I can ask if there are any challenging details or questions, so a big thank you to those friends of mine who are still in the profession. Similarly, although I visit Inishowen regularly, I no longer live there, so thank you to my friends who do, particularly Fidelma and Lily who were the original inspirations for the characters of Maeve and Leah.

Thank you to the team at Constable/Little, Brown UK who have published all of my books to date. I am very grateful in particular to my editor Krystyna Green and to Amanda Keats.

This year I changed agents after ten years when Kerry Glencorse left Susanna Lea Associates to pursue another career.

I am incredibly grateful for everything both she and they have done for me and I look forward to working with my wonderful new agent David Headley at DHH Associates.

Thank you to my parents and siblings who remain supportive and encouraging of my choice to leave a sensible career in the law for a more precarious one as a crime writer, and to the family who keep me sane and happy – my husband Geoff and our lovely lurcher Liath.

And finally, thank you to booksellers and librarians for their support over the years, and to you for reading this and the other Inishowen books. It is a series I love writing and I'm so grateful that readers enjoy it, too. Hopefully it will encourage people to visit.